"A thrillingly dark sequel for fans of fantasy and the supernatural. Trinity Rose Crane continues to turn magic into a reality with her writing."

Holly
@TheSleepyDinosaur

HELL'S KEY

TRINITY-ROSE
CRANE

This paperback edition published 2021 by Jasami Publishing Ltd
an imprint of Jasami Publishing Ltd
Glasgow, Scotland
https://jasamipublishingltd.com

ISBN 978-1-913798-27-7

The story is original, all names, characters, and incidents portrayed in this are fictitious. No identification with actual persons (living or deceased), places, buildings, and products is intended or should be inferred.

Visit JasamiPublishingLtd.com to read more about all our books and to purchase them. You will also find features, author information and news of any events, also be the first to hear about our new releases.

Acknowledgements

Firstly, I would like to thank Michèle Smith and everyone working at Jasami Publishing for helping make the release of my book possible.

Holly Richards for creating the amazing front cover and helping bring the book to life with her incredible illustrations. I especially love the artwork of the demons, they are very unique.

My parents for beta reading my book and my siblings for being there for me.

My friends, for dragging me away from working on my book whenever I need a break and listening to me complain about editing.

Lastly, my grandparents because I know you will read this to support me, but please skip any scenes in which the characters start to undress.

And lastly, my dog for regularly barking at me to take breaks and play ball with her.

Jasami Acknowledgements

The Jasami team is integral to the production of all of our titles. They are talented, creative and hardworking. Thank you.

Editors

May Winton
&
Joanne Tahaney

Marketing

Anna Dillingham
Kirsty Lawson
Rafe Petersen

Table of Contents

Hell's Key

CHAPTER
ONE

Enzo

Waking up, I groan softly. I struggle in the tangle of red silk sheets. Staring up through the sky light, I hear birds chirp above me. I rub my eyes, forcing them to stay open. Rolling out of bed, my feet sink into the deep red rug. The bed is empty. Alex must already be awake. A flick of my wrist and the lights blaze, illuminating the room. My feet pad on the floorboards as I walk out of the bedroom, down the stairs and into the grand kitchen. Alex's kitchen is twice the size of mine and there are two more in the mansion, not that she needs them. The mansion is fit for a queen, as is everything Alex owns. She settles for nothing but the best.

My feet tap on the cold tiles, I reach out for the coffee pot. Lights flicker in the hallway but we had turned them off last night. Curiously, I peer through the doorway, looking up at the diamond chandelier. The bulbs fade out as I enter. A bolt of energy shoots up the hall, flying at my head. Ducking, the blast shatters the mirror behind me. I flick my wrist, the light streams down the corridor. Heading down the hallway, I raise my hands threateningly. I assume whoever it is hasn't found Alex yet or they wouldn't still be here. I sneak forward, moving silently down the corridor. A small movement, I let out a surge of magic. There is howl of pain, I quicken my step. Turning the corner, I stop. A stream of fire strikes the wall beside me; it's a fire demon. I send out a bolt of magic, pinning the demon against the wall. Flames burn up the walls and rush over the floor hungrily.

My magic keeps ahold of my attacker as I make my way through the flames. I'm a warlock hellhound hybrid which gives me the ability to withstand fire. Approaching my aggressor, I see who it is. I could never mistake that curly hair and wickedly charming smile.

"Alex!" I release her from my magic's grasp in an instant. "What the hell are you doing?" I sigh in relief. We killed Silven, the demon who attempted, and almost succeeded, to free Lucifer a few months ago but we never know when the next problem will arrive.

"You shouldn't have done that." Alex leaps and grins. I hit the wall and I feel her hands wrap around my throat.

I pick her up off the ground by her waist and chuck her across the room. A wall of bricks sails in my direction but I cast a forcefield, laughing. It'll take more than that. Lifting my hands, I'm ready to attack. Rushing towards me at super-speed, she stops, our faces millimetres apart. She leans up and kisses me. I smile and grab her hand, snatching the magic reducing handcuffs from her grasp.

"You really think I would fall for that?"

"No, if I put them on you, Lucifer could escape." Alex is the type of person who would risk it. The flames racing up the wall are proof of that. "It was a distraction."

My legs buckle underneath me, I groan. Alex kicks me to the ground. Magic pulses out from my hand, aiming for her face. She blocks it easily. One of her hands sparks, ready to fire, the other steals back the cuffs. "Do I win?"

I glance down at my hand, considering the chance that I could blast her before she burnt my face off. Sparks jolt closer to my face as she waits. I don't have a choice but to admit defeat. "Fine." The sparks die out and she helps me up. "Any reason why you decided to try to kill me?"

"I was bored. You're improving but you still have no chance against me." Alex smirks, gesturing to the flames and they begin to die out and the house restores itself. "Now, you owe me breakfast for losing."

I shake my head fondly. "What do you want to eat?"

Alex snatches a handful of chocolate chips for the pancakes I am making. "I need those for the mixture." I bat her hand away.

"You can magic up more." She pops another handful into her mouth.

Alex is the Queen of Hell. She became the ruler after she overthrew her father, Lucifer. My magic is what is keeping him in Hell, I closed the rift that allows him to enter Earth. It's how we met. She came to torture me so that I would lock him up, but I offered to do it willingly. That was almost eleven years ago, and we've stayed friends. Then Silven, Lucifer's most loyal servant, almost succeeded in completing the ritual that would break the spell keeping Lucifer in Hell. Luckily, Alex inherited her mother's angelic ability to bring back the dead or I wouldn't be here. The stove fires up, I put the pancake mixture on the griddle.

"I bet Colt is missing your cooking right now." Alex jumps up on the kitchen counter.

"He's probably burned down the entire house by now." I smile. Colt is a vampire I have taken care of since his transformation. He is a great-grandson to one of my oldest friends. I promised to take care of her daughter and those who followed.

Alex snatches the pancakes the second I serve them. "These taste so good."

"Worth the wait?" I ask. I can make magic food instantly, but I find if I cook it myself it tastes much better. I get a nod, her mouth too full of food to answer. I take that as a compliment. I jump up beside her on the counter even though there are seats right next to us and dig into my pancakes.

My horns glint in the mirror as I brush my hair. My eyes glow a faint red colour which I inherited from my father who was a hellhound and goat horns from my mother, a witch. They died when I was young, but I still remember them like it was yesterday. A hip nudges me out the way.

"Stop admiring yourself in the mirror, I need it." Alex complains.

I sigh and step out her way. "I should probably go back home." I need to head back and check on Colt. I haven't seen him since yesterday and who knows what he could have gotten up to in that time.

"I have to visit my brother today anyway." Alex stops looking at herself in the mirror for a moment to talk to me.

"Text me when you're back from his and I'll come round?"

"Actually, they'll be coming here for dinner afterward to get away from their kids. You should come too." Alex smiles. "So you can cook."

"Why did you offer them dinner if you can't cook?" I pause for a second. "You always planned for me to come, didn't you? Why didn't you ask earlier?"

"Fine. The truth is Flint wants to 'meet you'." Alex rolls her eyes.

"He's already met me." I frown, I've met Flint a few times before and his wife, Jade. I attended their wedding, Alex invited me as her guest.

"Yeah, but he wants to do the pathetic 'big brother thing'. I've told him it's not necessary, but he's been pestering me and unless we do it, I'll have to kill him to shut him up." She jokes.

I roll my eyes. "Fine, what time?" Alex and I are dating... sort of. After defeating Silven, we got drunk and decided we wouldn't get romantically involved with anyone else, but we wouldn't label our relationship either. We did it because everyone I get close to dies and Alex has an obligation to protect her family at any cost and doesn't want to put someone in the way of that.

"Eight but get here earlier so you can cook."

"Okay. See you soon." I peck her cheek.

I jolt through the portal into my home. Colt is curled up on the sofa eating cereal soaked in blood. Two girls sit opposite him. Abby, his girlfriend, was possessed by Silven and her twin Holly, who is a werewolf. She was turned only a few months ago when Colt held a party and a rogue werewolf attacked the crowd. Colt has sworn to help her get used to the changes and he's doing a good job so far.

"Hello." I announce my presence to the three teenagers sitting in my living room ignoring my existence.

Colt jumps up like a skittish cat, his cereal flying in the air. Snapping my fingers, the bowl and its contents hover; I'm not letting that stain my couch. Colt is a vampire, he should have been able to sense me. He has never been very good at being constantly alert, that's still a work in progress.

"You're back early."

"Thought I would check you hadn't burnt the house down." It all seems to be in one piece, surprisingly. I'm not afraid Colt will hold massive parties behind my back, he'd tell me because I don't care if he does. Colt is more likely to destroy the house trying to cook or something similar.

"Yeah right, Alex had enough of you, didn't she?" Abby snorts. I glare at her. "I've had enough of you already."

Holly snickers, she is the quiet one of the group, she prefers watching us bicker instead of joining in. I do not understand how Holly and Abby can be related let alone be twins. Abby is the exact opposite from Holly. I feel sorry for their parents.

A knock on the door stops Abby from retorting back at my comment. I look, all three of them are here. Who the hell would knock on my door? The only other person who comes here is Alex and she wouldn't bother using the front door. She would just teleport herself directly into the living room.

"Please don't tell me you ordered pizza at nine in the morning." I shake my head, walking to open the door.

They did that before, waffles too. I can't say any of them are good chefs, it's understandable. I do cook for them most days. I open the door, a girl stands in front of me. Thankfully, there is no pizza box in her hand.

"H-Hello, is...is Holly here?" She stutters, eyes glued to my horns. I forgot to glamour them before opening the door...

Luckily, it doesn't matter, because this must be Holly's girlfriend, Selena. I told them to inform me if they were inviting guests. Selena is human, like Abby. My curly goat horns and amber eyes frighten most humans. Abby seems to be the exception.

"I'm Enzo. Holly is in the living room."

I open the door fully for her to enter. When Holly told Selena that she is a werewolf, they broke up for a month, then got back together. Selena decided she didn't care but it took her long enough. I don't think Holly should have gotten back with Selena. I know the supernatural is scary to humans but if it takes that long for someone to accept you for who you are, they aren't worth your time. I haven't said that to her. Firstly, she wouldn't listen and secondly Colt has made me promise not to. Holly was a mopey mess when they broke up. That was a long month, and I definitely don't want to deal with that again. She's happy now, I guess that is what counts. Selena slides by cautiously, speeding into the living room. I shrug, using magic to close the door. I'm used to people being afraid. I turn and walk into the living room to find out what they are doing today.

Abby

A knock at the door, interrupts my comeback to Enzo.

"You better not have ordered pizza at nine in the morning again."

He huffs, walking over to the door. Holly's eyes widen, it's Selena at the door. She jumps up to her feet, but Enzo is already opening the door. Selena is going to get a surprise, Enzo's horns and eyes are on full display. Selena knows about the supernatural, Holly decided to tell her. It was the right decision. It took a while for Selena to come to terms with it, but at least they're both happy now.

Selena rushes into the room. "There's a man with horns?" Her eyes wide in shock.

Enzo chuckles hearing her comment from the corridor.

"That's Enzo, he owns this house." I explain.

Selena has visited a bunch of times, but we have only invited her when we knew Enzo would be out. We didn't expect him to be back this early. Colt and Holly's traits are easily hidden, unlike Enzo's. We didn't know if she would be comfortable seeing him. Luckily, he didn't bring Alex, she would really freak Selena out. I like Alex, she is great. She helps me make fun of Enzo but she is extremely intimidating. Selena hugs Holly and sits down. "Is he joining us today?"

We have arranged a picnic with Kyle and Lily, our friends from school. The six of us are going to hang out in the forest behind Enzo's house. It is massive and Enzo owns all of it; he bought it so he could roam around as a Hellhound without humans bothering him. Enzo waltzes into the room.

"I am not joining you today, don't worry. I have better things to do."

Selena's eyes go wide, realising he could hear her. I must have been just like her when I first found out about the supernatural. It's so obvious when you know, but when you don't it's like stumbling around in the dark.

"What better things do you have to do?" Colt frowns.

"Prepare a dinner Alex sprung on me." He rolls his eyes fondly. "I'll be gone at seven tonight, don't wait up."

"You are going again? You two might as well live together." I shake my head; they spend almost every night and day together. I can't say much, Colt and I are the same. My parents have given up with Holly and I coming home on curfew.

Enzo snorts at the idea. "No. I'll probably be back before midnight. It's only dinner, and Flint and Jade will be there."

That's code for getting the family's approval. They like to pretend they aren't serious, but they are. I don't believe they have even labelled their relationship as 'official', let alone said 'I love you'. Though it's obvious they do. Alex came running to rescue him when he died. She didn't care about anyone but him at that moment. If that's not love, then I don't know what is. It is understandable why they are both being cautious about their relationship; all Enzo's past lovers died tragically, and Alex had never been in a serious relationship before because she's worried it'll interfere with her responsibilities. But it's too late for that, they are already there whether they like it or not. It doesn't matter, they have forever to figure it out. I just hope they realise it before I die so I can at least attend their wedding.

Kyle and Lily should arrive in half an hour, we plan to spend all day in the woods. They don't know about the supernatural, Enzo says they don't need to know. I wouldn't mind disobeying him, but Colt agrees with Enzo. I trust Colt, so it is the right decision.

"Do you need me to magic you up a picnic?" Enzo offers.

"No, we're good." Colt refuses.

"You made it?" Enzo splutters. "I feel bad for whoever has to eat it."

"I'm going to help." I add.

"Even worse, I'm glad I'm not eating it." He smirks, walking into the kitchen to tamper with the food most likely.

I sigh, lifting myself up off the cosy sofa. "We need to start packing the picnic."

Colt nods, standing up to help me.

To my surprise, Enzo is pouring himself coffee instead of using magic on our food. Colt opens the cupboards and fridge, taking out snacks. An entire shelf of the fridge is dedicated to blood bottles for Colt. I pack a bottle and hide it in the rug; I don't want Kyle or Lily finding that. There is no reasonable explanation for it. We baked cookies last night, hopefully they will taste good. We followed the recipe. I see a spark fall over the cookie tub. "Enzo!"

"You need them to be edible." He shrugs nonchalantly. I can't argue with that, he probably did make them better. It's a little disheartening because he didn't even try them first, he just assumed they'd be awful. I take the food from Colt and he stops, looking at my face.

"You've got bags under your eyes again. Are you still getting nightmares?"

"Yeah." I have been struggling to sleep, I keep getting nightmares from when we took down Silven. I don't remember much of it; I spent half my time under Silven's possession. I have tried taking medication from the doctor, but it hasn't been working.

"Can we see the nightmare?" Enzo asks, raising his hands. "I might be able to detect what's causing them."

I hesitate for a moment. I would rather not go back to the nightmare but I'm willing to try anything to make them stop. "Sure." He grabs the back of our necks with each hand and sends us all into my head.

Running, I bat twigs out of my way. Leaves blind my view as I charge through the forest. Branches crack behind me, the dark figure getting closer and closer. Panting, my heart beats manically in my chest. My eyes dart wildly for an escape. The forest is an endless abyss of darkness. Tears burn on my face, I thought we'd succeeded, I thought I had suffered enough. My feet drum rhythmically on the dirt, the grass is completely dead. I duck under a thick branch without losing speed. My lungs burn as I force myself to continue running. My vision blurs, the oxygen leaving my brain. My foot snags on a vine and I fly through the air. Landing flat on my face, I whimper in pain. A log connects with my skull, dazing me. I reach out, trying to stand up but a hand forces me back down. Gasping for air, dirt fills my mouth. I choke, pain throbbing through my body. My head jolts up as I struggle. I roll over and cough up clumps of dirt. Silven smiles, her hands close over my head. My eyes roll back as she possesses my body all over again.

Returning, Colt looks shocked. "Damn, every night? No wonder you don't sleep."

"I can get you something to take if you want." Enzo offers. "It'll taste disgusting but might be worth it. You look like death."

"Enzo!" Colt barks but doesn't disagree. He'd be lying if he did. I have looked in the mirror, it looks like I have two black eyes and hiding them with make-up doesn't work.

"I'll try it." It's worth a shot. The door rattles again, Kyle and Lily are here.

"I'll make myself scarce, I can't be bothered hiding my horns to talk to your boring friends." Enzo walks out the room and jogs upstairs.

"I'll get the door." I turn to leave.

"Wait." Colt grabs my hand, whisking me back to him. He pecks my lips. "You can go now."

I laugh happily, going to open the door. Passing the living room, Holly and Selena are in their own little bubble giggling together. They didn't even hear the knock. I open the large heavy door to Kyle and Lily on the other side.

"This place is huge." Lily says, admiring the house.

"Trust Abby to get a rich boyfriend." Kyle rolls his eyes.

"Hey!" I nudge him playfully. "Come in." I welcome them into the house.

Lily collapses on the sofa, moaning softly. The sofa is amazing. Problem is that it is white and Enzo notices whenever we accidentally spill something on it. Along with the McLaren, it's one of his most prized possessions.

Ten minutes later, we are walking out into the never-ending garden, leaving Enzo alone in the house to prepare for his dinner. We have a training session with him tomorrow at eight in the morning. He's helping Colt train Holly to control when she changes into a werewolf, they have made quite a lot of progress the last few months. She is also learning how to fight, because supernaturals are always in danger. We learnt that the hard way. In a matter of days, Holly was almost killed by a classmate, then I was almost permanently possessed, Colt got kidnapped and Enzo died unpossessing me. Sadly, we failed to stop Silven opening up the portal for Lucifer. Not that I could do much, as Silven used my body to do it. If it weren't for Alex, we would all be long-dead, and Lucifer would rule Hell and Earth. Demons flooded out of the rift, there were too many for us to fight. Alex killed them all in a minute, she is the most powerful being in the universe or that's what I've been told, and I'd never consider questioning it. Even though the threat has passed and Lucifer is still stuck in a cell in Hell and not returning to Earth, Enzo thinks it's important we both get training. I don't mind, except when it's that early in the morning. I am not looking forward to it. I tried to convince Enzo we would pay more attention if we had training at eleven o'clock, it didn't work. We stroll up the hill, a little into the forest.

"Damn Colt. Your father must be rich." Kyle looks over the acres of land.

"Yeah, he's a lawyer." Colt lies. Or it might not be a lie, Enzo doesn't speak much about his life. He's opened up more and more the longer we've got to know him. From what Colt has told me, Enzo has done plenty in his long lifetime. Some human jobs, some supernatural jobs. It would not surprise me if Enzo has been a lawyer. I can imagine he would make a good lawyer, possibly a judge. I smile at the idea of Enzo wearing a long curly white wig, holding a gavel. Maybe not a judge.

"Do you want me to take the basket?" Kyle offers Colt.

"No thanks." The basket is heavy to me, but it's like a feather to Colt. He also needs to sneak his blood out of it before Kyle and Lily see it.

Lucifer

I slump down in my cell. Alex and her beloved Enzo haven't visited me recently. I assume they are doing well together. I shake my head, love destroys you. I thought Alex, out of my two children, would know that. She has spent her entire life without becoming attached to any mere being. I believed she would never love anyone, except her brother. Even then, I thought the love for her brother wouldn't extend to sacrificing herself. I was wrong there too. Now, she has a boy toy, Enzo Thornhill, a man she is deeply in love with. It's sickening. Then there is Flint, he has a wife and children. I shake my head. My children are worthless.

A few millennia ago, I thought about the idea of having my own personal minions. I wanted them to be the second and third most powerful beings in the universe, after me. I pictured it, they would never question my authority and be obedient slaves I could use for my grunt work. I loved the idea, it was ingenious. I knew the only way to have such powerful slaves was to produce offspring.

I devised a plan to have two descendants. One with the second most powerful demon in Hell to make the strongest demon child possible. Then I would have the second with an angel, the mixture of angel and demon genes would be very potent. I wasn't even sure if an angel and demon baby was possible. But I wanted to experiment to see which one would be the most impressive offspring. If these offspring were successful, I thought I could produce more. I envisioned an army of powerful loyal servants to complete all my dirty work for me.

Getting Kath'tek, the second strongest demon, to produce my heir was simple. A little charm was all I needed. I had her impregnated in less than a week, then locked her away. She spent most of the next six months under sedation; she tried to escape every time she was awake. It was also easier to maintain her if she was asleep. She needed less food, didn't require a bed and, best of all, she couldn't complain.

To impregnate an angel, it took a little longer. Fifteen days to be precise. I caused chaos over Earth, killing more and more humans. I caused natural disasters, famine, and a plague. I sent my demons on the rampage. Every fifty or so accidents, an angel would rescue a dying human to restore the balance. I waited until the angel Maridth floated down to earth after I had caused a serious tsunami. I caught her and took her down to Hell. Our kinds aren't meant to interact. Demons can't access Heaven and Angels couldn't go to Hell, until I decided to change that. Before I kidnapped her, I experimented with lesser angels to find a way to get her into Hell.

Once I got her down into Hell, I put her in a cell and impregnated her. She was very tame for the first month of her pregnancy. She just sat in her cell, staring at the wall. It wasn't until she snatched a guard's knife and drove it into her stomach that she started to go insane. I'm surprised my offspring didn't die. Every waking minute, Maridth tried to kill her unborn child. She swore she would not give birth to a monster. I had to keep her chained up to a wall to stop her killing herself and the baby.

Along with dealing with my offspring's mothers in the nine months leading up to their births, I had been preparing for their arrival. First of all, I found a witch who would be able to forge a weapon able to kill both of them if they were to betray me. They would both be incredibly powerful beings, I believed it was important for them to have an off switch if necessary. Also, I made them a house with a maid in the human world because, though I wanted them, I didn't wish to raise them myself, in fear of being attached to them. Lastly, I spread the word about their existence to the supernatural world, hoping it would urge them to go after my children. Therefore, if they could survive to their eighteenth birthday, I would know if they were worth my time.

Flintagon was born first, I killed his mother the moment he was born. I didn't have any use for her anymore. She didn't even get to see his face. To my disappointment, Flintagon looked human. He had no obvious demonic marks. I remember pricking his foot and drawing blood for the weapon, the witch ready and waiting to take the sample to forge the dagger. I kept her alive, so I could take this precaution with any further offspring I had if these two were a success. The annoying, small, squidgy thing squirmed in my hands as I held him. I immediately sent him to Earth to be with the nanny for the real experiment to begin.

The day after Flintagon's birth, my mixed angel and demon was born. Alexagon, a girl. Evil sparked in her eyes the second I held her in my arms. She smiled up at me, red eyes boring into my own before returning to a more natural human colour. That is when I knew she would be the interesting one. She was the unique one after all, she's the only half angel to exist. I took a vessel of blood from her foot before sending her off to go with her brother.

The eighteen years passed quickly; I would be lying if I said I wasn't excited to find out the results. So, on Alexagon's eighteenth birthday, I went to visit them on Earth. I watched from a distance as they went about their usual boring day. They went dancing around the village, drinking in the woods and Alex played with knives. I'd heard what they had done in their last eighteen years. In the beginning, I had spies following them. That didn't last, Alexagon killed them all. I changed tactics to listen to supernatural gossip. Over the first eighteen years of their lives, Alexagon's biggest achievement was destroying the biggest coven in the world but Flintagon's achievements were uncertain. He was always there with Alexagon but he didn't particularly make a name for himself by doing anything special. For a final challenge, I decided to send a wolf pack after them, the most powerful one I could find. I watched from a distance as they took down the pack.

The experiment was a failure. Flintagon barely did anything, he's the biggest wimp I have ever seen; a fully fledged demon with no sense of how much power he wields. Alexagon, she was different. She attacked them with no mercy. I would have taken her back if she didn't care so much for her brother. I should have raised them separately; they had formed a bond. One stronger than fear and admiration for me. If I wanted something done, I needed the reassurance they would put my needs before each other's. They are both failures.

I left them to grow up and become adults. I had hoped Alexagon would eventually betray her brother and join me, but instead he taught her compassion. She was attacked by one of the daughters of a witch she had killed when she slaughtered a coven. Instead of killing her, she sent her to a school for warlocks and witches. A school to help her. It would have been so much easier to kill her but, to please Flint, she learned to be good. If she didn't have him, she'd have known love is the downfall of all…

I had thought about trying again for the minions I desire to do my work, but I had been biding my time to ensure a new generation would be successful after the last was such a failure. I was assessing different breeds and experiments that I could do. I thought of trying for another hybrid. A demon and a witch would make a powerful combination. They are sworn enemies, I would love to see what that would make. I was very excited when I heard my son was dating a witch. I didn't think it would last, but now they are married and have children. Once I get out of this damn cell, take back Hell and get my revenge, there will be nothing stopping me from teaching his two young, gullible, yet incredibly powerful, children to be my slaves. Having Flint as my offspring will finally be useful for something.

CHAPTER
TWO

Enzo

I start getting dressed up, looking into my wardrobe for an outfit. I used to only own one suit because I very rarely needed one. I gave up on big parties and events about a hundred years ago. I have been to more since I met Alex; she has dragged me to quite a few over the past decade. I flick through the countless racks of clothes Alex has made me buy. Apparently, my old wardrobe needed an upgrade. I'm not complaining, I like the clothes. The gym clothes especially, she knows what shoes are comfortable.

I pull out a suit, it's Alex's favourite. I don't see the difference between this one, and the other twenty suits I currently own. They are slightly different styles, I guess. The black and gold blazer fits over the white shirt nicely. The tie matches the blazer. I look up at the painting hanging opposite my bed. It doesn't match the rest of my room. Alex moaned when I put it there. It was meant to be displayed in the living room where everyone could see it. I put it in my bedroom because I wanted it for me. She's an incredible artist.

The painting is of us at a sandy beach in Australia. We went there about three years ago. We spent most of our time surfing, drinking and eating ice cream. I think by the end of our trip, we had gone to every bar, nightclub and ice cream parlour in the city. Alex insisted on trying every flavour we could find. Her favourite was rum, no surprise. The painting is of us in the middle of the trip, a few hours before Alex's massive bonfire party. We are on an empty beach; Alex had manipulated the owners to close it for a day. In the painting, Alex is laughing as I'm running away from a massive wave she created. Much too big to ride. I remember the second the wave hit, I got swept away into the ice-cold water. Alex did too, her mistake. The art piece is beautiful and the detail is immaculate, each groove in my horns, every loose strand of hair from Alex's messy plait and the feather fluttering in her hair. She captures every detail from that moment, it's exactly how I remember the day. It's absolutely breathtaking.

I glance in the mirror, the suit looks good, but that isn't surprising considering Alex picked it. I brush back my hair. I'm cooking chicken cordon bleu for Flint. Apparently, it's his favourite. I adjust the collar of my shirt and jog downstairs. I turn into the living room.

"What the hell are you wearing?" Abby teases. "Kidding, it's a good suit."

"Looking good." Colt praises the outfit.

"Nice." Holly nods, she knows as much about fashion as I do.

"Thanks, I thought you would all be out." I check my watch, it's seven in the evening. They said they'd be back at nine, it's not like them to leave an event early.

"No, it started raining." Colt grumbles.

"Okay, well, have fun. Stay out of my liquor pantry. I notice when bottles go missing." I haven't actually checked, but I know they have been in there. The guilt crosses their faces instantaneously. "I'll lock it." I threaten. Colt and Holly can handle their alcohol; they are supernatural, with the ability to heal the damage of large quantities of alcohol. Abby does not, but that has not stopped her challenging them to a drink off.

"We'll keep away from it." Colt promises.

"Tonight." Abby's eyes twinkle.

I'm telling them to stay away from it for her welfare. "Goodbye, have fun." I wave before slipping through a portal into Alex's home.

Appearing in Alex's kitchen, I find it empty. Alex must still be with her brother. I start cooking, pulling ingredients out of thin air. Magically, the breadcrumbs make themselves while I focus on the chicken. Picking out a suit took longer than I expected. I don't dress up often, I don't want it to look like I've tried too hard.

Dinner is in the oven and the washing up starts to do itself. A minute later, magic swirls from a portal in the main living room. I turn around, Alex stands there with Flint and his wife Jade, without their kids. Alex has two nephews, she has been texting me pictures of them all day. One of them is ten, the other is three or four, I can never remember. Currently, they are being looked after by their friends. I've met her nephews before and helped Alex babysit them, not that Flint or Jade know that. Alex gets bored caring for them by herself. Alex loves them to bits and is a great aunt, but the problem is that Jade and Flint promote reading or good behaviour as fun activities. They don't like the knives and martial arts Alex tries to teach them. She tried to show them art, but that didn't work out either. She has nothing in common with the kids, I'm sure when they are older and want to disobey their parents, she will become their best friend.

"Hi." Flint puts out a hand, like it's the first time we've met.

I shake it obligingly.

"Nice to see you, again."

I shake Jade's hand next. Alex rolls her eyes behind Flint, pulling a face at me. I try not to laugh; Flint trying to be serious and Alex making fun of him literally sums up their relationship. I know this means a lot to Alex, even if she won't show it. Flint is the most important person in her life, it's crucial to her that we get along.

"I'll serve up dinner." I suggest, now the awkward handshakes are out the way.

"I'll help." Alex jumps in, grabbing my hand.

We walk into the kitchen. She grabs me by the shoulders, looking up and down. "Damn, that suit." She admires the outfit. "I have brilliant taste."

I chuckle. "Don't look too bad yourself." I eye her up.

"Excuse me! Not too bad?" She scoffs in offence.

"You're gorgeous." I murmur.

The dress is stunning on her, off the shoulder, tight red lace that shows off all her curves. I tilt up her chin. Our lips touch, it feels exactly like the night we first kissed. I remember cursing myself for not doing it sooner.

Alex groans softly. "This better be worth smudging my make-up."

"When is it not?"

"Good point."

She jumps up, legs around my waist. I hold her up in my arms, her back hits the empty fridge. Our lips part for a breath. She grins, her hair tickling my neck. She reels me back in, our lips colliding. My blazer slips to the floor. I pull back, kissing her neck, working my way down to her collarbone. Alex whimpers, starting on the buttons of my shirt. My hands go up her back feeling for the zipper.

"Ahem." Flint coughs.

I curse under my breath, not because he caught us but that he has interrupted. Alex laughs, and jumps down begrudgingly.

"I'll leave you to finish." Alex murmurs, winking.

I chuckle. "Yeah, I got a little distracted." I turn to Flint. "Dinner will be ready in a minute."

I serve out the chicken cordon bleu which luckily hadn't burnt. Sitting down, Jade takes the first bite. "Damn, you didn't just magic this up. You can actually cook."

Flint nods. "Yeah, even while being distracted."

Alex laughs. I smirk, I can't help it.

"It's been so long since I've eaten non-magic homemade food." Jade groans. "Children take up so much time."

"I'm glad you like it." I snap my fingers and a bottle of aged scotch sits on the table.

"My favourite." Alex uses her own magic to pour the glasses. Originally, she didn't have magic. She stole the amulet of sacrifices from the first witch's tomb, the amulet contains power which is given to the wearer. Jade flicks her hand, one of the glasses flies into her hand.

"I feel left out. I'm the only one here who can't do magic." Flint takes the floating glass from Alex.

"It's not our fault you're a weakling." Alex teases, smiling.

"Weakling? I said I didn't have magic, not that I couldn't kick any of your asses." He snaps back.

He's the son of Lucifer, he's definitely more powerful than Jade and probably me. He has the abilities of fire, earth, water and air. He can heal naturally and is practically invulnerable to physical pain. He's physically stronger too, Flint is built like a house.

"Well, you obviously couldn't beat me, and you'd never fight Jade… only one way to find out. How about Enzo?" Alex's eyes dance.

Flint sputters out his drink. "You seriously think he has a chance of winning?"

I can't blame him for being egotistical, he is known as the third most powerful being in the universe, after Alex and Lucifer. There is a chance I could beat him. He's out of practice and I have more experience, even if he is older. "Do you think you could beat me?"

I shrug. "Perhaps." Alex is right, only one way to find out.

"Toxic masculinity, right here." Jade chomps down on her meal, waving at the two of us.

"Well… we can either play cards after dinner or you two could duel." Alex grins, egging us on for her own amusement. "It's actually a very good way to judge this 'is he worthy' crap."

"I'm not here to see his worth." Flint lies.

"Yeah right." Alex snorts. "You have never wanted to meet anyone else I've dated."

"You've never dated anyone else, the closest you have come to a relationship is hooking-up with someone more than once." Flint backs-up his point.

"Still counts." Alex shrugs.

"Also, don't forget you wanted to meet me so you could threaten to kill me if I hurt Flint." Jade points out to Alex. "Then, you attempted to kill me when you thought I wanted to screw Flint over."

"That was an accident and even you admitted what you said on that call sounded suspicious." Alex defends her actions. "Flint and Enzo will duel for our entertainment, after dinner."

I roll my eyes at Alex. "Fine by me, if Flint's okay with it."

"Sure, sorry in advance." He's cocky, that can work to my advantage too. Underestimating someone is the easiest way to lose.

Dinner ends, and Alex drags us all outside immediately. She grabs the chocolate mousses from the fridge on our way out. She magics up cocktails for Jade and her to go with the mousse. They lounge on deck chairs, we stand on the patio. Why did Alex come up with this idea? I shouldn't be surprised by anything she comes up with by now. I take off my blazer, putting it on an empty deck chair, Alex will kill me if I ruin it. "What are the rules?"

"First one to give up loses. Hey! You'll crease it!" Alex snatches up the blazer I dropped and carefully irons it out with her hands.

"Oh, and don't let your ego get the best of you. Give up before you die." Jade adds, directing her advice at me. I understand why; her husband is the son of Lucifer. I am a warlock-hellhound with a revenge streak. I should have zero percent chance of beating Flint.

"You'll begin on three." Alex referees.

Flint and I stand opposite each other, he hasn't even taken off his blazer. He obviously thinks I'm not going to last long. "One!" Alex yells. "Two."

"Are you sure?" Flint checks.

"Of course." Jade and Flint both think I won't be able to get a shot in, and I'm not going to let them believe that. I'm not useless.

"Go!" Alex orders.

Charging forward, I pounce. Feet barely missing the branches sprouting from the ground attempting to trap me. That was easy to predict, if I'm correct he'll be like Alex and prefer close combat. My hands pulse magic, striking his face. He blocks my approach, his flaming fist aims for my face. I'm not wrong. I catch his fist. I'm half Hellhound, fire doesn't affect me and he knows that. It's a distraction. I duck, moving out the way of a huge wave of water.

"How did you…?"

I take him out at the legs, a bolt of magic thwacking his chest.

"Shit." Flint groans, landing on his back.

He hasn't planned any more moves, he thought I would be down by now. Obviously, he thinks I'm stupid and weak, even a hundred-year-old warlock could withstand this. I don't know who should be more insulted; maybe Alex because he obviously believes she'd date a useless moron, or me being considered a useless moron.

Before I can make another move, a rush of air sends my back cracking into a wall. Snarling, my teeth start sprouting out my mouth. I take a deep breath and retract the hellhound. I have a better chance against him in human form. Warlocks were invented to fight demons. Hellhounds were made to serve them. Flint's fist whacks my jaw, I stumble, smashing an electric burst of magic into his chest. He tumbles back. Jumping to my feet, I flip over his head. Flint yanks my shirt as I go over, crashing back down. Flint laughs, my back connecting with the dirt. I roll out the way as his heel jabs where my head had lain. Vaulting off the ground, my fists connect with Flint's face, sparks seeping between my fingers. In retaliation, the fiery sparks from my hand burn his face, while the other hand holds his shirt to keep him still. The ground shakes beneath my feet, I lose my balance and start to fall. A gust of wind causes me to fly backward, smacking my back into a tree.

The tree branches instantly trap my hands, next going around my feet. Branches close around my fingers, preventing them doing magic. My legs refuse to move, the tree roots working their way up my body. Shit. In a blur, his fist smacks into my face and blood splutters down my nose.

"Give up yet?" Flint taunts.

"No." I scrunch up my nose, he doesn't think I can get out of this. I can if I think logically.

"Wrong answer." The tree roots close over my entire body except my face, leaving it a target.

His fist connects with my jaw, it cracks. I hiss in pain. Flint laughs. "I'm enjoying this." Six more punches meet my face at super-speed, and he does not hold back on his demon strength. Spitting blood out of my mouth, it lands on his very expensive shoes. Adrenaline pumps through my veins. I can feel my magic building up, unable to escape from my hands. His fist meets my face again, harder this time. I howl in pain, a bolt of magic firing out my chest, bursting through the branches.

They disintegrate and the magic hits Flint. Soaring over the grass, he lands in a heap twelve feet away. I guess I didn't need to think of an escape, my magic did it for me. I had no control over it. Stumbling forward, I remove a dead, flaming tree root from my foot. Flint doesn't get back up to his feet. A harsh burn covers the left side of his face and his suit is in ruins, charred flesh visible under the clothes. I walk over to him and nudge him gently with my foot to see if it is an act. "Flint? You alright?"

He doesn't move. I look up to Jade and Alex. Jade stares in surprise at her husband, lying in the dirt. Alex's eyes are wide, the spoon hanging out her mouth.

"Holy shit Enzo."

Worried, I kneel down and nudge him again. Flint should heal in an instant. I roll him over, so his back is on the ground. He groans as I flip him over, limbs askew, right arm at the wrong angle.

"I give up." He murmurs, his jaw clicking back in place.

"I'm sorry." I curse myself. I should have let him win. I'm too damn stubborn. The magic got out of my control.

Jade appears at my side. "He's not healing like normal. Alex, give him your blood."

Alex slits her wrist, dripping some blood into his mouth. Her arm heals in a second, and so does he. The burns vanish and the limbs snap back into place.

Flint grunts, gathering up to his feet. "What the hell was that?" He straightens his suit, which is in tatters.

Jade flicks her hand, the suit restores itself. The tree I was stuck in flares in green magical flames. Alex glares at it. Closing a fist, the fire dwindles to nothing.

"Hell, Enzo. I didn't think you could do that." Alex laughs. "You okay there, Flint?"

Flint nods, no longer in pain, eying up the dead tree that had been alive five minutes earlier. The leaves are non-existent, compared to the other ones, which are covered in thick green leaves.

"How did you do it?" Flint shakes his head in amazement, thankfully. When I've accidentally lost control of my magic before, all I would get is a look of horror and fear.

"It's a long story." We make our way back to the deck chairs where the scotch is.

"Do tell." Jade encourages.

I take a glass of scotch and I start to explain how it happened. The fact that I got injected with a serum by some human scientists and that they were trying to get rid of my powers, but they did the opposite. Their mistake meant that I got enough power to torch them and break free. That happened when I was ten years old. Whenever I think I've got the hang of controlling it, I relapse and lose it again.

"Well..." Flint begins. "Explains how you beat me. That injection must have been some powerful stuff."

"Makes him worthy, huh?" Alex smiles.

"Well, I can't really fight him if I say no." Flint chuckles.

I was surprised when he didn't heal, Alex has no problem when we spar. Half an hour later after dessert, Flint and Jade leave through a portal to relieve their babysitter. The portal shuts behind them. "That could have gone better."

"I thought you were going to let him win when he got you pinned in that tree." Alex replies.

I frown. "You thought I would win?" That is not what I was expecting her to say. Flint is the Prince of Hell. I thought I had a twenty-five percent chance at most, as long as I got in some lucky shots.

"Of course, you have a lot more experience than him, your power radiates off you and you know how to use it. I felt the bolt of magic you shot out your chest from here. Flint is too cautious."

"I am sorry I hurt Flint." I say sincerely. I know she cares about her brother; he is the most important person in her life. Next, her nephews. She would protect them with her life.

"You didn't mean to, the duel was my idea. Besides, the only permanent damage you caused was to his ego." She laughs, coming over to my seat and straddling me. "Now, where were we before we were so rudely interrupted."

I grin, leaning up to kiss her, my hands already working on removing the dress. Alex starts on the buttons of my shirt. My heart pounds, as I draw her in, her lips tasting of chocolate. I chuck off my bloody shirt. Our lips part as Alex's dress goes over her head. I pull her down, kissing her harder, working away the rest of our clothes.

Lucifer

I deserve to be here, I was foolish. No, I had hope, that is what got me stuck in this predicament. I had faith Alex would end up like me. I believed she would be power-hungry and willing to betray her brother. That is not the case. She is practically a human, with emotions rather than a drive for power. What a disappointment. Out of my two children, she is the one I had faith in.

I would have been proud when she stole the amulet of sacrifices before I could, snatching it from right under my nose to take the power for herself. I was excited, I believed she had finally turned against her brother, and was taking the power for herself. Or that is what I thought she was doing. Instead, her intentions were to save her brother. I wanted to think she would put her own survival over his.

Even so, she should have never found out how to defeat me. I didn't tell anyone the plan, except Silven but I didn't account for Enzo. The bastard. He knew everything about the amulet, he is the only one who knew more than rumours. He possessed the only book about the first witch's amulet. It makes sense, he is the first witch's grandson after all. Not that he knows that. I stole the book from Enzo and recruited him to my army. Little did I know that he was able to resist my power to compel him, he faked it the entire time. He wanted to stop me as badly as the human I was going to sacrifice did. He told Alex's friend everything she needed to know for Alex and the others to succeed. Using all my efforts of planning, finding the tomb and gathering the sacrifices to defeat me.

I remember the moment Alex grabbed the amulet of sacrifices out of the witch's tomb before I could. Taking all that power for herself, it should have killed her. The amulet is meant to kill you, unless the witch thinks you are worthy of her power. The whole reason the amulet existed is because the witch wanted her power to live on after her death, but only to be used by someone worthy. So, she put all her power in an amulet, to be found by whoever was smart enough to find it.

Somehow, Alex was able to pass the test, I have no idea how. I never got to see the witch, that privilege was left to Alex only. It would have worked out, if Alex had never come back. I would have still been the strongest being in the universe. Life would have gone back to normal; I would have sat on my throne in Hell, plotting new ways to obtain more power.

It was probably her little act of heroism while in the tomb that caused the witch to like her. Either way, I underestimated her, and she threw me in a cell and took my crown. Alex has ruled for almost eleven years. It's finally time for me to get my revenge and take back my throne. My plan is foolproof this time, I will not let anything get in the way of me ruling Hell once more. I know exactly the way to do it; the problem with beings having human emotions is it makes them fragile and easy to toy with. Of course, I will use that to my full advantage. I know exactly who to start with to get Alex to kneel.

CHAPTER
THREE

Abby

I jolt awake to the clatter of pots in the kitchen downstairs. I check my alarm clock and curse. I have ten minutes until I'm meant to be at the training session, why didn't Holly wake me up? I rub my face, trying to keep my eyes open. Holly and I got back home just after one in the morning. Then, we had to face our parents' wrath; we forgot to text them asking to stay out. That lasted an hour, I didn't get to sleep until three. Now, Holly and I have to sneak out. Hopefully, Enzo will have a portal so we can get out without our parents noticing. We are grounded from all activities except school for a week. They will probably find out we've gone out in an hour, and we'll have to face another week, possibly longer. We can't cancel, training is important, and I think Enzo is already going to kill us. Our parents forced us to give them 'the parent in charge's phone number', to complain about sending us home so late. I'm sure he'll give us an earful too.

I throw on a random pair of leggings and loose shirt for training, I brush my hair quickly, pulling through the knots and tying it up in a messy bun. That'll do. I stuff an empty bag with a spare set of clothes for afterward, and my hairbrush. Lastly, I yank on my trainers.

I sneak into the bathroom, both my parents are downstairs. I brush my teeth, so at least I won't have bad breath. I'll shower and eat breakfast at Enzo's after training. Peering out the bathroom, I hear my parents talking happily downstairs. I knock on Holly's door quietly so to not alert them. She has a werewolf's hearing, she can probably hear my footsteps outside her room.

"You're up!" Holly sighs in relief. "I thought you fell back asleep when I woke you up earlier."

She woke me up earlier? I did fall back asleep, but it doesn't matter now. She ushers me into her room. A portal swirls inside. She scoops up her bag from her bed. "Let's go."

Soaring in, we land in the living room. I'm still getting used to portal travel. The swirling lights are enough to make anyone feel sick. Colt, Enzo and Alex are sitting on the sofa. Alex joins us occasionally; she enjoys sparring with us. Especially with Enzo, he's the only one who can give her any sort of a challenge. It's hard to believe she is the Queen of Hell, let alone that Hell is a real place. Even after all these months, I struggle to get my head around it.

"One of you needs to explain to me how the hell your parents got my phone number! And why they thought it was so damn important to call me at three in the morning!" Enzo insists.

"Our mum forced us, she wanted to speak to Colt's parents about responsible parenting and to find out why we weren't sent home earlier." I answer.

"Yeah, I got that from the call." Enzo snorts. "I meant why is it important to talk to me about it? You're basically adults, I'm not the one responsible for your actions."

He's right, we are eighteen and technically adults. But we are still in high school and under our parents' care. Damn, it's Monday tomorrow and I have a test I have not reviewed for. I shrug. "I'm not sure, but we're going to get hell when we get back home and they find out we snuck out."

"Yeah." Holly grumbles. She is not used to being in trouble with me. She is meant to be the well behaved one of the two of us.

"You snuck out? We went and compelled your parents to not question, punish or worry about you for anything involving us, then made them forget we were there, obviously. Enzo was meant to text you." Alex frowns.

"Yeah, I forgot, I fell asleep instead." He glares at two of us. "Like I was before their parents called."

"Yeah, we were totally sleeping." Alex winks at him.

Enzo blushes grinning. "Anyway, don't let them call me again."

"Sorry, and thanks." That makes our lives a lot easier for when we go back.

We walk out onto the field. A rack of weapons for us to choose from sits at the edge of our training area. I pick up a dagger, it's my favourite out of the bunch, Enzo told me some fancy weapon technology about how the dagger fits my fighting style, but I didn't understand a word of it. I just like how it fits in my hand. There are a few new ones, I assume Alex made them. She is a blacksmith, as a hobby. It's a weird hobby to have, but ruling Hell is not a normal job either.

Alex stands opposite me. "You ready?" She doesn't hold any weapons but knowing her she has about ten hidden on her. Before I can nod, she throws a punch. I duck and move to stab her stomach. She grabs my wrist and twists. I'm sent off my feet, my back hits the grass with a thump. I whimper in pain, Alex is ridiculously strong. "Oops, I may have been a little too hard on that one." She heaves me back onto my feet. "Are you okay?"

"Yeah, thanks. How did you do that?" I ask in amazement.

"It's a mixture of strength and the right movement." Alex explains. "You might be strong enough to do it. I'll show you."

She pulls out a dagger from no-where and points it at my stomach. "Take my wrist."

I clutch her wrist with both hands. Slowly, Alex talks me through the actions. I copy without applying force while she demonstrates. "If you do that, you should be able to flip them over your arm onto their back."

"Can I try it?" I ask.

Alex nods, stepping back a few paces while the dagger dances between her fingers. "Are you ready?" She runs, blade out, ready to stab me. I dodge, grab her and wrench. She sails over my arm, exactly how she had done it to me. A foot connects with my face. I sink to the ground, blood pooling from my nose. Alex stands over me, smiling. How does she do it every time? I have never gotten her to the ground and never will. "That is how you divert the move." She helps me up, yet again. "Oh, you're bleeding. I forget how fragile humans are."

I wipe the blood from my nose. "I'm fine. Can you teach me that move too?"

"Sure. It's not that hard." Alex starts talking me through it. "You just direct one foot to hit the attacker and the other catches your fall. Like a somersault in the air."

My eyes widen, as I watch her do a full three-sixty mid-air. It is not easy at all. I don't think I'm flexible enough to do that. Suddenly, Alex's hand shoots out. Magic soars out of her hand, up into the sky. Holly hovers in the air, inches from knocking me out. That was close. Dropping to her feet, Holly stands there "Thanks." She brushes off her sweatpants. "Do you want to swap?"

"Sure."

"Whoa, you didn't need to agree so quickly." Alex looks offended.

"I can actually get a shot in on Colt." I answer, it also gets me out of attempting that trick myself.

"Good point." Alex chuckles. "Fine, off you go."

I pick up my fallen dagger as a phone starts ringing. "Alex, it's yours." Enzo calls.

"Who is it?" She asks. "Then I'll decide if I want to answer."

Enzo picks up her phone to check the caller. "Esmeralda."

Alex sighs. "Fill in for me."

Enzo approaches Holly. "Come on, let's go."

I walk up to Colt. He grins, the sun is bathing his face, fang teeth popping out his mouth happily. He doesn't have a weapon, I put mine away for hand-to-hand combat. Colt darts forward, I know from experience he is going behind me. I spin around and punch him in the nose before he can kick me. Colt grabs his nose cursing, it clicks back into place by itself. In five minutes, it'll be like it never happened. Colt kicks my shin and I buckle to my knees. I groan, I have permanently bruised knees because I always fall for it. Colt's fist goes to punch me in the gut, I take it and flip him on his back like Alex had shown me. He groans "Good one."

"Enzo and you three." Alex gestures to us, instead of calling our names out individually. "Are you free tonight?"

"Yeah." Enzo answers. "Why? What does Esmeralda want?"

Enzo obviously knows whoever Alex is on the phone to. Maybe an old friend, but I didn't think Enzo had any, except Alex.

"Her and Hybrid got engaged. They want to speak to you." She beckons him over.

"Be back in a minute." Enzo jogs off.

I assume Hybrid is some sort of nickname. Alex likes to make up nicknames, she often calls me 'human' instead of my name. Colt is 'fangs' and Holly is 'wolf girl'. She doesn't have a nickname for Enzo. Colt's fist hits my face. I groan, I should learn not to get distracted. That's another one of my faults. I brush off my knees and stand up.

Ten minutes later, we break for breakfast. Enzo and Alex are already at the table. They left training early. Enzo has made French toast, our plates are on the table for us. Enzo is a great chef, he doesn't talk about his life much, but my guess is once he was a professional chef or at least took lessons. I scoop up a plate.

"Are you three free later?" Alex gestures her knife at us.

"Yeah, why?"

"It means you can come to the engagement party." Alex smiles.

"Who's engagement?" Holly's nose scrunches.

"Some friends of mine, I didn't think you'd care. You get booze and I promise there won't be any rogue werewolves."

Enzo sighs, shaking his head at Alex's joke. It was at Enzo and Colt's party that Holly got turned by a werewolf.

"Okay, what time and where?"

This hasn't been the first time Alex has invited us to random supernatural events. She throws many parties, it's incredible. Alex doesn't always know everyone there; she just wants a reason to drink alcohol with people and I can't complain.

"My house at nine. I'm sure Enzo will portal you there." Alex polishes off her French toast. "I have a party to plan." She kisses Enzo's cheek. "See you soon."

Alex disappears through a portal. She doesn't even stop walking, it appears, and she is gone.

"What are we doing until then?" I ask.

"Our homework?" Holly glares in my direction. I've been avoiding it all weekend. I need to review for my test too if I want to pass, but I really don't want to.

"We can do that in the morning." I argue.

"What, before school?" Holly shakes her head.

"Yeah, it's Sunday. Who would want to do homework today?"

"You actually believe you'll be able to wake up earlier enough to get it done tomorrow?" Enzo snorts.

I glare at him, even if he does have a point. I'd never wake up early before school. I'll probably do it if I get another nightmare, but if I manage to sleep, I'm definitely not waking up.

Enzo

Damn it, I have to dress up again. I stand in front of my wardrobe with no idea what to wear. Alex sent dresses for the girls and she told me to surprise her. Well, that is impossible. I flick through my wardrobe. It's been a long time since I've seen Esmeralda and Hayden; a year or possibly longer. Esmeralda and Hayden are the two humans Lucifer used as sacrifices so he could open the tomb and retrieve the amulet of sacrifices. During the process, Hayden got bitten by a werewolf and a vampire which turned him into a hybrid. Luckily for him, the werewolf part of him allows him to go out in the daylight. I met them because Alex wanted me to help him get used to his new powers.

I helped train him and the human, Esmeralda. It was eight years ago, before I adopted Colt. Teaching them was a good experience and helped me make fewer mistakes with Colt. I pick out my outfit and put it on. I jog downstairs, the three of them are ready.

"Finally." Colt stands, he has actually tried, which is surprising. He wears black trousers and a blue shirt and has even tied his hair back. He's neglected to cut it the last few months, it's almost to his shoulders now. Both Abby and Holly wear what Alex sent for them.

"Aren't you going to hide your horns?" Abby asks. "Your face is already scary enough."

"You know, I don't have to give you those sleeping potions." I retort, snapping my fingers and the glamour appears. I wouldn't hide them unless it was necessary but there will be humans at the party, and I'd rather not draw all the attention.

Abby snickers, her hand slipping into Colt's. "Let's go."

I roll my eyes, creating the portal.

We spawn at Alex's front door. I don't want to interrupt the party by making a portal in the middle of it. Alex would not be impressed by that sort of grand entrance.

Abby frowns. "This doesn't look like Alex's house."

"This is a different one."

Esmeralda and Hayden live in England, Alex owns multiple homes in the UK. She must have chosen the house closest to where they live so their human friends can get here. Portalling them and erasing their memories would be too much effort.

Walking in, a huge chandelier hanging over our heads casts light over the entire room. The ball room is massive, big enough to hold a thousand or so people. There are only twenty people in the room at the moment. My eyes pick out Alex instantly. She is stunning. Somehow, she looks even better than she did in the dress yesterday. She wears an oversized crimson blazer with matching trousers, no shirt and open-toe heels. Power radiates from her, filling the entire room. Her eyes meet mine, she smiles and beckons us over.

Sliding over with the little huddle of teens following behind me, I watch as they stare in awe at the massive building. The architecture is amazing, massive carved pillars holding up the ceiling. I make my way towards Alex.

"Nice suit." She winks. I didn't try as hard this time. I left out the tie and a few buttons on my shirt to fit the style of the party.

"Enzo!" Hayden, the hybrid greets me. "It's been a while."

It has, but Hayden hasn't changed a bit since the last time I saw him. He doesn't look a day over sixteen. He is actually twenty-six, like his fiancée. Esmeralda looks her real age and will continue to grow old like a normal human. That is what happens when an immortal and a mortal fall in love. One will grow old and die and the other will be frozen in time. The immortal one will then have to live an eternity without the other. It's a tough decision to make but sometimes it's worth the pain to spend seventy or so years together. There are ways to solve the problem, the human can be turned into a vampire but that is their choice. I'm glad Hayden and Esmeralda were able to make it work.

"Congratulations on the engagement." I smile.

I didn't really keep in touch after I helped teach them. Occasionally, I would see them at events that Alex organised but we rarely talked. I didn't want to get too close to them. I believed the best way not to lose any more friends was to not have them at all.

"Who is this?" Esmeralda smiles.

"Colt, Abby, Holly." I gesture to each one as I go through their names.

Ever since Holly turned, the two of them have been spending almost every day at my home, it feels like I've adopted two more teenagers.

"Let me guess. Vampire, werewolf and..." Hayden starts to guess, looking over the three of them.

"Human." Esmeralda finishes, pointing at Abby.

"How did you do that?" Abby exclaims in surprise.

"Alex told us before you got here." Esmeralda laughs.

Her face relaxes in relief, I roll my eyes. Humans confuse me sometimes. What, did she think that we are all telepathic? It's crazy what assumptions humans will make, it's why all their movies and books about us are so unrealistic.

More guests flood into the room, the clock striking nine. The guests are certainly dressed for the event. It's easy to tell between the humans and the supernaturals. A hand slips into mine, I turn to the side. Alex smiles. Hayden and Esmeralda talk to their guests. How many people do they know? I sip my whiskey. "It's nice of you to throw them an engagement party."

"I suppose, but it was really just an excuse to get you to dance."

"Excuse me." I raise my eyebrow.

"Did you really think I'd let you stay in the corner looking glum the entire night? If so, you're dumber than you look. Come on." Alex insists, dragging me by the hand towards the dance floor as the next song starts. Alex has hired an entire orchestra for the event.

"Do I have to?" I follow her to the dance floor.

"Yes." She puts her hands around my neck. "I'm sure you're not as bad as you remember."

"I wouldn't bet on it if I were you." The song is slow, thankfully. I'm not good at much else. I used to be... three hundred years ago. Dancing has changed a lot over time. I probably can't remember a lot of steps from back then.

"If it is really that terrible, we'll erase all the guests' memories of it."

I chuckle. "A bit extreme, don't you think? Fine."

I take her hands and I lead her into the dance. We begin to sway to the beat. I watch my footwork, counting the steps in my head, each one landing perfectly. I don't want to step on Alex's feet. She laughs.

"What?" I don't dare look up and lose concentration.

"I've never seen you look so scared." She shakes her head. She lifts my head up by my chin so our eyes meet. "You're doing fine."

"The song isn't over yet." I warn her.

The violin plays the last beat of the song and I dip Alex. I sigh in relief; the song is over and I only messed up once. I lift Alex back up. Her eyes shimmer. "That was good." She praises me, lips an inch from mine.

"It could be better." I murmur, lips going onto hers. Her arms wrap around the back of my neck, I grin. Pulling her closer, my hands go around her waist.

"I knew it!" A voice yells behind us.

Our lips part, unfortunately. Alex looks over my shoulder. I turn with her.

"I knew you two would get together." Esmeralda chirps.

I force a smile, I'm glad she had hope for us, but did she really need to interrupt? It is her engagement party, I guess we should be polite.

"Yeah, that was obvious." Hayden slides in beside her. "I knew the second Enzo walked in, surprised it took you two so long."

"Yeah." I think about it. It took dying to make me realise it, but it was worth it.

I never thought of being with Alex before I saw my life flash before my eyes and realised what I'd been missing. Luckily, I got a second chance, and I didn't waste it. Everything happens when it is meant to, I guess. Who knows if it would have worked out before? I can't say either Alex or I have ever been good with commitment. Whoever I love dies or gets seriously hurt because they know me. Colt, Holly and Abby would know. I'd only known Holly and Abby for a few days before a demon possessed Abby to get to me. That is only one example. I could give a few hundred more. Alex was so afraid of losing her brother, she spent her life protecting him. She hates how vulnerable it makes her; she didn't want any more burdens, or any more ways to be heartbroken than she already had. Alex has spent millennia with Flint. She wouldn't know what to do without him. Luckily, Alex can't die on me, and I can take care of myself which is why we were willing to try without making a big deal about it.

"You can't say much, took you ten years to propose." Tina, an old friend of ours, appears behind Hayden.

"She has a point." Alex adds.

I remember when I met Tina ten years ago. She is a witch and a friend of Alex's. We were both recruited by Lucifer for his little army when he wanted to steal the amulet of sacrifices. Fortunately, for me, Lucifer's mind-control didn't work, and Tina had been released from its hold by Alex. We met when Tina was snooping through Lucifer's things. I went there searching for the book he had stolen from me. I don't remember where I got the book, but it had a lot of information about the amulet, and I didn't want Lucifer to have it any longer than necessary. Turns out Tina was looking for the same thing. I snap out of my thoughts to the sound of laughter.

"I should probably find Colt, I fancy blood and no doubt he probably does too." Hayden smiles.

He fits in with new people easily, being supernatural did not change that about him. I sigh. The three of them are probably already drunk. I'll have to magic them all sober when the night is over. They have school in the morning. I swig my whiskey, it'll take a long while until I'm drunk. Esmeralda starts talking to Tina. Esmeralda fits right in with supernaturals, even if she is human. Abby is the same. They would probably get on quite well.

"Let's get out of here." Alex whispers in my ear. I'm all for that idea. We walk away from the conversation, they don't notice as we leave and go off to one of the adjoining rooms.

Alex leads me into a kitchen area, a little away from the party. There is no one in this room. Alex wraps her arms around my neck, pulling me down to kiss her. It's not that she is short, quite the opposite. She is five foot eleven without heels, but I am six foot four if I don't include the horns sticking out my head. They add a few extra inches. My hands wrap around her waist and I kiss her. It's easier without my horns in the way. Alex draws back for a breath and goes back in for another kiss without a word. My hands race down her back, grabbing her ass. We finally have no one to disturb us. I smile, drawing back to look at her eyes.

"Come on, we have about thirty minutes until someone comes looking for us." Alex un-does her own blazer.

I grin. Going back down for more, the lights flicker and go out. Alex's head turns, her hair hitting my face. Without warning, the windows smash. Clouds of smoke begin to fill the room. I spoke too soon. My hands flare up with magic ready to fire. A shadow moves in the corner of the room. Blasting it, the blender explodes. The smoke disperses at Alex's command. The lights return and the attacker is nowhere to be seen. A blur from the ceiling and pain strikes my back. I collapse to the floor, groaning. I roll over and fire blindly.

"I have her." Alex stands there, pinning a woman against the wall.

"Thank god it's you." The woman sighs.

"Who the hell are you?" Alex snarls.

"Tessa. Tessa Baer."

"What do you want?" Alex kicks her leg.

The woman whimpers. "I'm an assassin."

"You aren't doing a very good job." Alex thwacks her head against the fridge.

"I'm not here to kill you! I'd never! You're my hero!"

Alex turns and arches her eyebrow at me. "Why are you here then?"

"I came to warn you, a bounty has been put on your head. And his…" She gestures behind her, roughly in my direction. "And all your family; your brother, his wife and their kids."

"If you aren't here to kill us, what's with the dramatic entrance?" Alex questions her.

"A test. Do you know how many people pretend to be you? I mean you can't blame them, but it made it a lot harder to track you down." The woman is telling the truth, her heart rate didn't jump once, even with being pinned down by Alex.

"Make one wrong move and I'll kill you." Alex releases her.

"Thank you!" She turns to face us, a bruise already forming on her forehead. She'll probably have a concussion.

"Tell us about this bounty then." Alex urges her impatiently.

"All the assassins want in on it. Normally they'd be stupid to even try anyone of your standing, but it's a lot, and I mean a lot, of money. No one has taken yours yet, but people are researching ways to kill you. The others have been targeted." Tessa reaches into her pocket and hands over a piece of paper.

"I'm only worth a billion?" Alex snorts. "Seriously?"

Tessa frowns. "Did I write it wrong? It should say ten billion. Enzo and Flint are a hundred million each, and Jade and the kids are ten million individually. Honestly, with how easy it was to jump Enzo, he should only be worth a million."

"Hey!" I scowl. I could have easily taken her.

"Don't worry, your profile report was very kind. It described you as a good-looking, very talented, extremely powerful hybrid with anger issues. Seems like they got the last part right."

Alex laughs. "I'm starting to like her."

I snatch up the paper and decide not to respond to that comment. "Who ordered the bounty?"

"Lucifer."

Alex's face falls. "Lucifer ordered these hits? Can you prove it?"

"Yeah." She pulls out her phone and shows us a video from Lucifer's cell as he waves to the camera and talks about the hit job. It's true, Lucifer ordered the hits. Somehow, he got access to a phone.

"Why do you want to help us so badly? Isn't it your job to kill for money?" Alex hands it back to her.

"Yeah, and they deserve it… well some of them do. I came to warn you because you are my idol, and I don't want you to die. Also, Lucifer sounds like a dick."

I can't tell if the glazed look in her eyes is from her head injury, or if she is star-struck by Alex. It's hard to tell. Either way, she's not lying.

"It was really easy to find you by the way."

Well, Alex doesn't really keep a low profile, and the assassination attempt doesn't sound odd at all, except that the order is from Lucifer. He knows that no measly assassin, even a supernatural one, could kill Alex, or any of us. Even me, which Tessa doesn't seem to believe. Normal assassins in the supernatural world don't have any enhanced strength or speed, but they all have one unique supernatural ability that is often inherited from the family. That still wouldn't be enough to kill one of us. Lucifer is planning something greater, which means we need to stop it, or we'll be screwed.

"Thank you for the warning, but I'm sure we will be fine." Alex says confidently.

"You're welcome. If I can ever help you again, let me know. I could be your personal bodyguard."

"That's what Enzo is for." Alex jokes. "Go enjoy the party as you're here. I need to talk to Enzo, alone."

We watch her go bounding into the party, then look at each other with the same expression. Lucifer is coming out of the woodwork again and he's trying to distract us. But he knew we would assume that. We have to be cautious.

"I'll go check he's in his cell." I answer before she has the chance to ask.

"I can do it." She insists.

I shake my head. She should be with Esmeralda and Hayden; they are the whole reason we are here and she's a lot closer to them than I am.

"I'll be back in less than an hour. You won't even realise I'm gone."

"I will, but okay. One hour at most, I'll be counting. Also, be careful." She kisses my cheek.

I smile. "Alright."

"We are getting soppy, aren't we?" Alex snorts. Classic Alex, that is just how she is. She has to back it with a sarcastic comment. I love that about her. She sighs, doing up her blazer. "See you later."

She walks off onto the main dance floor. I check the doorway to make sure no-one is looking and create a portal to Hell. Time to find out what Lucifer is planning...

I land in Hell and the heat is overwhelming. Normally, it's not this bad, but I'm in human form. Hellhounds can endure the heat better, but it's much harder to communicate. Being part hellhound is the only reason I'm not a charred skeleton right now. I stand in front of the castle; it's made of mud like bricks and is older than Earth. It shocks me that it is still standing. It's not been well kept, Alex had to do countless renovations to it. Marching in, the throne room is empty. None of the demons would dare enter it without Alex's consent. They are all terrified of her. They only come in to work, then they leave.

The cells are six stories under the ground floor of the castle. There is an entire prison down there, but Lucifer never used it. He preferred to kill them and get it over and done with. Alex could probably have found a way to kill Lucifer, she is the only one with the ability, but she hasn't. Death is too good for him; it would give him the relief from pain. He does not show it, but it eats away at him that his daughter was able to outthink him and kick him off his own throne. That is worth keeping him around a little longer.

My shoes tap on the stone spiral stairs and I make my way down to the last floor. Demons come down here to guard and feed the only prisoner. I walk down to the furthest cell in the prison. Lucifer leans on the bars, smiling satanically. "I've been waiting for you to show up."

I glare at him. Of course, he was. I bet he's imagined exactly what I'm going to say too.

"Whatever you're planning isn't going to work, so you might as well give up now, or we will kill you." I threaten him.

"Oh, that's no fun, is it? I just wanted you to visit, I was hoping you would bring my daughter with you, but I guess her lap dog will have to do."

"You sent assassins after us to get a visit? It's rather pathetic to be honest."

He snorts. "You're here, aren't you? In one piece too." He looks me up and down.

"You sound surprised."

"No. You could take out a few assassins, you aren't completely useless. You are the grandson of the first witch after all."

"Very funny." I roll my eyes sarcastically. He can come up with a load of bullshit when he wants to. Probably part of his elaborate plan to escape.

"You didn't know?" He smiles. "It's true, if you don't believe me, ask Alex. She knows, I'm surprised she didn't tell you."

That is his plan, to get between me and Alex. He wants me to believe him and ask Alex. I don't know how this is meant to fit in with his plan to escape, but I'm not falling for it. He would need to come up with a much better lie. My mother would have to be thousands of years old, older than Alex or Flint. Alex killed most of the witches and warlocks who were older than her when they started an uprising to kill her and Flint thousands of years ago. It's impossible, but it's nice he's keeping himself busy with these awful plans. If he thinks I'm going to ask Alex, he's going to be very disappointed. "I've had enough of your bullshit." I shake the bar, it's secure. Now, we just need to find out who put the bounty out for Lucifer. Probably one of the guards.

Lucifer nods. "Very well, I look forward to our next visit." He waves as I leave.

He's stupid to think he'll be getting another visit any time soon. I walk out of the castle and create a portal back to Earth. I have a party I need to get back to.

CHAPTER
FOUR

Abby

There are only a few people at the party when we arrive. We are ten minutes early, I'm sure there will be many more once it hits nine. That is what always happens at Alex's parties; this will be my third party I've been to since I met her. She hosted one in our honour when we defeated Silven. I got very drunk; it was an accident. Everyone else in the room kept refilling theirs and I did the same. The difference is they struggle to get drunk, and I am the exact opposite. I had the worst hangover the next day, Enzo fixed it with magic, thankfully. Colt's hand slips in mine, I smile.

"Damn, she did all of this in a few hours?" Holly admires the house.

The house looks very formal. Candles in an iron chandelier cast light over the room, an entire orchestra gets ready in the corner. Violins get pulled from cases, it's very different from the other parties. They had modern music from a DJ and the clothes were more fitting for a club. This is like a ball, I think, I've never been to one. I'm glad Alex gave us dresses, nothing I own would fit this party. Alex talks to two people. The woman wears a large diamond ring, her hand entwined in a man's. I assume they are

Esmeralda and Hayden. We approach them and I frown. The woman looks like she is in her mid-twenties and he looks a few years younger than us. They must have at least ten years between them, which wouldn't be so bad if he wasn't so young. They can't really be a couple.

Alex introduces us to them. "Esmeralda and Hayden." She gestures to them.

"Hello." Hayden's fang teeth peer out of his mouth, they retract just as quickly.

I remember what Enzo had said, he is a werewolf-vampire. Vampires are immortal. He could be older than Esmeralda but still look sixteen because she's mortal. I remember Enzo saying that Alex became ruler of Hell about ten years ago, and Esmeralda and Hayden helped. That means they got together when they were both sixteen. In the ten years since then, Hayden has not aged a day and Esmeralda looks ten years older. I think about Colt, he is twenty. I often forget because he looks eighteen and goes to school like a normal teenager. He goes to school because he missed the chance after turning. It's harder for vampires when they first turn because resisting the urge to drink human blood is incredibly hard to control. It's strange to think that one day I will overtake him in age, appearance wise.

"Let me guess, you are a werewolf." Hayden points out to Holly. "You're a vampire."

"And you are human." Esmeralda adds.

"How?" Do supernaturals have some sort of sense to find others like them? I know some can pick out scents...

"We got told before you came."

That makes more sense. People start to flood inside on time. The adults begin to talk among themselves. Colt pulls me away. Holly follows us, Selena couldn't make it because she had something to do. We find our way to the booze table. There is plenty of it, along with a bartender at the next table for cocktails and other fancy drinks. There is a list of drinks on a chalkboard behind the bartender.

"Why does Alex never have beer?" Colt looks up at the board.

He has a point. She only has the stronger spirits and a few mixed drinks that probably have as much alcohol. I'll have to be careful with my intake, or I'll end up like I did before. I want to last the entire night. Colt orders our drinks from the bar; I've never heard of half of them. They all have fancy names I don't recognise. The bartender mixes the drinks expertly and pours them into three glasses.

We take them and move to the side of the party. The room is packed full of people we don't know, unlike school parties where I know almost everyone. I sip my drink, it tastes good, but I still have no idea what it is. The band starts playing and people fill the dance floor, the music is slow, and they sway gently to the beat. I never learned ballroom dancing.

"Want to dance?" Colt offers.

"Sure." I look out to the dance floor; I have no idea how to start. Hopefully, I can pick it up.

Holly laughs. "Good luck." She pulls her phone out. "I need to video this."

I flip my middle finger at her as Colt pulls me away.

Edging onto the dance floor, I realise I don't know how to do this type of dance; I'm used to modern dancing. This one is old-fashioned. Colt laughs at my bewilderment.

"I've never seen you second guess dancing. I'll walk you through it. You'll be fine."

"You know how to do that?" I wave to the crowd dancing.

"Sort of, Enzo is a good dancer, old-fashioned only though. I learnt a few things from him."

I chuckle, imagining Enzo dancing. He has always refused at any party we've been to before.

"Fine, let's go." Colt spins me into a gap on the dance floor.

Colt swings me around, the world blurring, we move too quickly for me to comprehend exactly what we are doing. We move back and forth, Colt laughs. He swings me around, dancing amazingly, leading me along. The music slows down for me to catch up. We sway gently, hands together; I can do this.

"I'm going to twirl you outwards then throw you in the air." He murmurs in my ear.

"What?" I squawk.

"Three...two…" The music begins to speed up. "One."

I spin out of his arms, spinning gracefully outward then back in. Colt's hands wrap around my waist and I sail up in the air. He catches me and spins me around, I laugh. I go back down, landing on my feet. Then the final beat plays and I dip.

"Well done." Colt praises. "For your first try."

"Translation: terrible but you're too nice to say anything."

"No!" Colt refuses. "You were great because you had an amazing lead."

I chuckle. "Good point, I did." The song changes and slower music begins to play.

"This song is easy. It's a box dance. I'll show you." Colt takes my hand. It's a step-by-step movement, repeated in a circular fashion as we go around the dance floor. My feet follow easily. I'm not completely untalented.

"You are good at this." Colt says, honestly.

"Well, it's not that hard." I hold his hand in mine. My foot takes a wrong turn, crushing his foot. "Or not, sorry."

"It's okay." He smiles, eyes shimmering in my direction.

I'd kiss him but I would lose track of the steps. I don't want to destroy his feet, even if they will heal.

Another song plays and I don't step on Colt's feet, somehow. "See you're getting the hang of it." Colt says confidently.

"Don't jinx it." I warn him. If I step on his feet now, it's his fault.

Colt rolls his eyes. "I'm not, don't worry. Do you want to get another drink?"

"Good idea." I grin. "We've probably abandoned Holly for long enough."

We reach the table where we left Holly, but she's gone. The table has a new set of people, where did she go? I look around the room. I spot Alex and Enzo dancing. Colt was right. Enzo can dance, very well in fact. He leads Alex around the dance floor with ease. I scan the rest of the room, but it's packed. Holly is only five foot four and shorter than most of the people in the room. There is no way we can see her over all their heads.

"Maybe she went for a drink? Let's check the bar." Colt leads me away from the crowd.

Colt orders drinks again. I couldn't see Holly on our way around the hall. We have different cocktails; I watch the bartender make them. Fire flares from the drink as he makes it. Taking the glasses, I cautiously take a sip. It tastes good. Sitting up on a stool, I scan the small bar area again. Thankfully, my eyes catch Holly. She is talking to a woman who is obviously flirting with her. I'm proud of Holly for talking to someone by herself. Normally she is too shy. I might need to remind her that she already has a girlfriend, but Holly doesn't look like she is flirting back. The woman continues to talk to Holly and touches her arm. The woman stands out in the crowd, she is wearing a cloak over a full black outfit. She looks like a typical hunter from a movie. Her hood remains up, even inside.

The woman looks up as we approach. She looks like she is in her early twenties, but she could be any age, it depends if she's immortal. The woman has gentle facial features and grey eyes with wavy black hair. She would look very approachable if it wasn't for the thick red scar on her face. It starts just above her lip on the left side of her mouth and ends halfway down her chin. There are similar scars racing up her forearms.

"Hey, who is this?" I ask.

"Tessa Baer." She smiles wildly. "Nice to meet you!"

"Nice name, I'm Abby."

"Colt." We introduce ourselves. I slide my spare hand into Colt's by instinct. He smiles fondly in my direction.

"This party is wonderful, isn't it?" Tessa chirps up.

"Yeah." Holly agrees, not that she has been to many other parties to compare it to.

"Do you know Alex?" She sips her drink.

"Sort of, she's dating our friend."

"Enzo?" She chips in. Is she another friend of theirs? I'd have to ask. "Where are they? I have something urgent to discuss with them."

"Over there, talking with Hayden and a few other people." Holly points them out in the room.

"Don't go too far, I'll be back shortly." She winks at Holly before leaving hastily, cloak flapping about her.

"Should I remind you that you already have a girlfriend?"

"You thought she was flirting with me?" Holly looks taken aback.

"She winked at you, yes, she was flirting with you." I shake my head. I sometimes wonder how she and Selena got together.

We sit down at a random table. Our cocktails are almost gone, we'll need refills soon. "You two don't have to stay with me." Holly downs her drink. "I'll find someone to talk to."

"No, it's alright." Colt shakes his head. "We have to keep an eye on you, make sure you don't run off with any hot, dangerous looking strangers again."

Holly rolls her eyes and drains the rest of the drink.

"Hey!" A voice comes from behind us. We turn, Hayden stands there. "You three okay?"

"Yeah. We're good."

"Good, good. Colt have you ever played vampire beer pong before? I need someone to play with."

"No, but I'll try it out."

"Great, you'll enjoy it. You two are welcome to join us. Also, if anyone asks, it's wine." He leads us away into an adjoining room which is much quieter than the hall.

Hayden pours out drinks, including blood, in a set of labeled cups. It looks like normal beer pong, except it's only on one side of the table.

"Okay, it's like beer pong, if you get the ball in the cup, the other one has to drink it." Hayden explains. "Each cup has a different type of blood in it." I look at the array of labelled cups.

"Rat blood?" Holly's nose shrivels.

"It tastes terrible, like rotten meat." Colt shakes his head.

"How do you know?" I ask in concern.

"I drank it by accident, it was in the house. Turns out it was for one of Enzo's potions, not for me to drink." That answers why he would drink rat blood but not why he knows what rotten meat tastes like.

"You go first." Hayden passes over the ping pong ball.

Colt chucks it, it pings off a cup. He curses. Hayden chucks the ball, and it falls into the pig blood. "Not that bad." Colt picks up the alcoholic blood mixture and downs it. Colt normally sustains himself on pig and cow blood. Colt goes again, it lands in fox blood. Colt curses.

"Why is fox blood good? It smells terrible." Holly holds her nose.

Hayden shrugs. "Depends. It's more by the vampire's preference. It's a little salty for my taste." Hayden shoots it down with ease. He aims for the insect blood, which sits directly next to llama blood. It sinks into the insect blood. Hayden cheers. Colt groans, pinching his nose and chugs. Coughing, he puts down the empty cup. "That's awful."

"I know." Hayden laughs. I'm not going to ask how he knows; I assume a different game of blood pong? Hayden fits in with us perfectly, he doesn't just look our age, he acts like it too. He picked beer pong over the fancy drinks at the bar and he's awfully good at it. I guess, if people didn't know his real age, they'd treat him like a teenager instead of an adult, which means he never got to properly grow up.

"Abby, take my turn so he might actually end up drinking something." Colt passes over the ball.

I scoop up the ball. "What do you want me to aim for?"

Lucifer

Footsteps pound on the ground. Dear old Enzo got my message. He charges up to the gate of my cell with purpose. "What a shame, I thought you would bring my daughter with you." I lie; I planned for it just to be him. He's her knight in shining armour, I knew he would offer to check on me so Alex could continue with whatever mundane task she was doing. A measly assassin attempt isn't much, but it is worth a visit. Besides, no one would even dare to take on Alex, even for all the money in the world. That's why an assassin called Tessa Baer went instead of a real assassin. But that was only step one of my plan, this is step two.

"An assassin, really?" Enzo scoffs. "Whatever you are planning, don't. Or we'll kill you," he threatens.

If he could, I'm sure he would. He's powerful but he hides it. He thinks the injection the humans gave him when he was a child was to remove his powers, but it was actually to enhance them. I would know, I was the mastermind of the operation. I wanted to experiment on supernaturals, I've always been interested to know if I could take and give power at will. I picked the supernaturals for my experiment carefully. I only wanted the best. After I picked them, I kidnapped them and sent them to the facility. I chose Enzo because he was a hybrid, a mix between a retired Hellhound pack leader and the First Witch's daughter. I'm not sure how his mother snuck past Alex all those years ago, but that doesn't matter now.

The injection I forced the humans to give Enzo was a final experiment after I had had my fun. It was a syringe full of my blood, I wanted to know what it could do. I thought it would kill him as it had killed all the other subjects. One drop and the power consumed them. It did the opposite for Enzo. I remember the small, feeble, boney child tied to the metal table, barely able to breath. His ribs were so bruised from experiments. He wasn't healing correctly due to the lack of nutrients in his body. Then my blood went through his veins, and he shuddered and jolted over the table. I thought he was dying, it looked that way. He showed all the signs the others had before their deaths. Instead, green and red magic began to hurtle from his body, attacking everything in sight. It was wonderful to watch. The skinny, tattered boy exploding with new energy. He has not used that gift to its full potential ever since, it's such a waste. I snap back to Enzo standing before me. I cannot get distracted by my excellence, not until I am free.

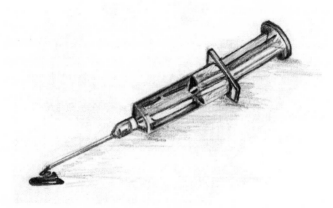

"You didn't die, did you? And you are in one piece." He shouldn't be so offended by the assassins, it's not like they could kill him.

"You sound surprised." He shakes his head.

Enzo thinks that I believe he's weak. That works in my favour.

"No, you aren't completely useless. You are the grandson of the first witch after all."

Enzo snorts. "Very funny." He thinks I'm kidding him. That is not a surprise, Enzo is the type of creature who needs proof.

"You don't know?" I smile. "It's true, if you don't believe me, ask Alex." That makes him smile.

He thinks he has figured me out, that I have just accidentally revealed my grand plan, that my purpose is to get between him and Alex. He's not wrong, I am, but I'm also smart enough to know he trusts Alex completely. He would never ask her if I'm telling him the truth because that provides the opposite impression. I'm her crazy father and she is his loyal girlfriend. It would be insane to even think what I'm saying is true. Hell, he'd probably trust a stranger before he'd listen to a word I say.

"I've had enough of your bullshit." Enzo snaps at me as I smile and storms off.

He will be visiting sooner than he thinks. I know that I need to send him proof, reminding him where he got the first witch's book from isn't enough. I need a big gesture that screams it in his face, so he can't ignore it. I have already planned it. My present will be arriving at his doorstep tomorrow morning and phase three of my plan will begin.

CHAPTER
FIVE

Enzo

I pop back into the party. I check the time; I was in Hell for an hour and twenty minutes. I head directly for the bar, where I'm certain Alex will be. She sits on a stool, ordering her favourite.

"Make that two." I say to the bartender.

"You are late!" Alex tuts.

"Sorry." I scoop up my drink. "Didn't miss anything, did I?"

"No, the only hot guy left, and it was rather boring after that." She grumbles. "But he's back now. See." Alex points to a random person entering in the hall, from an adjoining room, holding a girl's hand.

"Well, I think he's taken." I roll my eyes.

"Damn, you are right. I guess you'll have to do." She smirks playfully. "What did Lucifer want?"

"Attention, I think he's lonely in his cell."

"Well, he better get used to it, he's going to be down there for a long time. Thanks for going."

"You're welcome. We need to find out who sent out the order for our execution on his behalf."

"Yeah, I've warned Flint. I'll track the bounty back to its source tomorrow morning."

"I'll help." I look out at the ballroom. "Have you seen the three annoying children who I can't seem to get out of my house?"

"They are drinking." She points to a far-away table.

"Abby is going to die of liver failure one day." I sigh.

"Don't worry. After her fourth drink, I told the bartender to switch to non-alcoholic." Alex winks. "She's too tipsy to figure it out, but not drunk out of her mind either."

"That is a brilliant idea." I might do that myself in the future. I'm surprised I'd never thought of it before.

"You're welcome." Alex shrugs.

"Let's dance." I put down my cocktail.

She fakes a gasp. "Did you just offer to dance with me? How can I be sure you are really Enzo?"

"You have a caramel chocolate bar in your left suit pocket." I answer.

Alex laughs. "Yeah, it's you." Alex always carries chocolate with her, and caramel is her favourite flavour. "Alright, let's dance, but I'm leading this time."

Guests start trickling out about midnight and now there is only a gaggle left, including the woman, Tessa, who we met earlier. She chats chirpily to everyone with an incredible amount of energy. She is not like any assassin I have ever met. They normally appear, kill their target and disappear. They are supposedly dark and mysterious, and you don't see them unless they are about to kill you. Tessa is definitely not like that. She carries weapons at least, that's what the cloak is hiding. I look at the three drowsy teens laughing at the simplest thing in the corner.

"I should make those three go to bed." The three of them double over laughing, clutching each other for support. I think Abby is the most sober of the three of them, for once. "I feel like their dad."

"You are, sort of."

"Yeah, but I only remember adopting one." I chuckle.

"Come back after?" Her eyes sparkle.

"Definitely, but I will have to wake up early tomorrow to get them to school." Geez, I am their dad, at least when they are drunk or hung-over; they are self-sufficient the rest of the time.

"That's fine, just don't wake me up when you leave in the morning."

"I won't."

I portal the drunk trio to my house. Colt crashes into the wall, laughing. I roll my eyes. He's meant to be the sensible one. Holly clings onto Abby for support. I lead them upstairs, making sure they don't fall down. They crawl into their rooms and crash immediately. Holly and Abby have their own bedrooms; they stay here often enough. Colt will drive them to school in the morning in his pick-up. He will be sober by then. They are all going to regret tonight in the morning; I will probably have to force them out of bed. Loud snores come from two of the three rooms. I sigh and teleport back to Alex.

I reach the house, Alex is magicking away decorations. Outside, the band pack their instruments into a van. "You are back earlier than I expected." She grins. "You can help clean up."

"I think I forgot to check Colt was asleep. Let me just..."

"You aren't getting out of it." She laughs, dragging me back inside.

I groan. "I thought you had a cleaning crew for that."

"Yeah, you. No, I do have cleaners, but they won't be here until the morning." She flicks her hands to send the decorations away. I join in and magic away a stream of soft yellow lights from around the room. "Enzo!" Alex yelps, the lights tangling around her body.

I laugh. She yanks at the cords, falling onto her ass. She wiggles a finger, and they disappear. Damn, I thought it would last longer. "That's it." Alex sends a table flying for my head. I chuckle, ducking out the way. She laughs, her smile lighting up the room. Another table, I dart out of its way. Plaster falls off the wall where the table hits it. I scramble behind a pillar, magic bolting at her.

***

Waking up on a couch, I rub my head. Alex's arms wrap around my half naked body, trapping me in place. Gently, I remove her arm. She murmurs. I slip out from her embrace. She reaches out in her sleep. I smile and take a photo on my phone, without flash, I can tease her about it later. I use magic to change my clothes and get clean. I don't have time for a shower. I leave Alex to sleep, before portalling back to my own home.

At home, I start cooking to stop the teenagers moaning when they wake up. I whip up batter and set it in the pan. Waving my hand, magic wafts the smell of pancakes up the stairs. That'll get them to awake. I once went to wake them myself, that didn't work out very well. They grumbled and moaned and fell back asleep. I ended up throwing cold water over their heads, then Abby got sick. She blamed me for it, but I bet it was just a normal human cold from the weather. It was just a coincidence.

Fifteen minutes later, the stack of pancakes awaits, and a head appears at the doorway. Abby, dressed and no longer covered in the stench of alcohol. Colt appears behind her along with Holly. They have an hour until their first class, and it'll take twenty minutes to drive there.

"Thanks." Abby shoves a pancake in her mouth without adding any toppings or syrups. Her hair is pulled back in an average ponytail and dark bags sit under her eyes. Colt barely manages a nod. He was the drunkest out of the bunch, somehow. I think Hayden might be to blame. I don't want to ask how many he had,

"Selena is meeting us at the gates." Holly puts down her phone. "She wants to know how the party went."

Abby nods, without a word. I flip another pancake onto Holly's plate. More mixture sizzles in the pan for myself and Alex. I'll send it to her with magic. They sit in silence and I pull open the blinds. They curse in unison, shading their eyes. I laugh, serves them right for drinking too much. The front door rattles.

"Selena isn't meeting you here, right?" I ask.

"No." Holly double checks her phone.

"I'll go." Colt heaves himself up from his seat. I flip the pancake to allow it to cook on the other side. "Who are you?" I listen to Colt talk to the stranger.

"I'm here to see Enzo Thornhill, is he here?" The person replies, the voice is familiar, but I can't figure out who it is.

"Yeah, I'll go get him... Hey! You can't barge in here!" Colt protests.

I turn to where the intruder will enter. One hand ready to use magic to pin them when they walk in, the other holds the spatula.

My hand freezes as the person turns into the doorway. The spatula drops from my hand. Colt stands behind the woman. How the hell is she here? She should be long dead. Very long dead, five hundred- and twenty-three-years dead to be exact. Her hazel hair is cut up to her shoulders instead of down to her waist, like it used to be, but it looks like her. The same blue eyes I remember. My stomach drops, ready to throw up. It can't be. It's an illusion. Kicking back into action, I send out a jolt of magic that flings her against the wall, as the magic closes over all her limbs.

"Who are you!" I demand.

"It's me, you haven't forgotten my face, have you?"

I haven't forgotten. Her face is exactly how I remember it, from the freckles on her nose to the yellow flecks in her eyes but it can't be her. I dart across the room and grab the side of her face; she screams as it burns.

"Remove the glamour, now!"

"No." She whimpers. "It's me. I swear. I-I can prove it. For your second birthday, your father carved you a hellhound, you carried it around everywhere." I loosen my grip a little. That's true, I did. "And I-I taught you your first spell. You accidentally knocked out your father."

I break my hold on her, no one knows that except Colt and Alex. They would never tell anyone. Well, Colt may tell Abby and Holly, but definitely not a stranger. I drop her down to the ground. It's proof, for now.

"How?" Is all I can manage to say, struggling not to throw up, my insides clenching. I watched her die in my arms. I checked her pulse; she had stopped breathing.

"It's a long story." She shakes her head.

"Who is she?" Colt pipes up.

"I'm Adeline Thornhill, Enzo's mother."

Somehow, it is. After five-hundred years, she pops up out of nowhere. A lot can happen in five-hundred years. "It's nice to see you, son." She wraps her arms around me. I wrench myself back. She may technically be my mother by blood, but I don't know her. Not really. I knew her for six, possibly seven, years and that was five hundred years ago. That is less time than I have known Alex.

"You're his mother?" Abby smiles. "Damn, you look like his sister."

"You three need to eat, you have to leave for school in ten minutes." I order. "Come in here." I lead her into the dining room. I need to find out what the hell is going on.

She turns back, looking at the three of them as I pull her away. "Are they your children?"

"Close enough." I mutter, drawing a knife.

"Enzo!" She yelps as I extract her blood. That hasn't changed, my mother is terrible at reading people. She is the most predictable person in a fight. I magic it into a test tube and do the same for myself. "You don't believe me?" Her voice sounds hurt.

"Of course not." I snort, trusting her from that little anecdote would be foolish. It was simply enough that I wouldn't kill her straight away.

"Oh." Her shoulders droop. "I am your mother."

I use magic to test the blood and look for similar DNA. I've done work on forensics before. Magic is only efficient with knowledge. I'll believe the results. Blood is something you can't forge. Magic swirls around the tubes before it falls over a sheet of paper, displaying the results. I snatch it up and read. My heart drops... they match. She is my mother. I watched her die, along with my father and then some wacky scientists took me to do mad experiments.

"How?" I repeat, looking at her, making sure she is real.

"I was dying, my heart stopped but I was saved. Someone did chest compressions, I was in a coma for two years."

"Who was it?"

"I'm not sure. They wore a cloak, I never saw their face, they wouldn't let me see."

Odd story, who else would be there at the time? We lived alone away from the village, and we didn't have visitors. A better question would be who would take care of a stranger for two years and then not let them see their face? I'm not convinced.

"How come you have only found me now?" I ask, after five-hundred years she suddenly shows up on my doorstep. Why decide to visit now?

"I thought you died with your father." Sadness crosses her face.

Colt's head pops in the room. "You okay?" He mouths behind her back.

I nod. "Bye, have a good day. Text me if you need anything."

He nods, leaving us alone so I can get answers.

"I heard you were alive a few years ago but I was too afraid to come."

"That's not it." I frown.

"What?" Her face falls in disappointment.

"There is something else." I can tell. No one randomly barges into your house after half a millennium to say, 'I'm actually alive'. Not after they've had all that time to do it. Besides, her heart rate isn't helping her case.

"You've changed." Her shoulders droop. "You never used to be so paranoid and uptight. You got along with everyone in our village." She smiled softly reaching for my face.

"I grew up." I answer, batting away her hand. "What do you want?"

"Are you not happy to see me?" she asks, softly.

"Depends, why are you here?" I'm not just going to start trusting her because she is my mother. A blood relationship doesn't mean shit.

"Lucifer went after me." she admits. "I didn't know who else to go to."

She wants my help, that makes sense, I suppose, but why would Lucifer go after her?

"My magic is not what it used to be; I can't defend myself anymore. They burnt down my house."

"So, you always knew where I lived?" I calculate. She came right here; she knew where I was and never visited. Not until she needed something.

"Yes, I did. I thought I'd been gone so long you might not want to see me."

Bullshit, she just didn't bother. "Why would Lucifer attack you?" I quiz her story.

"To get back at you, of course. You have really pissed him off."

Well, that's not a surprise, but why target my mother? I didn't know she was alive... To get her to visit and kill her later after I think I got her back. I curse, I need to talk to Alex.

Abby

Colt leaves to answer the front door, Enzo looks as confused as us. It's not Selena or Alex, she's never used the door. A yelp, not from the intruder. I jump up in my seat. Enzo is ready, his arms lifted. One holding the spatula as a weapon, the other ready with magic. A woman comes through the doorway. She doesn't have any weapons ready, but that doesn't mean she isn't going to try to kill us. The woman has crinkled hazel hair and cold blue eyes that brighten at the sight of Enzo. The spatula drops from Enzo's hand, his face is deadly pale. The sparks in Enzo's ready hand dwindle. The woman stares wordlessly at Enzo with a grin on her face. Colt appears in the doorway, perfectly fine.

The three of us stand, unsure if we are meant to be attacking the intruder or not. Enzo stares at her like she is just going to disappear into thin air. Do they know each other? Suddenly, Enzo flares back to life and pins her against the wall with magic. He speeds across the room.

"Who are you?"

The woman's face falls. "You don't recognise me? Has it really been that long?" I look back to her face, she has horns. Why is that not the first thing I noticed? I guess I'm used to it, I barely notice Enzo's now and her horns are identical to his, except her left horn is complete.

Enzo growls, his hand burning her face. "Tell me who you are?"

The woman whimpers in pain, rambling an explanation, I can't quite hear, she speaks a little bit about a birthday and Enzo drops her to the ground. Slowly, the burn on her face heals by itself.

"Who is she?" Colt asks the burning question.

"My name is Adeline Thornhill." She smiles.

I look from Enzo's face to hers. Holy shit. She is his mother. She only looks ten years older than him, but she is a witch after all. Enzo told us both his parents were dead. Do ghosts exist? Enzo grabs the woman's wrist.

"Come with me, you three eat or you'll be late for school."

He disappears into the dining room before we can ask more questions, though I don't think he would be able to answer them. He looks as confused as we are, which is not a good sign. Enzo seems to know everything; he's always predicting our moves in training before we even know we are going to make them.

"Is something burning?" Holly asks.

"Shoot." Colt grabs the pancake cooking on the grill. Grabbing my water, he throws it on the fiery pancake.

"Hey!" I pretend to moan.

"I'll get you another glass." He goes back to the water pitcher leaving the ruined pancake in the sink.

"I thought Enzo said both his parents were dead?" I accept the new glass.

"He did and Enzo doesn't lie." Colt sits back down to finish breakfast. "Not about that anyway."

"She's not a ghost, right? She's alive. Do ghosts even exist?"

"Ghosts do exist but no, she's alive."

"Do you think she faked her death?"

I come up with theories. The only way to be revived would be Alex bringing her back, and even that only works for a limited amount of time after death. I know Enzo's mother has been dead for more than five hundred years. Alex could never revive her.

"That would be sick. No one would fake their death in front of their five-year old son."

"In front of? You mean Enzo watched them die?" Holly asks.

"Yeah."

"Who cared for him?"

This is the most we have learnt about Enzo's personal life ever. He will sometimes mention the places he's been, but not in detail. He thinks we'll pity him, and I can't say we wouldn't. We are doing it right now.

"I've already said too much."

"Please." I beg him.

"Fine, I'll tell you in the truck." Colt stacks dishes on the side. "I'll meet you there in a minute."

Holly and I walk over to the pick-up. "Dibs on the passenger seat." I call out.

"Damn it!" Holly curses. "I call the next ride!"

"You can't do that." I hop in the passenger seat.

"Why not?" Holly snorts.

"Fine, it counts." I shut the door. "I take dibs on all future rides after your turn."

Holly jumps in the back seat sighing. "I should have seen that coming."

I laugh. Colt enters the driver seat. Holly and I are learning to drive. Enzo has been teaching us. He's a surprisingly patient instructor, though we probably have Colt to thank for that. In the rearview mirror, I can often see them share glances where Enzo obviously wants to say something, but Colt stops him. Colt pulls out onto the open road, out of earshot.

"So?" I urge him to finish his story.

"Scientists killed his parents to take him and experiment on him." Colt states bluntly. "They took him and did a bunch of lab experiments. Enzo didn't go into detail about what they did. They were trying to manipulate his DNA to make him human. He escaped about five years later."

"What did he do after that? He was ten years old."

"Murder, mostly. Revenge for his parents. They were all rich, he took their money and lived off that."

"Do supernaturals often get experimented on?"

"Sometimes, by those crazy enough to try." Colt shakes his head. "It doesn't usually end well."

I swear the entire supernatural world is messed up. Colt was turned by a teacher and disowned by his family. Holly was turned by a rogue werewolf. I got possessed by a demon and killed a few dozen people. I still get nightmares, even though it's been months since it happened. But I can't imagine my life being any different, we've adapted surprisingly well.

Colt pulls up in the last parking spot, the rest of the cars are empty. We are running late; we have about two minutes until we need to be in registration. We jump out the truck and walk over to Selena, who is tapping her foot impatiently on the concrete. "We should leave Enzo to deal with his mother. So, do you want to get ice-cream after school?"

"Hell yes!" I smile.

"Me too." Holly smiles. "Selena. Want to get ice-cream later?"

"Yes! You three can catch me up then. You're all late, I've been waiting for ten minutes." She complains, looking at her watch.

"We got distracted." I defend the group. It is not our fault that our lives are so interesting.

"Well, you two only have one minute to get across campus." Holly and Selena are lucky, their class is in the building in front of us, while mine and Colt's is at the opposite end of the school.

"I can do that." Colt scoops me up. "Bye."

I laugh. "Bye." I wave.

Colt speeds along the campus at full speed. I laugh, we really shouldn't be doing this. The wind catches in my hair. The world blurs around us. I clutch on tightly, holding my breath. No one will see us; Colt moves too fast. A benefit of being a vampire. We skid to a stop outside the door to our classroom. I check the time; it took us ten seconds.

"Thanks for the lift." I kiss his cheek and jump out his arms.

"You're welcome." He grins, opening the door.

Entering, the class is already full and we slide into our seats on opposite sides of the room. The teacher glares at the two of us but doesn't say a word. She doesn't like either of us very much, not after she caught the two of us in her room during break a few weeks ago. Lily nudges me.

"Did you do the homework? I need to copy." I curse, I didn't do it.

CHAPTER
SIX

Lucifer

Enzo will be getting my little present right about now. He'll know it's from me, if not I'm sure his mother will tell him. I doubt I'll get a thank you card from him. He's not polite enough to do that, his mother didn't get a chance to raise him properly. They'll have that opportunity now, thanks to me. Enzo didn't know she was alive; his dear old mother was too scared to go and visit him. He is no longer the sweet, young, innocent child she could scoop up in her arms that she remembers. He's a man with blood on his hands. He grew up with very little parental input and it shows. That is what I would change if I ever had offspring again. I'd teach them. Making them learn my ways young may prevent their emotional side kicking in.

I'm certain Enzo will think this gesture is some sort of trick. It is not. I haven't planned to kill his mother or hurt her in any other way. I only got her house burnt down to push their paths together. That's the closest I came to harming her. But I am not responsible for what Enzo does in the next few days which could lead to unfortunate events.

In my cell, I have had time to reflect on what got me here in the first place. Emotions. All beings have them, apparently. I did not account for them in my last interaction with Alex and Flint which led to my demotion from ruler of Hell. I've been studying any visitor I have had to see how they react with others. I haven't had many people visit; my offspring, their consorts and a few random Hellhounds. I have learnt what different emotions do to people. That people build emotional relationships over time or because of their blood ties. Not only that, I've learned how to toy with them until they break. I plan to get my revenge by inflicting not only physical pain, but emotional pain too.

I have been confined in this cell for too long. I have not been let out for any reason, not even torture. I did get temporarily relocated when Silven tried to free me. A failed attempt, but it gave the demons faith I would rule again. That's all I needed her to do. I slump down in my cell. I cannot even lie down; the floor isn't big enough. My back has been bent for years but I don't have to wait much longer. My next step will happen in approximately three days.

I have calculated each day in my head perfectly. I cannot let any time escape if my plan is to work. It has been ten years, eight months and six days since I've ruled. I bet Alex has been enjoying her time on the throne. She has been taking her position for granted, controlling the demons' every move while never spending anytime in Hell.

She has put more regulations in place, she cares about the humans' lives over the demons' fun. That is why they will all very happily join my side to take back Hell. Once I finish using them, I can scold them for their betrayal.

Enzo

The sound of a portal appearing comes from my living room. Alex has woken up. I said I would help her find out how Lucifer managed to take out a hit on us. It could have been a guard; they have access to him but can't break him out. The only person who could do that is Alex or whoever she grants permission. That list consists of myself and Flint. We'll find out which guard it is quickly enough, once I find out what to do with Adeline.

"Enzo?" Alex calls out.

"Wait here." I gesture for Adeline to sit down.

"Who is it?" She pesters but I ignore her and walk out the door.

Alex holds a pan in her hand, a burnt crispy pancake glued inside. That is never going to come off.

"I guess this is why I didn't get breakfast." She laughs. "Since when do you burn things?" She drops the pan back in the sink.

"I got interrupted." I rub my head. I completely forgot about the pancakes. Chances are Colt will never let me live it down, I always make fun of him for burning things.

"You look stressed, what's up?" She puts down her bag, the weapons inside clattering together.

"Alexagon?" Adeline exclaims behind me. I thought I told her to stay in the dining room until I work out what to do with her.

"Enzo, do you have a sister I don't know about?"

"No, I'm his mother, Adeline." She grins.

Alex glances in my direction, refusing to believe Adeline until I say something. "Yeah, she appeared at my doorstep this morning to say she was alive, and Lucifer was trying to kill her. The mother thing checks out but Lucifer trying to kill her hasn't been confirmed."

"Okay..." Alex nods slowly. "I understand the stress now and will forgive you for forgetting breakfast."

I can't help but chuckle at that. "I'll make more."

"Good, I'm starving. I'll call Tessa. Her number might come in useful after all. I'll see if she knows about the hit on…what's your name again?"

"Adeline Thornhill. I've heard great things about you Alexagon."

"I go by Alex now." Alex states bluntly. "I'll be back in a minute." Alex puts the phone to her ear and walks into the other room so Adeline can't eavesdrop.

I magic up a new pan and chuck the burnt one in the bin, it's no use to me anymore. I start mixing up more pancake batter. Adeline looks to the doorway where Alex has left.

"Do people often waltz into your house uninvited?" Adeline asks, passing me the flour.

"You did, don't do it again." I retort. "Alex is allowed here whenever she wants."

Adeline watches as I stir the batter, as if it were some sort of trick she hadn't seen before.

"How come you know the Queen of Hell?" She asks, eyebrow raising.

I frown, that is a rare question. I'm sure every supernatural knows how we met. It was at the same time Alex overthrew Lucifer. Then there is the story of his near return. Those stories spread like wildfire. Most of the demons spread them around, supernaturals are nosey people.

"I helped her keep Lucifer in Hell, twice." I point out.

"Yes, I know. I was a little late on it, I don't keep up with anything supernatural. I found out she overthrew him six years after it happened." She shakes her head. "No, I merely meant how come you're still in contact?"

I listen to her heartbeat, I can't help it. She isn't lying, it's true. I haven't seen this woman in years, she may be my mother, but I don't have to trust her. I trusted the woman I knew five-hundred years ago. She is different, time has passed, trust must be re-earned.

"You didn't answer my question." Adeline looks up to me.

"He couldn't resist me." Alex struts into the room, grinning.

I chuckle. Well, she isn't wrong, but I think it goes both ways. I sure hope she doesn't randomly ask anyone else if they want to go to Rome at three in the morning.

"Tessa is coming in half an hour." Alex jumps up on a stool. I slide pancakes to her, then more to Adeline.

"So, you two are together?"

"Yes, and we're going to find out if your story is bullshit or not." Alex smiles.

"You don't think I'm telling the truth?" Adeline's face scrunches up in annoyance, as if it's absurd for us to doubt her, despite the odd circumstances. "Enzo you believe me, right?"

"No." I snort. She wouldn't be able to tell if I were lying, but I'm not sugar coating anything for her.

"Well, I suppose we need this Tessa so I can prove my story."

"Alright." I shrug. I flick my wrist and the dishes do themselves while I dump blueberries on my pancakes.

We fall into an uncomfortable silence. I was never the kid who wished that their parents weren't really dead. That they would come back, out of nowhere. I never dreamt of seeing them again, or what I would say if I got the chance to speak to them. I knew they were dead, and they weren't coming back. That is how death works. I honoured them by avenging their deaths then continuing with the rest of my life.

I need to discuss with Alex how we will find out who gave Lucifer access to the outside world and how they will be punished. However, I can't bring that up with Adeline in the room, in case she is not here for the reason she said she is. Then we'll have to figure out what to do with her, depending on her true objectives. I scrape up the last of my pancakes. I put down the plate, the clatter is loud in the silence.

"So..." Adeline starts. "What have you been up to recently?"

Alex and I share a look. Neither of us know what to say, Alex is more of a conversationalist than I am. She rolls her eyes, knowing I am waiting for her to start.

"Well, I mean other than raising your children together." Adeline adds.

Coffee spews out of my mouth. I choke, laughing. She doesn't understand sarcasm apparently.

"Well, Enzo, why did you not tell me we had children?" Alex raises her eyebrow.

Adeline frowns. "Those kids who just left... I thought you said..."

"My sort of adopted son, his girlfriend and her twin." I correct her, though the other two are becoming more like my children too. I do enjoy their company and will miss them when Colt decides to move out, but I would not admit it to their faces. Colt is the easiest one to mistake for my child.

"Oh, okay. Sorry."

We fall back into silence. Thankfully, Alex's phone rings. "Tessa is ready. Can you open a portal for her?"

"Gladly." I wave my hand to summon a portal.

Tessa appears out of the mirror of swirling magic, bouncing up and down. She wears the same cape from the party only with her hood down. She wears brighter colours than yesterday; a purple shirt and black jeans.

"I have the information you want!" She chirps happily.

"What did you find?" Alex asks.

"There was indeed a contract put out on the name of 'Adeline Thornhill'." Tessa explains. "Another family took up the hit job but then they all died trying to take down a specific individual, who no one in their right mind would try to kill, especially for the money on offer. It was awfully low for someone of that stature." Tessa shakes her head. "I couldn't track it any further to see if anyone had taken on the hit after. Maybe with a little more time I could find out, but chances are no one did. The Kim assassin family only died two days ago, and it was only made official yesterday. People won't be taking on their jobs for at least a couple of days, sometimes it's even a week or two after. It's a form of respect."

"So you're saying that she does have a price on her head, but it's not likely someone tried to kill her in the last twenty-four hours? Or at all." Which means she is lying.

"Yes, it'll take some time to get information and concoct a plan to kill her. She'll have at least two weeks until she is in any sort of danger again."

"But my house got burnt down! How do you explain that!" Adeline insists.

"It could be true. There are some rogue disrespectful assassin families who wouldn't wait, but I don't know any personally. Other than a fling I had with one of them..."

"How did you get this information?" I ask, cutting her story short. We don't have time for it.

"My brother. See, I got cut out of the family after I purposefully let a hit who was worth over a million dollars go. It's not my fault, they were so kind and sweet when I was scouting them. I couldn't murder such a nice werewolf. He did kill someone, but I'm pretty certain it was self-defence, even if the victim's family wanted him dead. Anyway, my brother is one of the most important assassins there is, he has the highest number of official kills on record."

Her last name is Baer which means her brother is Ace Baer. I've heard stories about him, he's very powerful. Her family line has the power of telekinesis.

"We need to see your house." I demand. "Where do you live?"

"She lives at 24 Limber Road." Tessa interrupts.

"I do." Adeline agrees. "Surely the fact someone put a hit on my head is enough, Lucifer wants me gone!"

"Lucifer? He didn't put a hit on your head, a random demon did it."

"But demons don't know how to use phones." Adeline defends herself. "Or any type of technology for that matter."

"They could learn. If they have hands, obviously. I can't imagine tentacles or claws would work on a screen." Tessa shrugs. She's right, one must have learned somehow to help Lucifer.

"What's the name?" Alex asks.

"I couldn't pronounce its name if I tried. Demons have wacky names, except you Alex."

Alex shakes her head but has a little smirk on her face, she loves having a little fan. "Do you know how to spell the name of the demon who ordered the hit?"

The names might be different, but chances are both contracts on us and Adeline were put out for Lucifer by the same informant. If Adeline is telling the truth, that is. That demon is his outside source, and we will have to kill him in retaliation. In a bad way. Torture will need to be involved or other demons will think it's okay to disobey Alex.

"I have it on my phone, I'll text it to you." She taps away at her phone.

Alex checks the message. "It's as we thought, one of the guards." She looks over at me. I bet it's Stewaroid. He's an asshole, I've never liked him.

"Oh! Oh! I could take the hit on Adeline! Then you would be safe. It could buy you at least two weeks."

"We'll see if that is necessary. Let's go visit this ruin of a house." It's the only way to see if it's true or not. Tessa has brought up more questions than answers. We can worry about protecting her or not after we know everything.

"24 Limber Road, which country?"

"England."

England is pretty far from Canada. She doesn't have an English accent. "If you were in England, that portal must have been hard... considering you said your magic isn't working properly."

"I was terrified. It was probably the adrenaline, I'm lucky I made it."

"Okay then." I whisk up the portal. There is no point arguing the possibility here when the answer is a portal away.

"Of course, anything to make you believe me, son." Adeline jumps in.

Tessa skips after. I go to enter. A hand grabs my wrist. "What happens if it's not true and it's a trap?"

"I assume we'll kill her, bat her around a little first." I think aloud. "Why did you have something particular in mind?"

"That sounds about right, we may also get battered around. Your mother is much older than you, remember."

"True but if I can take out Flint, I'll be fine. If not, I'll hide behind you. Come on, before Tessa talks Adeline's ear off." I grab Alex's hand as we swirl through the portal.

We land in the middle of a boring old street. This is not the house I imagined. Most immortal beings have large, expensive houses because they have forever to accumulate money. Most of us live in secluded areas away from humans. Some who do conform to human life normally switch cities after a few years before people start to pick up on the fact they haven't aged. The house sits in the middle of a long line of identical houses that fills the entire street. It's a very human environment and a very average house. Well, it used to be. Adeline's house is in ruins, there is nothing left of the ceiling. The bricks are stained with a thick coat of ash. The fire is out, but it must have burned for hours. The door swings loosely on its hinges. Her story is adding up so far, but she could have set it herself.

Carefully, we enter. The first room is a narrow hallway. Small and convenient, a few threads of a coat remain on a metal hook. Melted plastic with a shop's logo sticks to the coat, it looks like it used to be a bag. There is a sooty shoe rack, with no shoes on it. There is barely anything left in the entire house. Through the doorway to the next room, I see springs sticking out of a sofa lying on its side, ruined feathers all over the floor.

"Is this proof enough for you?" Adeline waves around what used to be her house.

I did not expect the house to be in such a state. She is a witch, after all. A few waves of her hand and she could sort it out. I thought the house would be inhabitable, not in smithereens. If the fire was supernatural, it would burn faster. I step over broken bricks.

"Whoever did this, didn't know what they were doing." Tessa calls from the kitchen.

The kitchen is the worst, the stove is non-existent. It barely looks like a room, sunlight streams in through the ruins. Walls are smashed in like something heavy hit them.

"Someone tried to use the gas from the cooker to explode the house." Tessa surveys the room. "They didn't let enough gas out before they lit the match. It turned into a raging fire instead."

"You were in the building when this happened?" I look over at Adeline, it seems impossible for her to have not noticed. The gas in cookers has a smell, so humans can tell when there is a leak.

"I was asleep, I didn't wake up until the explosion went off."

"Okay, why didn't you put out the fire by yourself?"

"I'm not as strong as I used to be." Adeline admits. "I knew I had to get out of here. The fire was raging. I did the first thing I could think of."

That is to travel halfway across the globe to me, apparently. Which, admittedly, is less draining than putting out a fire. But it's nice to know she only thinks of me when she needs help, not to let me know she was alive or anything. I was still a kid when she came out of her coma, and she didn't even bother to check if I was alive. She just assumed it and moved on. I shake my head. I can't dwell on that, it's hardly important; that time has come and gone.

"So, you just freaked out and teleported to Enzo's house?" Alex investigates.

"Yes."

"How do you know it was Lucifer?"

"The person who set it chanted his name before running away from the fire."

"Assassins don't do that; it probably wasn't an attempted hit. It was someone different." Tessa pipes up. "Maybe the demon who ordered the hit? If he heard the family who took on the job had all died, he might have taken it upon himself."

She has a point. Assassins are sly people trained from birth, they don't make mistakes, or their family will disown them, like Tessa's did. Assassins are all about reputation; they want a perfect record. If Lucifer threatened the demon, they could have gotten desperate enough to do it themselves. Demons do not know how to work household objects which is why the hit failed, but then why didn't the demon just slaughter Adeline. That is what they do best. Alex glances at me, I know she is thinking exactly what I am. We'll have to visit Lucifer. Just like he wants us to.

"Okay, Tessa you will go back to Enzo's home and keep an eye on Adeline. Enzo and I are going to investigate the demon." Alex takes charge of the situation.

"Of course!" Tessa nods trying to be serious, but she has a large grin on her face. "You can count on me. I will not let her leave my sight."

"What? What more can I do to prove it!" Adeline grumbles. "I thought you would trust me! I am your mother."

That last sentence forces a wince. 'Mother'. That is true, but I don't want to call her that. Her story is suspicious, I would normally just dismiss any random person who comes to my door. She's lucky I'm giving her a chance. Mother or not, I will not put Colt or the others at risk for her.

"Alex and I will be back soon. If the kids come back before we do, keep them away from her."

Tessa nods. "Will do."

We barely know Tessa either, but she was willing to sacrifice her job to tell us about the hit on us. She is obsessed with Alex, that is no joke. I would put more faith in her than Adeline.

I whisk up a portal. "See you soon."

"I could come with you, to help prove my innocence." Adeline insists.

"You can't go to Hell, you don't have demon blood." I correct her. "Goodbye."

Tess grabs Adeline's wrist and drags her forcefully through the portal, an authoritative air to her. Alex laughs, as they disappear. "I think I've found my own little personal assistant."

"It looks like it. Let's get this over and done with."

The heat overwhelms my body, pits of fire swarm the dry earth. Not all of Hell is a fiery pit, Hell is actually split in half. The fiery burn-your-flesh off half, and the icy half that could freeze your blood while it's still in your body. The other side isn't very popular, not many demons can survive there. It's more of a wasteland than this part. Demons bow towards Alex as we make our way to the castle. They have to. The doors open with a flick of her hand.

"Which demon has been working for Lucifer?" I ask as we enter the throne room.

"Stewariod." I knew it. "I plan to talk to him, he cannot lie to me. Lucifer wants us to visit. We can't give him what he wants." A serving demon scampers by. "You! Get me Stewariod."

It nods, running away. Alex kicks her legs over the side of the throne. "I miss having servants when we are on Earth." I think that's Alex's favourite part. The demons must follow her every command. She is their ruler, if they don't, she gets to punish them. Which will be happening to Stewariod in a few moments.

Stewariod marches up to face Alex on her throne, he bows obediently. Alex sits up straight in her throne, a smirk crossing her face. She has already chosen how to punish him.

"Did you put out a bounty on the head of a woman called Adeline Thornhill?"

Stewariod nods. "Yes."

That is not a crime, he can admit to that. Even if he had killed someone, that is no big deal in Hell. That is a demon's sole purpose in life. It is praised. Alex has stopped them doing stupid things like plagues, but she cannot stop them from doing their job. They do go to Earth and kill. However, if their intent was to hurt their Queen, that would be treason.

"Why pay an assassin, why not do it yourself?" Alex interrogates him.

"Because I'm very busy."

"But the assassins you ordered died? What did you do after that?"

"Got another demon to do it." He admits everything that is not against the law.

"Who?"

"I don't know, one of the rodent ones."

Demons have rankings. Alex and her family are at the top, then it goes to the dukes and duchesses, named demons and eventually just demons who don't have names and are more animal-like. They're like pets for the stronger demons. No wonder it did a bad job, but that does mean part of Adeline's story is adding up. "Why did you try to have her assassinated?"

He freezes, unable to give a reason. Demons are excellent followers, but they are terrible planners. They cannot concoct a plan if they tried, but they have enough of a brain to follow one.

"I did it because…" He trails off, unable to think of an excuse.

"Surely you have a reason, if you couldn't wait to kill her. I just want to know." Alex shrugs.

"A-a friend asked me to." That would be valid, but demons don't often use the term 'friends', they like calling their 'pals' disrespectful names.

"Who?" Alex urges him on as he sweats, using his brain for the first time in his long life.

"Um…"

He must know a few dozen demons who he would willingly throw under the bus, but he can't think of any in his panic. There is no chance he wants to protect them; demons don't do that. The only one he will not tell on is Lucifer, who has probably threatened his life, and, for some reason, he's more scared of Lucifer than Alex.

"Tell me who asked." Alex demands impatiently, eyes blazing with fire.

He fidgets on his spot, fiddling with his tentacles. "No one."

"So, you lied?"

"No!" He fidgets, sweat falling down his face. "It was…" He looks up into Alex's eyes.

"Tell me the truth and I won't punish you." Alex is obviously lying, but the demon is too stupid to tell.

"Lucifer." He blurts out. "Lucifer made me do it."

"Why?" Alex orders.

"Because he wanted to mess with you! He thought you were enjoying yourselves too much. He wanted you to know that he can reach you, even from his cell."

"Alright. That means you were also the one who sent the assassins after us, correct?"

"Y-y-yes. Can I go?"

"Of course."

Stewariod's face sags in relief as he trembles. He spins to run away. Alex laughs, magic soaring from her hand and Stewariod flies to the ground. Marching over to him, she picks him up by his neck. The octopus-like flesh drips off his body, turning him into goo. The waxy substance turns into a puddle at Alex's feet. Blood curdling screams leave his mouth as his body parts from his head. A few demons who happen to be in the room at the time watch. Eyes wide as they watch him die with very little effort from Alex. I bet word of this will spread around the demons. Alex drops what is left of him on the ground.

"Does anyone else want to help Lucifer?" She offers the room, it remains silent. "No? Good. You." She points to a demon. I forget their name, there are too many to remember. "You will replace Stewaroid. Go." Alex sits back on the throne, the liquidated demon stains her hands and clothes. The demon hurries away. The goo disappears; demons fade away when they die. "If any of you cooperate with Lucifer, there will be severe repercussions. You work for me, not him."

I do not understand why they prefer Lucifer. He worked them harder, and he killed them for no reason at all. Alex treats them better, while still asserting her authority. But they liked his ruthlessness towards humans. She really didn't need me to come with her, but I can't say I didn't enjoy watching. Alex bats a strand of hair out of her face.

"Well, we sorted that out quickly. Want to go back now?"

"Sure." I whip up a portal.

We spawn outside my house. The door in front of us. "Why are we outside?" Alex frowns.

"Because I wanted to do this." I push her back against the door and kiss her. My hand goes around her back.

Alex pulls away grinning. "Why couldn't we do this inside? Don't want your mum to see now we know she's innocent?"

"No, I don't want Tessa fighting me for you." I answer truthfully.

Alex laughs, our noses touching. "Good point."

Our lips collide again, my stomach flipping. Damn, she is a good kisser. I leave a trail of kisses down her neck to her sharp collar bone. Alex gasps, as I work my way back up to her lips. Alex smiles, eyes sparkling. My hands go around her waist, hands going up the back of her shirt and reaching for her bra. As I am going in to kiss her, the door opens. Alex stumbles back, falling. I grab her hand, pulling her back up before she falls over. Colt stands at the door.

"I found out why the door was banging." Colt calls back into the house. Alex laughs. The sun is setting in the background, there is no sense of time in Hell. We must have been there a while, even if it didn't feel like it. "Are you two coming inside?" Colt asks. "Tessa and Adeline are waiting for you, and Tessa will not stop talking about Alex."

"Yes. We are coming." Alex sighs.

CHAPTER
SEVEN

Abby

My feet swing from the tree branch as I tuck into my ice cream. The lessons were boring, Colt and I had a cooking class. We were able to convince the teacher to let us sit next to each other. It makes the lesson bearable. We didn't actually get to cook anything, it was just a lesson about sanitation. I picked random subjects; I have no idea what I want to do with my life. Colt doesn't know what he wants to do either. Holly does, she wants to be a paediatric doctor.

The sunbathes our faces. I was surprised when I woke up this morning without a hangover. I'm glad I didn't, or I'd be hiding from the sun instead of enjoying it.

"Want to try mine?" Colt waves the spoon of honeycomb ice-cream.

I open my mouth and he feeds me. "Damn that's good." I give him some of mine, I chose strawberries and cream.

"It's nice." Colt smothers his ice cream in blood from a flask. The blood helps it go down more easily, but he can eat food normally.

I rest my head on his shoulder, looking at the almost empty park. A few children and their parents crowd the swings. I remember when Holly and I went to the park when we were little. There is one directly across the street from our house. We were allowed to go after dinner every day for an hour. We would always fight over the swing. We would spin each other around on the round-a-bout and push each other down the slides too. Holly had a watch, she could read the time better than I could, she would always make sure we were back home on time, or we wouldn't be allowed to go the next day.

My phone buzzes, I pull it out of my pocket. It's my mum, asking what time we'll be home for dinner. Crap, I forgot that Selena and Colt were meant to come with us for dinner, but we have to go around Enzo's later.

"What's wrong?" Colt asks.

He has forgotten too. My parents arranged it weeks ago. They have already met Selena a bunch of times, but they want to meet Colt too. They were very proud of the idea. "I need to tell my parents we are busy."

Colt curses. "Yeah, I forgot too. Arrange it for next week?"

I nod. They'll understand. Alex used mind-control on them. They are no longer grounding us or worrying about us when we don't come home. I talked to Esmeralda at the party, she and Hayden had their memories wiped for two years so they could continue their lives until they finished school. I can't imagine doing that willingly. I hated it when I couldn't remember what Silven did with my body. It makes sense; since Holly was turned into a werewolf, I have missed a few dozen days at school and my grades have gone down considerably, but we don't have much time left until we finish. The sun begins to droop in the sky after a few hours of talking. Colt yawns, stretching out his arms. He glances at his phone.

"I think we have waited long enough. Want to go back?"

I nod, jumping down from the tree. My legs give out, numb from sitting for so long. Colt laughs. "Are you okay down there?"

I smile. I jump to my feet, pins and needles throb through my legs. Colt chuckles while I try to take a step. "Frick you. Just because you don't have a natural blood flow." I curse him.

"Here." He lifts me up off the ground, swinging me in his arms. He begins to walk to the car.

I laugh. "Why didn't you do this in the first place?"

"It was fun to watch you struggle."

"Hey! That's mean." I grumble, but I can't help but smile.

"No, being mean would be leaving you here."

I laugh. "Good point, you would never do that."

"Is that a dare?" His eyes light up.

"No! It is not!" I warn him. Colt carefully places me on the ground. I howl, jumping to my feet. Pins and needles jolting through my legs. Colt runs away. The pins slowly fade as I chase him. I pass Selena and Holly walking hand in hand, talking to each other. I pounce on Colt's back; he is going slowly for me. Otherwise, it would have been impossible for me to catch up. Colt grabs my legs to hold me up on his back. "I hate you." I shake my head.

"I love you too." He continues onwards towards the car.

I smile. I wear Colt's hoodie over my outfit. A good thing about dating a vampire is I don't have to feel guilty when I steal his jacket; Colt cannot feel the temperature. I swear he only wears jackets so I can nick them when I get cold. I am not complaining.

Reaching the car, I drop from his back. Colt opens the door for me.

"Thanks." I kiss his cheek and climb in. He shuts the door behind me. Selena and Holly are still approaching the car when Colt starts the engine. "

Should I?" Colt's eyes sparkle.

"Obviously."

Colt steps on the accelerator. I laugh, watching Holly yells at us from the wing mirror. It's not as fun when you are the one who has to run a block after the car. We won't go further than a street. Selena murmurs something to Holly. Their hollering stops. Holly races forward. The car jerks, the seat belt catches my body as I get flung forward. The back wheels struggle. Looking back out the window, Holly is holding up the back of the car. I laugh, show-off.

Colt stops the truck and Holly drops the vehicle, cursing. Selena jogs up to the stopped truck. "Thanks babe." Selena kisses her on the lips.

"You're welcome." Holly blushes. They jump into the back of the car. Holly shakes her hand in pain, a red mark on it. The soreness will recover quickly. Colt starts the car, glancing out the window to check that no one saw Holly. Luckily for us, no one is on the street. Drawing out onto the road, we drive back to the house.

Colt draws up in front of the house. I can't spot any activity inside. The only way you can tell that someone lives in the house is when Colt's car leaves the driveway. Enzo doesn't use his car often; he doesn't have much of a use for it, except enjoyment. He doesn't even use the front door or curtains. Colt is the only one who makes it seem like the building isn't abandoned. Colt stops the truck. We jump out and he opens the door with a key. We all have keys but we don't really need them. If we really needed to, we could go through the back gate, Enzo never locks that.

I dump my backpack at the front door and kick off my shoes. We walk into the living room. A lamp flies through the air, right at our heads. I duck, Colt catches it before it smacks against the wall.

"Oh, it's you three. Hey." Tessa, the woman from last night, sits on the sofa. "Sorry about the lamp. I panicked."

What power does she have? She flung a lamp at us without moving. A witch, possibly?

Colt carefully puts the lamp back in its place. "What are you doing here?"

"Alex asked me to keep an eye on Adeline. We are becoming really close friends." Tessa grins. "They went to Hell to check out

Adeline's story. I have to guard her and keep her from hurting you three, but I don't think she will."

"Maybe we should be cautious of you too." Colt arches an eyebrow.

"The lamp was an accident. I didn't know when you would be back. I won't do it again." She promises.

"How does Alex know you?" Holly pipes up.

"I told her Lucifer wanted to assassinate her, her boyfriend and her family, instead of taking up the offer for myself. I would never do that! She is my idol."

She's an assassin? A supernatural assassin. I guess a paid killer is a good person to babysit a witch. They sit on the couch, Adeline doesn't say a word. The television is on, but Adeline is simply gazing out the window.

"Oh, good it's you and..." Tessa looks over Holly's shoulder to Selena. "Who are you?"

"She's my girlfriend, Selena." Holly holds her hand. I swear, their hands are glued together.

"You have a girlfriend? Damn, okay. I'm making coffee, anyone want some? I've had twelve today! I also got bored and made cake." Tessa stands. "Oh! We could all play charades. I have an app on my phone we can use."

Colt glances at me. I'm not sure how much sugar is in those coffees, but that amount of energy is not normal. Colt tugs me onto a spare seat. Settling on his lap, my feet go over the armrest. Tessa jumps back into the room with cake and coffee. Adeline looks at us, shakes her head and mouths 'Don't eat the cake'. I hope Alex and Enzo get back soon.

Tessa and Adeline aren't that bad, but the cake is awful. The coffee is surprisingly good. Charades is questionable. Tessa is winning by a long shot. I down my second coffee, curled up against Colt's cold body. The door thumps, who is that? The door has been used more times in the last few days than in the past months I've known Colt and Enzo. The only visitors they get are us three.

"Let's go check the door." Colt wriggles out of my embrace. I can't say no, it's Tessa's turn and I have no idea what she is doing. Eagerly, we walk off to the door. I roll up the sleeves on the oversized sweater so I can grab the door handle. Opening the door, a woman flies forward at us. Colt jumps in the way to stop her from hitting me. Enzo catches Alex before she falls over. They were making out against the door. Seriously? We've been stuck in here, while they take a snogging break? I shake my head. I hope they got their answers about Adeline. It does not surprise me that they went to check her story. If someone randomly appeared out of nowhere claiming that they were my dead mother I'd be skeptical too. "Are you two coming inside or shall I close the door and pretend you were never here?" Colt asks.

"We're coming." Alex sighs.

Inside, Tessa is still taking her turn. I have no idea what she is doing. Adeline has given up guessing and sips her coffee in silence. I think that is proof enough that she is related to Enzo.

"A car?" Selena still tries to guess.

"A person riding a horse obviously." Alex answers instantly, with only a glance.

"Yes!" Tessa spins, noticing them. "Alex! You are back."

How did Alex do that? That is the last thing I would have guessed. I move back to the seat with Colt. Adeline looks up from her statue-like position. "So?"

"Your story adds up." Enzo grumbles, he almost sounds disappointed with his findings. I must be wrong, why wouldn't he want his mother back? He is probably grouchy from us interrupting them.

"So, you believe me?" She grins.

"Well, yeah."

"Thank you!" She jumps up from her seat, hugging him.

Enzo pushes her away forcefully, "You're welcome."

"Will you help me, until I'm safe?"

"Sure." Enzo nods, like he doesn't know what to do.

"Thank you! I knew I could count on you son."

Enzo nods, uncertainly. Tessa interrupts the awkward interaction. "Alex, it's your turn."

"I'm good, thanks. You take my turn, Enzo and I will start dinner." She leads him away from Adeline.

Tessa nods. "Of course." Tessa loves Alex, she would do anything for her. That is what I have worked out from the last hour. She believes Alex can do no wrong. I have no idea how she came to that conclusion; Alex has killed thousands of people.

"How about we don't play charades anymore? Now we know Adeline is legit, please tell us all about baby Enzo." Colt smiles.

I hadn't thought about that. We can get all of Enzo's embarrassing childhood stories. We have all shared ours. My favourite is when Colt said to everyone in his school that he could climb a tree with his feet taped together. He then actually tried to do it and broke his leg. Adeline smiles for the first time this evening.

"Where do I start? Enzo was a ball of mischief from the start."

She goes on to tell us about how Enzo could use magic from the second he was born. He turned into a hellhound at age three, that he couldn't walk and got so irritated, that he set the entire forest on fire by accident. These were not the cute baby stories I was hoping for, but it's nice to know Enzo has flaws other than his lack of social skills.

My eyes droop to the amazing smell of pasta sauce and the warmth from the fire. My head rests on Colt's shoulder. Adeline goes on and on about Enzo. She is very proud of him, that is undeniable. That doesn't answer why she took so long to check up on him. Surely, she would have been desperate to see him again? I don't know enough about the supernatural to be certain. I still can't wrap my head around the fact Colt's mother disowned him for being a vampire. It's not his fault. Colt doesn't really like talking about his parents, or his life before becoming a vampire. Enzo is his family and that is enough for him. My eyes close out of boredom. I don't fight it, and drift off into a calm sleep in Colt's arms.

A cold chill touches my cheek. I blink heavily, yawning. Hot, steaming food sits on the table. Colt's lips touch my cheek again, waking me up gently.

"Thanks." I kiss him back. I take my plate; Enzo has fetched chairs for him and Alex. The room is not prepared for this many guests. I remove my head from Colt's shoulder so he can eat.

"I hope the kitchen wasn't too messy." Tessa eats. "I didn't realise how hard cakes were to make."

"It looked like someone had been murdered in batter." Enzo scoops up his food. Alex's feet go over the arm of her chair and sit on his lap.

"Sorry." Tessa laughs.

Tessa takes her turn to talk, the rest of us stuff our hungry faces. She speaks about her childhood. It sounds normal, except for learning how to kill people. Assassins make their first kill at eighteen, it's a rite of passage, which is insane. The food is amazing, much better than anything our food technology class makes. Enzo teaches Colt and I when we have a meal to make.

After dinner, Colt and I excuse ourselves from the room. Colt and I go to his room, it's nine already. Holly and I will probably stay the night. Selena too, she sleeps in Holly's room when she stays over. I pull out the textbook and Colt pulls out chocolate from his snack draw.

"I love you." I murmur as he feeds me.

He laughs. "I know."

I open the textbook. English, it's not too boring, but it's hard. We don't have much time until we take the exams, but after that we are free to live our lives. Colt groans at the sight of the book.

"Do you think we can convince Enzo to do it? A whisk of his hand and we get an A."

"You know what happened last time."

Enzo did the work for us, after we forgot to do it. We took the work without a second thought, neither of us proofread it. We'd always gotten As before. Last time, he played a prank and the work was awful. We both got kept behind for a detention after school. Turns out, Enzo had simply written the line 'please give me an A. I was too tired last night to do my essay.' in paragraphs. He said he would have written 'drunk' which was the truth, but he didn't want my parents to be contacted and told I'd been underage drinking.

"Good point, we better do it." Colt sighs, pulling out his laptop.

We have a system for the subjects we both take. We complete one load of work together, then copy it and change a few words for the other person. It is very effective and less of an effort for both of us.

Two large chocolate bars later, our English work is complete. I put away my laptop, yawning. Colt slumps back in his chair, rubbing his tired eyes. It's eleven in the evening, but there are still distant voices talking from downstairs. I can't hear much, but my guess is Tessa is doing the most talking.

"I should go have a shower."

"Alright, do you want to come back after or are you going to sleep?"

I consider it, I would love to hang out longer but I'm at the point where I may fall asleep in the shower. "I'll sleep, see you in the morning."

"Alright, see you in the morning." He draws me in for one last kiss.

I smile, kissing him back. My stomach flips, I lean in for more. Colt pulls my chair closer. "You know you could sleep in here." Colt suggests.

"Good idea, I'll just shower in the morning." I murmur, kissing him again.

Enzo

We drink and talk with Adeline for hours about her life the last few hundred years. There wasn't a lot for her to say. She has been living like a human the entire time. Ignoring her powers and living in a city for twelve years or so, then moving on. There is nothing exciting to say about it; human lives are boring. They work, sleep, eat and die. I can't imagine living my entire life in a system, as they do, without going insane. Adeline said she believed it was the only way to survive. Everyone thought she was dead, she stuck with it and lived among the humans. She hasn't used magic, even in her home, for years. Her idea worked; she has not been bothered by any supernatural incident until now. Thanks to Lucifer.

We are four bottles down on the liquor before the conversation slows down and people start to get tired. Luckily, I have enough rooms for all the new guests. Tessa is staying the night too. I offered, she has been useful and just sending her home seemed rude.

Alex's legs swing off my lap. "We should probably go to bed." I frown, it's unlike her to be the first to retire, but it's understandable. This is incredibly dull. "I'll show Tessa a room, you show Adeline." She conducts.

"Alright." I stand. "Come with me."

I lead her upstairs to an empty room. It has its own en-suite bathroom, a double bed and an empty closet. I whisk a hand; I assume with her magic being rusty it would be best if I made her clothes. They fill the closet, and the bathroom fills with shampoo and other toiletries she may need. Pyjamas appear on the bed. "Thank you for everything, I know you probably hate me for being absent from your life." She looks me in the eyes sincerely. Absent is one word for it, but I don't care enough about her to hate her. I'm only helping her because I'm the reason Lucifer is after her in the first place. If she were to die, it would be my fault. She'd die for knowing me, not because she deserved it, and

I have enough blood on my hands already. If she does make a wrong move, I won't hesitate to throw her out, mother or not.

"That's alright. I'll speak to you in the morning."

"Yes, I was hoping tomorrow we could bond a bit more and talk, I have so much to say." From my experience tonight, I really don't think she has a lot to say, nothing interesting at least.

"Sure." I shrug, I'm sure Alex will tag along to keep me entertained. We also need to find out if Lucifer is planning anything else. Adeline will want to get back to her human life as soon as it's safe, and I won't complain about getting her out of my hair.

"Goodnight."

"Goodnight son."

"Don't call me that."

"But…"

Slamming the door behind me, I cut off whatever she was going to say. I put her in the room furthest down the corridor. I hear Selena and Holly whisper in her room. Abby's door is open, I can't see her, I assume she's sleeping with Colt. I make my way back up the corridor to my bedroom.

The door is slightly open. Alex sits on my bed, holding a bottle of whiskey. She has changed her outfit to a backless, short, red jumpsuit with a low neckline. Straps of a bikini on her shoulders. "Now that they are all sorted out, we can go have fun. I think a beach in Greece has just suddenly closed." She grins waving the bottle.

I laugh, I understand why she was so eager to finish the night early. She just wanted to lose all the extra people in the room. I create a portal. "Let's go then."

"I knew you would be up for it." Alex grabs my hand, and we disappear.

Sunlight floods the beach, sparkling water lapping against the sand. The heavy scent of salt floods my senses. Damn, it feels good to be here. Seagulls call over our heads, the beach is empty. The heat burns my skin, the breeze gently drifts by. Alex smiles, proud of herself. "I knew you would enjoy this." She flicks her hand and my outfit changes. My clothes disappear leaving me in swim shorts. Sand sinks between my toes.

"Now I'm enjoying it too." I laugh. I should have seen that coming.

"The view is exquisite." Her eyes sparkle, looking down at my chest.

"I could say the same."

"I know you could." She smiles back.

I kiss her, drawing her in. Her scent is light and fiery. Her lips go on mine, happily. The bottle drops from her hands, and she wraps her arms around my neck, pulling me into her reach. My stomach flips and I press my lips onto hers harder, trying to smother any millimetre of distance between us. Alex's hair tickles my neck. I can feel the magic pulsing off her body. She groans clutching my head against hers. She gasps drawing back for a breath. I smile, kissing her nose. Her hair brushes my shoulder, her lips nibbling my ear.

"I would like to continue, but I really want to try out the jet skis." I smile, that's no surprise. She'll want to race too. Alex leans in, kissing me again instead of letting go. "Damn you know I can't resist that smile. That's just mean."

I kiss her back. "That's not my fault, you made me smile."

"Good point." Waves crash against my feet.

Alex tugs me down onto the sand.

Waking up, I groan softly. Sand covering my body, I rub my head. We drank about six bottles last night. Alex lies in her bikini next to me. She clings to one of my arms, sleeping softly. I feel in my pocket for my phone. I have spells on it to make it constantly charged and waterproof. Good thing too, after Alex threw me off the jet ski. I curse, it's half-seven in the morning at home. The others will already be waking up. I should probably get back before they realise I'm missing. Alex murmurs gently on my arm. I don't want to wake her, but I don't have much of a choice unless I leave her here. I move her hair out of her face and kiss her forehead.

"It's not morning yet." Alex groans.

I chuckle. "Even you can't manipulate time."

"I can try." Alex rubs her eyes, then curses. I flick my hand, the sand she had gotten in her eyes disappearing. "Thank you."

"You're welcome. I need to go back."

"Are you sure about that?" Her eyes sparkle mischievously.

"No." I lean down to kiss her. They can get themselves breakfast today. Alex smiles triumphantly, knowing she has won. Her nose brushes mine. My phone rings, it will be Colt undoubtedly asking where I am. I groan, it continues to ring.

"You should answer that." Alex sighs. "Before they think your mother kidnapped you or something."

"Good point." I pull away and answer the call. "What's up?"

"Where are you? I searched the entire house for you! Tessa is attempting to make French toast and Adeline is worrying about you." He moans.

"Alex and I went out. I'll be back in a minute." I hang up.

Alex sighs, listening in on the conversation. I shouldn't leave them with Tessa and Adeline much longer, though. It's not that they aren't old enough to look after themselves and trust Tessa, her heart rate says everything. She'd do anything for Alex, her devotion is not fake. I just don't trust Adeline; something is off about her.

"Before we go." Alex puts her sand-stained jumpsuit back on. The make-up she had been wearing yesterday was washed off by the sea. Her hair curls over her face and she irritably bats it out of her eyes. She looks up, catching me staring at her. I grin, eyes meeting hers. She rolls her eyes, smirking. "Before we go, are you okay? What with your mother appearing out of nowhere."

"Yeah, but if I need an excuse to escape the situation, you need me for something, okay?"

"Of course. I need to be in Hell for an hour or two, but I'll try to keep my phone on me. Be careful. I know she's your mother, but don't let that fool you."

"Of course." A blood relationship does not mean that someone has your best interests at heart. Lucifer tried to kill both his children for power, and he won't be the last. It happens rarely, most families are closely knitted together. If Adeline is how I remember her, then I would like to get to know her, but Alex, Colt, Abby and Holly are more like my family than she will ever be.

"See you later."

"Will do." She grins happily.

I lean down to kiss her goodbye. She puts a finger to my lips. "You know if you kiss me once you will want to do it again." She has me there. I can't help it if she is irresistible.

Alex smiles and backs up into a portal to Hell. I create my own portal. I land in my living room. I changed my outfit as I went through. I switched to a sweater and jeans and boots. The gaggle of teenagers are devouring cereal. The two adults are in the kitchen talking between themselves. I do not want to see what Tessa has done to my kitchen.

"Finally." Colt raises his eyebrow.

I yawn, I suspect Alex and I got four hours of sleep at most. Sand stains my hand, I magic it away quickly.

"Sorry I'm late. Nothing happened while I was gone, did it?"

"A small fire, Tessa burnt the toast, Adeline broke her shower and Selena accidentally stabbed herself with a spoon." Abby explains. "But other than that, it's gone quite well."

I sigh. I leave for a night and all that happens. I wouldn't have left if Tessa wasn't here. The teens can look after themselves, but Adeline is here too. Tessa would help protect them. Turns out, Tessa caused most of the problems but all is easily fixed with magic, luckily.

"Also, Abby crashed your car." Colt adds.

"What?" I snap. I have forbidden them from driving my McLaren until they learn how to drive. Firstly, to prevent my car getting damaged, also because they could easily kill themselves in it.

"Hey!" Abby shoves Colt playfully. "That's not true."

"Yeah, I just wanted him to pull that face." Colt laughs.

I shake my head. I should repair my kitchen and send Tessa home. I'm sure she doesn't want to be stuck here while Alex is away.

Walking into my kitchen, I see black ash races up the walls. To be fair, it's been in worse condition. I wave my hand and it all repairs itself back to its original state.

"Do you want toast? I've been taking chef classes?" Tessa motions to the burnt French toast. "Where is Alex?"

"No thanks." I watch as pans and pots clean themselves in the sink. At least Tessa is putting her telekinesis power to good use and cleaning up after herself. "Alex is in Hell. I can portal you home if you like."

"I probably should get back." She agrees.

"What do I owe you?" I ask, I can't forget to pay her for her work. Her information was very useful.

"Nothing. I'm just excited I got to help Alex out. Tell her to call me!"

"Of course." I lie. I flick my hand, a few thousand dollars in hundred-dollar bills slip into her pocket. I can't let her work for free.

"Great! I'll be on my way. I hope the washing up isn't too hard." The pots drop into the sink. I create a portal for her to go through. "Bye Adeline. Bye Enzo."

Colt leans in the doorway. "Could we get a portal too? School starts in ten minutes, and Holly and Selena want to go home."

I sigh; I am their parent. "Sure."

Ten minutes later and I'm left with Adeline. She pushes away the French toast, she has nibbled her way through half a slice.

"God that was awful, but the girl tried so hard. I didn't want to disappoint her after the children refused to eat it."

"I can cook you something else." I offer, chucking the leftover toast in the bin. The burnt egg is black on both sides of the bread. How Adeline was able to consume it without throwing up beats me.

"No, I'm okay thank you." Adeline dabs her mouth with a napkin. "Is Alex coming?"

"Later, she has business to do."

"Does that mean we can talk? Just the two of us?" Her eyes sparkle.

"Yes, I should teach you some self-defence." I plan for us to do something with a minimal amount of talking. She should learn it as well, if she wants to survive Lucifer.

"Good idea. We used to do it all the time when you were little."

We did, she taught me a lot as a kid, so did my father. He was better than she was. My mother was better with her magic, my father with his fists. Now she doesn't even use her magic. They were the best days of my childhood. In the winter, my father would create a fire whenever I got cold. The weather is nice today, we can train outside.

"Come with me then."

I pass her a staff; I am not letting her near a sharp object. She is out of practice and I would rather not arm her with a knife. She holds the staff correctly, that is a good start. "When was the last time you were in a fight?"

She frowns, in thought. "I don't remember. Humans aren't as aggressive as our type. When I worked in a bar, I had to break up a few then."

"Alright." I don't have much hope she'll do well. "I'll do some attacks, try and block them."

She nods, focusing hard. I shadow a head blow and scoop out her legs instead. She squeals, toppling onto her ass. I laugh, that was too easy. Adeline scrambles to her feet. "Alright, I'm very out of practice. Go again."

I nod. I swing the staff effortlessly and it thumps her shoulder. The next jab hits her chest. She falls over again. In an attempt to redeem herself, she grabs the end of my staff and tugs. I hold my ground. I flick the staff up and it whacks her on the chin. She groans, that will leave a bruise.

"You are better than I expected." She rubs her chin.

"I had to learn quickly, or I would be long dead." I help her to her feet.

"How so?" Adeline asks.

I shouldn't have prompted the conversation. That's my fault. "I killed a lot of people and a lot of people tried to kill me."

"I didn't know. I would have come back, if I had known you were alive. What did you do after you lost your father and I?" She asks. "You survived the ambush obviously."

I swing the staff in her direction, she ducks down. That's a decent start.

"I was taken and experimented on. I escaped, killed anyone related to the project in revenge, took their money, found an abandoned cottage in a village, and lived there." That basically sums up the first twenty years of my life. I am not ashamed of anything I have done.

"You did all that?" Her eyes widen.

My life has been more entertaining than hers. No surprise there. I lived in the cottage for six months before a supernatural cult heard what I did, tracked me down and asked me to join their ranks. I accepted their offer. I was young, naive and needed guidance, and I got it alright. There were hellhounds, warlocks, werewolves, witches, assassins and even a few demons. I learned everything I needed from them; they were amazing teachers. The only thing I needed to do was help kill people in return and never argue back. All their targets were guilty of something. Not all of them deserved to die, but I needed to survive.

It wasn't until one named Jesse killed a child and wasn't punished, so I killed him myself. But I wasn't as smart as I thought I was, they caught me and tried to kill me in retaliation. The cult didn't have any members left once I was done. That was the second time I lost control of my power, that injection was strong. I have tested my blood before, but I have never been able to work out the formula they used. It wasn't natural, that is for certain.

I nod. "Of course I did it." I poke her with my staff. "You need to focus."

She tumbles back, her balance is dreadful. Her staff falls out of her hand, falling with her. I hear a clang of silver beside me. I shake my head at her attempt to grab a weapon. I'm surprised she is strong enough to do it. I spin and bat away the knife. It thwacks the grass harmlessly. I duck, knowing exactly where she will aim. I jump backward over her shoulders and slam her in the back, going through the manoeuvres swiftly that I have practised over a thousand times.

"Shoot, I thought I had you."

"You're lucky I'm not using magic." I roll my eyes. She would have no hope. This is simple, mundane fighting. Selena could do better than this.

"I am. I understand why you did all that as a child." She dusts the mud of her hands. "You had no one. I'm sorry that happened to you."

What has happened, has happened. I hate pity, it doesn't solve anything. There is no point in compassion. I don't expect people to forgive me because of my age at that time either, I did what I did, and I stand by my actions.

"A similar thing happened to me; my mother died when I was a baby."

Ah, so she has turned it into a competition. I hate it when people do that. 'Who has it worse' really isn't a contest that should be held. It's worse than pity.

"Okay." I wave the stick and it weaves between my fingers gracefully.

"I was well looked-after by my father. He's the one who taught me to fight." She smiles. "I wish I remembered what he taught me."

"Why don't you try?" It may be her only hope of learning how to fight.

"Okay. Pass me the knife. He loved knives." She puts down the staff. I sigh, giving her the knife.

Frowning, she holds the handle carefully. She puts the tip of the blade between her thumb and forefinger. She flicks the knife in my direction. It moves swiftly through the air. I lift a hand; it freezes the tip near my forehead.

"I did it! Sorry, I didn't mean to aim for your head." She chirps. "Wait. Give me two more. I want to try something else he taught me."

I offer the knives. She holds the three knives at the tip. I have a feeling this one will go wrong. She chucks the knives. They spiral out of control. I dodge the knives with ease, and they land in the grass ten feet away in random places.

"Damn it!" She moans. "I thought I got it."

"I'll teach you." I suggest. I know what she is trying to do.

Adeline grins. "Really! Thank you!"

I laugh, I can't say our time together has been boring. My phone rings, Adeline practises the move again. She's also attempted a few magic spells. Nothing taxing, it's hard to believe she has lost her power. Supernaturals who live among the humans usually use their powers in their own home. Adeline's power has become dormant due to the lack of use. I didn't know that was possible. I've researched it, but I couldn't find anything, it's not normal for a witch or warlock to completely stop using their powers. I step away to pick up the call.

"Hey, how is it going?" Alex asks.

"Better than expected." I admit. I was expecting a lot of awkward silence to be honest.

"Well, I hate to disturb you, but I have an actual problem and I would really like your help but if you don't want to because you're with your mother, I totally understand and I will find a way to do it without you."

I smile, I like it when she asks for my help. "What is it?"

"Well, I promised to babysit Flint's kids while they have an important meeting, but some demons are being assholes. I really need to sort them out, it'll only take half an hour, tops. Flint wants you to stay at his house with them. All their toys and other things are there. Also, he would prefer you do not bring Adeline."

"So, you need me to babysit while you kill a bunch of demons?" I honestly thought I'd get to kill some too, but I guess babysitting isn't so bad. I've been doing it all morning anyway.

"Basically. I did tell Flint he could send them down here to me, but apparently it may scare them."

I chuckle. "I can do it. When do I need to get there?"

Flint and Jade's meeting is important; they have started an organisation to help supernatural kids. Their progress has been slow so far, but it's growing. The hardest part is probably convincing people that you're trying to help, even if you are Lucifer's son.

"About ten minutes."

"I better go then."

"Thank you! I'll talk to you soon, I miss you." The line beeps as she ends the call. I put away my phone. I am not very good with children but it's only for half an hour. They are well behaved children, I'm sure it won't be that hard. "I need to go."

"Why?" Adeline's shoulders droop immediately. "I thought we could try another trick. We are having a good time."

"Alex needs me to do something. I won't be long. Feel free to roam around. There are acres of land or there is plenty of food in the kitchen."

I had to buy a stockpile of food when Colt started to live here, then more when Abby and Holly began staying round too.

They cannot magic their own food and they would bug me every five minutes for a snack. So, I gave in and my cupboards are constantly full.

"Are you sure Alex can't wait?" Adeline groans her hand loosening on the knives.

"No, she needs my help now, it's important."

"More important than spending time with me? We haven't seen each other in five-hundred years!"

"And who's fault is that?" I glare at her. She can't try to use that to make me stay. It's her fault we don't know each other, it's not my job to fix it.

"Just don't let her boss you around. I've seen what you are like around her. She told you to be cautious of me, didn't she?"

"She did, but I would be anyway. I'm not stupid."

Adeline frowns. "You went on that entire and, quite frankly, unnecessary mission yesterday. My story was true, you admitted that yourself."

"Yeah, and if it weren't for Alex's help, we probably wouldn't have been able to prove it. So, you should probably shut up before you say something you'll regret."

I don't think she's in the position where she can judge anything about my life. Especially criticising Alex for asking me to do one small task, while she is asking for my protection after disappearing from my life for the last five-hundred years. It's getting more and more tempting to kick her out. If she keeps it up, she'll be out before the week is over, Lucifer or not.

Adeline sighs. "Fine, go if you must."

"I don't need your permission." I growl. I open up the portal and disappear.

I land at Flint's front door, I'm not going to let myself into his home, even if they are expecting me. I rap the door. It opens by itself and I walk inside. Jade is in the kitchen, running past at the speed of light. Flint does up his tie in the middle of the hall.

"You should probably meet the kids. Ricky! Kai! Get down here!" Two children pop their heads around the banister. The oldest is ten years old, the other one is three.

"Enzo!" Ricky, the older one chirps happily, bounding in my direction and wrapping his arms around my leg. I guess they remember me better than I thought.

Flint raises his eyebrow. "You've met before?"

"Yeah! Enzo always looks after us with Auntie Alex." Ricky tells Flint. Well, I guess that is no longer a secret.

"Very well, I guess you don't need to meet them then." Flint rolls his eyes. "We won't be long, thanks for doing this."

"Yes! You two don't get up to any trouble for Enzo." Jade kisses each child on the head. "Goodbye sweet peas. Bye Enzo." I wave them off as they go through the portal.

"Parents gone!" The little one, Kai, jumps in joy. "Let's go!" He pulls on his brother's hand.

The two kids scramble up the stairs. I frown, I do not understand children. I am only here to stop them doing anything stupid or dangerous. They should be fine.

A moment later, they appear with their arms full of sheets and pillows.

"What are you doing?" I watch as they clamber gleefully onto the sofa, taking the cushions with them.

"A pillow fort!" They start spreading the sheets out over the floor. A pillow fort? What is that? I watch in confusion as one climbs up on a chair, trying to hang a corner of a sheet on a curtain hook. The three-year-old, balances on the sofa edge. The child stumbles on his little feet and begins to fall headfirst.

"Shit!" I run out and catch Kai before he headbutts the floor. I understand why they waited till their parents were gone to start; it's dangerous, which means their parents would probably not approve.

"Thanks Enzo." The child bounces off the sofa to get another sheet, unfazed by the fall.

"What does shit mean?" Ricky asks, looking me dead in the eyes.

Fuck. I mentally curse this time; I'm not repeating my mistake, even if the damage has already been done.

"Shit, shit, shit." The toddler sings, taunting me.

I restrain myself from cursing again. "Don't say that word."

"What, 'shit'?" Ricky grins in joy.

I could have said worse. Still, I don't think Flint and Jade want to come back to their children singing the word 'shit'. "Yes, don't say it."

"Only if you help us and magic more pillows." Ricky bargains.

"What?" I'm being blackmailed by a ten and three-year-old. I don't let anyone blackmail me, I just threaten them back and if they don't comply, seriously injure them. Unfortunately, I cannot do that to children, my only option is to admit defeat and help them.

"You are a warlock. You have horns!" The baby babbles. "We want pillows!"

I sigh. Waving my hand, the pillows duplicate themselves, along with the sheets. "What do I need to do?"

Sitting in the middle of a fort is not how I planned on spending my day. We had to peg up a billion sheets to tables and chairs. I had to use magic to put some up and keep it from collapsing in the middle. The pillows take up more room than the children in the fort. They roll around in the cushions.

"I really don't have to be in here with you." I try to convince them to let me leave.

"No! You are the prisoner." Kai climbs a mountain of pillows eagerly. "And I have trapped you in my castle!" Children have very wild imaginations, but I guess it could be worse.

Ricky jumps into the tent. "And I have come to save you!"

He aims a pillow at Kai. He falls off his tower onto a floor of pillows. Kai attacks him with an equal amount of vigour. Ricky's supernatural strength sends Kai flying into the air and to the other side of the fort. Where are the well-behaved kids who could sit for hours reading? I think they've been possessed.

"Don't hit each other!" I moan. They have never pulled anything like this when Alex is around.

"Fine." They both grumble, at least they listen to me. "We'll hit you instead!"

"What?" I squark, two pillows thwacking my face. This is not what was supposed to happen. I was meant to be the prisoner who didn't have to do anything.

"Get Enzo!" They scream.

Crap. "No!" I warn them. "Don't!"

They laugh harder, pillows hitting my arms. I scramble out of the fort. Maybe I should have let them hit each other. The pillows bounce off my leg and arm. What do I do? Children are confusing creatures. Weight tugs on my back, the mini child clambering on. How did he get up there? His legs wrap around my shoulders and the pillow hits my head repeatedly as the other one pounds my mid-section. What did I do to deserve this? I wave my hand, the child on my back floats off and plonks down on the edge of the sofa that is not covered in sheets. The other child goes to join him. They giggle, jumping back up to their feet.

"Again! Again!" A pillow connects with my shoulder. I whisk them back onto the sofa. They zoom through the air laughing... they're enjoying it. They jump back up like boomerangs and go in for the kill. They pelt me with the cushions, one in each hand. I lift my hand, magic forcing them into the air. They dangle above the fort, giggling.

There is a laugh from the doorway. I spin. Alex stands there shaking her head. "What the hell have you three been doing?"

I lower the kids to the ground, they groan in disappointment. I don't understand it. I once lifted a person into the air and they trembled at my feet, terrified about what I would do next. These kids simply enjoy it.

"Enzo said shit, then he helped us build a pillow fort, then we attacked him with pillows, then he made us fly in the air!"

"I assume the first event led to the others?" Alex walks in. "Now drop the pillows and leave Enzo alone."

"Okay." They put down their weapons obediently.

"How come it works for you?" I complain as they listen to every word Alex says without an argument. They don't try any of their evil tactics on her.

"Because I don't let them walk all over me." She chuckles. That's not insulting at all. "Now, kids, you are doing it all wrong." She waves her hand, and they hold even bigger pillows. "We'll fight Enzo together."

"You have to be kidding me." I curse, the three of them charging forward.

I duck as the pillows beat me from all directions. I thought Alex was saving me from these evil children, not helping them. The feathers blur my vision so I can't use magic against them in case I hurt someone. I guess I'm going to have to stoop to their level. A pillow appears in my hands at will.

I restore the house to its original state, magicking away all the feathers from popped pillows into an abyss somewhere. The pillows often got stuck on my horns. I pluck a feather out of Alex's hair. The kids are sitting in the kitchen having a snack.

A portal appears and Flint and Jade appear in the cleaned-up room. A feather vanishes out of my hand, hiding the last of the evidence. "You kept the place intact." Flint sounds surprised. "Normally they take advantage when a new person is taking care of them."

"Yeah, you should have seen it when Alex babysat for the first time." Jade laughs. "Ricky made her create an entire house out of chocolate, but it melted on all of them. They were stuck in a gooey mess when we returned. The kids were so sick afterwards."

I chuckle, so much for not letting them walk over her. Alex got manipulated by the children as well. She nudges my side. "Shut up." She mumbles.

"Thanks again." Flint takes off his blazer. "You should come for dinner some time."

"Sounds good, we should probably get back." I'd forgotten about Adeline waiting at my house. It's been much longer than half an hour. I got distracted; I should have left when Alex got here. Well, there is nothing I can do about it now. Serves her right for the crap she said earlier.

"Are you sure?" Jade checks.

I nod. I would leave Adeline longer, but Colt and the other two will be back soon. I'd rather beat them there; Tessa is no longer there to keep an eye on Adeline.

Alex grabs my hand. "We'll be back soon. Also, he did screw up. They learned the word 'shit' today and forced him into making a pillow fort." Alex tells on my failed babysitting.

"Hey!" I thought I'd gotten away with it, but Alex would never let that happen. I should have known.

"Bye." Alex pulls me into the portal before they can complain.

Landing back in my home, I shake my head. "You couldn't let me win, could you?"

"Of course not, I wasn't going to let them think you were a better babysitter than me." Alex laughs. "Let's go see what Adeline has been doing. She's probably mad that I kept you for so long."

"Well, her opinion doesn't matter." I snarl.

"Did something happen?" She frowns.

"Nothing to worry about. She just said something." I squeeze her hand. Adeline walks into the room, stuffing her face with a sandwich, a coffee in her other hand and a bandage wrapped around her forearm. "You're back! I've been practising that knife trick!"

"I see you haven't had the best time with it." I inspect the scratches on her body from what looks like many failed attempts.

"I've gotten pretty good at it." She disagrees. "I can show you, if you like?"

"Sure." I need to check she isn't going to accidentally kill herself. There is no point keeping her here if she is just going to kill herself at my house. I might as well let her go.

An hour and a half of training later, Alex and I have helped her learn a few more moves. I heal her wounds with ease. I taught Adeline to create a bolt of magic and fire it. She could barely manage ten bolts before her magic ran out. Her power is weaker than a ten-year-old warlock's. I hear Colt's truck pull up in the driveway. They're back already and will want food.

Alex puts her weapons on the rack. "You would be best with a spear point knife. I can make one, if you would like?"

"That would be nice, thank you." Adeline nods in appreciation.

"I'm going to get the whiskey." Alex walks back to the house.

I go to follow but an arm grabs my wrist. "Enzo, wait. I want to apologise."

"For?" I frown.

"Alex, I judged her too quickly. I guess I was just worried about you, but I see she makes you happy. Please forget everything I said earlier."

I nod and walk away. I'm not forgiving her, but I don't have the time to argue. At least she has a little more sense.

CHAPTER EIGHT

Lucifer

The wait is agonisingly painful. I can practically smell the freedom beyond the bars. The time is so close. My plan is being laid down, piece by piece. The next step is my freedom. I have been waiting for this moment for years. The ache in my body for the sweet release of freedom is overbearing but I cannot let it get the better of me. Not yet. Getting ahead of myself and not contemplating every possibility is what got me in here. This time, I will not be defeated with such ease. Alex may be stronger physically, but emotionally? I will crush her like a bug. The list of people she cares about has grown longer since we last went head-to-head. There is Enzo, her nephews, Jade. She would die for all of them, not just her brother. She has melted the devil dagger which is the only weapon that could kill her and Flint, after she stole it from me. Or she thinks it's the only one, but I plan to use more than just weapons to hurt her. I will feed off her emotions to win.

It's been a few months or so since Silven died. Her sacrifice was not pointless. It was all part of my elaborate plan, for she possessed a human who is free of her now. The girl she possessed is the first one to live through a demonic possession in two millennia. There is a reason why no one is able to survive it. The sword the angels made to free them from possession was destroyed many years ago after I got my hands on it. The human still holds a smidgen of Silven's power, and she doesn't even know it. I will need that power in my attempt to escape. That is why I allowed Silven's plan to go forward. I had an informant help me pick which two teenagers would be a good match for my plan. Abby and Holly fitted perfectly, Abby's curious and brave personality mixed with Holly's intelligence and timidness would intrigue Enzo and Colt enough to keep them around beyond an obligation to help. They would become actual friends without them realising I had any involvement in it happening. I just needed to introduce them, so I turned one into a werewolf so they would get close to Enzo. Then Silven would pick the other one for her plot because of this closeness. It was the perfect plan. And it worked. They even believe Silven did it alone, but she wouldn't have even made it into a body if it weren't for my help. She was never the brightest bulb, but she was loyal and useful to me, even after her death.

The minion I had called upon appears at the cell bars. The demon grins from ear to ear. I beckon him closer and tell it what to do. I might not be able to go to Earth, but they can. I need it to do something for me. I may have delivered Enzo's mother to him, but he won't trust her, let alone like her and I need him to, for my plan to work. I'm sure it would happen over time, but I can't wait that long especially when a well-orchestrated event can easily make it happen. A life-or-death situation, where she can conveniently help save a life. Enzo would appreciate her then. "And remember, don't be seen doing any of this. The human you use can't see you." I picked out the human for it already, otherwise the demon would never get it right.

Abby

I wake up in my own home for once, we didn't stay that long at Colt's yesterday. Colt drove us home around eight, we didn't have any homework to do. My parents finally met Colt which made them happy. We had a second dinner, which none of us complained about. It was not a patch on Enzo's, but my parents are decent cooks considering they don't have any professional experience. I had to distract them while Colt added blood to his plate, pretending it was ketchup. Overall, it was a good night.

Stretching out on my bed, I realise it's only Wednesday. Three more days of school until the weekend. I don't have any interesting lessons today. I'm not looking forward to it. My phone pings. I pick it up. I'd been texting Colt till late last night; he doesn't need as much sleep as humans. I lost track of time and passed out mid-message. It's him asking if I want to bunk off school for a training session. I don't think that even needs to be a question, I'd pick training over school any day. I'll ask Kyle for an update on what I missed later.

Begrudgingly, I pull myself out of bed and reply. Colt messages back that there will be a portal in my bedroom for Holly and I in thirty minutes. Enzo has also offered to give us a driving lesson. I'm surprised we are going over today, I thought Enzo would want to spend time with his mother. He probably does, but not alone. I imagine it's like when our parents see a childhood friend in a shop or something. They have so much to tell each other but, at the same time, they don't know what to say because it has been so long.

From the little I have heard about Enzo's parents, he had a pretty good childhood. Up until the point they died, obviously. He has always spoken highly of them and the idea that the same women wouldn't go looking for him is surprising. Enzo didn't look very happy to see her, understandably. I bet Colt would be the same if his mother appeared out of nowhere after she abandoned him. I imagine he'd tell her to go to Hell, but they never had a good relationship before he was a vampire either. I think the only reason Enzo hasn't kicked her out is because she is in danger for being related to him. He'd think it was his fault she died, and he believes in protecting the innocent. It took a while to understand how his mind works. Colt explained it simply to me. 'Kill the guilty, protect the innocent'. That is what he is doing now.

I knock on Holly's bedroom door. She opens it, her head like a bird's nest and eyes drooping heavily. She looks worse than I do. "What?" She grumbles, sleepily.

"Want to bunk off with me?"

She nods, she used to be strongly against breaking any rules, now she doesn't care. I guess Colt was right when he said supernaturally changes you. Holly is definitely more badass; she has stuck up for herself a lot more. A few students used to make fun of her for being smart, they don't anymore. I still don't know what happened, she refused to tell me. It's all good changes though.

"Give me ten minutes." The door shuts.

"What did you ask Holly?" My mother asks behind me.

I groan. If only I had wolf hearing, then I would know where my parents are before I make plans they wouldn't approve of.

"It's for school." I lie.

I feel guilty for using the mind-control Alex put on them. She made it so the phrase 'It's for school' forces them to let us do what we want without worrying. Alex said we could take advantage of it whenever we wanted, whether it was supernatural or not, but then I would feel worse. It feels bad enough to keep the entire supernatural world that we've become involved in a secret. Holly and I did discuss telling them, but we both decided it wouldn't be a good idea, we don't think they would react to it well. Not after it took them six months to accept that Holly was a lesbian.

"Alright sweetie." She smiles. "Have fun."

"Thanks. Bye." I walk into the bathroom for a shower.

Eventually, we reappear in Enzo's living room. He sits eating breakfast with his mother. He talks back to her, smiling, which is better than when I saw them yesterday. Alex is nowhere to be seen, probably busy. She spends every free moment with Enzo. Enzo looks up as we enter the room.

"Are any of you hungry?"

"No. We ate." I refuse, though the croissants do smell good.

"Training or driving first?" Arms wrap around my waist. I look up, Colt. He's put up his hair in a mini bun to keep it out of his eyes, it looks good. I tug a strand out and he shakes his head, smiling. It falls over his face, now it looks perfect.

"Driving." I vote.

"Yeah." Holly agrees.

"I guess we better get to it. Who's going first?" Enzo stands up leading us outside to the garage to Colt's truck.

I get in the driver's seat of the truck. Enzo sits in the passenger seat. Adeline sits in the back seat with Colt; Enzo won't leave her alone in the house because he doesn't trust her, so she has to come with us. Holly wanted croissants so decided not to join us until it was her turn. I start up the engine and hold the wheel. My foot sits on the clutch and the brake. I slowly release the brake and move over to the accelerator. I start the car and we work our way down the road. Swiftly, I turn the wheel, following the road. My hands move over the gearstick. Most people listen out for the engine to know when to change gear, I listen for Enzo's growl. We make our way down the road. There is a new traffic light that has never been there before. Enzo put it there, it's a glamour. I go through the gears and the pedals and wait at it.

"She's good." Adeline speaks up. I don't think waiting at the light is overly impressive, but I'll take the compliment. We wait at the red light; Enzo could easily change it to green. I think he does it to test my patience, to see if I'll push it and go straight past. I won't, he's the one grading me. Some time in his life, he became legally allowed to teach people to drive. I don't want to ask what year it was or what type of car existed at the time, but he does a decent job, so I'm not going to question it. The light turns green, and I start up again. The traffic light disappears.

Ten minutes down the road, there is an intersection. There is a glamour of cars around the intersection and another behind me. All the cars have a large 'G' on their hood to indicate that they are a glamour, a few real cars do go down this road, but not many. Carefully, I wait for the cars to pass then make my turn. I remember the first time I did one. I crashed into an oncoming car, but luckily the illusion just went through us. Enzo didn't get too mad. "Turn left here." Enzo instructs.

I listen looking behind me before making the turn.

"You forgot to indicate." Adeline points out.

I curse, she is right. I'm the worst at indicating, it's easy to forget. I continue along the road. There are a few cars behind me, I check my speed monitor. Enzo loves to make them beep at me if I'm not going fast enough, Colt has tried to make him stop. It hasn't worked so far. I gently accelerate to the speed limit along the quiet road.

An engine roars behind us and a real car comes down the road. Enzo waves his hand, and the illusions disappear. He doesn't want to confuse the driver with all the lines of perfectly uniformed cars. I glance in the wing mirror quickly, lights appear on the car in the distance. I frown, checking the road, hands firmly on the wheel. They look like they are going pretty fast. We are coming up to a bend, they'll need to slow down. Enzo's brows furrow in concern, I can feel the tension in the car as it gets closer. I check that I'm in the lines fine so the car can pass with ease, the engine is purring and not growling. I'm at the speed limit. I flick my eyes to the mirror again to get another look.

"Shit!" Enzo curses, hands rising.

Suddenly, our car smashes forward, spinning on impact. I grab the wheel with all my strength to try and control it, my foot on the brake but the car spins off the road. My head slams forward, catching on the airbags. The metal crushes my legs. I howl in agony. My head is spinning. The glass shatters, the car smacking into a bush. My back throbs, the force flinging me forward in my seat. Luckily, the seatbelt catches me.

In a daze I lift my head, pain burning throughout my body. I try to move my legs but it's useless. I howl in anguish, coughing in the dark pit of smoke. Hands grab my arms and drag me out the broken car window. Throbbing, my legs are forced out of the small space between the metal and the seat. I wheeze, landing on the grass.

"Abby? Abby? Talk to me." Colt's ash coated face fills my vision, panic in his eyes. "Are you okay?" He pats out the flames on my sleeve.

My eyes try to focus on his eyes. "I-I" I cough. "I can't move my legs."

Enzo kneels beside my body. "She's hurt."

"No shit, Enzo." Colt swears.

I chuckle, pain jolting through my lungs. My eyes struggle to keep looking at Colt; they refuse to focus. The soft touch of magic envelopes my body, some of the pain easing as Enzo checks me over to find the problem. The issue with being human is that I do not heal like the others.

"Concussion for sure, her spine might be fractured and a few cuts and bruises." Enzo concludes.

"My spine?" I panic. I thought my leg must have been broken at worst after being trapped in the metal.

The pain numbs down, Enzo's hands moving. "I can fix it. Ten minutes and I'll be done."

"Let me help." Adeline kneels by my still body. I can't move.

"I really don't need help, thanks."

"Let me help please. You can lead. I'll just lend a hand."

"Fine." Enzo starts ordering her to do things. I feel Colt's hand slide into mine, I smile. Enzo's hands start pulsing magic through my body. "This might hurt, I have to put your spine back into place."

A large snap, I bite down on my tongue to stop a scream. He continues, instructing Adeline on what to do. Medical procedures are not a flick of the wrist, unfortunately.

A few minutes later, the pain subsides and I collapse in relief. Enzo steps back to give me space. "Move your left leg." He orders. I obey, it bends perfectly without any pain. "Now the right leg." I do the same thing, then get to my feet gently. I'm fine, thankfully.

"Is it painful?" Adeline asks.

"No. Thanks."

My eyes can finally focus on Colt, the fear in his face vanishing. "How are you feeling?"

"Exhausted but other than that good." I check my leg again. "Thanks for getting me out of the car."

Or I would be dead. The flaming car burns steadily from the hood. Enzo waves his hand, diminishing the flames before they reach the gas tank. The car is a total write-off.

"What happened?" I rub my forehead, ash appearing on my fingers.

"That idiot driver crashed into you. You handled the car well; it could have gone much worse if you hadn't steered it." Colt praises my driving.

"Where is that bastard?" Enzo stands up from the dirt scowling.

We walk over to the other car, Enzo marching in front. The car is totalled a few meters away from the truck. We reach it, the driver is unconscious in his seat. Luckily, the car isn't on fire. Enzo's fist smashes the window in, dragging the man out by his collar. Eyes glowing, Enzo dangles his body in the air. Blood smears the driver's face.

"Are you going to help him?" I ask, he does not look like he's in good shape.

Enzo scowls. "Why would I do that? I thought we'd bat him around a little before we ditch him here." That sounds more like Enzo. "He fractured your back. You wouldn't be able to walk properly, if at all, if it wasn't for magic." Enzo chucks the man to the ground, like he is a bag of rubbish. He groans loudly.

My eyes widen, I didn't think about it like that. I knew Enzo could fix whatever was broken. I didn't think about what would happen if the injuries were permanent. Never being able to walk again, that would be agonising. There would be so much I could never do again. All because this man crashed into us while speeding. I'd be angry, I'd want him to suffer like I would be. Enzo zaps the man and he groans, doubling over.

"Wait." I order.

Enzo hesitates, hand hovering. "Why? Do you want to do it? You could probably break his leg with that log." He gestures to one in the undergrowth.

I am okay. I am lucky that supernatural power goes beyond science. Not many other people would have been so lucky. I don't want the man to do it again, but he's human. He should be punished the human way for what he did, which is prison. "He should be punished by humans. Not us."

Enzo snorts. "We can't call the police and be here. They'll want statements and get us involved with the human law system. Then he'll get off scot-free, look at him. He's got plenty of money, he'll buy a great lawyer and buy his way out. He won't receive a prison sentence, Abby."

"Enzo has a point." Colt agrees.

"How do you know?" I quiz him.

"I used to be a lawyer, but I got pissed off with the legal system and quit the profession." Enzo states bluntly. "Men like him get off all the time, it does not matter how good your lawyer is, he'll bribe the judge or the jury."

My shoulders slump. He's right. We can't call the police and expect him to go to prison. He couldn't be charged for injuring any of us, because we are all fine now. The only proof would be the state of the car, which will show that we should all be in hospital or dead. No one would believe we were that lucky. But he'll do it again unless he is taught otherwise. Enzo looks ready to kill him, but I'm not violent like him. Neither is Colt.

"There must be a non-violent way." I suggest.

"I agree with Abby. We should just be thankful that she recovered." Adeline inputs.

"What do you propose then?" Enzo's shoulders droop disappointedly.

Good question. "Um… could you, I don't know, mess with his thoughts? Make him scared to do it again?" Manipulation is something Enzo can do by using his magic on the brain.

"You want me to make him into a good person?" Enzo frowns. "It's not as much fun, but I could." Enzo drops down next to the half-conscious man and grabs his forehead.

The man's eyes burst open, rolling back into his head. Enzo quirks a smile, trusting him to do it might have been a bad idea. Enzo lets him go a moment later, the man falls unconscious and starts floating to his car.

"What did you do?" I ask, hoping he didn't do anything else.

"He is now so terrified of speed that he'll never be doing it again. Nothing else, don't worry."

"Why were you smiling then?" Colt backs me up.

"I had a glance at his life to see what would help scare him the most. I didn't expect it to be so sad and embarrassing." Enzo explains. "We should go."

The man's car rolls forward to a road sign and the damages change to make it look like a different accident, not involving anyone else. He waves a hand, the truck is eaten up by a moving portal.

"How come we have to walk through portals?" I quirk a smile, trying to lighten the mood.

Enzo waves his hand and the portal soars in our direction and eats us up.

The lights flash before my eyes, I fall into the colourful abyss. My head spins. I drop and land on a couch, feeling dizzy. I hold my stomach to try and stop it from churning. Enzo laughs, also appearing. I guess I know my answer; it makes portalling ten times more nauseating.

"What about his ambulance?" I ask. We should have done that before we left.

"He is calling it himself, I used magic to make him conscious so he would survive until they arrived to pick him up." Enzo grumbles. "He'll be fine."

"Only because I forced you. You wanted to leave his phone outside the car and make him crawl for it." Colt growls at Enzo.

Enzo shrugs. "Same thing."

I smile, that sounds about right. Colt is the sane, sensible, caring one of their duo. He rolls his eyes, jumping into the seat next to me.

Adeline turns to Enzo. "You didn't torture him that much, did you? While you were inside his mind?"

"Not really." A mug of coffee appears in his hand.

"Hi...Why are you all covered in blood?" Holly panics entering from the kitchen. "Did you get ambushed by a demon or something?"

"No, an idiot driver." I correct her. "We're fine."

We catch her up on the story while Adeline lectures Enzo about how messing with people's heads is technically mental torture. I didn't think about it like that, but he's better off now than he was before. He almost killed himself along with us. It won't matter what Adeline says, Enzo won't regret what he has done.

"Your back is fine now, right?" Holly checks worrying about me.

"Yeah."

"Colt, the car dealership is open. Do you want to go get a replacement?" He pulls out his bank card. "I'm not letting you drive my McLaren to school every day."

"Damn it." Colt laughs. "Yeah, I guess I'll have to get my own McLaren."

"Go for it, but you aren't having mine." Enzo scowls at him. Enzo is very protective of his car, I don't know why. He repaired it when it went into a tree but is letting Colt get a whole new truck after this one is crashed. He could obviously have afforded to replace it but chose not to.

"Can't you just fix my truck instead of buying a whole new one?" Colt asks.

"I can fix it, but it would be good to have a spare." Enzo answers while passing over the card. "We keep crashing cars."

Colt takes it. He does have his own card, but I imagine Enzo's has more on it.

"Want to come with me?" He gestures to us two.

"We aren't actually driving it are we, I think we've had enough of that for today."

"No, just looking." Colt glances over to Enzo and his mother.

"Oh, okay. Yeah, let's go." I nod, finally understanding; he wants to leave Enzo with his mother so they can spend time together alone. "Good idea." We both turn to look at Holly, who hasn't said a word.

She sighs, dragging herself from the sofa. "Fine. I'll join you."

Teleporting into the car showroom, it looks posh, to say the least. Rich people are waltzing about the room, eyeing up what's on offer. Cars spin on large displays, two floors worth filling the pristine white room. Immediately, a dealer appears next to us as though we summoned him. I expect the dealer to shoo us away to be honest; we are not dressed up and look too young to buy a car without an adult with us. We should have brought Enzo.

"Colt. Nice to see you, what are you looking for?" The man says.

"I'm not sure yet, go annoy someone else please."

The man chuckles. "Sure." And walks off at Colt's request.

"How come they know you?" Holly asks before I can.

"Enzo used to drag me here all the time. He has a garage full of cars and a racetrack in some isolated forest."

"Seriously?" I raise my eyebrow.

Enzo is rich, that is obvious from knowing him. But a racetrack in Canada and a bunch of cars is not what I expected him to spend his money on. That is more Alex's style. Enzo only drives his McLaren, I would assume he'd drive the others regularly if he had them.

"Yeah, but apparently it's not a patch on Alex's but I've never seen her's." He moves over to a maze of cars. We follow, unsure of what all the signs about the cars mean.

Colt chooses an electric blue mustang. Apparently, Enzo likes them too, which is why he picked it. Enzo and Adeline are fighting in the training room when we get back. From the bottles on the coffee table, I would say neither of them are sober. Hopefully, they won't seriously injure themselves or each other.

CHAPTER NINE

Enzo

I yawn, half-awake and tired. Alex and I spent a few hours last night trying to work out if Lucifer had any other tricks up his sleeve which we need to prepare for. There is a small list of demons to keep an eye on, but nothing else. She had to leave for business, which translates to killing someone. I would have joined her, but I didn't want to leave the kids alone with Adeline. I don't think she plans to kill them, but I'm not going to risk it. She did try to help drag them out of the car when we went off the road, then proceeded to help me fix Abby's back. Her help wasn't necessary but arguing with her would have left Abby in pain for longer. I check my alarm clock, it's five in the morning. The house is completely dead, Holly and Abby didn't stay over. The house is as quiet as it's going to get. I drag myself out of the bed and change to sweats.

I wander into the gym in my home, there is a secret bar behind it. There are a dozen trap doors and passageways.; Colt's found a few, but not all of them. There is even an underground bunker. I put in my earphones and start on the treadmill. I had to use magic on the earphones for them to work in my ears; the music would be too loud for my supernatural hearing otherwise. A number of things in my house work with the help of magic: the bins empty themselves, the beds make themselves, dishes clean themselves too. All the boring human tasks I simply don't see the point of doing. Being supernatural can be a pain in the ass and very dangerous, so I might as well make the most of it.

Two hours of exercise and a shower later, I come downstairs to find Adeline already there, gazing outside sadly. I never asked how she felt after the attempted assassination and her house burning down. I guess I've normalised it, shit happens, and you get over it. If I were to dwell on everything that has happened to me, I wouldn't have any fun in my life. I have to enjoy life while it's good, because everything could change at any moment. It's something I have learned over my long life. Enemies can pop up out of nowhere.

I don't plan to ask Adeline about her emotions, that is beyond my willingness to bond with her. I helped her with a few more knife tricks, which I suppose I enjoyed. I still haven't forgiven her for what she said about Alex, or for her excuses for not coming to visit. I have made up for some of it by bashing her about during training.

"Coffee?" Adeline asks, standing up and going over to the pot.

I nod. "Yeah, thanks."

I text Alex, asking when she will be over. Hopefully, we'll get to spend longer together today. I open the fridge and take an apple. Colt won't be up till the last minute for school, he was up until late last night binge-watching a TV series.

"Do you have any updates about the hit on me?" Adeline passes me the cup of coffee.

"Tessa has taken on the job, which means you are safe from assassins for now, but Lucifer will know his informant was discovered and could try again. It should only be a few days till we know for sure." Last night, Alex and I both agreed Lucifer would have a back-up plan and that it's best to wait until we're certain his entire plan has failed.

"Thank you. It means a lot to me."

"Okay."

If she thinks I'm doing it for her, she is wrong. I may have known her once, but I don't anymore. If she was to die, I wouldn't be sad. I would feel guilty because she got killed because of me. I want to avoid that guilt.

"I was wondering if you have any spell books? I thought I could try practising some simple spells and start learning again."

"Yeah, come with me."

I lead her to the library. The room is split in half; one half stores human books, both old and new, and the other half are supernatural. Walls from the floor to the ceiling are filled with books, the sky light shines over the dark oak bookcases.

"Well, I see you take after your mother. I once loved all of these books. I had much older versions. I wish I had never given up my magic. I was just so scared after I lost you and your father." She strokes the spines of the books.

Gently she picks up my book about the first witch, the title 'Year of the Witches' scrawled across the front page. I stole it back from Lucifer after Alex overthrew him. It's all about the amulet of sacrifices, its power and about early witches and warlocks after the first witch was born. After she was born, more began to appear, born from human parents. It was one in millions which isn't many at all considering the population size back then.

Adeline strokes the book. "You have this? That amulet was so powerful, no wonder Alex was able to overthrow Lucifer using it. It contained all of her magic, I'm surprised Alex could endure it, only the people with a pure heart could withstand its power."

I frown, it is common knowledge the amulet was powerful, but no one knew that only someone with a pure heart could withstand its power. The known story is that Alex grabbed it first. She shouldn't know the rest.

"My mother would be so disappointed to see me right now. So out of practice. Unlike you." Adeline carefully puts back the book.

"How do you know all of that?" I interrupt.

"Because I owned the book before you. It's part of our family history." Adeline explains. "The book says the holder of the amulet sees the first witch, like a dream. I would be surprised if your grandmother didn't mention you to Alex. She would know you exist, even in death. She knows everything. Did Alex never tell you?"

"What are you on about?" I ask her directly.

"Your grandmother is the first witch. I didn't get to tell you as a child, I wanted to wait till you could understand what I was saying. I assume Alex would have found out when she met her."

Lucifer told me the exact same thing the other day. He said Alex knew too. It can't be a coincidence. Lucifer sent her to mess with us. It explains why she was so hostile towards Alex yesterday. Magic surges from my hands, the bolt hits her in the chest. She screams in agony. I grab her by the collar of her shirt, thwacking her against the wall. "You work for Lucifer, don't you?"

"No. Enzo, let me down, please." She begs. "I swear…" She chokes as my grip tightens.

The door opens, Alex stands there. "What the hell did she do?"

"She's working for Lucifer." I throw her to the ground carelessly.

She wheezes. "I'm not. I swear. I was just telling him about his grandmother, and he lost it."

"Lucifer told me the exact same lie the day before you showed up." I hiss.

"Your grandmother… Oh shit. Okay. What did she tell you?"

"That she was the first witch, and you knew about it, which is bullshit." I would believe the first half with enough proof; she did have a daughter. No one knows what happened to her. She just disappeared from history, it was assumed she was dead. The second half not so much, if Alex knew, she would tell me.

"Okay… it's true." Alex corrects me.

"What?"

"Which means she knew because she is the daughter of the first witch, not because she is working for Lucifer."

Adeline gets off the floor. "I told you." She brushes off her jeans.

"Wait, you knew, and you never told me?" I turn to Alex angrily. I dismissed the idea when Lucifer told me, I dismissed it when Adeline told me because, out of the three of them, I trust Alex. I believed she would tell me, yet she was the one holding back the truth.

She curses under her breath. "I can explain. I didn't know when I met you. I mean, she told me she had a grandson and when I met him to stick around. That the power she gave me would be at its strongest when I was close to you, but she refused to tell me your name. She said I would know when I met you."

"Wait, what?"

I snatch the book from Adeline and flip open the pages. I read one of the passages I had tabbed. I read the entire book after I took it back from Lucifer. I skim the page. It says that one of the witch's descendants could not take the amulet of sacrifices but if the person who received her power is closer to one of descendants, the power would be stronger.

"If you're near me, your magic is stronger."

"Yes. Which is why, after I was certain, I didn't want to say anything. I thought you would be mad, that you might think I'd only stuck around to use you for the power it gives me."

"When did you know?" She should have told me, no matter what reaction she thought I would have. Admittedly, the thought she was using me would have crossed my mind, but not for long. I'd have asked, but believed her if she said it wasn't true. We were friends after all.

"Eight years ago? It was after we killed those werewolves. The magic you used was incredible, especially for a half-warlock and the fact we were friends after all that time."

"Why didn't you tell me when you were speculating about it? We could have found out sooner by investigating it together?" I insist.

"Well, I obviously didn't think of that. You know now."

"Would you have ever told me?" I scowl.

"Yes... Probably. I was trying to find a situation where I could tell you without you wondering how I knew."

"You were going to lie to me about how you found out?" That makes it even worse. I trust Alex, I've told her things I have never told anyone else. I hate telling people about my life, but I felt comfortable telling her. And she kept a secret from me, and she planned to lie about how she knew to stop me getting mad. Truth is, if she'd told me back then, saying she'd just worked it out, I wouldn't have been mad. Maybe a little ticked off that she didn't mention it earlier, but I could have helped her find out sooner. But we have been dating for months and she's never bothered to bring it up. "Are you fucking kidding me?"

"I feel like I've opened a can of worms." Adeline edges for the door. "I'll leave you two." She slips out the room.

I turn to Alex scowling.

"Yes! Shit. I should have known this would bite me in the ass. I'm terrible at this. I should have bloody known I'd make a mistake." She shakes her head at herself. "I'm sorry, I was an idiot." I stand there, unsure what to say. "I don't normally stay with someone long enough to have arguments. So, what happens now?"

"I need to go." I can leave, Adeline isn't here to kill us, and Colt will be going to school in a minute anyway. I march out of the room before she can argue. I walk into my garage. It's either go for a drive or a drink. The door slams behind me and I spin, thinking it's Alex.

Colt stands there. "You know the mustang is ready to be picked up."

"Let me guess, you want to skip school and get it with me?"

"You read my mind." He grins. I create the portal.

We get to the dealership, the car is sitting just outside the showroom. I do the final signature for it and they pass over the keys. As we leave the shop for the car, I chuck the keys to Colt. "You can drive."

"Wait, what? You're letting me drive it first?" He catches the keys. "Damn, what did you and Alex fight about?"

"Get in." I slide into the passenger seat.

Colt starts the engine, then looks at me. "What happened?"

"Are you seriously going to pretend you didn't listen in through the walls?"

"Okay, you got me there." Colt chuckles, the car purrs as he pulls away from the curb. Steadily, he continues out of the car park. "It's a long ride back, Enzo. You are not allowed to portal us back. We have to test her out, so talk."

"I could portal myself back."

"You can't portal in a moving vehicle, and I'm not stopping." Colt argues. I raise my eyebrow, he has learned that trick from me.

I sigh. "What do you know already?"

"Well, I heard…"

I explain what Colt missed in the conversation. He bursts out laughing as I finish.

"What?" I can hardly see what was funny about it.

"You are ridiculously smart, yet you still didn't figure it out. You're the only one with a copy of the book. Even I could see how that connects."

"I never remembered how I got it."

"Because you had it all along, obviously."

I pause for a moment, thinking about what he said. "Alex didn't figure it out either."

"She did, it prompted her to look, and she found out the truth."

I frown. He has a point. It does make sense now I have been told. It explains a lot about my powers and why I was taken from my parents to be experimented on. If my kidnappers knew, I would be an amazing subject.

"See, I don't think you're mad about your heritage or even at Alex. I think you're upset you didn't figure it out sooner."

I glare at him. "That is seriously all you have to say."

"Well, let's look at this factually. Is it a shock you're the grandson of the most powerful witch to exist? No, your power has always been abnormally strong. Two, you know you'd have done the same thing in Alex shoes. You have to know all the facts before presenting them to someone. What or who else is there to be mad at, other than yourself."

"You for starters, for being a smartass."

"Because I'm right."

I pause to think about it for a minute. It would have been so much easier to have known all these years. Controlling my power is extremely difficult, but if I knew why, it would have helped me understand and control it better. To know why I was dragged from my home as a child for experimentation, why I was chosen. Then, knowing the answer was right under my nose this entire time... I do feel stupid. Alex knowing does hurt a little, but it's not her fault that I didn't know five hundred years ago, when I really needed to know.

"Fine. You are correct. Happy now?"

"You admit I'm right? You're lucky I'm driving, or I'd use my phone to record it. This is a once in a lifetime occurrence."

I roll my eyes. "What do you think of the car?" I change the subject before he can insult me more.

"I think that you can take your time fixing my truck." He smiles.

I roll my eyes, I should have seen that coming. I will fix his truck when we get back. It'll take an hour at most. "We will have to race one day."

"Not fair. You'll obviously win." Colt smiles.

"Okay, I guess you don't want to then."

"No, I didn't say that. I just think I should get to drive the McLaren a few times when we do. You know, to make it fair. It is the faster car between the two."

"You wish." I chuckle. "Maybe one lap. If I am feeling kind that day."

"I'm holding you to that."

We return to the house and I start fixing the truck. Colt is taking the mustang to Abby and Holly's for a ride. Selena too, if she is with them. I duck under the truck, footsteps echo on the floor. "Who is it?" I call out.

"It's me, Adeline. Alex went searching for you after you disappeared, are you two alright? She was panicking a little."

I nod. "Fine."

Blue surges of light start blowing up the tyres. I look inside the crushed burnt hood. It would probably be easier getting him another truck, but it is his first car, so it has sentimental value. It will need an entirely new engine, airbags and front seats. Probably pedals too. There is almost no space between the seat and where the driver's feet are meant to go. If Colt didn't have super strength, it would have been impossible to get Abby out with her legs intact. The back of the car is completely smashed from the impact but will probably be the easiest part to fix.

"Can I help with the car?" Adeline asks. "I know a bit about them from living with the humans. I had to learn how to fix my car."

I think this is a little beyond changing the oil or a wheel, but I should probably be nice after slamming her against a wall. "Sure, sorry about almost killing you."

"Don't worry about it."

I could instantly fix the truck but if I miss something, it would be in worse shape than it is already. I find it best to take my time with the more complicated things. I wave my hand and the engine pops out of the hood and onto the floor.

"That is unsavable. Look at it." Adeline pokes it. "But these circuits aren't. I could put them back correctly."

I smile. "Alright, you start with that."

An hour and a half later, I rub my brow. It's fixed, thankfully. I had to create a few dozen parts but it's in one piece. It was a good distraction.

"We need to make sure it works now." I close the hood. "Do you want to drive it?"

Her eyes light up with joy. "You'll let me drive it?"

"Well, if it blows up, I'd rather not be the one driving." I joke.

"Good point." She takes the keys out of my hand. I jump in the passenger seat again. "By the way I do have a driver's license."

"I know, I saw the car in your driveway when we visited." I wouldn't let her drive if I didn't think she could. I don't want to repair it again.

She rolls down her window as we start off down the road. She changes between the gears perfectly fine. They are not clogged up. The engine purrs well. There are no signs of smoke or sparks.

"I understand why you checked if I was telling the truth. You hadn't seen me in centuries. You thought I could have changed, and I was no longer the loving mother you remember, but I promise that is not true."

Why do they always wait until they start the car to talk? I look out the window, we aren't going too fast, I could jump out of it but that is a bit too dramatic.

"You thought I'd changed and it's true. It would only be logical to think you had too."

She has changed; my mother used to make magic seem so easy, the power she had was incredible. I used to be awe-struck by the sparks.

She nods in agreement. "I did. Your name isn't well received when people hear about you. The people you've killed is an endless list, then the child…"

"No. I did not kill a child." I snarl. A witch, stuck at the age of five attacked me. Stopping at an inconvenient age happens, most who stop at an old or young age normally glamour themselves to their desired age. The witch pretended to be a child to manipulate me so I wouldn't kill her. It almost worked, I struggled to do it, and even the thought makes me feel sick to this day.

"But…"

"I swear I didn't." The idea that people believe it makes it worse. I didn't know that many people found out. I thought I'd covered it up well, despite it being broad daylight in a busy city.

She nods slowly, as if she doesn't really believe me but doesn't have enough proof to disagree. "Anyway, I realised that shouldn't have stopped me. You have helped me so much these last few days which just proves to me how stupid I was for not coming back."

Well, I'm not going to disagree with her. She should have visited me or let me know she was alive. I've spent over five-hundred-years believing she was dead.

"People have done what Alex did before, haven't they?" She quizzes. "You don't trust many people, do you?"

People who don't know me could figure that out. I spent centuries alone before I met Alex, then I took in Colt and he got close to Abby and Holly. That is just what happens in a long life. People die, you drift apart, many things can happen in time.

"Well, I hope we can continue meeting up after it's safe for me to go home."

I agree. "Sure, sounds good."

***

I wake up alone. I check my phone again. I still haven't responded to Alex's messages; I don't know what to say back. There is a new one from her, saying she is coming over whether I like it or not. I swear, is she serious? That was ten minutes ago. It's eleven in the morning, I've slept in. Adeline and I talked for hours last night. Colt will be at school with Abby and Holly. I scamper out of bed and get dressed. If Alex says she is coming over, she is coming over. I can't stop that. I should probably be at least out of bed before she arrives. I yawn and pick up my comb. The sound of a portal opening comes from downstairs.

"Enzo? I'm here!" A voice echoes throughout the house. I groan, she is already here.

A yelp and a thud, the sound is similar to someone falling down the stairs. I drop the comb and run down the stairs. A lamp shatters into pieces. Alex ducks behind the couch as Adeline's magic soars through the air. Adeline's hands rise again, Alex sends out a bolt of power and she skids along the floor.

"What the fuck do you think you are doing?" I curse, looking at Adeline.

"I'd like to know that too." Alex frowns.

Adeline stands abruptly. How the hell did she do all that? Her magic is out of practice. Adeline ignores us both, magic flying at Alex. She blocks my approach with ease. My hands flare, magic soaring. It hits her, and she doesn't budge. She laughs, hitting me harder. I soar across the room, my back breaking through the wall. Through the thick mass of brick dust, my hands burn with fire. Lost her power my ass, it's perfectly fine. I groan, trying to scramble out of the rubble. My arm throbs, stuck under a cluster of rocks. With my free hand, I throw off the rubble. My wrist aches, flopping in the wrong direction. It's broken, I flick it back into place with a groan.

Running back into my house, through the new massive hole I hear, "You didn't even put up a fight, did you? Too scared to hurt Enzo's feelings? At least that's one good thing about you."

Alex is on her knees, hands in power-reducing handcuffs. Rope keeps Alex's feet from moving. Adeline is strong, but there is no way she could have tackled Alex. She's there by choice for some reason. I lift my hand to cast magic. A knife goes to Alex's throat.

"Don't or I'll slit her throat."

"What the hell do you think you are doing?" That knife can't do anything to Alex. She heals faster than I do.

"Let's see, shall we?" Adeline crosses the knife over Alex's upper arm. It cuts perfectly through the skin like a regular blade. We wait in silence. Two minutes of silence and her arm does not heal.

"What weapon is that?" Alex glances down at her arm.

"Another family heirloom. Could even kill Lucifer." Adeline boasts.

I curse, I can't just blast Adeline out the way and expect a good outcome. Alex is tied up securely, I can't magically un-tie her without Adeline noticing.

"It can kill Lucifer? I could have used that a few years ago." Alex chuckles.

"Let her go." I demand. Alex still hasn't broken herself out yet, and I don't know why.

"Listen to me and you won't want me to." Adeline smiles. "I lied when I said I hadn't been practising magic. I didn't visit because you didn't need me anymore, until I heard you were dating this scum."

"Hey!" She yanks Alex's hair. "I saw that. You only wanted to bloody date him to use him again, didn't you?" She sticks the knife in Alex's neck a little.

"You are a bitch, aren't you?" Alex shakes her head. "I have no idea what you are on about."

"You are a monster! You took Enzo from me as a baby. You killed my husband and tried to kill me." She snaps. "Now you want to use him for the power he gives you!"

"What are you on about?" I bark, noticing how close the knife is getting. Alex doesn't seem to care.

"When you were four, and were taken to that awful lab facility, it was her doing some wicked experiments on supernaturals. She was trying to make you stronger, not weaker. It was her!" Adeline insists. "Now, she is using you because you make her stronger."

"Where did you hear that bullshit?" Alex snarls. "It's not true."

"She's lied to you before. She has probably lied to you a bunch of times before. It was all her!" Adeline screams in anger.

Yes, Alex lied but that does not mean she is a kidnapper... Well, not of children. She would never do that, or experiment on them either. That I can be certain of. "Why should I believe you? Where did you find this out?"

Alex's face falls to pure horror. "You don't believe her, do you? Enzo..." Her eyes widen figuring it out. I'm humouring Adeline, exactly like she is. Alex grins, her hand slipping out of the cuff… she's not stuck. She never was. She just wanted answers.

"Why shouldn't you! I did everything to convince you to trust me! I told you the truth, about your heritage, her using you, I even helped to save your stupid little human friend in that car crash!"

"Did you arrange that crash?" I ask. Hurting a young innocent human on purpose is a whole new level of low.

"No! Lucifer did for me. He told me everything about how Alex had kidnapped you after he rescued me all those years ago. I would be dead if it weren't for him! He should be free, not this disgrace of an angel. He sent me a message about how she was still using you and I had to come and stop this madness. I thought I could try and convince you she was a monster, but after everything I did, you still trust her over me. I realised I was too late." The knife goes further into Alex's throat. "So, now I have to do this myself."

Well, I was right. She is working for Lucifer, but my reasoning was wrong. Lucifer knew I wouldn't believe him so he sent Adeline to get Alex to admit she lied to me. We have been following along with his scheme for the last few days like puppets on his strings. I am lucky Colt and the others aren't here. Hell, I should have been able to work it out correctly. This is all my fault. What doesn't add up is why Lucifer saved her all that time ago. It is completely out of character for him. He could have convinced her that he did, but there isn't the glassy look in her eyes from mind-control. She really believes Lucifer.

"Why would he save you?" I quiz her.

"To make up for his daughter!" She snarls. "He nursed me back to health."

She is not describing Lucifer. He probably took advantage of the situation, to save the daughter of the first witch, as a tool for the future. Well, it was a good move. But how did he know about the kidnapping? If he showed up in time to save her, it means he was there when it happened…

He did it, replace what Adeline said about Alex with Lucifer and it all adds up. He is the one who ordered those scientists to experiment on me and he saved Adeline to use her in the future. That bastard!

"You should be helping me kill her." Adeline grins. "You can kill her if you want." She smiles.

"I'd rather you didn't." Alex's feet are free, burnt rope on the floor. Adeline is too angry to notice.

"You don't have a choice!" Adeline's hand goes down with the knife.

Alex grabs her arms and wrenches downward. Adeline flips over Alex's arm and hits the floor. A cut crosses Alex's chest. I blast Adeline in the jaw.

"Bitch! You have manipulated him! Son, you don't understand. You are on the wrong side."

"That's you." I blast her again.

She stumbles back in pain. Alex stands, ripping the cuffs in half. They clatter to the ground. Now Adeline is in trouble. Alex's hands burn with roaring fire, it soars in Adeline's direction. She screams out in anger, face burning away.

A bolt of magic sends Alex through another wall. "You tried to kill me last time and it didn't work. It won't work this time either."

This isn't going to happen the way she believes it will. Firstly, the last time didn't happen the way she thinks it did. Secondly, this time Alex and I are working together. Firing, magic hits Adeline in the chest. She snarls, hair flying over her face. She is more powerful than me, but she doesn't want to kill me which I can use to my advantage. Alex soars through the rubble and attacks, red eyes glowing. I quirk a smile. She means business now. Alex growls, objects in the room flying and thwacking Adeline all over her body. I jump in to help, my hands glowing with fire; I can't let her have all the fun.

Adeline sweeps a wave of magic in my direction. I fly back landing on the couch. I freeze in my position, unable to move.

That bitch, it's like trying to move through water. I try to pull myself off the couch. Adeline grabs Alex by the throat, choking her. Alex's arms and legs are glued to the wall behind her uselessly. We have to be able to access some sort of movement to use our powers.

"I'm the first witch's daughter. You can't beat me." Adeline laughs drawing out the blade to kill Alex. Alex bashes her head into Adeline's and drops back to the floor.

My body breaks free. Adeline wipes blood from her temple. She may have Lucifer's powers helping her, but she doesn't have Lucifer's body. I surge all the power in my body and blast it at Adeline's chest. A searing hole rips through her heart. Adeline's eyes are wide, as if she could already see the other side.

"Enzo?" She whimpers. Alex drops her fist.

I pounce off the sofa, rushing over to her body. Tears prick in Adeline's eyes, her mouth moves but no words come out. Her eyes slowly drift away from life, the agony slipping away from her face. My heart drops, I can't help it. She is my mother, biologically and I will always have those memories of her when I was a child. But there is no way I could pin her down. Alex was holding back, she didn't want to kill her, for me. Killing her was my only choice. I lay her carefully on the floor.

"Holy shit Enzo. If I knew we were going to kill her, I could have taken her out ages ago." Alex stares.

"Do you want me to fix that?" I wave to the wound on her chest.

"No, it's just a scratch, I'll be fine… Do you want me to bring her back? We can cuff her first, obviously." Alex waves the knife near her arm.

"No." I shake my head. I cover Adeline's mouth to stop her feeding her blood and reviving her.

"What? Why?" Alex retracts her wrist. "If she escapes the cuffs, I'll knock her out. It'll be fine."

"But then what? We could never let her go and there is nowhere to put her. She can't go to human prison for obvious reasons, and she can't go to supernatural prison because she can't enter Hell. This is the only option."

"You want to leave her dead?" Alex checks.

"Yeah." It may not be the happiest conclusion, but it's the only sensible one. I would rather she was dead than risk the lives of the people I really care about. Colt is my family, he's the one I need to worry about. Then there is Alex, she tried to save Adeline, even after she attempted to kill her. It's not worth it.

"Okay, if that's what you want." Alex puts the knife away. "Thanks for the help. I probably didn't deserve it."

"What do you mean?"

"I lied to you, she didn't. You had every right to believe her, but you didn't."

I chuckle. "You've done a lot of messed up shit, both of us have, but neither of us would torture children. I hardly think you need to thank me."

"I would like to assume you wouldn't believe it, but I did mess up not telling you about your grandmother and everything. Basically, I'm trying to say I'm sorry."

"It's okay."

"Why? I know what trust means to you and I still lied. And I didn't do the best job at meeting the parents." She looks down at Adeline's dead body.

I shake my head. Alex almost died trying to protect my feelings by not killing my mother the second she acted out. My mother who was working for Lucifer and tried to kill someone I care about. Something we only found out because Alex let herself be captured so Adeline would talk willingly. She isn't even trying to take credit for it either. Worry clouds her face, it's the first time I've seen her scared.

"I love you."

Alex quirks a smile, relief flooding over her face. "I love you too."

"Good." I grin. "Or this would be awkward."

"Are you accepting my apology?"

"Depends if you are hiding any other secrets from me."

"No. I swear on Hell." Alex promises.

That's good enough for me. "Then I forgive you." I lean in and kiss her gently.

I trust Alex with my life and that is not going to change. I cling onto her tightly, it may have only been two days but, hell, I missed her. Alex catches onto my neck, pulling me in. I don't think I could ever give it up.

Drawing back, our eyes fall on the dead body gawking at us. "You know, I was worried I'd have to beg you to forgive me, which we both know I'd never do. So, I can't say her death was for nothing."

I chuckle. "Didn't you just do that?" I tease her.

"No, I never said please. I asked you to accept my apology. It's different."

I'm not going to argue with that, I would never win. "Where did you go yesterday? You have sand in your hair."

"I went to the beach in Greece. There was business I needed to sort out there. Speaking of which we should bury her." She glanced down at the dead body. "Are you certain you don't want to revive her? There is no going back after she's in the ground."

"I am." I nod. She was not the mother I remember. There is not much that can be done about it. "We should go bury her then."

"Where?" Alex looks down at the body.

"With my father." I scoop up her body. I owe her that much.

CHAPTER
TEN

Abby

Colt drives up towards the house, along the empty country roads. School was actually okay today, our teachers were a lot more relaxed, probably because it's getting closer to the weekend. Holly curses in the back of the mustang. "When will the truck be fixed? The seats are tiny back here."

"It is fixed, I'll use it tomorrow." Colt promises turning into the long driveway to the house. Smoke rises from the building. "What the hell."

The car speeds up, racing up to the front door, a gaping hole in the wall beside it. He quickly swerves in front of the house. We jump out of the car...

The house is in ruins. Large gaping holes in the walls, there is nothing left of the doorway. The ceiling droops where the support has been destroyed. Lights swing down hanging on their wires. We run inside, plaster dust filters down from the ceiling.

"Enzo? Enzo!" Colt screams at the top of his lungs. I jump over a chunk of plaster, peering in all the rooms. Holly does the same, carefully making her way up the broken staircase.

"Enzo?"

I can't see him anywhere. Both Enzo and Adeline are gone.

"Enzo!" Colt yells so loudly it echoes off the walls.

"He's not here, Colt." I shake my head. "Call him."

Colt nods, grabbing his phone, fingers moving so quickly it's a blur. It starts to ring and continues as we wait for Enzo to pick up. Panic rises in my gut. I would say it was Adeline, but she is not strong enough to take down Enzo. I saw her, she could barely lift a knife with her magic. Tessa possibly? Or it could be a random threat we don't know about.

"This is Enzo Thornhill. Do not leave a message at the beep. I didn't pick up for a reason." Colt's phone chimes.

A curse, Colt tries again. The line picks up. "Alex? Where the hell is Enzo? The house has fucking holes in the walls!"

"Hello to you too. Enzo is fine. I am too, thanks for asking." Alex says through the speaker phone. "Now, how do I put this simply. Adeline turned out to be a psycho killer working for

Lucifer. Enzo killed her. We just had her funeral. I'll come fix the house in a minute. Try not to lean on anything."

"What?" Colt yells down the phone as it cuts out.

Adeline did this? How? She was so weak, unless she was faking it? If so, she is very powerful. Or I should say was very powerful; there is almost nothing left of the building. Enzo killed her. I don't think I could kill my own mother, even if she was trying to kill me. But I guess he didn't have a choice. She must have been pretty banged up if Alex couldn't bring her back... unless he didn't want to. Hopefully, he's okay.

The blue and purple swirls of a portal appear, Alex walks through it like she is on a catwalk.

"What is going on?" Colt insists.

Holly jumps over the banister, avoiding the ruin of stairs. "Alex! Where is Enzo?"

Alex sighs. Waving a hand so the couch fixes itself and she sits down. "Exactly what I said on the phone. We just held a funeral for her. Enzo is visiting Lucifer since he caused all of this." Alex says as the house slowly restores itself to its original state. "And that is what happened to us today. What about you guys?"

"Did you and Enzo make up then?" Colt asks.

I heard about the argument they got into. Sounds like they made up.

"Yes, we did. I should really go help Enzo. We need to punish Lucifer. I assume you children are hungry. Want to order pizza or something you guys like?" She suggests. "We'll be back at some point, when we decide what to do about Lucifer."

The walls reconstruct themselves, furniture moving to exactly where it was before. Alex's hands wave. The scorch marks disappear from the walls, effortlessly.

"I'll order pizza." Colt starts on his phone. "Holly, do you still like pineapple on your pizza?"

"Yeah. I do." She nods.

Colt shakes his head at her answer. I quirk a smile, he has been trying to convince her the pizza would be better without it. He can't say much, he dips his in blood. I'm the only normal one of the three of us.

"Alex, do you want anything?"

"Hmm? No, thanks." Her hands stop working on the house. "Done. I should go." She frowns, looking at the lamp for a moment, it moves a quarter of an inch then stops. "Have fun." She smiles brightly. "Also, Holly, Enzo said he would transform with you tomorrow to make up for today."

I forgot; Holly transforms into a werewolf every week. If she doesn't change for a long time, she gets agitated and moody. It happens to everyone apparently. Enzo changes with her and teaches her new tricks. Holly can transform in two minutes now. Alex doesn't say another word and waltzes into a red portal to Hell. If we were to go through the portal, we would die. We don't have hell blood; the heat would fry us to ash instantaneously. Or that is how Alex described it. I didn't ask her how she knows that. I don't know if I'll like the answer.

Colt rubs his face and flops onto the sofa, putting his phone away. We fall silent, there is not much to say. Adeline is dead, she pretended to be so nice when we met her. She helped Enzo fix my back after the car crash. When we trained with her, she couldn't stop apologising when her knife nicked me by accident. I suppose anyone could be acting, you never know their true intent. Poor Enzo has to deal with that his mother is dead. He had to kill her. That's the trouble, there is no law for the supernatural, it's each to their own. Except for Hell, which has Alex. To think life was normal a few days ago is beyond me. I slump next to Colt, he wraps an arm around my back, his cold hand gently stroking my arm. I used to shiver at his touch, the chill from the lack of body heat forcing my body to react in goosebumps. Now, it feels normal, and I can barely tell.

I bite into the piping hot pizza, fighting the urge to spit it out. My mouth burns like it is on fire. Colt laughs. "You are pulling faces again."

"It's not my fault." It's the damn sauce's fault. Colt got stuffed crust, my favourite. Holly sneakily switches a slice of her pizza with Colt's. He picks up the slice without realising. I grin at her, she smiles back. He dips it in blood and takes a bite. He chokes, pulling a face. We both laugh as he runs over to the bin to spit it out.

"Well, that wasn't dramatic." Holly raises an eyebrow sarcastically.

Returning from the bin, Colt wipes his mouth with a napkin. "It tastes like rabbit. I don't get how you can eat it."

"God, you're right." Holly's eyes widen and she drops the pizza. "I knew it tasted familiar."

"You two are gross." I shake my head. "Why would you eat rabbit?"

"Enzo loves them, it's his favourite thing to hunt." Holly pushes away her pizza and takes a slice of my ordinary cheese pizza instead.

"Hey!" I go to slap her hand away, but she moves too fast. Stupid super-speed,. "You can eat your rabbit pizza."

Holly chuckles, munching down on my pizza. I pick up another slice. "I think we need drinks to get rid of the taste."

Colt pulls a face. "Beer anyone?"

"Yes please!" I call, as he jogs off to the fridge.

An hour of eating and drinking later, we sit with the empty pizza boxes, except for the forgotten pineapple pizza. I think Colt has finally persuaded Holly to turn away from her love of it. Holly takes her turn to get the beers.

I lean over to whisper in Colt's ear. "You added rabbit to her pizza, didn't you?"

"No. Maybe." He grins, which does not help his story in the slightest.

I nudge him. "You are evil!"

"She tried to feed me her pineapple pizza, and you knew. You let me put that in my mouth, who is really the evil one here?"

"You! You fed my sister rabbit as a prank."

"She eats it anyway." Colt defends his actions. I roll my eyes at him and stretch out on my side of the sofa. It's slowly getting dark, the sun setting gently. Alex and Enzo are still not back yet.

"When do you think…" At that, a body soars across the room, crashing into the floor.

I jump from my seat onto my feet. Alex coughs, body limp on the floor. Alone. Crap, what happened? Her eyes flutter, who could overpower her? Holly's beer smashes on the ground and she rushes to Alex's side, nudging her. She groans; she's alive. Alex lifts her head weakly. Horns sticking out of her head, massive grey wings coming out of her back. I would take a moment to admire them, if they weren't covered in blood.

"Who did this to you?" Holly asks.

Her eyes flutter gently. Blood pools out over her chest. I can see it heal through the torn shirt, but it's slow. Especially for her. The portal closes, Enzo doesn't come through with her.

Enzo

I sit on the edge of the bench, brushing the dirt off my hands. She's buried. We sit in the exact place where I was kidnapped all those years ago. It is still a forest, that has not changed. I bought the land to prevent that happening. I installed the bench years ago, it still stands, ivy locked over the handles. My parents don't have tombstones, there is a tree with their names engraved in the bark instead. The village that used to be close to our cottage is gone, along with my family home. That is what time does. I lean back on the bench. Alex's head sits on my shoulder.

"You okay?" She asks in concern.

"Yeah. I'm fine." I answer honestly.

I am fine, I think I knew my relationship with my mother would end badly. It wouldn't be any different from any other one I've had. My hopes are low with every new person I meet. Except Alex, she can't die. That is the most reassuring thing there is. Colt has lived with me for two years with only one major incident. It's the best I could ask for. I am still scared he could die but that fear will always be there. Hopefully, I'll be there to stop it if the situation arises.

My hand stretches out, closing in and out of a fist. Lucifer caused my life to go sideways. I should have known, the sick psychopath. No wonder he gives me that taunting look, like he knows more than he should. He's been messing with my life for years.

"You are pissed off at Lucifer." Alex reads my thoughts. "I know, but how can we punish him? If we try torturing him, he'll just laugh. It'll make it worse for you."

I nod in agreement. He invented torture, nothing we could do would even remotely affect him. He would laugh at our attempts, which would only piss me off even more. The fact he is not the ruler is the best punishment possible. He loves the throne, it's the only thing in the world he craves. There is nothing more we can do. Killing him would relieve him of the self-hate he feels at being overthrown.

"Going there will prove he got to us." Alex continues. "But he is obviously planning something, we need to find out what it is."

"Let me talk to him." I respond. "I'll boast that I killed Adeline, maybe thank him. See if that messes with his plan. He may not show emotions on his face, but it'll be in his damn eyes. If I could make them stop twinkling for one second, it will be worth it."

"Are you really willing to do that?" Alex brushes hair out of my eyes. "You would have to do a very realistic performance."

"I know, it's worth a shot though, right?"

"I suppose so. I wish he would just leave us alone and admit defeat." She sighs.

"Well, it would be no fun if he did." I smirk at her.

She laughs. "That's true. It would be too safe, who would want that?"

I grin, kissing her gently. She smiles, eyes dazzling in the light. Leaning in as my phone goes off.

"We could ignore it?" Alex suggests.

"But what if it's Colt? We left the house in a state, he's probably panicking. I should have left a note."

Alex sighs heavily. "Fine."

I feel for my phone, it stops ringing as I pull it out. Alex's phone follows immediately after. She picks up and mouths. "Colt." I knew it. He is the only person who calls me, except Alex. She explains where we are and hangs up.

"I'll go repair your house and sort out your children while you try to piss Lucifer off. I really think you've got the fun option out of the two of us."

"I do" I smile. "Come join me after?"

"Of course, I will." She kisses my cheek. "Now I'll go sort these children out. Don't have too much fun without me."

"I won't." I promise.

She stands up, creating a portal. "Love you, bye."

I grin and she disappears before I can say more. I look back to the graves.

"Goodbye."

I smile down at the graves sadly. I hope they find peace in death. If that is a thing. Adeline got caught up with Lucifer, which messed with her head. Lucifer has that effect on people, he can make anyone do his bidding, he has no respect for any other person. That is what makes him so evil. Evil is the inability to love, which makes him able to do the things that others would deem unthinkable or make them do the unthinkable. I stand up and walk through the glowing red portal.

I walk up to Lucifer's cell, he grins from ear to ear, a sparkling glint in his eyes. He's happy I'm here. I relax back on the cell door opposite Lucifer's without a word. I wait for him to speak and he tilts his head, looking at me. I can almost hear his mind whirling. I wait for him to start the conversation; I'm not doing it. That's how it always starts.

"You almost had me." He laughs finally. "So close."

"What do you mean?" I ask, letting Lucifer lead the conversation. I need him to talk, not me.

"You are hurting." His eyes spark. "Why?"

"I'm not hurting." For someone with no emotion himself, he does an awfully good job at reading people.

"You're lying to me. You want to ask me a question. Don't you? Well, I'll answer it for you. Yes, yes and yes."

"What questions? I don't have any." I already know the answers. I may have been late to figuring it out, but I know the answers now.

"I did send your mother to kill Alex, I did know you would end up killing her and I did kidnap you as a child. How does that make you feel?"

This isn't going anywhere. We know he wants to hurt us, but he wouldn't just toy with us for his own amusement without a motive. He would think it was a waste of his time. Especially trying to kill Alex, that is more than fun. Nor would he let some slave do it, he wants to do it himself. Lucifer wants to escape, but I just don't see how this will help him. He knew Adeline would fail.

"Nothing. I barely knew her." I shrug.

"Enzo, we both know that is simply not true." He laughs bluntly. "You are telling me the fact that I killed your father, made you kill your mother, kidnapped you as a child and experimented on you, which completely ruined your childhood, has not fazed you at all?"

I remain silent. I don't think I can answer that question without my heart rate spiking. My jaw clamps shut, fist closing. I can't have him know he's getting to me.

"My favourite experiment that I conducted on you has to be injecting you with cyanide. You were sick for weeks. I thought you would die. Or that time when someone dressed up as your father pretending to rescue you. You opened that door, thinking you would be released, then." He chuckles. "We just took you back in. You cried for hours and hours, asking about your father until you worked out that he was dead, and it was all a hoax." Lucifer sighs. "Or that last one, that was the most successful experiment. I'm sure you want to know what I did."

"Why should I care?" I fight the urge to open the cage door and punch him in the face. He'd just laugh.

"Because you do. You want to know why you have this boiling rage you can't control."

I take a step forward. "No, I don't."

"You don't want to know why you killed your mother, why you've killed so many people in rage, in revenge." Lucifer grins. "Yet, you could never save any of your friends, could you? It's because deep down, you didn't care if they died, did you? Colt is going to end up the same way as the rest of them, and I know you'll blame me for everything I did to you but, deep down, you'll know it was all your fault."

"Shut up!" I snarl. I grab him through the bars, my hands burn through his clothes.

"You're only upset because you know it's true." He taunts.

I howl, smashing his face onto the metal bars. They burn his face, he shakes his head lightly. Pain does nothing to him. Lucifer looks into my eyes. "Enzo. You stupid boy." His black pupils fill over his eyes, smothering his red irises.

"You are trying to use mind-control?" I snort. We both know that is not possible. He's tried before and it didn't work.

"I'm not trying." Lucifer's head tilts. "You will do everything I say no matter what it does to you."

I laugh, shaking my head dropping him to the ground. This is too good to be true. Lucifer is so desperate he is trying to take control of my mind. He tried to recruit me to get the amulet of sacrifices and used mind-control. It didn't work. No one knows why, the only fact is he can't do it. This is the best revenge I could ask for.

"You are really that pathetic." I shake my head.

"You wish I was." Lucifer's hands shoot through the bars and grab my head. My eyes roll back, images playing out in my mind.

I soar back in time through his memory, back to the research facility. I watch all the other experimental subjects die, one by one after being injected with a substance. I watch from the back of the room as their mouths froth and blood pools from their eyes. Their bodies tearing themselves to pieces from the inside out. Energy explodes out in their last moments, the power too much for their bodies to contain.

We flash to a new scene, Lucifer plunging an empty syringe into his own arm. He draws out a tube of blood from his body. He passes it over to a researcher. "Here. Give this to the boy."

"It'll kill him." She holds the tube. "Like it did to all the other subjects."

"One way to find out. If one of them can be successful, it'll be him."

The researcher and Lucifer march into a room. My limp, boney form lies before my eyes. I had forgotten what I used to look like. I've come a long way from that boy. Hollow cheeks, you can see every rib on my shirtless body, millions of scars over my papery skin. Dirt and blood smears my flesh, my nails are broken, and my hair is long and unkept. My eyes bug out of my face, the bags underneath making it look like I have two black eyes. The researcher adds another liquid and the blood turns green. The needle dangles above my head, I fidget. Begging for her not to do it, my tears well up but don't fall. I'm not even hydrated enough to cry. The needle stabs into my arm. I start to spasm. My horn starts cracking.

We jolt out of the memory. Lucifer's blood. He injected me with his own blood. The other liquid was just to change the colour to disguise what it really was. The unusual, uncontrollable power comes from him. "You bastard!" I swear, grabbing him by the neck.

His eyes go black once again, I tighten my grip. "Let go." My hand stops. "Good. Now, you'll do everything I ask." Gasping, I double over out of my own control. Lucifer looks down on my crippling body. I wheeze. "I told you I wasn't just trying. I was succeeding. In a few seconds, you will be mine."

My head swarms, agony throbbing through me. My muscles spasm, my legs giving out underneath my body. How? I can feel his filthy hands claw over my brain.

"The harder you fight it, the more painful it will be." His black, soulless eyes bear into mine. "I'd tell you to simply give in but it's fun to watch you struggle."

He's wrong, there is a way out. There is one way out before he takes control of me and makes me his personal slave, then who knows what he'll force me to do. I can't let that happen.

My shaking hand reaches for my waist; a knife tucked away into my belt. There is no way I'm letting Lucifer use me to escape and kill Colt and Alex. I could never live with myself if that happened. This is the only way I can make sure that doesn't happen, whether Alex can reverse it or not, it's a risk I'm going to have to take.

I fight my body which is slowly giving in. I take the knife and plunge it into my chest.

It freezes, halfway into my chest. Lucifer's hand reaches out through the bars. "I'm not letting you do that." I fight his strength, trying to force the knife in. I'd rather die than follow his rule and lose everyone I love. That's not happening. I've already lost so many, but none of them are as important as Colt or Alex. I have a few seconds left. I wrench away, with all the strength I've got left. My eyes droop, mind clouding. My own thoughts being overthrown by Lucifer. My hand slips down against my will.

Lucifer

I chuckle, looking down at the boy's limp body. He tried so hard to fight it, but it was inevitable. The knife sticks out his chest. I wiggle my foot through the bars, kicking him. He groans. Alive. I knew he wouldn't have it in him to kill himself in time. I can't wait till I release him from my hold and let him see what he has done. After I finish using him, of course. I'm certain Alex will arrive soon to check on her beloved. We need to move quickly.

"Get up!" I order him.

My slave rises at my command. A shiver of joy goes down my spine. Enzo, doing my bidding. This is wonderful. I could never control him before, I concluded it was because of his emotions. He is emotionally strong. That is why I sent his mother. The torment of old memories, of how I tortured him and turned his loving mother into my slave to use against him. Reminding him of the pain he had shut out. It crushed him like a bug. Emotions are so powerful, I never realised what I could do with them. He came to me, hurting, in emotional pain. Then, I fed off it, hurting him more, allowing me to take control of his mind. I knew saving his mother would be useful one day. She was so grateful to me for saving her life she would believe, or do, anything I said. No mind control needed; she was terrified of death. I only spared her life because I wanted the first witch's daughter at my beck and call. I thought it would be amusing, and it certainly has been. I tap the bars, they clink against my nails.

"Open the door, minion."

Enzo lifts his hand, opening the door without complaint. I smile, proud of my accomplishment. Alex should have killed me if she really wanted to rule Hell. My escape was inevitable. I did it with no work at all. I strut out of the cell, finally able to stretch out my arms without hitting the walls. "Take off the chains." I point my wrists at him. Wordlessly, he does it without any expression. They un-click. The power floods through my body, reassuringly. I smirk, hands sparking. I missed it so much. I can feel the immeasurable power pumping through my veins, fuelling my every movement. I'm back.

"Magic me a syringe." I wave a hand at him dismissively.

He nods, it appears in his hands. I don't need an amulet for power, I have a slave who can do all of that. He is part of the first witch's bloodline, and I get to use all of that power. The power he doesn't even know he has. I fill the syringe with my blood and stab it into his skin.

Spasming, he falls back onto the ground. There is a minute of pain and agony, he flounders around on the floor. I watch his eyes glow, bugging out, ready to pop. If they do, that's not going to be pretty. He stops moving, I kick him. He gasps, rolling onto his side, vomit spewing everywhere.

"Disgusting, get rid of that." I snarl.

Enzo stands and, without even moving his hand, the vomit disappears. Flint's blood kills people, Alex's blood revives the dead. I knew my blood must have some sort of special property. I used those test subjects to find out what. Enzo was my success. It gave them demonic power. It's marvellous. I can create energy; the only catch is that I can't for myself. The reason it worked on Enzo, and not the others, is because he's already from Hell.

"Don't try to control the power." I tell him. He's spent five-hundred-years trying to fight it. I want to see what he can really do.

Now that exhausting step in my plan is completed, it is time to take back Hell. With a new sidekick to replace Silven, it will be easy. Not only is Enzo more powerful, he is also Alex's lover. She won't kill him, which makes my return absolute. Enzo stares forward, waiting for his next instruction. On queue, the events I have planned in my head for so long unfold before my eyes. Alex turns from the stairwell.

"Pretend you're not under mind control." I instruct Enzo.

He nods, grabbing my throat automatically. I thought Enzo would have more enthusiasm than this, it's highly disappointing.

I glance over to Alex, her mouth hanging open in shock. What a beautiful sight to see. She shouldn't have left her vulnerable other half in my hands for that long. But I knew she would. She blinks, like she is trying to figure out if this is real or not.

"How did he get out?" Alex lifts her hands.

I thwack Enzo around the head. Alex sends a bolt of fire; it burns against my skin. I curse in pain. I grab Enzo, flipping him onto his back, putting his body before mine as a shield. Alex's hand hovers, not moving. Enzo fidgets.

"Don't break out." I murmur. He stops.

"Hand over Enzo or I swear I'll kill you!" Purpose burns in her eyes.

I'd like to see her try. "No."

She howls, the ground erupting behind me. I fly into the air, thwacking the ceiling before falling back down. Enzo runs over to her, out of my reach. I stand, air rushing by. The torches lose their flame. Alex grabs Enzo's hand protectively. There is no more work for me to do. "Enzo, kill Alex and enjoy it." He won't succeed, she'll have to run at some point. She could overpower him, but she won't because she cares about him, while Enzo will be throwing everything he has at her.

I tell him to enjoy it so that when he remembers it, he'll feel sick to his stomach.

Snapping at Alex, he grins. Her eyes widen even further. "Oh shit. Enzo, seriously?" A pellet of unnatural, blood-red magic slams Alex in the chest. I think that answers her question simply enough. "Fuck." She scrambles up from the ground. "He wanted you to come down alone." She's right. I did. She just figured it out a little too late, which I also planned to happen. She outsmarted me once, that is not happening again. I've been planning this for over a decade.

Alex doesn't attempt to attack Enzo. I knew she wouldn't. She may put in a few blows, but she isn't going to risk killing him. She may be able to revive him, but she knows I could snap my fingers and mutilate his body beyond saving.

Enzo doesn't hold back, another blast causes blood to pour from her nose. I watch Enzo mercilessly slam another bolt of energy into her chest, puncturing her lung. She gasps for air, tears of pain springing up in her eyes. Enzo grabs her by the throat, laughing.

"I'm sorry." She mutters to him gently.

Show time! Alex's eyes go a deep red and wings sprout out of her back, she got those from her mother. The horns are from me. She howls, Enzo hits the wall. She isn't going to try to sweet talk him out of brutally killing her, she knows it won't work. Nothing can stop him at work. Alex's wings flap, violently swiping Enzo in the face. Releasing his hold on her, he stumbles back.

"Nice try." He snaps.

I could really do with some grubs while I watch them fight. I've been craving some well-cooked hell-worms for the last ten years. Enzo slams his fist into her jaw, normally they would both heal instantly, but they are playing with powerful magic. It'll be like when humans get wounds; bloody and painful. In return for the punch, she sends an arrow of elemental magic out towards his chest. Enzo flies back, his body snapping on the stairwell. He screams out in agony.

Alex pounces, wrapping her legs around his neck and pulling out a knife. He grabs her legs and flings her over his head. She groans, landing on the ground with a satisfying thwack. The most interesting aspect is that they both know each other's moves from years of training together and learning from one another.

Alex jumps back to her feet before Enzo can stomp on her chest. That doesn't stop his demonic magic flowing.

Alex howls, the flesh on her face burning horrifically. She could beat him... if she killed him. I bet the small piece of him that is left wants her to kill him. Alex's wings beat Enzo down to the ground. A larger pulse of magic, powerful enough to kill a city of humans, sits in Alex's hands. She hesitates, for a mere moment. It redirects to hit me. I sidestep out the way, watching it continue down the corridor. It hits the wall but, instead of shattering, it rebounds in my direction. Before I can move, it hits. I judder, struggling to keep on my feet. I grab the wall for support, I'm out of practice. That's why I have Enzo. He pounces on her like a rabid animal, dragging her to the floor.

Hound teeth peering through his mouth, his back snapping. He's transforming into a beast. Alex punches him across the room, the beast in him whimpering in pain. That poor punch doesn't stop him, he soars in her direction, teeth sinking into her rib cage hungrily. She grabs him, trying to peel him off her body but it's useless. Blood splatters and flesh sits in his mouth. Tearing through her skin and shredding it. He chuckles, spitting out what looks like intestines. Alex screams out in pain. Pure, retching agony. Not only physical pain, but emotional pain as well; the person ripping her heart out is her love. Joy is running through my body. She howls, Enzo hits the wall. Whimpering, his legs don't move to get back up. He doesn't need to; Alex is too weak to fight back. White, cracked bones stick out her bloody chest where Enzo has bitten and clawed away at her organs. Her hand goes out, a portal appearing. She reaches for Enzo's body, his teeth snap. There is no way to rescue him, taking his body won't help.

"Don't bother returning." I smile at her, knowing she will. For precious Enzo. Alex stumbles through the portal, staggering away in defeat. The pain and hurt in her eyes as she disappears is one of the best sights I've seen in my long life. This memory will be replaced by a better one; when I kill her myself. I'm going to do that with my own bare hands.

I walk over to Enzo's limp body. I kick it hard. "Get up!" I order him. Groaning, he limps to his feet. The wounds over his body heal, he must have gotten some of Alex's blood when he was trying to rip her to shreds. It was a genius move. I smile, marching up the stairs. "Follow me!" I instruct him.

My eyes fall upon the throne, it has not changed a bit since I was banished to that cramped cell. Marching up to it, my finger touches the armrest. Shoe dust marks stain the throne. Alex mistreated it, of course she did. It must be cleaned of her filthy prints. I look down at the beast by my side. I sigh, it's a shame he can't do anything unless instructed.

"Change back, wear clothes, then clean my throne."

Enzo nods. No words coming out of his mouth. "And address me as 'Lucifer, Ruler of Hell'." I remind him.

I know Enzo is cursing inside. The aggressive, sizzling anger in the back of his eyes, under the glassy look, fills my soulless body with joy. He transforms into a warlock, fully dressed in the regular clothes that he owns. Cleaning supplies from the human world appear in his hands. He starts to scrub the throne, hatred in his eyes. I could get any other demon to do that for me, it's a very simple, mundane task. I just enjoy watching Enzo do it.

Two minutes later he has the throne sparkling. I sit upon it, grinning. It was always made for me; it's existed for as long as I have. I have the throne back; I rule Hell once again. All is right with the universe. My hands stroke the wood. Sadly, even with Enzo, my position as the ruler is not guaranteed. Alex is alive and will already be plotting her revenge. But I have planned for that too. I wouldn't release myself from that cell without planning every step, all the way to ruling all three plains: Hell, Earth and Heaven. But that is in years to come. Currently, I will be happy for Hell to be mine, with millions of demons at my beck and call.

"Enzo, I need clothes. What do you think would look good on me?" I ask him, just to taunt him further. I know he helped pick out the rags I have been forced to wear for the last decade.

His mouth opens to say something. I have to be specific in my wording, or he'll find some way to screw me over. I know it, I have control of him, but he'll be constantly fighting it in that little mind of his. "No sarcastic comments." I add.

His mouth closes, taking a moment he finds a new response. "A black button up suit with boots." He answers honestly.

"Yes. Do that for me." My outfit changes to what he describes, my hair shortens too. He's the best servant I have ever owned. "Now, listen." I lounge on my throne, in pleasure. I have time to kill before they try to rescue Enzo. I plan for them to succeed; Enzo is only half of my plan. I need someone else to retain the throne. "I bet you want to know how I did it."

"I know how you did it." Enzo responds.

"How?" I ask him to see if he is smarter than he looks.

"You ordered your demon to fake the attack on Adeline and send her a message..." He starts.

"Nope. There is much more to it. It started with Silven." I gloat.

Enzo goes silent and nods. I can see him cursing himself in his head. Mind whirling, trying to figure out how much I've screwed with their lives over the last few months. Perhaps longer.

"Come here." I beckon him, my long nail glistening in the torch light.

He steps before me. Swiping my hand across his face, my nail cuts through the skin. Cursing, he grabs his eye, blood dripping through his fingers. I haven't damaged the eye, I still need him to be able to see. The cut will scar so, whenever he sees his face, it will remind him of our time together. Just to piss him off that little bit more. Enzo steps back out of my reach, wiping his face with his sleeve.

I can't reveal my plan to him, he'll be going back soon. I might as well get some use out of him while I can. "I need you to fetch me something. It's in a building not far from here." I stand walking over to a bookshelf. I draw out a book, ashy pages flapping. I rip out a map. I knew Alex would never bother looking through my possessions. She barely came down long enough to be named ruler. She abused the title. I hand over the page.

"Here. Go to this location."

Enzo takes it obediently and pockets it into his belt. "I will." A small pause. "Lucifer, Ruler of Hell."

I grin, that is how it is meant to be said. All the demons will sing it. "Don't do anything that is not in my best interest and be quick." I demand. I will need him back shortly.

A nod. "Yes, Lucifer, Ruler of Hell." He excuses himself and walks out of the room, on his mission to recover my artefact. While he is busy, I should let the demons know I am back in charge and here to stay.

Marching out into the fresh new day, fiery storms whirl around my body. Demons appear in my presence, staring in awe and surprise. This is what I craved down in the cells, their heads bowing as I walk above them. My power submitting them to a state of panic and obedience. They do not question my power, they know if they did, they would die a miserable painful death. I stare out into the plain, small tweaks of the landscape made by Alex, ruining the creation I made out of blood, sweat and effort over thousands of years. I will have to fix it once she is out of my way for good. The buildings are too well kept, demons need caves, not houses. It's from all her time on earth, she is trying to treat my demons like humans. Pathetic excuse of a child.

CHAPTER ELEVEN

Abby

Alex groans, her wings filling up most of the room. We managed to get her on the sofa. Well, Holly and Colt did. I watched and supported them while they did it; I am not strong enough to lift her with the huge feathery wings attached to her body. Colt checks her chest, blood pools over her. She should be healing a lot quicker than this.

"Can we feed her her own blood?" Holly asks.

"No. It's already in her, it won't make any difference. I need bandages and a warlock." Colt instructs.

"I'll get the bandages." Holly runs up the stairs at full werewolf speed.

"How are we going to get a warlock?" I panic. Enzo didn't come through the portal with her, she told us she was meeting him in Hell. Which means Enzo could be in bad shape too, wherever he is. We won't know until Alex wakes up.

"Try to call Enzo. If he doesn't pick up, call Tessa." He chucks me Alex's phone. I take it and dial Enzo in hope that he will pick up. The phone doesn't even ring and it goes straight to his voicemail. I find Tessa's contact by clicking the notification bar where there are a dozen texts fangirling over Alex.

She answers before the first ring could finish. "Alex? What's up?"

"Tessa? Do you know a warlock?" I ask.

"Who is this? What are you doing with Alex's phone?"

"It's Abby, we met at the party. Do you know a warlock?" I pester her.

"Oh, you. The one with the pretty sister. Yeah, I know a bunch of warlocks, or I did, not many of them are still alive. Why?"

"Can you bring one to Enzo's house? Alex is hurt, she needs help." I feel bad for adding the last sentence. It is true, and I knew it would make her move faster and ask less questions.

"Give me a minute." She hangs up immediately.

Holly and Colt start wrapping up Alex's wounds in bandages. Enzo has given us simple first aid lessons for moments like this. Alex jolts upright on the sofa, Colt flies across the room, hit by one of the wings. Alex coughs up blood, her hand going over her bandaged chest. She lies back down groaning, her eyes struggling to stay open.

Tessa appears in the middle of the room with a warlock. The warlock is a young man dressed in all black leather with scars streaking over his face, weapons holstered all over his body. "Oh. My. Devil." Tessa squeals. "You have wings? That's incredible."

Colt stands, rubbing his cheek. "Yeah, don't get too close."

The warlock doesn't say any words, he clutches onto Alex's arm. A light grey stream surrounds her body, the wound on her arm slowly heals.

"I didn't want to waste time calling all the warlocks I know, so I brought my brother." She points to him. "Ace is great at healing people. It's his assassin ability; it is what makes him so special. It happens to one in every twenty thousand assassins." She boasts. "Is Alex okay? What happened to her? Who did it?" She scowls protectively.

"We don't know, she hasn't said anything." I shrug. We need to know if she met up with Enzo before this happened, or if he is hurt too.

Tessa nods. "She will soon, my brother is the best. The healing will match that of any warlock."

"Why do assassins need healing capabilities?" Colt asks, stepping back while Tessa's brother works. "Isn't your job to literally do the opposite?"

"Yeah, it is, but healing is the best gift for an assassin to have. It means they can heal their own, as we can get pretty beat up on the job. They are like the field medic of the family on a hit job. But that is not how my brother uses it. He heals his victims without them noticing, till they believe they are invincible. He starts with the little things, no broken bones falling down the stairs, they don't get hurt when their hand slips on the kitchen knife, so by the end of the week they are throwing themselves off buildings thinking they are some sort of god. They technically kill themselves." Tessa explains. "People do crazy things when they believe they can't be hurt. Once, someone shot themselves out of a cannon. Let's just say, I'm glad I wasn't the one who had to clean it up."

That is a very twisted way to use a healing ability. I mean, Tessa is right, he is an assassin who hasn't killed anyone with his own hands. He lets their gullibility and curiosity do that for him. I mean, who wouldn't test the limits when there aren't any consequences?

Alex jolts upright, Tessa's brother dodges a flapping wing skilfully. The wings glamour away. Luckily, the glamour also means they cannot attack anything either. The horns disappear from her head.

"It's done, Tessa." Ace growls, his voice barely audible; it's so deep. "Now, can I go back to my job? They don't kill themselves, luckily, or we would be out of a job."

"Yeah, thank you brother." She smiles. He disappears in a cloud of smoke. I guess the movies got something right.

Alex pounces off the sofa and enters the kitchen without a word to us. We follow her, we need answers about what is going on. Colt is desperate to know if Enzo is alright. I want to know too. Alex was going to meet him and came back battered to a bloody pulp. The only hope we have that he is okay, is if she got ambushed before meeting up with him. If Enzo was there, we don't know what condition he's in; Alex is supposedly unkillable, and she was in bad shape. Enzo will be much worse. Alex grabs a bottle from Enzo's pantry. "I need my phone." She waves her hand at me. I take it from my pocket and pass it over. She starts texting someone, we wait anxiously. How the hell can she be texting someone like nothing has happened? Putting down her phone, she looks up to the group of us. "None of you are safe, you need to find a place where Lucifer can't find you. He's already got Enzo, and I'll be damned if I let him take anyone else for revenge. That is, before I stop him, of course."

"Wait, Lucifer has Enzo?" Colt splutters in panic. "Is he hurt? Is he alive?"

"He's alive. But if you see him, don't trust him, you must message me immediately and leave." Alex instructs.

"Why can't we trust him?" Colt demands. "What in the hell did Lucifer do to Enzo?"

Alex takes a deep breath. "Somehow, Lucifer manipulated Enzo. He forced Enzo to let him out and he attacked me."

"Lucifer attacked you? I thought you were stronger than him?" I frown in confusion.

Alex laughs sharply. "I am but no, Lucifer didn't attack me. That demon has never done anything for himself in his life, he made Enzo do it. The bastard knew I wouldn't kill him."

"Hold on, Enzo is being controlled by Lucifer?" Worry clouds Colt's eyes.

"Yes, I don't know how Lucifer did it, yet." Alex doesn't look scared at all, only pissed off.

Lucifer has escaped his cell and taken Enzo. Yet, she is perfectly fine and functioning after almost dying. Well, maybe not perfectly fine, she still has scratches over her arms and face.

"How did Enzo beat you? You are definitely stronger than him." I ask. I know Enzo is a very powerful warlock, but he can't match Alex. Not even close.

Alex produces a syringe from her pocket. "This was on the ground; I think Lucifer injected him with it. I need to find out what was inside. Enzo's magic wasn't natural, it was bright red. That is why I need you to go find somewhere safe to hide until I figure out what to do."

"I'm not going anywhere." Colt argues. "Enzo is my family. I'm helping you save him. The substance in that syringe could be deadly."

Alex shakes her head. "You don't get it, do you? Lucifer has had ten years to plan his revenge and take my throne. Throughout Lucifer's thousands of years of existence, he has only made one mistake, which was underestimating me, and it cost him his throne. He'll be more thorough in this plan than any he's ever created. Each and every possible gap filled. It's not like when you three took on Silven. Lucifer has a brain. He's ruthless, has no emotion and an excellent understanding of people. I can't charge in there and expect to live; Lucifer knows your next move before you even think of it."

"I know, but I can't leave Enzo." Colt insists.

"Neither can we." Holly and I join in. Lucifer sounds beyond awful, but we cannot give up on Enzo and let Alex do all the work. Enzo may have been reluctant at first, but he helped both of us and almost died for us.

Alex sighs. "None of you can go to Hell, you are all going to get yourselves killed. So, no. None of you are staying. This is exactly what Lucifer will want." Alex argues. "Now, I need to figure out his game plan."

"We aren't hiding." Colt frowns in defiance. "Besides, Lucifer hasn't done the ritual. What is the point of hiding if he can't come to earth?"

"Demons can, it only prevents him. I bet in three days, you'll see 'natural' human deaths double." Alex plots. "Look, I'm not going to fight you it is a waste of my time. But think about what Enzo would want you three to do. Also, Tessa, thank you for your help. You may leave, I don't need you getting hurt either."

"No, I'm with these three, we are helping." She sides with us.

"You are all very likely going to die if you stay, and I would rather not face Enzo's wrath if that happens."

A swirl of a portal and a random man walks in the room. Who the hell is this? "Flint, what the hell are you doing here?" Alex snaps. Alex's brother, Flint. He doesn't look like how I imagined he would. He is very tall, at least six foot six, blonde and looks like a bodybuilder. Why would he work out so much when he has a crazy amount of super strength? He wears an expensive suit; I guess wearing designer clothes runs in the family.

"I got your message. Jade took the children to safety. I have come to help." Flint explains simply. "Jade wanted to come, but the children cannot care for themselves and we couldn't get hold of Esmeralda or Hayden."

Alex howls in anger. "No one listens to me. I could eviscerate all of you right this second, keep that in mind. None of you can help, it is what Lucifer wants. Hell, this conversation might be in the plan that came from his twisted mind."

"And you think you can outsmart him by yourself?" Flint laughs. Damn, he has some confidence to challenge her, especially after that threat. I mean, he has known her for their entire lives. "Look, Enzo almost killed you, are you honestly going to say you don't need help? By the way, whoever Tessa is." He looks over at the group of us. "I have no idea how you got my number, but thank you for telling me what Alex neglected to let me know in her text."

"You're welcome." She smiles.

"I don't need help, I did it last time on my own, if you remember." Alex retorts. "I need to find out what is in this." She holds up the syringe. "This is a waste of time." She gestures to us. "Do whatever you want, I'm not responsible for your actions."

I think that means we are helping. Alex yanks out the stained plunger.

"What are we meant to be doing?" Colt asks. We have no idea how to start a war with Lucifer.

Alex sighs. "I don't know, there is literally nothing you can do. You aren't from Hell, and you have very little experience. The only thing you can do is stay alive. Flint, you can help me with this."

He smiles. Alex scowls. "No, you haven't won the argument. I could do it without you."

Colt urges the two of us away, along with Tessa. We enter the next room. A red mark stains Colt's cheek where the wing whipped him. "Is your face okay?" That should be healing quicker than it is, but it was done by Alex.

He wipes some of the blood from his cheek. "I'm fine, but if we want to be of any use, we need a way to go to Hell. That is the only way we can make sure Enzo comes back in one piece."

"That is impossible." Tessa refutes the suggestion. "No one without demon blood has ever gone to Hell. Trust me, many have tried. My uncle did, no one has seen him since. We are certain he burned to ash. That is how it's recorded. The pictures are horrific, and I kill people for a living. I mean, if we do try and it goes wrong, there are no second chances. We'd be toast and that is not how I plan to die. I plan to die after fulfilling my dreams, then doing something heroic to be remembered forever."

"If you need demon blood, can't we drink some of Alex's?" Holly asks. "Then it would be in our digestive system."

"It's not that simple. I mean, there is a tiny possibility it would work, but the second it left your system, you'd fry up without warning. You'd have to drink every few minutes, which isn't practical at all." Tessa shakes her head. "Your best chance would be to trick Hell into thinking you were a demon using a spell."

"Who would you go to for that spell?" We don't have a warlock to help us anymore.

"Honestly? Enzo; he's the only warlock who has been to Hell, but we can't reach him, and Alex is busy. I'd say Jade or Tina. Tina would be best because Jade has kids to look after." Tessa calculates aloud. "We should go there. I can take us to her house, I should probably call her first." Tessa pulls out her phone. "Give me a minute."

My phone rings. I pull it out of my pocket, it's Tessa. The call ends. "Sorry, my finger slipped."

"How do you have my number?" I frown. "I never gave it to you."

"I have everyone's number who was at the party. Being an assassin is not an easy job. I can also recite their names, jobs and supernatural traits, if they have them." She puts the phone to her ear. She has all of our phone numbers? How? I shake my head; I probably don't want to know how she did it. Tessa talks on the phone with the witch.

Colt takes my hand, pulling me away a little. "Abby, I should warn you, if we do find some way to get into Hell, you might not be able to go. It'll be even harder for a human to get in than one of us."

I didn't think of that. I often forget I am the only human in the room. It's only obvious during training or other scenarios which cause their powers to manifest themselves. I hate the idea of not being able to help. Sitting here waiting does not sound like a fun job, but I might not have a choice. "Okay, thanks for the warning."

"I didn't want you to be disappointed." Colt wipes fresh blood from his cheek. I pull out a tissue from the box in the room and wipe his cheek. The gash isn't too deep, it'll heal soon enough. "Thanks." He smiles gratefully.

"Tina is in, she is creating a portal for us now." At that moment, a swirling green portal appears in the middle of the living room.

"Wait, shouldn't one of us stay here to help Alex and stop her storming into Hell without us?" Holly points out. She's right. Alex may take it as an opportunity to leave us hanging. It wouldn't surprise me; she doesn't want us interfering and putting our lives in danger. "I'll stay back." I offer. Here I can help, unlike Hell, where I might not even be able to go.

"Okay." They agree.

"I'll text and keep you updated on what we are doing." Colt promises, kissing my cheek goodbye.

They slip through the portal with nothing else to say. I hear a curse from the dining room. I should get in there, at least they have booze.

Alex sniffs the substance. Flint touches it. "It's blood." Alex concludes immediately. She puts down the syringe.

"You are right." Flint nods in agreement.

"Of course I'm right." Alex rolls her eyes. "We need to find out whose it is; blood is not a poison or a drug to boost your magic."

Sounds like they don't need me, they are coming to conclusions by themselves. Alex looks up to me. "Abby, could you bleed into a tube?" Alex asks, a test tube appearing in a rack.

I roll up my sleeves. "Can I ask why you need my blood?"

"We need to compare it to all types of blood to see which being it belongs to." Alex responds. "A demon could have snuck anything in there. And whoever it was, I'm going to kill it."

"We also need to test it for any drugs." Flint pricks a knife into my elbow, diving the thin needle blade into the flesh.

I wince, holding it over the test tube. Flint cleans off the blade then continues to do the same to himself. "What sort of drugs?" I can't imagine steroids working on supernatural powers. I could be wrong.

"There are supernatural drugs. Some can increase your power for a short period of time, but it's not worth it. The after-effects are terrible, and they are highly addictive." Alex takes my full vial of blood. "Some are taken for fun, or the thrill. Most humans can take the fun ones without dying, like vampire venom and pixie dust." Alex's magic swarms around the two glass tubes. She chucks down my portion of blood, it clatters on the side. "It's not human blood, but that is not much of a surprise." She picks up Flint's blood.

"How do you know Enzo?" Flint tries to strike up a conversation while Alex concentrates on her work, looking between the blood sample and the empty syringe case. I suppose the magic allows her to test similarities.

"He's my boyfriend's brother." I don't actually know their official relationship status. Enzo is too chill to be his father, but they are family.

Flint nods. "Alright. It's good of you to help. You aren't supernatural, are you? You should be careful; do you carry a blade?"

"Not on me." Colt has suggested it before, but I live in a human world where you are not allowed to carry switchblades in your pockets. I also go to school. I would never take one there. They just worry about me because I'm human and I don't have any built-in weapons.

"You should carry one." Flint advises. "For now." He produces a small flick knife from his pocket. "Take this, it's highly effective; the tip is stained with poison. Be careful not to stab yourself with it."

I take it, sliding it into my pocket. "Thanks." I don't think I'll be doing anything 'human' like for the next few days, so I don't need to worry about carrying it anywhere inappropriate.

Alex swigs more of the whiskey before turning back to the blood. She pours in a mixture of mine and Flint's. Flint frowns. "Alex, no one's blood will be human and demon."

"I swear, there is some human blood in it." Alex shakes her head. "The blood is old, the DNA has very little evolutionary signs compared to Abby's." Alex relaxes back in her chair. "Lucifer wants us to find out, or he wouldn't have left it there for me to pick up. He doesn't make mistakes like that." She rubs her face.

The test tube starts to sizzle, the blood is reacting somehow. Alex's eyes light up. "Flint your blood is killing Abby's. It's rotting it away instantly on contact." She admires it.

I sit up at the table, watching the sizzle slow down to nothing. "Alright, that's not it." She puts down the tube. "But it is very similar to Flint's. An early demon; there are elements of a human in it." Alex concludes.

"How does that help us?" I frown. I didn't think a human/demon hybrid could exist. Enzo has never mentioned that in any of his lectures. "Is it common?"

Alex curses. "Flint, wait a minute." She disappears at full speed and returns in a matter of seconds. She opens a book, it looks old, probably from Enzo's supernatural history collection.

Flint leans over and reads it. I peer over, but I do not understand a single word on the page. It is in a different language. Latin, I assume. "What does it mean?"

"The whole point of the supernatural is to balance out the circle of life." Alex reads. "It started with angels and demons, the good and bad, then humans who are neither, they are neutral. See, humans are meant to be based on a mixture of angels and demons. Anyway, throughout time more subsections evolved from those three, like vampires, werewolves, warlocks and assassins. However, demons evolved to be less human-like and more animal-like. That is why Flint and I look fairly human compared to the other demons, it's always why we are stronger."

I hadn't thought about it before, but Alex and Flint do look awfully human compared to other demons I have seen. They were creatures with talons, scratchy skin and more like animals that had been chewed up and spat out. The only things that Alex glamours are her angel wings, horns and eyes. The rest of her looks human; she doesn't have scales, claws or other animal features. It would make sense if they were related to humans in some way. Alex curses. "I know whose blood this is. It explains how a demon never got caught giving him the syringe." Alex chuckles sharply. "It's because they didn't have to. It's Lucifer's blood."

Flint's eyes wide. "What?"

"The blood is almost identical to yours, Flint. Pure demon blood with a few human aspects. It obviously has power, like ours. I suppose it makes sense Lucifer's blood would do something special. Most early demons had abilities like it." She flips through the pages.

Old parchment pages flip out to make one massive demonic family tree, sketches with the name for each person. It starts with one at the top, labelled 'royal family'. Lucifer sits at the top of the page with the mothers of his children. Next, Alex and Flint. That tree ends, it obviously hasn't been updated recently with Flint's kids. Going to another branch, Silven and other demons fill the page. There has to be over a hundred, but over half are recorded as dead. They have children too, a mixture of demons. Then another section of more animal-like demons. It is showing the different levels of demon rankings in Hell. I didn't know it was so complicated.

"How were demons made?" I frown.

"Like humans. They materialised in their own worlds. Hell, Heaven and Earth. It started off with Lucifer and Angel Moroni. Then a human, a mix between the two species. Humans were made to be the neutral beings between the angels and demons. If there weren't humans, time wouldn't be necessary; demons and angels never die and no other supernaturals would have been created as evolution wouldn't exist. Anyway, skip a few hundred years, and more and more humans appear. I don't know all the details. But more appeared until enough were produced that they could keep their own race going."

"But where did Lucifer and the angel come from?"

Alex shrugs. "That's as much of a mystery to us as to humans. Lucifer might know how he came to being, but he hasn't bothered to share. The other demons who could possibly tell you are long dead. I know the first witch came from a human, if that helps. It was the world doing its job, balancing everything." My eyes widen, she says all this casually, like it's information I should already know. Demons and angels just came into existence, then humans. Now after thousands of years of evolution, we are here. And still, no one knows how. That is a mind-boggling amount of information to take in at once. Especially, considering I have never even thought about it before. From what Alex has just said, humans are powerless demon/ angel hybrids.

"So, this is Lucifer's blood." Alex holds the syringe. "It has given Enzo a large amount of power. It must be his ability, like mine is bringing back the dead."

"Do you think it's how he got control of him?" I think aloud.

"No, Enzo would have had to magic him the syringe." Alex rejects my idea.

"But he was injected before, remember. As a kid, if that was Lucifer's blood as well, he already had some blood in his system." Flint brainstorms.

"The shot all those years ago could have been Lucifer's blood, but Lucifer would have been able to control him ten years ago, if that was the case." Alex rejects his idea too.

"How did Lucifer get control then?" Flint asks.

"I assume Lucifer knew Enzo would kill Adeline and feel guilty about it. It would hurt Enzo and make him vulnerable to a mental attack." It's hard to think of Enzo as vulnerable but she has a point. Mind-control is taking control of someone's entire body, while they are still conscious inside. It's different from possession where they have no control or recollection. If Enzo didn't want to think, it would be easier for Lucifer to get in. Alex puts down the syringe. "At least we know what is fuelling Enzo's power. Lucifer won't give Enzo any more power, it could kill him."

Alex sits back in her chair. "That's the easiest part. He wanted us to figure that out. The reason why is more difficult." Her perfect brows furrow. I have no idea why he would want us to know how he did it. To boast? I don't know. Alex said he's twisted, I'm not exactly sure what it could represent.

"We should..." Flint's words are cut off by a phone ringing.

Alex picks up her phone. "It's Enzo." She answers the call and puts it on speaker. I know Enzo's phone can get signals from Hell, there is some sort of spell on it. But it won't be Enzo, it'll be Enzo under mind-control or Lucifer with his phone.

"A-Alex?" He stutters. That's Enzo's voice, it sounds weak. The line buzzes. Enzo screams, voice echoing through the phone. I wince, the noise is painful to my ears.

"He's fighting it." Alex holds her phone closer. "Enzo, what is Lucifer doing?"

"I don't know. I've got..." The line fades, Enzo groans in pain. "Shit, he's..." It goes silent.

Perching on the edge of my seat, I listen in. Hopefully, he can tell us something. Faintly, I can hear fire crackling in the background. Alex grasps the phone tightly. "Enzo?"

"Yep. I've...box." Enzo howls. "I... can't open." He stumbles on his words.

"You can't open a box, well that's helpful. Is it special in some way? If so, how?" Alex bombards him with questions without checking up on his well-being.

"Blood." Enzo sputters out.

"It has blood inside? Or needs to be opened with blood?" Alex pushes.

"Open. It is- Crap!" A bloodcurdling scream from Enzo's mouth. He mumbles something I can't hear, and the line cuts out.

"Why didn't you ask where he was? Or if he was okay?" I insist.

Alex raises her eyebrow. "He's in Hell, obviously. The connection was pathetic. And asking if he's 'okay' is a stupid question and doesn't help us, it does the opposite to be honest. It wastes our time, we need information that can help him, not comfort him. Enzo has confirmed he is not Lucifer's end game, but what is in that box is. If he is still using Enzo, we have time."

Alex smiles. "But what we still need to work out, is if Lucifer knew there was a possibility Enzo could break out of his control. If he did, this information could just be setting us up for a trap."

"He wouldn't think that far into it. I thought you said he was confident. Surely he would assume his hold on Enzo is unbreakable." I argue.

"He's confident, not stupid. He'll have everything planned, including the words coming out your mouth right now."

I'll have to trust her on that. "Did either of you hear what Enzo murmured before it cut off? Was it important?"

Alex bites her lip. "It's not important."

"What did he say?" I frown.

"He asked me to kill him, again." Alex explains.

My eyes widen. That is important. Enzo wants to die? That is not a good sign. We can save him from mind-control. He can't die, it would break Colt. "Again?"

"Yeah, he asked when he was attacking me."

"Well, he knows that's not happening."

Alex and Flint pause, not a single word coming out either of their mouths. They share a glance, excluding me.

"You want to kill him?" I squark. "Are you serious?" I thought Alex loved Enzo, but she is considering killing him? And so much for Alex telling me Flint was the good one of the two of them. He's on board with the plan.

"No, I don't want to." Alex growls. "You love Colt and your sister, right? Now, imagine one of them is going to destroy the entire world. You can either kill them or not, but if you don't, they will kill everyone on Earth. Which means they would still die, and take your parents and friends too. What would you pick? There is a chance I could save him with my blood, if Lucifer lets me get my hands on him."

I pause, thinking. I could never kill Holly or Colt, for that matter. I wouldn't have the guts, even the idea makes me feel queasy. I physically couldn't do it, even if it was to save the world. I guess that makes me selfish, they would die anyway. Hopefully, that is never a choice I have to make.

My phone vibrates in my pocket, cutting off my thoughts. I check it, one message from Colt and one from Holly. Colt's message says they are with Tina, and they are working on a way for us to get into Hell, that it may actually be possible. Holly text tells me that Colt is panicking about Enzo, and any good update would help him. I start a message back; I don't know if it's good news or not.

Enzo

I trudge along the rough Hell dirt to the location, fighting each step I take. I tried to kill Alex, it didn't matter how hard I tried to stop. I don't have any control over my own body. I'm a small voice in my head while Lucifer controls the rest. I can try and fight it. Hell, I am trying, but it's not working. The most I could manage was to mouth the words 'Kill me' to Alex. Dying would help a lot more than living at this point. Lucifer is not going to let me go any time soon. I'd rather die than serve him. He's got something sick planned, no doubt. I don't know if Alex saw me ask or not. It is a hard ask, I know, but she's smart enough to know when to let me go. I fight my moving feet, but they refuse to cooperate. I struggle to reach for my phone, but my hand barely twitches.

Demons ignore me as I stomp past them. They are used to seeing me here, there are dozens of them in the area. All of them are part of Lucifer's loyal army. They accepted Alex as Queen, but she restricted their bloodlust, and they hate her stricter rules. Once they hear Lucifer is back, he won't need to force them to serve him. They'll die willingly. I follow the map, leading me far across the plain. How far away is it? Squinting, I can see a small hut made of clay and dirt. I assume that is where I'm heading. I fight to reach for my phone; luckily, Lucifer hasn't taken it from me. I go to sigh in annoyance, but I can't. Even not being able to do small acts like that pisses me off. Screaming at myself to turn around is not going to help at all, nor is fighting it. I should wait until there is a good opportunity.

I reach the small squat building; it looks like an old-fashioned witch's hut. There is a small door, made from hell ash wood. A few of those dead trees sit around the building. I swing open the poorly fitted door. There is a yelp from inside. Who would be here? I left all demon life a mile back. Walking inside, I see an old woman wearing chains, trembling. Wild eyes meet mine; the woman looks like she hasn't showered in years. Dirt stains her skin, her hair is one massive knot and the smell is awful.

"W-who are you?" She whimpers.

"I could ask you the same question." I glare at her. Lucifer never mentioned that someone would be here. Does he know? I should warn him when I get back. I curse myself. I shouldn't care what Lucifer thinks.

"My name is Annie." She shakes under my gaze. "Lucifer trapped me here, please save me."

I have so many questions. She definitely isn't a demon, which brings up the question: how is she here? Lucifer must have done it, somehow, but why? She could know something about Lucifer's plan. But I can't ask her, my mouth refuses to move. It's not in

Lucifer's best interest, which means she does know something. "I'm looking for a box for Lucifer." I say instead.

"Oh, you work for Lucifer." Her shoulder's droop. "I shouldn't have hope. I'll get the box." The chains drag on the floor, she walks to a cabinet and takes it out. Cuts and blood enclose her wrists where she has struggled to get out of the chains. How long has she been here? The woman takes out a small wooden box with gold engravings. I snatch it up and her wrinkled hand grabs my wrist. I pause for a second, then wrench it back. I watch her eyes light up like stars. "You are under mind-control."

"No." I snort. "Get out of my way, you old hag." That is definitely not what I want to say. I want to say 'yes, now tell me what you know or else.' Irritatingly, I can't do that.

"You are. I see it in your eyes." She smiles. "I can tell you how to get out of it."

I like the sound of that. "I don't need to know. I said I'm not under mind-control."

She shakes her head. "If you want to..."

"I've been here long enough." I snap.

No! For demon's sake.

I start marching out the door. I can't do anything that is not in Lucifer's best interest and finding out how to escape his torment is not on that list. Getting him this box is. My hand closes over the doorknob, the box disappears from my hands. The woman holds it. "I'm going to tell you how to break out of it, but you have to help me after."

I snarl, my hands rise. Hot red magic blasts uncontrollably out of them. She thwacks the wall, whimpering and falling into a crumpled heap. The box lies on the ground, out of her reach. Power drums through my veins, throbbing throughout my body.

"No!" She begs.

That's it, my hand lets out a black bolt of magic. She screams, the bolt hits her chest, body parts fly across the room in an explosion. A trail of liver smacks my face, a few measly pieces of body scatter around her home. Killing her was not necessary, I didn't even mean to do it. I just meant to shut her up. I don't have control of the power I wield. That is the worst possible situation for a supernatural, no story ends well for those who struggle with their own ability. An eyeball sits on the box, I bat it off and pick it up. I catch myself in a mirror; my eyes are a mixture of black and red, nothing like their natural fiery colour. My skin is much paler, and my cheeks are more sunken. The injection did that, the power is barely containable.

I storm out the hut, I have what I came for. I continue back down the path, the box clenched tightly in my hands. I look down at it, the box is old, but well-preserved. Hell doesn't have dust, but I suspect it hasn't been touched in centuries. The gold is tinted a faint red. It's not human gold, it is from Hell. It's a very rare metal. My fingers itch for the clasp. It doesn't have a lock. My will fights for the clasp. If I can open it, it'll give me a clue. A single clue would be better than nothing. Struggling, my fingers move. They retract. My feet won't stop going down the path. I need to look inside it before I get back to the castle. Focusing, my hand quickly jabs out and tries to open the box. It refuses to open. I try again. The box stays shut, there might be a spell on it. The important part is that I can move my own hand. My hand shakes as I focus on trying to do a spell. My legs continue moving on towards the castle. The spell refuses to leave my hand. The box has a small dip at the front; it can be opened with blood from the person who it belongs to, Lucifer. All that effort, for nothing. I can't open the box with magic. Unless there is enough of Lucifer's blood in my system. I could open it with my own blood. My hand shakes as it reaches for my dagger. If I open it, Lucifer certainly will be able to tell. Then he'll know I can break out of his hold, even for a moment. I can't give that away too quickly. Knowing I can do small movements by myself has to be good enough for now.

I should warn Alex, if I can. I don't have much to tell her but, if I can tell her anything, it has to be worth a try. Lucifer can't track phone calls; he doesn't understand technology. Gathering everything that is left of me, my hand jolts back and forth inside my pocket. I grasp my phone, I can feel the resistance as I pull it out. I would call Colt, to reassure him, but that won't help ensure his safety. Alex's name is first on my speed dial. Trembling, sweat drips down my face. My hand hits the dial, the phone hovers in my free hand, there is a voice in my head telling me to let go and stomp on it. The chest sits under my other arm, safely tucked away. I wish I could throw it in a fire.

Alex picks up, thankfully. My finger itches for the decline button. "Alex?" I manage, impressed I have enough control to stay on the call. My legs have stopped carrying me to the castle. Pain throbs through my entire body as I fight the movements.

"Enzo? What is Lucifer doing?" She asks.

All my effort is put into holding onto the phone. "I don't know. I've got..." The connection buzzes, fading in and out. My muscles start to spasm under the pressure. "Shit. He's..." The phone drops from my hand. I groan, luckily my knees buckle. I drop close enough to be heard. That works.

"Enzo?" My name echoes out of the phone.

"Yep. I've... box." There is no point trying to speak in full sentences. I will never get them out. My jaw clicks, fighting my words. "I can't open." I howl in anger, I should be able to talk, this is agonising. I should have died when I tried to kill myself, fast-healing is a curse sometimes.

"You can't open a box, well that's helpful. Is it special in some way? If so, how?" Alex pesters me for useful information.

I am able to quirk a smile which is greeted with a wave of pain. "Blood."

"It has blood inside or needs to be opened with blood?" Alex asks.

"Open." I want to ask her if she thinks I should risk opening it. Personally, I don't think it's a good idea, but she may have a plan to stop Lucifer. If opening the box would help in any way, I would put all my effort into doing so. Even if it killed me, it would be worth it to stop Lucifer. "It is- Crap!" My body shudders, the mind-control throbbing through my skull, trying to take back its place. I scream out in agony. Before I can manage to say anything, my hand snatches up the phone and ends the call. Mentally I curse myself; I had more to say, especially about the women there. I gather myself back to my feet and, against my will, start walking back to the castle. I try to grab my phone again, but I can't.

I reach demon civilisation, none of them live near the hut. I have no idea who that woman was, but the demons must be wary of her. The path widens, worn away from thousands of years of use. The castle doors stand before me, they are a lot uglier knowing they don't belong to Alex. I welcome myself inside. To no surprise, Lucifer is lounging on his throne. He smiles at the sight of me. I hand over the box. "I collected the chest, King of Hell." I hate saying that. I want to wash my mouth out with poison.

"Good job. How was your call with Alex?" He draws a knife.

How does he know I called Alex? Did he have a spy on me? I didn't see a demon following me. Surely, they would have tried to stop me. Unless...

"I wanted you to call her." Lucifer grins from ear to ear. "I told you, you could only do things in my best interest and you did just that. Why, did you think you were able to fight it off?" He laughs bitterly. "I just made it painful so you would think you were doing something against my wishes. See, I've been planning this for ten years. There is nothing that will happen that I have not planned to the letter."

That entire call, he knew it would happen. He left me with my phone on purpose, that point of weakness in the control wasn't me. I hadn't gained back any of myself, that was all him. He tricked me into thinking I had. Everything I told Alex, admittedly very little, was just helping Lucifer. I'm an idiot, no wonder he could take control of me, I'm weak.

"See, I knew you would want to tell Alex everything. That is why I sent you to get the box, instead of a demon. Then, I let you tell Alex, there was more to my plan. She'll think she has more time to prepare and take my throne. Really, she doesn't have much time at all." I fell for that, I should have worked it out. I did the opposite of helping. "Pass over your device." Lucifer puts out his hand.

I hand it over; I don't have a choice. He frowns. "This is a phone?" He touches the screen, the light shining in his eyes. "I might need you to teach me how to use it. I mean, I don't know what I was expecting." He shrugs pocketing it.

He takes his knife and draws his own blood over the box. The lid pops open. I can't see inside. Lucifer picks up an object. He smiles, holding a dagger. It's identical to the one Alex melted down ten years ago. The one that can kill her and Flint. "She should have known I would have a spare." Lucifer shakes his head in disappointment. "Anyway, you. Now that I'm done with your real emotions, I might as well shape them how I want. It'll make you able to serve me without instructions." Lucifer's eyes go black. "You want to serve me, you are willing to die for me, you don't care about Alex or the teens you have taken under your wing. You want to watch them die. You hate them all, you want to serve me till the day you die."

My eyes go wide looking into his. I can feel my own emotions fade. No, no, no. He can't do that. That is not how mind-control works. You can control their actions but not their emotions. I hated the fact I was forced to smile while attacking Alex, but I still felt awful while doing it. He cannot take that away, it is the only piece of me left in my body. I cannot let him do that, but my eyes won't look away. If this works, there is nothing to hold me back. "You don't love Alex." Lucifer continues. "You want to see the world burn. You only care what I think." His eyes change back to a harsh red.

Lucifer places the blade into my hand. "What do you want to do with this blade?"

"Drive it into Alex's heart." I speak truthfully. There is nothing I would like to do more. "After I kill Flint." She loves Flint. Her brother means the world to her and his death would cause her more pain than her own.

"That is music to my ears." Lucifer grins.

CHAPTER
TWELVE

Lucifer

I dangle Enzo's phone in my hand. "This is a phone?" It's not what I was expecting. Last I heard, they were massive bricks with very little electronic power. Times change, I suppose. I pocket the device; I might need to contact Alex later.

I open the box with my blood and take out one of the objects. This was my back-up. Ten years ago, Alex took my amulet and threw me in a cell, but I had enough time to instruct Silven to do the last few tasks before Alex rounded up my loyal followers. All the items I need are in this box. I pluck out a second devil dagger, Alex is a fool to believe I didn't have a spare.

I look down at Enzo. I could tell there was some restraint in his fight with Alex, he's stronger than he gives himself credit for, and I can leech off that. But I need him to be fully focused on tending to my every need. Fortunately, my power can go beyond controlling someone's actions and can control their emotions as well. My eyes go a deathly black. Time for the next phase of Enzo's mind-control.

I convince him that I am the most important thing in his life, that his love for Alex is non-existent and that his son and friends mean nothing to him. Now he is completely at my mercy. I hand the dagger to Enzo, he'll be doing all the dirty work. I should check my plan has worked; I don't want anything to be ruined. It was difficult enough to make Enzo my slave, but worth it. "What do you want to do with this blade?"

"Drive it into Alex's heart and watch her die. After I kill Flint." He added the second half all by himself. I'm impressed. I know he won't fail me. I look at the rest of the chest's contents. They are for the next phases of my work.

I need to build up my army for when Alex arrives, which will be soon. She'll come charging in to save Enzo and she will get him. I need Enzo to distract Alex and break out of his mind-control, he is hardly a long-term solution. I need to be the most powerful being in the universe, which means my next step will be to acquire significantly more power. That will happen when the Enzo Rescue team comes charging into Hell. Once they 'succeed' in their mission to rescue Enzo, my job will be much easier. Alex will be less determined and ruthless after she has her precious Enzo back. She doesn't care about the throne, it was just a bonus for overthrowing me. She cares more for her family than what happens to Hell. She'll lie to herself that the throne is important to her, but it's not true. Her panic and urgency will drastically decrease once she knows I don't have my hands on the one she loves. This will benefit my plan as Alex works better under pressure. I learned that from past experiences. She'll want Hell back to ensure their safety is permanent, but it'll be a lot easier to kill her when she has them by her side, instead of in my clutches.

I know this for the same reason that I know Alex will have taken herself to Enzo's home instead of her own; it comforts her that Enzo is not gone forever. Also, his family and friends will be there. Who will help her take him back? I expect Alex, Flint, Colt, Holly, Abby, Tina and Tessa will be coming through that portal. I had to learn their names for my plan, I'll forget them as soon as they are irrelevant. Alex and Colt will be there for Enzo.

Flint will be there for his sister and the fate of his wife and children. Abby and Holly will be there because they do not want to be left out. Tina and Tessa will be there as friends of Alex. They will have gone to Tina for help to get them into Hell. They will need demon blood running through their veins, but I'm certain they'll figure out the way to do it. Tina will be very willing to help after the gift I sent to her an hour ago. I hope she enjoyed it.

I did consider the possibility that Alex would trick them and leave them behind, but I reevaluated, realising that she respects them too much to control their lives, even if she has the power to.

Getting into Hell won't be as hard as they might think. Well, not for Abby at least. Silven possessed her, which means Abby still has some of her power. This happens so a demon can visit Hell while still in the human form they have stolen. Abby is the first human in millennia who can freely enter Hell. I remember when the sword still existed, I used it for experiments on humans who lived through demon possession. In Hell, they could use some of the powers their possessors had. In a sense, they replace the demon who died inside their body. For Abby, Silven was expelled then killed, but I'm certain it won't make a difference.

Enzo tucks away the dagger, the glint of mind-control is dull, I can barely tell it's there. I slide the box under my throne, I won't need it for a while. Enzo's hand rests on the blade, ready to pull it out to kill any second. I gave him the last dagger with the ability to kill Alex and Flint so he can stand a chance against her, but I do not want him to kill her. That right is reserved for me. He needs to keep them busy for me. For an hour, perhaps? Partly for my amusement, partly for the plan. Enzo will get to keep the blade; I don't need a weapon to take down Alex. I need power. That is next on my agenda.

I miss fiery Enzo, this one is boring. I still enjoy using him, I know he's going to remember doing this and hate himself. "Fetch me some hell worms. Fresh." I order.

I suspect we have a little while until they arrive, and I miss the sweet taste of food. I cannot die of hunger and Alex took advantage of that. I haven't eaten in ten long years. Enzo disappears to fetch my worms. I stand, leaving my comfortable throne and making my way to the armoury. Demons rarely use weapons, but the few with hands could do with them.

I open the doors. Alex, the bitch. The armoury is nothing like I left it, I am certainly going to need to redecorate. The weapons are on display, shining under the lights. None of the buckets are crammed with weapons or scattered over the floor. The small fires on the walls light up the room, making the weapons sparkle. It's disgusting, it looks like a showroom. This is not what demons want to see, they don't care what they wield. I walk over to a chest, opening it. Rows and rows of daggers sit inside, the container was labelled 'poison'. I shake my head in disgust. Who cares if their blade is poisonous or not? A stray demon walks by the door. "You." I point at it. "Did Alex do this?"

The demon jumps to answer me. "No King, Alex made a demon do it."

The grey sludge's eyes light up with the simple fact I am talking to him. That is what I like to see. They have not lost their joy in my presence over the last ten years. I will always be Hell's ruler, that is inevitable. I have been alive since the beginning of time; I am alive for a reason. Not to live in a cell, but to rule Hell and, eventually, everything else. Alex was created because I was bored and wanted to experiment. Boredom is common when you live for hundreds of thousands of years, but it is not to be fixed with children. They are nothing but a nuisance. I thought I would leave them be and it would all be alright. I was wrong. Well, they won't be alive after this.

There is a new door in the room. I sigh, I don't think I'm going to like what is on the other side. I swing it open. I am correct. My eyes catch a pair of shoes and an entire outfit. I examine the shoes, high-heel boots, obviously Alex's. This room is full of training equipment. The punching bag with my face on it is sweet. I don't know what most of these human machines are. I have spent some time on Earth, enough to know I hate it. Humans are grub for us to thrive on.

Demons do most of the work in Hell, it's the reason they are alive. They are only here to serve me. I know they've missed killing as much as I have. That is why they are going to enjoy what is to come. I leave the room. The demons know I'm back but they need to arm themselves ready for Alex's arrival. I can't wait. Marching out of the room, I grin.

Walking out, I look for the first demon to pass. I pick it up by its slimy collar. "Gather the other demons, tell them to come to the castle. No delay." I order.

Scampering happily, it speeds away as fast as it's slime trail will allow. For the first week of incarceration, I was furious at the demons for caving into Alex's power so quickly. It didn't take me long to work out that they were waiting for my return. Demons are only useful if they have a leader, they only accepted Alex because they wanted to survive. They were not able to take her on by themselves and they doubted my ability. I don't blame them, it's the worst moment in my existence, no one should be overpowered by their own child. I should have killed Alex and Flint when I knew they were failures as my personal slaves. I let them live because I wanted to see what they would do, and if they would ever live up to their name. That is the mistake I made. Demons won't question my rule now. They have to submit to my power; they know I'm stronger.

I sit on my throne, crowds upon crowds of demons enter the room. They mutter and hop around in excitement of my return. Most of them should already be in the building. I never shut the demons out of the castle, they lived here as much as I did. There were only a few places in the entire building that were forbidden. Execution comes to those who disobey. Alex did keep a few in the palace, as servants. Demons weren't made to sort closets. It is to my benefit that she treated them as such, they appreciate that

I'm back and will fight to keep me. I don't need them, I could get rid of Alex by myself but it's more fun with an army. It also proves their loyalty. I chew down on the fresh hell worms, cooked to perfection. I sent Enzo off to my pantry to get a cup and the fiery alcohol for my toast to the demons to build their morale.

Ten minutes later, the throne room is filled with demons, they continue outside. Enzo rushes to my side, passing over the glass. I sip the crisp liquid. I haven't had a drink in ten years. This is well-deserved. "Demons." I begin. "I know I failed you once." I admit. "But not this time. Alex treated you as personal slaves." I growl. "She treated you as house pets and refused to let you kill at will. She protected the humans over you. But you know I won't. Help me defeat my disgrace of a daughter and I promise you not only Hell, but Earth and Heaven too." They cheer. Not that they can say no to my demands. I will defeat Alex and take over Earth and Heaven, but that is a few steps in the future. If I rush it, then there will be nothing left to achieve. A little struggle is fun every once in a while. "First, we will get rid of Alex..." I start with my plan, to the extent that they need to know. Demons work at their best if they have the information they need.

They hear the next step of the plan and immediately jump into action. They charge for the armoury, to mess up the terribly sorted work Alex has forced them to do. I can't wait for her to get here. That is when the fun will truly begin.

Abby

Colt and Holly are on their way back, they said they would be no longer than ten minutes. Apparently, they think they have found a way to enter Hell. It's risky but we have to try it, otherwise we'll never find out if it works. We are trying it here, at Enzo's house because Alex or Flint are the only ones who can create a portal to Hell. Alex is drawing on a chalkboard that she summoned for her game plan. So far, it includes her, and, after an argument, Flint too. I tried to tell her we would be joining, she laughed at me.

Alex draws up a map. "We can't portal anywhere inside the castle, there are wards up to stop it. We can probably sneak into the throne room through a back entrance. He'll be expecting us to storm through the front door."

The floor-plan is impressive, the details go all the way down to secret passageways. Alex stares at the board, deep in thought. She has not gone insane with panic; it's almost scary how calm she is. If Colt or Holly got taken, I would flip out. The castle is massive, Enzo's house could fit inside it fifty-fold.

Flint nods in agreement. "He would have demons everywhere; does it matter which room we enter from? The second we get there, he'll know."

Alex sighs. "You have a point. I really want to storm in the front door." Alex swings a pair of handcuffs in her hand. "It would also mean we wouldn't have to sneak through the entire castle to get to the throne room. Besides, Lucifer knows every move we are going to make."

"You obviously think that your plan can outsmart him, or else we wouldn't be going." Flint argues, his face drops. "But this isn't your real plan, is it? This is to trick Abby and I."

"No."

I cannot tell if that was a lie, but I assume it is. She doesn't want our help, so she won't include us willingly. I can't imagine how she is expecting to do it alone.

"What's your plan?" Flint demands.

Alex flips the board, on the other side is a detailed plan on getting in and out. I frown at the board, it has a lot of words, less pictures than the fake one. I'm going to pretend not to be insulted by that. Nowhere in her grand plan does it suggest taking back Hell; it's a rescue mission. "Are you just letting Lucifer take Hell?" I ask.

"No." Alex snorts. "Hell is mine, but we need Enzo back first. With that crazy blood power, he would be very useful in my takeover. This is step one."

"I bet this is another fake and the real one is on your phone. Hand it over." Flint demands.

"You aren't having my phone." Alex snorts. "But you're right."

"Alex." He growls.

"It'll be much better if I do it alone, also Lucifer will expect it. He knows you all want to come help, you're stupid if you really think it'll work."

"We have to come." I insist. "You almost died."

Alex snorts. "No, I didn't 'almost die'. That is a tad dramatic, I would've survived. Besides, this time I will be prepared."

"Alex, that doesn't mean you are going to win." Flint disagrees.

Alex is a genius, but refusing help isn't her smartest move.

The sound of a portal pauses the conversation, the four of them flash through a swirl of green energy. Tina is not what I expected, she has dark auburn hair and wears a professional suit. Alex raises her eyebrow, looking over at them. "I assume you found out you can't get in Hell."

"The opposite actually." Tina smiles. "Well, I think we can. You'll have to let us into Hell to test it out."

Alex sighs. Only demon blooded creatures can create a portal into Hell, which means we can't even test the theory if she won't let us. "Why are you helping them, Tina? I thought you gave up living an exciting life to become a lawyer."

"I did, but this concerns my own welfare. If Lucifer kills you, he'll kill me next, and it won't be a pleasant death either. I expect torture, limbs being sawn off, the whole deal."

Well, that is uplifting and comforting.

"He won't go after you, he probably doesn't even remember your name." Alex reassures her.

"A pack of demons interrupted my trial today, killing everyone in the building. I barely made it out in one piece; he's been in power for less than a day. So, I'm here because I want my head still attached to my body by the end of the week, instead of on a pike." Tina thinks we can win, that is promising. Though it sounds like she would happily change sides if she had more of a chance of survival working for Lucifer.

"Okay, he remembers you. I understand, you are pissed off. I will fix it."

"No, we are all going to fix it because I don't trust you to do it on your own. Besides, whatever we do, Lucifer will know. That is why you will let us help, then create a side plan of your own which none of us know about. Then, you kick his ass, and it all goes well."

Alex smiles. "No catch?"

"You can't use me as bait."

"Alright." Alex laughs, putting her hand out. They shake and bring it into a hug. That is all it took to convince Alex to allow us to help? I mean allowing her to come up with her own side-plan doesn't sound like a great counteroffer, but she is the one who has defeated him before.

"Alright, now we are all going, we need any Hell artefacts you own to link ourselves to you and to trick Hell into letting us in."

"I can do that, but you'll die. That's really the best you could think of?" Alex snorts.

"Honestly, no. I have no clue how to do it, these kids only gave me half an hour. I assume you know a way, but you wouldn't say so unless we were going to get ourselves killed doing it the wrong way. So, I made up that bullshit."

"But you couldn't get to a portal to test it, unless I create one."

"Haven't you forgotten the map, with all the portals to Hell I own?"

A pause. "Fine, I'll tell you."

"You told me there wasn't a way for us to get in Hell ten minutes ago." I argue. She was adamant about it.

"I was lying. There obviously is, Lucifer took my mother to Hell and she was an angel. I found his journals which explained how he did it. You'll need hell worms."

"How will worms fix our problem?" Holly frowns.

"Like all food, the nutrients from the hell worms you ingest enter the bloodstream. Hell worms are high in protein, therefore a large quantity will enter the bloodstream, which means you won't fry to death. You are what you eat. Supernaturals naturally have a faster metabolism which means they'll need to consume one every three to four hours." That is a very scientific way to get into Hell, I thought there would be a ritual or some scary magic to make it work. Eating a worm does not sound too bad. I didn't realise what I learned in science would be that important. "You can't eat one though." Alex gestures at me.

"Why can't I?" I really don't want to stay behind, which, now thinking about it, is sort of crazy. Hell sounds sort of terrifying.

"Alex worded that wrongly. It's not that you can't, it's that you don't have to. Your cells became partly demonic when Silven possessed you. She may not control you anymore, but the rest of the signs of possession are still there. Don't worry, it won't harm you." Flint inputs. Alex glares in Flint's direction.

"Wouldn't your blood have fixed that?" I ask Alex. I was told her blood would purge everything demonic from my body after Silven possessed me. If they are wrong, then I will be dead the second I walk through the portal.

"No. It's like when I resurrect someone. They don't forget their death. There's always evidence of what happened, whether they can see it or not. For you, the proof Silven possessed you is that you have demonic cells. But, like Flint said, they are completely harmless; it's how demons enter Hell after they possess a human body."

I can go to Hell, without help. That's better than being left behind. I get to be useful, even if I am human.

"If that is all it takes to get into Hell, how come no one has ever done it successfully?"

"Because you need something from Hell to get in and all the demons are banned from bringing hell worms to Earth. Also, no human has survived possession in millennia to test it out themselves." Alex explains. "I can get them now."

Flint laughs. "No, absolutely not. You'll 'accidentally' portal near the castle and attack Lucifer by yourself. I'll do it."

Alex sighs. "Fine." Her hand whisks up a portal for him.

"I'll be back soon." Flint nods, walking through it.

Alex laughs after the portal disappears, taking Flint with it. "I knew that would work. I would never do such a mundane task as picking up a few dozen worms. Alright, we should prepare you all for Hell while we wait."

We make our way to the small armoury in Enzo's basement. Weapons clutter the room, there are more than I can count. Alex flicks through a few weapons. "There should be enough here for you to pick from. You all need to change; this is not a jeans and t-shirt event. Preferably, you should wear something like Tessa. Nice, practical, easy to fight in, with plenty of pockets." Tessa grins at the complement given by Alex. "I assume you don't own assassin clothes, so…" Alex waves her hand, and clothes sit themselves upon the single bench in the room. Each pile of clothes has a name tag. I pick mine up. There are reinforced trousers and a shirt, it weighs a ton with all its extra protection. A long black cloak with countless pockets to hide weapons flutters around me. The boots have two-inch-thick soles with a strong grip.

"I need to fetch a particular weapon from my own home. I'll be back soon, be ready by the time I'm back." She creates a portal to her house.

I take the outfit to my room. Changing takes twenty minutes; there are half a dozen straps for weapons, buckles and protective gear. The trousers are tight but flexible. At least we will get to use the skills Enzo taught us. I tie my hair up into a bun and tuck away the loose strands.

I leave and go back to the armoury, Colt is already picking his weapons. He wears a tunic; it looks fairly old-fashioned, but he still pulls it off. Colt flicks a knife in his hand. "It suits you." He smiles.

"Thanks." I grin, I know nothing about what knives are best to kill demons. Last time we used what we could find. Colt wraps a hand around my waist, our lips connect. I smile, kissing him back. "Help me pick out weapons?"

"Of course."

The weapons weigh down my clothes even more; it'll get lighter the more I lose. That's why we need so many. A portal appears, Flint waltzes through it. Alex came back a few minutes ago, dressed up in a tight black and burgundy assassin outfit. Flint holds a few wiggling pouches of worms, dirt staining his suit, hands and face.

"Have fun, Flint?" Alex smiles.

"No. They kept running away." He hands over the pouches to the four who can't go to Hell freely.

"Don't eat any yet. We are going to have a proper meal while we discuss the plan. I'm starving."

"Don't we need to get there straight away?" Colt argues. "Lucifer has Enzo!"

"Yes, and us spending twenty minutes eating and ironing out a plan won't kill him." Alex explains. "Come on, Tina can magic us food."

Tina rolls her eyes as we make our way upstairs.

Alex starts to explain the plan, which is surprisingly simple and slightly concerning. If Lucifer is an evil genius like Alex says he is, there has to be more to it, which I suppose is Alex's secret plan. We go in, all from different angles of the palace. Lucifer will be stationed in the throne room, but there are about four entry points. We'll charge in and fight the hordes of demons. Alex will handcuff Enzo; we'll take him back as quickly as possible. There she can undo the mind-control. "Well, that's all of us, except Abby."

"What? What am I doing?" I finish off the hotdog. Alex was right about having food first. I didn't realise how hungry I was until food was put in front of me.

"You are sneaking around the castle to see if there are any props Lucifer has lying around that could tell us his plan."

"Because I'm human." I complain. I may be human but I'm not useless, it's insulting. "I can help."

"And you are." Alex rolls her eyes. "I chose you for that part because you are the one Lucifer is least likely to worry about if you are not there. Tessa can go with you; he doesn't know she is coming. You'll be paired because it's the safest way to travel, not because you are human, understood?"

She has a valid point. Lucifer won't care if I'm there or not, he doesn't even know my name and I hardly come off as threatening.

"Fine. How will I know when to come back?"

"Circle your way to the throne room, it's the room with the massive doors, and hopefully we'll be ready to go when you get there." Alex suggests. "You are looking for anything that could be dimension-wide destructive." Alex finishes the discussion and produces watches from the air. "These will set a timer when you need to eat another worm. It gives you a half an hour warning, so you don't have to eat the second it goes off."

Colt, Holly, Tessa and Tina strap them to their wrists. The pouches of worms are tied to their waists. Holly pulls one out, a look of disgust crossing her face. The worms are black tar-like creatures with razor sharp teeth. I'm glad I'm not eating them. "We have to eat it alive?" Holly pulls a face.

"No, you can kill it first. They have more flavour if they are alive, that's all." Alex informs them.

Colt downs it, full worm at once. He chokes, black sludge leaving his mouth. Holly pulls a face of horror, gagging as it goes down.

"It's awful." Tessa squirms.

"How can you eat that?" Tina looks at Flint and Alex. "It tastes like… I don't even have words." She summons a flask and swigs it. "The taste stays!"

"It's not that bad. It's an acquired taste." Alex rolls her eyes. "I'm kidding, I have never dared to eat one."

"I think you should eat a worm." Tina argues. "For karma."

"That's not how it works." Alex laughs.

A phone buzzes, Holly takes hers out and curses. "It's Selena." She picks it up. "Hey, I'm so sorry I'm not there. I got, um… sidetracked?"

Alex raises her eyebrow. "Alright, any questions while we wait for this very necessary call to end?"

Tessa slides next to Alex and whispers in her ear. "You are doing it because she's human, aren't you?"

"Yeah, keep an eye on her for me." Alex winks at her.

I scowl angrily. "I can hear you!"

"Human hearing is that good?" Alex looks impressed.

Holly rejoins the little circle. "Sorry, it was Selena. I forgot to tell her I wouldn't make our date. Alright, let's go to Hell." Holly attempts to smile.

Flint and Alex make separate portals for our different lines of entry. Tessa and I are starting on the roof of the building. Tessa pulls out a knife in preparation. I smile goodbye to Colt and Holly, my heart already pounding in my chest. Questions of panic race through my head. If the worms don't work, then they'll fry instantly and if Alex's assertions about Silven are wrong, I will fry to death and that's only at the first step... There is only one way to find out. Gulping, I step through the portal into Hell.

The wave of heat hits me like a slap in the face. It's painful, like needles pricking my skin all over. I'm alive in Hell. My eyes widen at the sight, we are on a massive rooftop with large watchtowers above us. The brick is a muddy red-brown colour and ready to crumble under our feet. Leaning over the edge of the castle, I see that Hell is literally a fiery pit. There are a few twisted dead trees. Ash scatters the ground like leaves. A random pit of fire ignites down below, leaping ten feet in the air. My eyes widen, fire just appears? We could be standing, then be charred to smithereens with no warning. The entire world looks dead, there is no sign of life at all. The only source of light is the fires burning through the dry soil. A hand grabs my shoulder, I squeal. Tessa laughs. "I lost you for a second there... it's different to say the least, isn't it?"

I sigh in relief; if she is okay, that means Holly and Colt made it in one piece. "Hi."

She gazes out from the ledge. "Don't touch the soil. It burns." A thick red burn scorches her bare arm along with a few flecks of remaining soil. "I say we should avoid touching anything unless we have to. I'm pretty sure anything here could kill you. We should have asked for more pointers, but it's too late now."

"Where should we start?" I ask, we have no idea how to get around, Alex was just trying to get rid of me.

"Well currently, two demons from the east watch tower are heading our way. I was thinking, let them get a bit closer, kill them, go through the tower to get inside the building." Tessa explains.

Spinning around, I see two demons charging our way. They are exactly how I remember them from when they crawled their way up from Hell to kill us. Death lingers in their eyes. They are getting very close. I draw a dagger, Tessa turns. Chucking her dagger, it shoots through the first demon's slimy head and spins, flying into the other demon's skull before landing back in Tessa's palm. They fall to their knees. Somehow, they aren't dead. Tessa jumps on a body and stabs the demon. It lets out one last squeal before dying. She holds the furry being in her hand as a shield against the second one.

Before I can jump in to help, the dagger in my hand flies out my grasp, killing the second one, slicing it in half. Black goo streams out their remains. "I didn't do that." I frown.

"I did. Telekinesis, remember?"

"Wow, you are an incredible fighter." That was impressive.

"I'm going to pretend not to be insulted by your surprise, considering it's literally my job." Tessa pants. "They are a lot harder to kill than humans. That's for certain. Humans are just one quick well-placed slice."

I scoop up my fallen dagger. "Sorry." I forgot that Tessa is not just a talkative fan of Alex but a highly trained assassin.

"It's okay, you won't be the first, or the last. Being underestimated is actually useful at times. When my uncle was murdered at a family event, my family completely overruled the idea that it could have been me. It was shortly before I was disowned for being too nice to my hits." She laughs. "I did it, they still have no idea." Tessa pats down the furry beast. "I got paid pretty well, my aunt ordered the hit. She couldn't do it herself, too suspicious."

She killed her uncle-in-law for her aunt? I want to know what he did, but this really isn't the place. We are in the open and I'm certain if there were demons in one watchtower, there will be more in the rest. Personally, I'd rather avoid them. "Let's go." She puts down the body and we jog to the door and into the castle. Sneaking inside, we make our way down the rocky stairs; there is barely enough room to put a foot. They spiral further than the eye can see. Carefully, I slowly make my way down, feet struggling to keep a grip on the cracked rock. I hold onto the wall for support, it'll be a miracle if we don't slip down. "Whoever designed this place was a dreadful architect." Tessa complains. "There's a safer way to get down if you want."

"Please." I beg. This is worse than not knowing if we would be burnt to a crisp going through the portal. One wrong step, or a stair crumbling a little more when I put my foot on it, will lead to a certain and painful death. My feet leave the ground, Tessa hovers behind me. We fly downward, spinning dizzily around on the steps. We stop at the doorway into the castle, Tessa places me down on the last step. That is one way to get down. Tessa brushes off her cloak. I draw a weapon and grab the metal handle.

Opening the door, I peek out; there are no demons. The hallway is dimly lit with torches on the wall held up by metal, just like I would expect to see in a dungeon. We need to search the rooms for clues, but I have no idea what would be considered suspicious. Tessa waves for me to follow, sneaking down past half a dozen doors. I jog after her, I'm glad she knows what she is doing.

CHAPTER THIRTEEN

Lucifer

Proudly looking down at my subjects, they skip in glee to their tasks. It's been years since they have had some proper enjoyment. Alex took their precious freedom away, not allowing them to kill whoever they please. There will be a mass murder spree to make up for the last ten years, once Hell is secure. Possibly a volcanic eruption where the sulphur sticks around for centuries afterwards. What is left of my army will appreciate it. I expect to lose twenty or more percent of the demons to this feud, but it will be worth it. I will never be confined in a cell again. This will be a short first battle, as soon as I get what I want. Alex will get what she wants dearly too; Enzo. It will be like an exchange, but with a lot more blood. I plan for this little quarrel to give her a false sense of security that I'm not as clever as I am made out to be. That she may win, without risking her life and dying by my hand. Sadly, that day is not today, but it will be very soon.

I look down at Enzo, standing like a soldier. He hasn't moved in minutes. It must be very uncomfortable, but it's nothing compared to being cramped up in a cell. Enzo's face is solemn, almost defeated. I quirk a smile, he used to be so cocky, with a smug smile on his face during visits to my prison. I wish I could be there when he can feel again and truly experience everything he has done. I'm not sure what will repel him more, hurting his loved ones or working for me. I do wish I could keep him a little longer; he has an endless amount of potential. Experimenting with his new power would be entertaining. A random spark leaves his hand; the second dose of my blood may have been a mistake. He's finding it hard to control his power, but it was the only way to ensure he could fight Alex successfully. He took that dose of blood much better than the first one he had as a child, that one came so close to killing him. He will struggle once I let him out of my control, emotions running high and his powers out of control, unable to reach out to anyone for fear he will hurt them. His friends won't support him, thinking I'm playing a mind-game by giving him up so easily. I grin, it'll make him an emotion driven mess.

Enzo's ears perk up like a bloodhound. I hear the faint sound of multiple portals to Hell opening. Three to be exact. They are splitting into groups, that's smart. Three groups, that's an easy solve. Alex and Tina will charge through the front gate because they are the headstrong duo. Flint cares about the wellbeing of the kids so he'll come through the side door with Colt and Holly. Abby won't be with them, she'll be with her own bodyguard, Tessa. They'll come from the back door, more secretively. They'll be late, Alex will stall Abby with a meaningless task as she's human and much more likely to die if she joins us. I'm sure she'll get here eventually.

"Enzo, lead this one for me." This is where I mess with Enzo's head then set him free.

"My pleasure." Enzo smiles genuinely.

"One more thing." My eyes bore into his. "Kill Tessa for me, then your mind-control will end, and you'll no longer serve me."

Enzo nods without complaint. I feel like a murder will make his experience worse, but I can't kill one of the stars of the show before it has even begun. Tessa will be an adequate sacrifice. I count three, two, one…

Alex and Tina storm through the large arched doors, rocks crumbling as the doors cruelly slam against them. Alex has no respect for my home. Enzo's eyes light up at the sight of her, craving to rip her head off her body. The demon's heads turn to their prey, hungrily. The girl, whose rule they were forced to live under, finally in their grasp for sweet revenge. Alex's hands light up, flames racing up the walls. I sigh, I had hoped for a better entrance than that. Each demon has control of one of the four main elements: fire, water, earth and air. She has all four, thanks to my spectacular genetics, and she picks fire. The one demons live around. Hardly frightening. Tina's hands glow with magic, her powers will be dulled simply by being in Hell. I hope she is heavily armed, or it'll be a quick, boring fight. The ground shudders, floor erupting. That is more like it. Demons fly against the walls into the burning fire. Craters destroy the ground. I don't move from my throne Alex won't reach me, there are a few hundred demons and Enzo in her way.

The next set of door bursts open, Flint and the younglings pounce in. The two children gawp at the sight of me. That is what I like to see, the extreme fear in their eyes. I don't show my face on earth often, many have died at the sight of me. I cause their spines to shiver and their hearts to beat rapidly enough to stop completely. I am death, that is what they see when they look at me. The guaranteed solitude of the painstaking death of all humans.

Enzo charges through the demons to get first dibs on Alex. I admire the view as his magic bolt strikes her against the wall. I might as well enjoy the show, I've been waiting for it for the last decade. It's well deserved.

Enzo

Snarling, I charge in. Alex is my target, the selfish bitch. Tessa next, when she decides to show up, Lucifer specially requested it. The sparks fly out my hands uncontrollably, they blast Alex in the face. She thwacks into the wall, laughing.

"I thought it would take Lucifer longer to throw you at our mercy." Alex winks. "I'll try not to make it hurt too much."

"I'm not promising the same." I snarl, sparks flying like wildfire.

Tina is stuck under a sea of demons. They are leaving Alex alone, Lucifer instructed them; she is mine. I block Alex's measly attempt at a fireball. I'm a Hellhound. She knows that. The ground splits between my feet. Howling, I jump before I drop into the lava pit. Alex's knife flecks my neck barely missing me. I can't believe she is meant to be a good warrior. I grab her frozen arm, her knife stuck in the stonework, and flip her onto her back. Alex groans, connecting with the floor, her hand latches onto mine. Shit. My head smacks the stone, blood spewing. A foot pushes my head down, grinding my complete horn and head into the brickwork. Howling in pain, I struggle to get back on my feet. Alex thrusts my head in deeper. Gathering my strength, I drive upwards, sending her flying off my back.

The second set of doors burst open as Colt, Abby and Flint enter. I laugh, is that her idea of back-up? They are going to lose terribly. This will hardly be a fight. Alex's foot connects with my jaw, thanks to my brief distraction. Time to draw out my deadly weapon; I take out the silver knife. She laughs, taking out her own. Unfortunately for her, mine can actually kill her. I aim for her side, Alex counters it.

"Sorry." A heavy weight launches itself on my back, fangs sinking into my neck. Colt, he has no respect for his mentor. I howl, without raising my hands magic blasts him off my back. He cries out in agony finding his way into a crowd of death hungry demons. Serves him right.

I dodge her blow for my head. Power hits my chest, flinging me into the wall, freezing me in my place. I howl in anguish. Alex smiles, knife going to my neck. She wouldn't dare kill me; she still cares, even if I don't. She tilts her head, inspecting my face. "Your eyes are different." A fire starts behind her but, unfortunately, she doesn't care to look back. Struggling, my knife hand wiggles. She restrains my moving hand. She curses. "Lucifer, they look like his eyes; emotionless."

"I'm going to deliver you to Lucifer." I promise. "He wants to do the honours of killing you himself."

"If you were under mind-control I would be able to see your true emotions in your eyes. I'm breaking up with you." She stares into my eyes. "Nope, nothing. You should look heartbroken under all that fog. There is no emotion hidden in that brain of yours." Alex pulls out power-reducing handcuffs from her belt. "I should have known Lucifer would do some shit like this."

Now that I've listened to all that bullshit, I fling the knife downward. It impales her foot, Alex doesn't react. I glance down, blood pools out of a hole in her shoe. The cuffs click around my wrists. Her power releases me back to the ground. "Not so tough now, huh?"

A demon flies in our direction after a misfortunate blow from Flint. Alex slices the demon in half, turning it to ash. I laugh, my bones begin to snap. Ears stretching across my face. The handcuffs stop magic, not transformations. My hands deform, fur growing and pads forming on my palms. The cuffs slip off like butter. Concentrating, I transform back into a human from my half-hell beast state. I scoop up my blade, she should have taken it when she had the chance. Alex's back is turned to me, my opportunity to kill her before me. But I can't, Lucifer wants her. He left me Tessa. I lift the blade, aiming for Alex's left shoulder. A loud crash and smoke fills the hall. Tessa bursts into the room, a small figure disappearing in the smoke with her. Abby. She's the last of the little gang to show up.

"Tessa!" Alex snaps. "I was getting there."

The smoke is clearing through the empty windows. Demons scratch away at Flint, Tina is battling with her blades, Colt is lying in a broken heap, Holly is a snarling wolf running on adrenaline alone. They are failing, horribly. It's a miracle they are all alive. Taking my gaze back to Alex, I force down the blade.

"No!" A voice breaks out and a weight tackles me down to the floor.

I snarl, Tessa's fist hits my jaw. I groan. "Nice try, little girl." A flick of my hand and the miserable excuse of an assassin sails off my body. I hear her knock a few demons on her way. It's sweet that she is trying to save her idol. Alex floors a dozen demons.

Tessa jumps on my back again. "I won't let you kill her!" I grab her arm and fling her over my head. I smile, little does she know I've been especially instructed to kill her, I just have to capture Alex. It'll be easier with her out the way. Magic charges from my hand, aiming for Tessa, whimpering at my feet. I howl, pain spikes my chest, a silver point through my heart. How dare she?

Her hand goes up again, I catch it. I'm not letting her throw any more knives. I drag her to her feet, driving my hand into her chest. I hear a rib crack. She gasps for air. Pain strikes my stomach and I throw her onto the ground. A bloody blade sits in her hand. I loom over her; fun's over. I fire a bolt of black uncontrollable magic at her. She screams, the sound of agony echoing through the entire room, the walls shaking, dust falling down from the ceiling. In a dark haze, her body writhes wildly, eyes rolling back in their sockets. I hold my ears against the noise, the entire room pauses.

I look over at Tessa juddering on the ground, black sparks fly from her chest. Tears stream down her face. "Remember me." She whispers. "Please."

I smirk, proudly. Lucifer will be happy. Tessa explodes. I soar back, stumbling into a pool of demons. One last horrific scream rings out, before leaving the room in deadly silence. The position where Tessa's body lay is empty. Ash flutters around the room like snow. I did it, she's dead. She went out like a firework.

My knees buckle, eyes closing against my will before I can fully enjoy my victory. Collapsing on the ground, I watch as they all stare at the space where Tessa used to be as my eyes shut.

Waking up gasping, I'm myself. Thank the devil. I jump to my feet, when I get my hands on Lucifer, I swear he will not live two seconds. My life flashes back to the last twenty four hours. My stomach churns, what the fuck did I do? The throne room is silent, they all stare at one spot. Red hot ashes fly around like dust. I can count each person in the room; Abby is near the throne, Alex and Flint are a few meters away, Holly is bloody but, on her feet and the same for Colt. Tina is here for some reason, looking woozy from blood loss. The only person left would be Tessa. Red sparks crackle in my hands; I killed her under Lucifer's influence. I remember what he said before the battle. Kill Tessa for me, then your mind-control will end, and you'll no longer serve me. It worked. She's dead and I am no longer under Lucifer's will. If only killing myself had worked. None of this would be happening. There is nothing I can do to change the past, but I sure can kill some demons now. Lucifer smirks in my direction, knowing exactly what I'm thinking. He gets up off his throne, walking down to the middle of the room.

"Why have you stopped?"

That's all the demons need, the short moment to process Tessa's death is gone. I lift my hands and the dangerous sparks begin to fly without a thought. Flicking my wrist, a demon screeches, flesh sizzling. More sparks fly out of my fingertips without my control.

I charge into the battle, there is no time to think about what I have done. Countless more demons swing through windows, ready to attack. Alex turns, a fire bolt hits my chest before I can get out a word. I groan, stumbling back. My clothes are in ruins, I pat out a jumping flame.

"You killed Tessa!" She snarls, hands ready to fire. A demon pounces for Alex's neck, I raise my hand and it vanishes to dust. She frowns, demon ash caught in her hair. "A new trick, huh?"

"Probably." I can't lie, he wouldn't let me go unless it helped him in some way. "I don't know what it is yet."

Alex grabs a stray demon around its chubby neck, squeezing it hard till its head pops from its body. The black oily blood trickles down her hand. She quirks a smile. "You didn't threaten to kill me in that sentence... Enzo, you're back?"

"I think so…" My eyes trail to the scorch mark where Tessa lay.

"It wasn't you. You know that. Lucifer is who we should be blaming." Her eyes dart to the throne, where he sits protected by a horde of demons.

I duck as a flying demon swoops down. "We need to get out of here."

Alex chucks a dagger at a demon crawling over someone, I can't see who. A wolf howl wails over the sound of the clattering silver. Holly charges forward at closing doors.

Abby

Scouring the sixth room, I can smell smoke. The ground is trembling under our feet, doors flying off their hinges and leaks leaving puddles on the floor. All from the fight downstairs. Tessa leads me to the next room. It's like the last room we were in; dimly lit, messy, full of supernatural artefacts, a surprising amount of old parchment books and practically no furniture. Tessa seems like she knows what she is doing. Tessa leaves the doors open, we make our way from room to room.

"Could it be possible that it is hidden? Shouldn't we be pulling books to see if there is a secret passageway?" I ask.

Tessa shakes her head. "No, I don't think so. That's too predictable, Lucifer is smarter than that, from what I've heard."

"You know a lot about Alex and her family, huh? Why are you obsessed with her?" I try to strike up a proper conversation, the silence is eerie.

Tessa glances up from her concentration, inspecting the room meticulously. "She overthrew Lucifer back when I was thirteen. My family were on my back, belittling me for caring too much. Then I heard the story about how she did it. She overthrew a man more powerful than her to save people she loved. It made me believe that my parents were wrong, that I wasn't weak simply because I cared. That lesson stuck with me. I've read everything there is to know about her."

I want to say her family did care about her, but she told us before that she had been disowned. The only person she has contact with is her brother. Supernaturals always try not to feel, I think Lucifer is the only successful one, in that regard. I don't understand why they do it. Tessa sighs. "We aren't going to find anything."

"How do you know that?"

"Lucifer wouldn't leave the key to him winning or losing in an abandoned unguarded room. Not if he's like how he's made out to be. Alex just sent us on a stray quest to keep you away from the action. I think we have carried out our task long enough. We should be able to sneak in through the back gate. That's where we might actually find something. That's if you want to. There will be hordes of demons." Tessa informs me.

"Yeah." I'm glad she is on board with not being sidelined. "You think what we are looking for is in the throne room? Surely that is dangerous, Lucifer knows that is where we will attack."

"Which makes it the perfect hiding place, don't you think? When I was young, I hid my journals in the armour box full of old weaponry. No one ever found them."

"That makes sense. How are we going to sneak around a huge room full of demons?" I ask.

Tessa detaches a small round bomb from her belt. "I make a grand entrance while you run. The only furniture will be the throne."

"How do you know? What if there are more seats or stairs?" I quiz her plan.

"It's a throne room, what else will be there? If there is a secret passageway, or hidden equipment, you will find it near the throne. If I'm wrong, you can curse me before a demon eats your head off."

The last time I fought demons there were only a dozen or so, and it did not go well. I would be dead if Alex hadn't shown up in time. I would rather have my head attached to the rest of my body. Tessa better be right. Jogging down the corridor, we have only encountered two demons so far; we have seen others but avoided them. We stop at the large dark oak doors. This is the throne room. My gloved hands grab for the door handle.

"Last chance to change your mind." Tessa draws out the smoke bomb.

"No, let's go."

Tessa kicks in the doors and pulls the pin, smoke clouds the room.

I cough, running in. I barely catch a glimpse inside before the smoke engulfs the room. The ugly sludge animals are snarling, I see sparks and people. I can't tell if we are winning. I cover my streaming eyes and rush to the centre of the room. The throne is unmistakable. Tessa was right, it is the only piece of furniture in the room. Tripping, I hit the stairs leading to the throne. I make it, scrambling up the steps. I feel my way up, trying to locate a lever or similar object.

"Tessa!" Alex's voice screams over the sound of weapons clattering and screams of agony. "I was getting there!"

Sounds like Alex had the same idea as Tessa. She was just trying to get rid of me, the task of looking for evidence of Lucifer's next move was bullshit. She thought it would be in this room, not the rest of the palace.

Claws grab my foot; I yelp as I fall back. Brandishing a blade, I attack blindly in panic. A dozen light cuts scar the rotten face. Focusing, I drive the blade into its side. The demon chuckles, grey spit staining my face. How did Tessa do it? How did Enzo teach us? Everything I have been taught, for a moment like this, leaves my brain. Teeth glimmer in my face. I squeal, blocking the approach with my arm. The teeth sink through the fabric into my flesh. I whimper, swinging out my arm, its grip loosens. I kick it in the chest with all my strength. Stabbing it in the head, it snarls. Tessa made it look so easy. There must be a certain spot to kill it. The ground shakes and I fall back. It's an earth demon. Scampering away, I climb the stairs desperately. I point a new weapon at arm's length in the beast's direction. Clicking the bones in its body, it moves up the stairs slowly. A scream, I pause.

Looking around, the entire room is frozen. I follow their gaze, seeing the same sight as them. Tessa jolts on the ground like she's having a seizure. Sparks fly out her chest. A deafening explosion, the ground trembles. I shield my eyes; the light is blinding. The light fades, ashes fall from the ceiling like rain... Tessa is gone. There is nothing left of her except scorch marks where her dying body used to be. She is dead, Enzo stands over her without expression. He killed her. My heart sinks, Tessa can't even be saved by Alex. There is nothing left of her to save. Tessa wanted to be sure I was okay risking my life, I should have asked her the same question.

A tall figure moves in the room. "Why have you stopped?" The demons lurch back to life. Talons dig into my leg. I kick the demon away. I dart for the throne; I need to finish what Tessa and I started.

Reaching the throne, I feel its armrests for buttons. I touch the chair, what could you hide on a chair? The frame is old wood, that stings my hands, and leather. I draw out my knife, it could be hidden within the chair. A demon pounces in my direction and I howl, ducking out the way. Waiting for impact, it doesn't come. I look, the demon is gone. I sigh in relief.

"You're welcome."

Staring up, I pause in horror. Lucifer stands before my eyes. Horns, pale skin and lanky like a stick. Pearly white teeth grin at me, making my blood run cold. He's not what I expected, I thought he would be like Alex or Flint. Human looking, but scarier. My heart beats rapidly in my chest, I want to run like hell, but I can't. I watch his red eyes dance in delight, boney fingers reaching out for my knife. He plucks it out my shaking hand, my stomach churning. His burning hot skin strokes mine. "You don't want to do that." He waves to the chair, where I was about to rip open the leather. My mouth turns dry as I try to speak. He laughs, the noise painful to my ears. I struggle to breath, sweat pools down my face.

"Don't worry, if I wanted you dead, you would be." He plays with the blade. "I have something much better for you."

Goosebumps rise on my arms. "Wh-wh-what do you want?" I stutter.

"You'll see." He motions over at two demons. "Take her."

They grab my arms. "No!" I kick out uselessly. The back doors open. I howl, I can't reach any of my weapons. The dry flesh rubs on mine as I fight to escape. The demons pay no attention, I cry out. Holly howls back, charging in my direction. "No!" I warn her. I don't want her to end up like Tessa. I could not bear that. I know I'm not going to my death. Lucifer is right, he could have killed me just then, but he didn't. Holly refuses to listen, jumping at the demon on my right arm. The demon swats Holly away with ease. Flames dart dangerously close to my face, the demon on my left howls. Its skin is hot to the touch. It lets go, screaming in pain. I wrench away from the remaining demon, its claws digging in harder. I whimper.

Alex's hands rise again as a swarm of demons soars out of the sky, blocking her shot. The massive doors shut in my face. I howl. With my free hand I pull out a small spear attached to my leg, jabbing it into the sluggish flesh, the demon screeches. I feel the hand loosen. I kick it in what I think is a knee and bolt for the doors.

Two more demons block my exit. I curse, darting in a different direction, there has to be another way out. My heartbeat accelerates as I hear the demons gaining ground behind me. I grab an old piece of armour from the wall and fling it to the ground. Panicking, I dart into corridors, unsure of which direction I'm going in. There has to be another way out.

I spin into a new part of the castle, meeting a dead end. A small crowd of demons stand at the other end of the corridor, I curse. There are no exits except the empty window frame. Demons charge at full speed. I gulp, it's a long way down, three stories and a lot of fire. I feel for my weapons, I grab the first hooked ones I can find; they'll have to do.

I climb out the window and hang from the edge. I dig in the dual hook swords, they have a special name, but I forgot what Alex called them. Plunging one into the castle wall, it stays firmly in the stonework. I let go of the ledge, gripping the handle for dear life. A crack, the stone crumbles around the sword. I attempt to stick the other one in but it refuses to wedge into the rocks. Before I can try again, I fall. Sailing downward, the wind smashes against my body. Preparing for impact, I protect my face, trying to land on my feet.

Crashing, my limbs explode in pain, the jolt of invigorating agony taking over my body. I howl; that was not the best idea. I try to move my arm but it refuses to respond. My eyes droop, I fight the temptation to fall unconscious, and force my legs to work. Stumbling to my feet, shooting pains jolt through my legs. Limping, I try to focus on an escape route. My eyes meet a huge portal which is red and black, high enough to reach the sky. That must be an exit. Taking a challenging breath, my lungs burn. I have to make it to the portal.

I listen out for demons; they haven't followed me outside. I hold a dagger in my bloody palm, sweat drips down my face. The soil burns through my wrecked shoes. Forcing my feet to move forward, I get closer and closer to the portal. It should take me back to Earth. My eyes fight to stay awake, blood drips out of my hair. I did not fall correctly; I whimper in pain.

Dragging my left foot along, I reach out for the portal. I can feel its power radiating off the surface. I'm going to make it out, hopefully the others do too. There were about a hundred demons coming in from the windows as I was dragged away. Sighing in relief, my fingertips touch the swirling portal. Earth is one step away. I push my feet to move, I stay stationary. My achy feet are relieved as they begin to float.

"Thought you could get away? That's sweet." Lucifer's harsh, venomous voice hisses.

The last second, I am here. I am so close. My eyes droop, I drive my knife backward in one last effort. Lucifer plucks it from my shaky hand. "Nice try. I like it when they struggle, it makes their failure that bit more entertaining." My heart sinks in my chest, eyes drooping. He has me. There is no other option than to give in. My eyes flutter shut, my limbs giving in.

CHAPTER
FOURTEEN

Lucifer

I dangle the girl from my hand, the full weight of her body in my grasp as she falls unconscious. I love it when they try so hard to escape. I like to wait till the last moment to intervene, it makes their wallowing sadness more entertaining. The girl, Abby, is the reason I wanted them to do a rescue mission. The entire 'kill Tessa' gambit was a distraction so they wouldn't focus on Abby. It worked like a treat; nothing has gone wrong so far. I pass the unconscious girl to a demon. It is a surprise she was able to run away; she is only human but did a better job than I can believe.

The demon runs away to lock the girl in a cell. She can't escape but I'd enjoy watching her try. My disgrace of a daughter and her little crew have left. They had to after the next wave of demons arrived, I expect they will be bickering about the loss of Abby instead of celebrating the fact I gave up Enzo. Maybe not celebrating; he did kill one of their little pals, but I had to have a little fun. Tessa was the most insignificant of the group. I would have liked Enzo to kill Colt, the results would have been devastatingly good. I have bets Enzo would kill himself in guilt but, regrettably, Colt will be a leading man in saving his girlfriend. I need that to happen. They won't be coming back any time soon, I have at least a week, which is plenty of time for the next stage of my plan.

Marching back to the prison cells, I find the girl lying in her cell, curled up in a ball. There is a small pool of blood around her head. "Go to my closet and take out a shirt and bring it back here, along with some water." I order one of the demons I set to guard her. "And you, visit Earth and gather some food and other human things for her." I need her to live if I'm going to rule. Humans are fragile beings, in need of food, water and general welfare. I unlock the door and flick her face. She groans. I do it again, her eyes flicker and she sits up. Holding her bleeding head, she slumps against the wall. "Good, you're awake." I nod in pleasure.

Abby's eyes widen to the size of boulders and she stumbles back to the corner of the cell. Peeling her eyes away from my face, she gazes longingly at the open door. I snap my fingers impatiently for her attention. We both know she is not going to run; firstly, because she has questions and secondly because she knows it will be a bigger failure than last time. If she does try, then she is dumber than I thought. She looks around the bleak cell, it is the only one without scratch marks covering the walls. My cell; I thought putting her in this specific one would be poetic. The little girl's eyes turn back to me, her fragile mind whirling.

"Why am I here?"

I suppose that is a decent question to start with. I need to tell someone my plans and she will not be leaving my grasp until I kill her. Also, leaving her clueless seems awfully rude, she should know that she is helping me make history. Lastly, I can get a few snippets out of her to see if events on Earth are going to plan.

"You are here to complete a purpose. I need you to help break me out of Hell and gain more power."

Confusion falls over her face, mouth opening and closing like a goldfish. She had no idea what I would use her for, which is a good sign that Alex doesn't either. That is no surprise, I am always a thousand steps ahead of the game. I sigh, beckoning her to follow. I didn't break out of prison and take back Hell to sit in a cell again. She can't go anywhere while I'm with her. Cautiously, she stands. "Hurry up." I wave my hand, forcing the air to move her along. Stumbling, she jogs after me without complaint, even with a heavy limp. Jumping out of a window when you have fragile bones is an idiotic idea. We climb up the stairs.

"How am I going to help you do this?" She asks, in concern.

I nod, marching quickly, knowing that she is struggling to keep up as it is. I just enjoy watching humans struggle. She whimpers, trying to keep up while looking out for an opportunity to escape.

"You can help me by dying."

"W-what?" She stutters in alarm. "You're going to kill me?"

I laugh, she reeks of fear, her chest moving so fast you'd think she was about to explode. Although, the best part is her eyes; the eyes are the window to the soul and hers are petrified. "No, not yet. What do you know about possession?"

Relief, mixed with concern, floods her face. I can see the cogs churn inside her head, trying to work under pressure. I know that the demon enters the body and takes control. The person they control is basically lost within themselves. If the demon dies in their body, they die too and if the demon leaves then the human dies and the demon goes back to Hell."

"Correct. What about in your case?"

"I was lucky. Alex's blood compelled Silven out of my body. It's the reason I had semi-control when she possessed me. I was given blood just after she took control. It wasn't enough to compel her to leave, but enough to disrupt her control." The gullible girl explains. "Why do you want to know?"

I already know all the answers, but I need to know how much they understand. "That's unimportant, just answer my questions or you'll lose your hand." I need her alive but not her entire body. I will cut off limbs very happily if it becomes necessary, or I get bored. "The dead vessels of the demons, where do they go when they die?"

"Um… they get buried?" The girl holds onto her arm, trying to hide the fact she is shaking violently.

"No, they are brought down to Hell and burned." If humans found the bodies and did an autopsy, then we would be discovered, so we burn our dead in a pit of fire.

"The bodies can go to Hell because they have demonic cells."

"Indeed." Alex actually taught the girl something decent. "Which is how you came down here without any assistance. It's quite unlucky that you didn't get to eat those scrumptious hell worms like your friends."

"How do you know that?" Her brows furrow.

I scoff, is she questioning my intelligence? The answer is simple, I don't understand how no one has ever figured it out. It's simple physiology. I knew, even Alex could figure that out. "I rule Hell, I know all the ins and outs. Question my intellect again and…" I pull out a dagger at lightning speed, holding it over her wrist. She flinches back in terror. "I will cut your hand off, finger by finger then make you watch me eat it."

Abby steps further away, nodding. I hear the little human heart accelerate in her chest, anymore and she'll die. I have spent millennia torturing Earth, I can read humans like an open book. She is terrified for her life, her friends and what I might do to her. "Alright, is that all you know?"

She nods wordlessly.

"Did it ever occur to you that if you got Silven's ability to come to Hell, then you would be granted her other abilities?"

She shakes her head. "No."

"Well, I know, because I remember when de-possession wasn't a thing of the past, before I destroyed the sword. The humans could have their possessor's power while in Hell."

I inform her. I remember that day vividly. A human waltzing into Hell after finding one of the portals located around Earth. I experimented on it before I killed it, obviously. The outcomes were remarkable. It makes sense, the demons can come to Hell in human form and use their abilities, why wouldn't the de-possessed human do the same? They still have demonic cells.

"But wouldn't I notice if I could do demon magic?"

"Look at your leg." She is still limping, but it's obviously not as bad as when she walked out the cell. The healing process has sped up because she's in Hell, it is also why she didn't die from a three storey fall out of a window. "As I had to use Silven to get out, you are going to be my new and improved version that I get to shape however I want."

"What do you mean, used Silven? She tried to set you free, and she failed." She quizzes me.

That means Alex does not know I set that entire operation up, just as I expected.

"Which was part of my plan. It links to a different task you can do for me." I have had plenty of time to figure it out.

I want to kill my children and Enzo, but I can't just yet. If I kill Enzo before finishing the ritual to break the spell keeping me in Hell, I won't be able to escape until a new hybrid warlock-hellhound comes into existence. Only they can bind magic from two dimensions because they are from both. If I killed him now, the spell would continue to work, as it's linked to each dimension, not just him. Alex and Enzo were desperate to ensure there would be no loopholes for me to escape, except they missed one. Enzo may have reinforced the spell after Silven almost succeeded in completing the ritual, but it doesn't change that fact she already killed the necessary sacrifices. After she failed to complete it, the power to finish was left in the vessel she possessed. Now all I need to do to complete the ritual and free myself is to force Abby to draw the freedom bird onto the portal to Earth, working like a key into a lock. After the ritual is finished, I will no longer need Enzo alive because the spell will no longer be effective so he can't be used as a bargain chip against me. Using Abby to open the portal will be painful for her but she'll live. I specifically made sure Abby would be Silven's vessel because I knew they would never expect me to take a human whom they would see as an unnecessary hostage. Therefore, they wouldn't pay attention to her which made it easier for me to kidnap her.

The girl's face falls. "Wait, you were behind what Silven did?"

"Yes, and I made that werewolf turn your sister." I explain my genius to her simple mind. I lead her into an empty room, old parchment books filling the four walls. With time there comes history, I have read very few books that I own, I prefer the hands-on experience. Unnin, the demon I sent to Earth, hurries in our direction, catching the door before it closes. "I found what you asked for King." Unnin presents a human bag, full of objects.

I snatch it from him. I'll look at the contents later. "You may go." He scutters away.

"You are the reason my sister is a werewolf... You bastard. You are the one who put her through all that pain?" She growls protectively, despite her fear.

"Yes. So, you know that in Hell you possess some of Silven's gifts, correct?" I lead her on.

"How does that help you?"

"I ask the questions here." I scan the bookshelves. "What do you know about the demon monarchy?"

The girl's eyes inspect the room, not for a means of escape but to prevent herself from looking into my eyes. Blood drips from her palm where she repeatedly scratches it anxiously. "I know that you were first, then there's a whole hierarchy down to nameless demons, then more under that."

That's a simple way to put it, I was hoping for more details and depth to her answer, but it's a start. Demons evolved in the opposite way to humans. The human theory of evolution is the idea that they evolved from animals, like monkeys. For demons, we started off fairly human, like myself, and evolved down to more animal-like creatures.

"Yes, anything else?" I urge her on. Alex and Enzo must have taught her a little.

"Um... The ones at the top of the ladder have extra abilities?" Her voice rises as if she is asking a question instead of making a statement. That's an obvious one. She has been around both my offspring.

I take over. "Yes, you are correct. The list goes on but the important point to note is that I am on top." I chuck a book off the shelf in her direction. A squeal, she darts out the way of the book. I glare in her direction. "Pick it up."

Wordlessly, she does what I say. She opens the book.

It is about the hierarchy of the demons, with descriptions of their abilities along with pictures, if she doesn't understand. She squints at the words. "What language is this?"

"You can't read it?" I picked the Latin adaptation; the demon version is much better, but I'm not going to waste a demon's time teaching her the language.

"I might." She looks back at the book desperately. "It's Latin. I know a little Latin." I don't think a vague knowledge of the language will help her. "That word says demon."

I sigh. I will have to explain it to her. I thought she would know old Latin, what else would they learn at human school? I flip through the first couple of pages until I find Silven. She was higher up in the rankings than I let her believe. The reason she was the only one I ever let provide important assistance, or be my 'right hand demon' as she called it, was because her purpose was to serve me.

"That's Silven..." She stares at the picture. "She's a duchess of Hell?" Abby reads the words under the picture.

"Yes. Daughter of Mammon. Mammon was the Demon of Greed. His ability was stealing power from other demons." She has no idea where I'm going with this. "That power got passed on to his daughter Silven, which is now in you."

"Silven can steal others' powers? Now you think I can." She concludes. "That's why you took me. I'm not a hostage, you are going to use me as a weapon."

"Exactly." I praise her.

"Wait, does that mean you can't kill me? Or you wouldn't be able to defeat Alex?" She asks hopefully.

"Don't get any ideas about trying to kill yourself to be the hero and stop me. Enzo already tried it and, as you can tell, it didn't work."

"Enzo tried to kill himself?" Her eyes widen, I guess that thought hadn't crossed her mind. Dying nobly for a cause greater than yourself is a hard choice when you don't believe you deserve to die. I don't believe I have to worry about Abby.

"He failed miserably, but yes, he did." I scan the dustiest part of the shelves, to my luck there is an English to Latin dictionary. I chuck it to the girl. This time she catches the book in her hands. "Take those books with you, you are going back to your cell." She will need the entertainment. I have a few more preparations to attend to before I need her again. She nods, walking with me out the room.

Back down in her cell, the demons have done their job. The girl has a bucket, a bowl of water, and a bed. The cell is much better than when I lived in it. There is a small torch to illuminate it and allow her to read. I'm not being nice; the bucket and water are to prevent mess, and the bed is cursed. If she sleeps on it, she'll have nightmares. I want her to be shaken up, I like the scent of fear. She walks back inside. I don't bother to take any weapons from her; she isn't going to do much with them, or her mobile device. There is no cell service for her phone. I throw the bag of human objects into her cell. "I suggest you use the bandages for your wounds." I need her alive. I hope Abby has basic knowledge of first aid. She's going to need it. She flinches away from the bag. I sigh. "Vale." I test her Latin.

"Bye." She watches as I lock the door.

Enzo

Portaling back, I stumble against the counter in my kitchen. Wiping a blood stain from my cheek, I groan. Lucifer must have sent his entire army on us. We barely made it out alive. I grab my jaw and click it back into place. The wolf on the ground starts to transform back into a human. I take off my jacket and cover her with it. She shifts back to her human form. Colt is panting on a chair. They shouldn't have come for me. I knew it would end badly. Tessa is dead and Lucifer took Abby. There was no way we could get her back without us all dying in the process.

Holly stands, wearing the jacket buttoned up. I lift my hand to magic her some more clothes then pause. I lower my hands; it could go wrong and I don't want to hurt her. Holly's eyes glow a dark yellow colour in anger. We all know what is about to happen. "Why are we back here? Abby is still in Hell! Lucifer has her. Lucifer! Didn't you see him? Didn't you see what happened to Tessa?" Holly screams.

"Holly…" Colt starts before she interrupts.

"No, Colt, I almost had her! Why on earth did you drag me away?"

Colt rubs the healing scratch marks on his face. "You would have died or been taken with her."

"Not if you had helped me save her!" Holy growls. "Abby is human, what could he want to do with her except kill her?"

I take a deep breath. She has a point; Abby doesn't have an ability that Lucifer can use to his own advantage. She could be a bargaining chip, but what for? If Lucifer really wanted to make

Alex give up Hell, he would have taken Flint. "Look, we will get her back, but yelling about it is not going to help."

Holly turns in my direction. "We can't trust you. You could still be under his control."

"She has a point." Colt agrees, stepping back from my side. I'm not under his control, but I can't prove it. He set me free for a reason, we don't want to risk it. I pass Colt a pair of cuffs and offer my wrists. He puts them on. Alex marches out the room.

"Where are you going?" Holly argues. "We need to go back."

"Your sister will be fine." Alex walks into the living room towards a chalkboard. She whisks her hand; the board wipes out two options and writes more branches off one idea. "Lucifer is not going to kill her."

We follow her, looking up at the board. "You knew he was going to take Abby?" Holly snarls. "And you didn't stop her going?"

Alex glares in Holly's direction. "No, I had an inkling he would go after her, which is why I tried to lie by telling her she couldn't eat hell worms, but then Flint opened up his big mouth. So, I sent her on a pointless quest with an amazing bodyguard, but they decided to interrupt."

"There must have been some way for you to stop her."

Alex raises her eyebrow. "Excuse me? I warned you all about the risks and all of you accepted them, you can't blame me. If I held her against her will, you would be equally as pissed off as you are now."

Holly growls. She is panicking about her sister, which is understandable, but this isn't going to help get her back. Especially blaming Alex. If Holly thought Lucifer was scary, she should see Alex all fired up.

"I'm with Holly. If you knew Lucifer may have wanted Abby, you shouldn't have let her go." Flint argues.

Alex takes a deep breath. "You can't blame me for decisions Abby made. I put her with an assassin out of harm's way. It's not my fault she went rogue, and I did try to save her. If you want to sulk, go for it, but don't do it around me."

"How did you know he would want Abby?" Colt intervenes.

Tina collapses on the sofa. "But don't say it in front of him." She glares in my direction.

"I'm wearing chains, I'm not going to do anything. The mind-control is gone."

"And we know that because?" Tina quizzes me. "This could be part of an elaborate trick."

Alex grabs my hands and unlocks them immediately.

"What are you doing?" Tina argues. "He could kill us."

"Lucifer needs Abby to open the portal to grant him his freedom, Lucifer won't have a use for her anymore if Enzo's spell isn't stopping him. Then he has every reason to kill her."

"He could kill us." Tina points at me.

Alex sighs. "One way to find out. Test him."

"How? You keep your memory in mind-control." Tina asks. "I could use magic to test him, but that type of magic has never been my strong suit."

"I'll attempt to un-manipulate him." Alex grabs my hands, looking into my eyes and murmurs a string of Latin. Magic pulses between our hands as she works. She stops, letting go. "He's fine."

"You normally take longer than that." Tina frowns suspiciously.

"There was nothing to take over. Look I'll prove it. I'm pregnant."

"What?" I squark, Flint does the same.

"See, he's back to normal. I'm kidding by the way." Alex smirks. "Kids are annoying."

"Why did that come to your mind out of everything you could have said?" Tina laughs.

"Apparently it scares men the most. I think it works." Alex shrugs.

Laughing, Tina winces, holding her head. "I think dying would have been a better option. Enzo, you owe us big time."

I roll my eyes. No one forced her to come, but she's right. "Fine."

I rub my sore wrists. My hands spark a little, I frown. I would not be surprised if Lucifer was pumping demons with his blood to make an invincible personal army. I'd offer to fix up wounds, but I don't know if I'll accidentally hurt them instead. That blow that killed Tessa wasn't meant to make her explode. I grip my fist. Alex stands in front of the board while everyone watches her, waiting for her to explain. "Okay, no more bickering. We know Lucifer has two goals; revenge and ruling all three plains: Earth, Hell and Heaven. Starting with Hell, obviously. He needs Abby to open the portal as, technically, the ritual has already been completed by Silven, when she was in Abby's body. I put the wards back up, but she can reopen them. She'll wallow in a cell for a few days while he gains power and is ready to come to Earth and attack us." Alex reassures them. "For now, we can spend the next few hours sleeping, eating and having a memorial for Tessa."

"How do we know he wasn't shoving her through that ritual portal the second we left. He could be killing her this very second!" Holly argues.

"You're forgetting that she's also his leverage. We won't risk Abby's life by going in unplanned and getting ourselves killed. But if he's released himself and killed her, why would we wait to plan, letting him gain the power he needs to beat us? He'll wait. Believe me."

Holly doesn't argue further. I don't like leaving Abby in Hell, but there is no way for us to get to her and live. It would be dying for no reason. There is no way it could be successful; it would actually do the opposite. We would take immediate action if we thought that she was going to die.

Alex's phone buzzes, she curses. "Lucifer took your phone, right?" She glances in my direction. "I'll ask for a video call to prove Abby is in one piece, for Holly's peace of mind."

We wait in silence, until the phone beeps again. "Huh, he actually agreed."

The line rings and Lucifer picks up. Holly jumps up, running to watch over Alex's shoulder. The video shows a room that is dimly lit by a torch; she's in a cell. The room has a bed and a bag with few objects spilling out of it; a water bottle, food wrapper and books. Abby looks up at the phone while sitting on the bed, bandages wrapped around her limbs and her head. Scratched hands hold up a book near the torch, allowing her to read. "Say hello to your friends." Lucifer's voice calls through the phone.

She carefully puts the book down and smiles. "Hi." She steps closer to the bars. She looks like she has been dragged through a bush then thrown down a staircase. "The injuries weren't my fault. She tried jumping out a three storey window to escape." Lucifer interjects.

I sigh in relief, that is a good sign. Her room is surprisingly nice... for a cell. Lucifer has added a bed and she isn't going to die of dehydration or hunger. He has given her health care and entertainment too. I'm not saying it's a nice place to be, far from it, but he is treating her surprisingly well, like he wants her to live. He won't jeopardise his escape from Hell. "You all left me to save your own asses!" Abby screams, grabbing the bars.

Taken aback, I watch her shake them. I didn't think she would look ready to kill us, possibly pissed off, but surely she would want us to save Holly and Colt first? I shake off that thought; she is in a stressful situation, cutting her some slack is a must. I can sense Lucifer grin on the other side of the camera. "Tell them, Abby."

He knows her name? That might be even more shocking than Abby being ready to kill us. The camera gets closer, Lucifer focuses on her face.

"I hate all of you! You..." The phone camera slides. We face the ground. "Guys, Lucifer is trying to use me to..." The screech of cell bars. "Kill you." A stomach-churning scream and the phone screen goes black.

"Abby!" Holly yells down the phone. "Is she alive? We have to go now!"

She's brave for stealing the phone from Lucifer, but there will be consequences. I don't even know what they will be. I hold my breath, Abby has grown important to me, I treat her like I do Colt. I do the same with Holly. The phone screen turns to Abby's face. She is curled up in a corner, crying, but alive. "She's still alive."

The call ends. We stare at the screen; he didn't kill her. Abby knew he wouldn't, or she would not have risked it. Or, at least, that is what I hope. Abby is brave for doing it either way, her angry performance was very convincing and partly based on truth, I assume. Alex is writing every word Abby said on the chalkboard with a smirk on her face. "That girl not only stood up to Lucifer, but she also surprised him with that move. I underestimated her." Alex finishes. "We can sleep on what we have. Abby is alive and useful, which means she is going to stay alive for the moment."

"Lucifer needed Enzo, but we still rushed to get him!" Holly argues. "Why aren't we doing the same for Abby?"

"Lucifer was using him as a weapon, we had to get him to stand a chance at taking Hell back. If he'd stayed there longer, Lucifer would have pumped Enzo with his blood until none of us would have been able to take him on. Lucifer leaving Hell is not our biggest threat right now, he won't bother with that for at least a few more days."

"We know where she is! Can't we teleport into the cell, grab her and get out?" Holly yells.

"No, it's underground. Also, you can only teleport in certain areas in Hell." I explain. If it were that simple, we would be doing it by now.

"Fine, but this shouldn't have happened! Alex, you said you had your own little side plan or whatever!" Holly snarls.

"Yes, and she died, which was not what I was expecting." Alex defends her actions.

Tessa, she had a plan with Tessa. I ruined it, I killed her. I rub my face, taking a deep breath. I can't think about it as I don't know how my magic will react.

The rap of a hand on the door pauses the conversation. Holly stands, marching to the door and grabbing her bag. "Where are you going?" Flint asks protectively.

"It's Selena. I'm going to come up with a plan if you aren't."

Flint moves to stop her. Alex shakes her head. She'll be safe with Selena. Lucifer won't make any more moves just yet. There is only one more to be made, and that will decide who wins. Flint watches the door close behind her. I see a glimpse of Selena before they hurry towards a taxi. We aren't the most consoling people in the world. She will go cry, plan and pass out from sleep deprivation, then come back after realising that she can't save Abby by herself. Alex rubs her forehead. "I need booze and a nap before I can think straight."

"I'll get scotch."

"I'll have a bottle for myself thanks. Your best too, none of the crap hundred-year-old stuff. I want it old and strong. I helped save your life." Tina orders.

"I'll help you carry it." Colt stands.

Walking out, Colt doesn't say a word. He hasn't said much since we got back. He basically had to trade Abby for me. I open the pantry and search the bottles. Colt grabs my arm. "It's good to have you back." He pulls me into a hug.

I nod, releasing him. "Thanks. Don't worry, we'll get Abby back one way or another."

"Oh, I know. We all knew what we were getting ourselves into, it's no one's fault. Abby will survive. She is not as weak as you think."

"She stole the phone from Lucifer, I don't think she's weak at all." I chuff, passing bottles into his arms. I think we are going to need quite a few. I know I need it, and a shower. I need to wash away the feeling of working for Lucifer.

"How was it working for him? Bet he called on you like a dog." Colt quirks a smile.

"Don't." I shake my head. "I'd rather forget." I close the pantry door, ten bottles between us.

"That is what alcohol is for." Colt balances the bottles carefully. He tilts his head. "You have a scar on your face. Why isn't it healing?"

"Lucifer did it, the scar won't disappear. He's making sure I don't forget." I sigh.

Returning to the others, the bottles disappear from our hands before I can even get a word out. I'm left with my own, I pop it open. Alex lifts her bottle. "A toast to Tessa, for being a crazy daring assassin and... crap, I'm bad at this. Someone else go, so we can drink."

We look at each other. I killed her, my fist inches closed. The worst part is that I desperately wanted to please Lucifer by doing it. He made me enjoy it, knowing I hadn't gained control over my new surge of power, meaning I wouldn't just kill her. She exploded like a firework, except it was guts falling back down, not colourful sparks. My gut twists, I remember smiling at her. Tina and Flint didn't know her. Holly and Abby aren't here to say anything. That leaves Colt and I. I stand voluntarily so Colt doesn't have to.

"We knew Tessa for a few days, but she was willing to put her life on the line to help save me and I'm sure if she'd lived, she would be helping now. She wanted to be a hero and she is." But it cost her life. Death is so common in our world, it hurts so much in the beginning but we end up becoming numb to it. Each time I lost someone it hurt a little less, not because I didn't care as much, but because it happened too often to allow it to. Tessa's last words were 'remember me' and we at least owe her that much. She'll either be remembered as the woman who helped save Earth from mortal doom, or the woman who helped try to save Earth. It depends on whether we end up joining her or surviving. "Cheers to a crappy funeral for a talented assassin." I swig the bottle. Drinking, that is a talent all supernaturals learn quickly.

We drink for a few hours, none of us could be bothered to cook, Tina used magic to make pizza. I grab my second slice; I haven't eaten food in what feels like days. We are all on our second bottle except Colt, he's a light weight. Flint pulls out his phone. "I should go for the night. Jade said the kids won't sleep." He yawns, looking at the empty bottles. "I don't know how much help I'll be."

A portal appears in the middle of my living room. "I'll be back tomorrow morning."

Alex nods, face full of pizza. He disappears.

I grab another bottle; I always have a good stock for a reason. Each memory of Lucifer makes me want to drink more; I did everything he asked. I shouldn't have failed in killing myself. I don't have a death wish, but I would rather die nobly than live as a coward. It makes me sick to think about it.

"Enzo, tell us everything that happened between you and Lucifer. We need any information you can give us." Tina instructs. "And no promises that we won't make fun of you, because we will."

I glare in her direction and start at the beginning. They are drunk, their jokes can't be that good. I hide my hands, sparks randomly spasming from them out of my control.

Tina rocks back in her chair, gripping Alex. "You had to call him King of Hell?" Alex shakes her head. I look at Colt for help, he is smirking. The memory makes me want to throw up. If it didn't help, I would keep it to myself. I would die with the knowledge. Colt looks at the clock. "It's three in the morning, we should really go to sleep."

Alex groans. "You are so boring. Fine, we will get back to it tomorrow." Alex puts down an empty bottle. "With less booze." That would be best, we need clear heads if we want to outthink the mastermind. I pull myself off the sofa, I flick my wrist to get rid of the empty bottles. Splinters of glass fly upward and shatter to pieces before my eyes. I curse. "I will clean that up in the morning." I don't have time to bother right now. Tina let's her green sparks fly and cleans up the pieces.

"Show off." I play down the fact my magic is struggling to stay stable.

"I'll be going home, I'll drop by at some point tomorrow." She yawns, picking up the bottle she hasn't quite finished. "I'm taking this with me." She portals away.

***

As I come out of the shower, Alex walks into the room. She had stayed downstairs to finish up her board. I thought she would go home like the others did. Colt is sleeping in his room. The rest of the rooms are empty, it's the quietest my home has been in weeks. "Do you want a spare room?" I ask.

"Excuse me." Alex laughs. "I may be covered in dirt, but I saved your life, you can't banish me to a spare room."

I smile. "That's not what I was saying." I am worried about my magic; if I don't have control over it, I could do something in my sleep. "I don't want to hurt you by accident."

Alex shakes her head, smirking. "Aw, how sweet; you think you can hurt me. No way, you don't have to worry. You wouldn't get a shot in."

Laughing, I sputter out. "I must have imagined kicking your ass in Hell."

"I was being nice to you because I thought being Lucifer's little minion was painful enough. Next time I won't be as kind if you are going to be cocky." She threatens.

She has a point, she is stronger than me, undoubtedly. I smirk, leaning down to kiss her. Alex puts a finger to my lips, stopping my approach. "I have a question. When you asked me to kill you... did you mean it?"

I nod. "I did." I'm not going to lie to her, I'm not an idiot. "I didn't realise you noticed. Why didn't you do it? It would have solved a few problems."

"And let you get out of being teased for being Lucifer's personal handmaid? Never." Alex wraps her arms around my neck. "Besides, I need you; you're my back up plan."

"What do you mean?"

"For the last ten years, I have had an emergency plan, in case Lucifer ever got out and I'd run out of ways to beat him."

"So, you have a plan if it all goes sideways, but it includes me. That's why you needed me back so bad."

"It is. The plan has consequences, but I need you to know you're on board in case we get desperate enough to use it."

I don't like the direction this is going in. The plan doesn't sound like it will end well...

I'm right, I hate the idea. "Alex I can't do that." I refuse. She is insane to think I'd even consider it. "It's the dumbest idea I've ever heard."

"Your heart rate just spiked. It's brilliant, but you don't want to do it."

"You'll die." I argue. "I'm not going to assist in your suicide mission."

"How is this any different to you asking me to kill you. Which happened after you willingly stabbed yourself in the chest to try and prevent Lucifer taking control. I'm only doing the same."

It's not any different, except she's the one to die, not me. I couldn't help her. "I'd like to remind you that you didn't kill me."

"Yeah, because it wasn't necessary."

"Why do you want me to do it?" She knows other warlocks and witches who'd be much less emotionally involved.

"I don't know anyone else strong enough to do it. Also, Lucifer would never assume I'd choose you because he wouldn't believe you would do it."

"He's right, I won't."

"Fine, I'll have to find another warlock to teach me so I can do it myself. I have magic." Alex yells back.

I take a deep breath and look her dead in the eyes. "Is there any way to persuade you that it's a terrible idea?"

"No, unless you can think of a better plan."

I curse. I don't think that's possible. Her plan can get rid of Lucifer and is flawless to execute, except for Alex's death. If this is Alex's plan, there's no way I could be able to think of something better.

"I'd rather you kill me than anyone else. Besides, we might not even need to use it."

I pause, thinking it over for a minute. "It's not worth it."

"If Lucifer were to win, we'd all die anyway. Colt too."

"Don't use him against me!" I hiss.

"I'm not trying to, I'm just telling you what will happen if we don't do it."

She'll do it, whether I approve or not. Alex is stubborn and reckless. If she wants it to happen, it will. There is nothing I can do to stop her. I'd rather do it how she wants than argue with her in what could be our last few days alive. "Look, I'll… I'll do it. But we have to think of every possible alternative first. Even if we think of one harder to execute, we'll try it first."

"Deal. Thank you." She leans up and kisses my lips gently. "I'm sorry." She whispers softly. "I know it's a lot to ask but…"

I grab the back of her head and kiss her passionately. Who knows how much time we have left? Chances are one, or both, of us will die in the next few days, and I refuse to waste a second. Our kiss tastes of fear, pain, and adrenaline. I keep hold of her tightly, refusing to let her go. Alex jumps up, wrapping her legs around my waist. She tugs at my shirt and breaks for a breath. "I love you." She mutters.

"I love you too." I draw her back in for more. I rip open her shirt, weapon holsters clatter to the ground with it. We collapse on the bed, I work my way down kissing her from her neck to her stomach. Alex gasps, my clothes disappear, and she grins, pulling me on top of her.

CHAPTER FIFTEEN

Abby

Holding up the book into the dim light, I attempt to read it. Lucifer spoke of Mammon, the Demon of Greed, in the past tense; he is dead. He was second-in-command under Lucifer. It doesn't say how he died, but I have a hunch it was Lucifer. From what I have read, he was powerful. Almost as power as Lucifer. There were a few others, they are dead too. Except Asmodeus, he is alive. He apparently lives on the other side of Hell. The fiery plain is only half of Hell, there is a deadly cold side where Asmodeus lives, but he doesn't own it, Lucifer does. This half symbolises fire and earth, and the other air and water. The demons are named after the four different elements, depending on which one they have. Ignis demons control fire, Lymph demons control water, Mundus demons control the earth and Caeli demons control the air. Apparently, the different types of demons were separated to their side but most migrated to this side to be near Lucifer.

I flip through pages in the dictionary, I have nothing else to do except read the text. My phone doesn't work, I don't have service. I haven't tried to leave the cell; Lucifer was serious about cutting off my fingers. He is terrifying to look at. I shudder, pulling the blanket up around my shoulders. I'm not going to die, which is reassuring. I have clothes, food and medical supplies. I have basic knowledge of first aid, but if I get an infection from the filth, I'm screwed.

Footsteps echo down the corridor, I glance up from my book. Lucifer appears at the bars. I try not to jump at the sight of him, he holds a phone; Enzo's. Waving it close to the bars, I hear voices come from the speaker. I know who that is. The camera points at my face. "Say hello to your friends."

I gently put down the book on the page I was reading. "Hi." I walk up to the bars slowly, eyes directly on the phone case without looking up at Lucifer. I know that will take away any will power I have to go through with what I plan to do next.

"I didn't hurt her, she did that to herself." Lucifer informs them. I did jump out the window, but it's his fault for chasing me. I was so close to the portal; he must have been watching and waiting till the last minute to snatch me. He enjoyed it. The phone weaves on the other side of the bars, I need it. Lucifer has told me everything he is going to do and I need to tell them.

I wipe my clammy hands on my trousers and slip a blade into my palm. I take a deep breath. I need him to move the phone closer and keep them on the line. It's easy to see that Lucifer likes drama.

"You left me here to die!" I scream. Lucifer moves the phone closer to my face, that's good. He's too old to know how to zoom in, thankfully. "I hate all of you!" The phone moves within my reach. I stab Lucifer, aiming for his eye. I grab for the phone, whisking it through the bars. "Lucifer is going to use me to kill you." The iron clatters. I panic, my heart pounding loud enough that I can hear it. They need to know. "Silven could..." Claws rip the phone out of my grasp.

Fearfully, I look up, freezing at the sight of Lucifer's cold, dead, angry eyes. My stomach flips, the chocolate bar I just ate ready to come back up. Lucifer's hand clamps around my neck.

Choking, I struggle, scratching at his arm, trying to escape. He can't kill me, he said he couldn't. I drop back on the bed, a dagger flies and cuts through my skin before I can move away. Screaming, my left-hand throbs. Clutching my hand in agony, my middle finger rolls off the bed. Whimpering, I hold back tears. Lucifer scoops up the phone and marches away.

Gripping my hand, blood pools over the blanket. My finger lies in the middle of the floor. Retching, I aim for the bucket, vomit spewing over my clothes. Dizzily, I collapse next to the bag. I grab bandages, my left hand shaking. Focusing, I bandage up the stub of my finger tightly to prevent blood loss. Tying it up, I use a switchblade to cut the bandage from the roll. Blood soaks through, it'll slow down soon. Adrenaline pumps through my veins, I take a deep breath, wincing, my hand throbs. The lonesome finger stares up at me, I pick it up carefully. The pearl white bone is cleanly cut through. Searching, I pull out a sock from the bag and put it inside. I don't know what else to do with it, I sit back on the bed. It is made of hardwood and not much better than the floor. I lie on the blanket as a mattress. I close my eyes in an attempt to sleep the pain away.

The door to my cell creaks, I bolt up in the bed. My hand grabs for my knife. The doorway is empty. The cell door remains wide open. Is this some sort of trick to see if I will leave? I look down at my throbbing hand, can I risk losing another finger? Gingerly, I creep towards the doorway. My eyes look at the cell door, I am tempted to close myself back inside. The anger in Lucifer's eyes will be engraved in my mind forever. Glancing out, I see the corridor is empty. Who opened the door?

"Abby." A voice hisses. Jumping in surprise, I turn to the voice. Halfway down the corridor, Tessa stands, ushering me to follow her. She's dead, what is she doing here? I could be hallucinating from blood loss if I hadn't wrapped my wounds correctly. I did bash my head pretty hard too. Tessa runs back in my direction. "Are you okay? You look like you've seen a ghost."

She chuckles. "I used to think ghosts were real. When I was little, my brother and I used to stay up at night and search for them."

"You are dead. I saw you die." I insist, unable to process how she is here. There wasn't a body left, she went up in sparks.

"No, it was a ruse. I'm Alex's side plan, she told me before we left. I'm meant to be listening in on Lucifer and updating her. You weren't meant to be here. We need to go." Tessa tugs my hand. "Quick before any demon comes to check where you are."

"Where are we going?"

"To the portal. I'll drop you off. Hurry up."

I don't take any time to process it, she is alive and that is what matters. It was simply part of Alex's plan, which means we are winning. I run, Tessa pulling me along. Darting through corridors, we bound up a set of stairs. I don't take the time to think about how winding they are.

Up the stairs, I spot a demon. Tessa pulls me around a corner to a different room. It's like a labyrinth of identical rooms. A voice comes louder from the corridor. The door shakes, Tessa waves her hand. A chair tucks itself under the handle. "Where are we going?"

"Out the window." Tessa looks down. "It's a two storey drop. I'll catch you before you hit the ground." She promises. "It won't be like last time, you landed like a flat pancake." She chuckles.

"You were there last time?" I didn't see her.

"Yeah, but I couldn't get to you. Well done for making it that far. It was impressive, I thought you were going to make it, until Lucifer snatched you." Tessa pulls me up onto the ledge.

I look down, it is far, but not as far as last time. I trust Tessa will catch me. Her power is telekinesis, I've seen her use it. The wood on the door groans. I drop without another thought. We soar through the air, the ground getting closer and closer.

I tense up, my face stops inches from the ground. Tessa snorts. "The fear on your face, you thought I wouldn't catch you."

"You left it a little close." I stand up, brushing off the dirt. I can't see the portal. We are on the wrong side of the building. Tessa presses my chest against the wall. She hooks her thumb, referencing that it's around the next wall. We walk against the wall, ducking under window frames to prevent being seen.

My eyes spot the portal. Tessa looks around. I don't see any demons; they are all in the castle. We dart towards the huge glowing oval. Sprinting full speed across the dry soil, burning our feet even through our boots.

We stop outside the portal. Breathlessly, I pant. "Are you coming?"

"No, I need to stay behind to see what Lucifer's plan will be without you. I'll be fine, they'll think you broke out alone. We don't have time to chat. Go quickly, before a demon decides to look out at the view."

I nod. "Thank y-" The ground shakes. Lucifer, he always waits till the last moment. Tessa goes bug eyed, a hand appearing through her chest, holding onto her heart. "No!" I howl.

Laughing, Lucifer wrenches his hand back out of her chest. My own sinks into my stomach in sorrow. She can't die again. Dropping to my knees, I shake Tessa desperately. "Sorry." Tessa murmurs, her hand flickers.

A hand grabs for my shirt and I soar backward. The portal envelopes around my body, red, black and purple cover my eyes. She sent me through, I'm going back...

Gasping, I wake up. I'm in the cell, the door firmly shut. Did I not make it through? Lucifer caught me before I could go through and knocked me out. I remember Tessa, her heart rolling in the dry soil. She died twice... or once and it was all a dream. I rub my face; it must have been a dream. I check my hands; I count nine fingers. He would have taken another if it were real, right? Slumping back in the cell, I realise that it wasn't real. I dreamt the entire thing. I bury my face in my hands. Tessa is dead either way and I'm still here.

I pick up my book and scour the bag. To my luck, I find a small bottle of vodka. I should go through the bag and work out how to ration the food and water; I don't know if I'll be getting more. Struggling to hold the bottle in my left hand, I twist the cap off with my right. It bursts open, splashing a little on my shirt. I take a swig and begrudgingly return the cap to the bottle. I don't know how much longer I have in here, running out of alcohol on the first day is not a good idea. I may have to use it as rubbing alcohol if it comes to it. I take the books and my phone. I can use the flashlight, while it's charged. The torch is awful and is giving me a migraine. I continue translating the text, I wish I had a pen to annotate the pages.

My cell has no windows, I have no idea what time it is or how long I have been here. I have the supplies figured out. I put on the hoodie from the bag, leaving my wet shirt to dry in the heat. It's poorly cleaned. I only have water and nothing else to wash it with. I roll up a sleeve of the hoodie and strap on a weapon holster. I put the knife where it belongs. I have a switchblade in my pocket, just in case. I'm not going to take on Lucifer, but I don't know if I'll need it. I may know all of demon history and speak fluent Latin by the end of my capture.

Footsteps approach as I pull out the bandages to dress my finger again. A demon opens the cell door. It has patches of short orange-brown fur over its body, buck teeth and short arms. I imagine it's part kangaroo. The book says that demons came before animals. Demons are the animals of Hell; the more intellectual ones came from the humans. It waves for me to exit. I'll have to keep my old bandages on until I get back. I walk out as instructed. Hopping, the demon jumps up the stairs three at a time. The spiralling stairs look longer knowing freedom is not at the other end of them.

Entering the throne room, I see a small crowd of demons. No more than a dozen. Lucifer lounges on his throne, looking down on them proudly. He takes out a box from under the chair as I approach. That is where he kept it, if only I had found it earlier.

The demon hops away without another word. Lucifer is about to use me to take their power, yet they are smiling and talking excitedly in a language I don't understand. They follow Lucifer blindly without a question of their own well-being. Lucifer waves a deathly contraption joyfully.

"Ready?"

Lucifer

I pull out the device originally made for Silven. She could absorb other demon's powers, but she had her limits. If there were no limits, she could have taken my power. If that were possible, I would have killed her on the spot. It's the reason I killed her father, Mammon. He discovered his ability and attempted to kill me and take my place shortly after Silven's birth. Silven was weaker; that happens over the generations so there can always be a hierarchy. She could take on most demons below her, but Silven didn't take power without my approval. She was the perfect sidekick; did whatever I asked, worked hard, was loyal and served her purpose until the end.

Silven and I had planned to use her as a vessel to acquire more power for myself. Then I heard about the amulet of sacrifices, a large source of power which anyone could take, and I could never let anyone gain such abilities. I knew it was a threat as long as it was in the world. We put a pause to our operation and went after the amulet instead. So, when I was sentenced to my cell, I forced her to gather the evidence of our experiment and hide it. If Alex found out, she would have used Silven for her own gain and I wouldn't have been able to escape. We never got a chance to test it, but I'm certain it'll work.

I take out the collar from the chest. I had Silven forge it out of pure osmium. I don't know what it will do to Abby's skin. Demons are immune to most metals; their skin is too thick for it to penetrate, while human skin is fragile and weak. Fortunately, I don't plan for Abby to wear it for long. Osmium will conduct the power that Abby absorbs, which I can then use for myself. Abby's human body couldn't hold much without the collar. Silven would be better but I had to use her in my escape plan. "Ready?" I unclip the collar.

Abby steps away, staring at the device in concern. "A collar? What will it do when I wear it?"

"It will take the power transferred into your body so that you don't die during the process." I reassure her, clipping on the contraption before she slows down the process any longer with her irritating questions.

Screaming out in pain, the girl doubles over in agony. Tears stream down her face, the skin around her neck bright red where the collar clutches on. She grabs for the clasp automatically, trying to unhinge it. I roll my eyes, it looks sore, but this has to be done.

"Don't touch it, or I'll take another finger." The girl hesitates for a moment considering my threat like it was an offer. "Fine, I'll take the entire hand."

She stops, her hand coming away from the collar. The skin is hot, red and sore where she touched it. Tomorrow, I may add padding inside, or it'll burn the head off her body. Then she'll be dead, and I'll need a new plan.

"Alright, you are going to touch the demon and close your eyes. I'm certain one of your friends has shown you a memory. They touch your head, and you see what they are thinking. Imagine you are doing the same but instead of showing a memory, you will do the opposite and take it." I explain.

Abby nods, understanding what I'm explaining. Let's see how well. I wave for the first demon to approach Abby; she does not look in shape to move herself. Lifting her head with effort, Abby's hands reach upward. Wrapping them around his head, she closes her eyes, tears of pain trickling down her face. I watch carefully. The silver metal glows gently, the girl whimpers in pain. The demon withers at her touch. Fading away, he slowly dies. I didn't realise they would die, but their loss will be worth it. They'll die doing more than they could if they lived. The last of him fades and the girl opens her eyes. "What did I do?" She panics, looking around for the demon.

"Absorbed his power. Next." I order. We have no time to waste. The power from these demons is not a patch on what I already have. They are a test before I go for the more powerful demons."

"I have to do all of them." Abby touches the collar; the rash has spread to the rest of her neck and is growing further.

"Yes." I demand. I should cut another finger for her complaint, but that would slow down the process further.

I watch her take two more, the rash getting worse each time. The metal is affecting her lungs, each new breath is raspier than the last. I won't be allowing Alex to call today, Abby's new wounds might stir up her suspicion. I allowed it yesterday so that Alex would know that I haven't used Abby to open the portal yet. It lets her know that I am taking my time and going to come at her with everything I have and there is nothing she can do to stop me. I'm quite looking forward to ruining the plan she comes up with. The fifth one steps forward, blood drips down from the collar. She grabs their neck, barely reaching it. In exhaustion, her eyes remain closed between each demon. The fifth one disintegrates.

Abby stumbles forward, struggling on her feet. Eyelids fluttering, she face-plants the ground before the sixth one can stand before her. She didn't even make it halfway through. I kick her in the side, she refuses to stir. I sigh, removing the collar. Blood soaks her neck. Wheezing, she coughs, more blood splutters onto my shoe. She is deathly pale, like a vampire who hasn't drank in a week. I kick her again for her weakness. Silven would have done better. I usher a demon to my side. "Take her to her cell." I point to another. "Take a few demons and visit Earth. I want you to visit a hospital, kill the sick, they're a waste of space. Then take a doctor and mess the place up a bit so they won't notice the missing supplies. I don't want Alex finding out that we need a doctor. Remember to feed the human hell worms before taking them through the portal." I wave to another. "Go to Earth, bring the girl back human food and other supplies." I don't know what she needs to live other than food and water. Humans are fragile, irritating beings.

We will continue later. I hold the collar; power is like electricity and very conductive. The amulet of sacrifices has similar properties, which is why I knew it would work. Certain conductive metals, or jewels, can contain supernatural power with some help from magic. Objects will hold it until the power finds a new host which, in this case, is me. Abby's body immediately puts the power into the collar by survival instinct as she can't contain it. The collar wouldn't be able to take power by itself, it doesn't have the strength to draw it out of a supernatural being. It must have assistance.

The small ounce of power enters my veins, I grin. This is the beginning of a long process. I need to put some rubber or similar material between the skin and the collar, or Abby won't be able to do much more and I have a schedule to keep to. I check my list, the names of the demons who are going to die for my power are written upon it. I cross off the first five names. Demons are an endless supply; they reproduce faster than they can be killed. I lean back on my throne, enjoying the moment. I deserve this, this throne was made for me, I'm simply keeping it that way.

The demon I sent to Earth skips in proudly, holding onto a woman in a doctor's uniform. She shakes uncontrollably in the demon's grasp. Seeing us scares humans, commonly to death. She gawks in my direction, falling down like a domino. I can hear a heartbeat, it is faint, but she is not dead. That's a good start.

"Take her to the cell." I need Abby alive. The wounds look hard to treat; we'll use the professional, then kill her. The hospital killing was just a small announcement that I am back. It'll spread over the news, reaching Alex to let her know what I will be doing after I kill her.

It's painful waiting to kill Alex, I still don't know exactly how I am going to do it. I need it to be the most painful death in history. I should toy with her a little further. Hayden and Esmeralda were involved in my downfall. They didn't mean to be, they did exactly what I had planned. Alex, with Tina and Enzo, are the ones who ruined it. Esmeralda and Hayden were sacrifices in the ritual for the amulet but, thanks to Alex, they got to live. I should put an end to their little happy ending.

CHAPTER
SIXTEEN

Enzo

Groaning, I stumble out of bed. The rising sun shines through the open curtains. I take my phone, it's five in the morning. Sleeping is difficult; memories of the last few days replay in my dreams. Alex snores softly, fast asleep in one of my shirts. I walk downstairs into the training room. Weapons are scattered on the floor, the doors to my armoury open. The mess is extreme, I shake my head. Focusing, I wave my hand gently. The knives lift carefully and hover. I signal for them to return to their place. Of the ten knives, six find their way back to where they belong and four soar into the wall. Wrenching them out, I try again. They float to their box without a problem. This is a good start.

The memories of first trying to control my magic, all those years ago, come back to me. I didn't care at first; it helped with my mass murder sprees of revenge. I began to care when I would hurt friends by accident. It took me fifty-two years to learn to suppress it. I'm not going to do that this time, I'm going to learn to control it. Last time, I was young, naive and scared, but I'm not anymore. I'll need this power if we are taking on Lucifer.

Practice and concentration. I create a ball of energy the size of a tennis ball. Firing it at the nearest target, the blast obliterates the painted wood, splinters flying throughout the room. Sighing, I try again at the next target. The same sized orb, but weaker. The target breaks into tiny pieces, again. I take a deep breath, I can't get frustrated, or it'll get worse, not better.

I repeat the process, over and over again with countless targets, hanging them up by hand, slowly getting better each time. I blast another orb in an attempt to get the target to stay in one piece. The wood explodes into splinters as the magic hits it. I curse. I try again, for the fiftieth time. I watch as the orb smacks into the target, the seared wood smokes but remains intact. I did it. I go again and only a few stray splinters flutter to the ground. I attempt a different target. Fire flares from the centre, that's not normal. I wave my hand, the flames put themselves out. A laugh. I shake my head, it's Alex. "Morning."

"I've been standing here for the last ten minutes." Alex crosses her hands over my shirt. "You okay?"

"Yeah. I was just trying to..."

"Not blow everything up." She finishes my sentence, looking at the debris. "You are thinking too much because you are worried it'll go wrong. You put the fire out without causing destruction because you weren't thinking."

"That's different, I was putting it out."

"You could have made it bigger by accident." Alex explains. "You know I'm always right."

I chuckle. "Not always."

A bolt of fire aims directly for my head, I roll out the way. A second at my chest, I gesture a chunk of target debris, it blocks the ball of energy. Spiralling, a tornado of water soars in my direction. Sparks race out of my fingertips, creating a forcefield to block it. The wave hits and continues to batter down the forcefield. Alex is not going to stop. I should have known that saying she isn't always right was a mistake. I push the forcefield forward, transforming it to energy. The water splashes back, soaking Alex. Batting soaking locks out of her face, she blasts an elemental bolt.

"How dare you!"

Red magic hits the wall. I attempt to blast her back, trying not to overthink it and miss her, skimming by her face. Before I can blink, Alex pins me to the floor. Her red eyes dance, knowing I will have to use magic on her to escape. A spare fiery hand wraps around my neck. I said I wouldn't worry, so I won't. My hand pulses, a bolt knocking Alex on the chin. Flying, she thwacks the wall. "I told you." Alex gloats. "You are just a scaredy cat."

"You were right." I admit. I'm not going to deny it again, I'm not stupid.

"Good." Alex nods in triumph. "Now come on, I'm hungry."

Alex tucks into the cinnamon roll she requested. She stuffs her face, smiling. "I think I missed your food more than I missed you." She jokes.

"Thanks." I chuckle, watching her take a second. Nice to know her real feelings.

"You're welcome. We need to discuss game plans." She magics coffee. "Want to finish telling me what you did for Lucifer?"

I sigh, I suppose it has to be said. "Sure." I start where I stopped yesterday. Alex sits patiently until I finish, without giving me any taunting comments. I can see her holding them back at a few points.

"He always planned to let you go, we need to figure out why. He could have kept you, used you to help him win but chose to let you go. It is part of whatever he is planning to do."

"He probably just thinks I'm not significant enough to count as a threat if I'm against him."

"But you almost killed me, which means you could do the same to him." Alex shakes her head.

"But you didn't try to kill me, he would." I point out.

Alex shakes her head. "You took down Flint, which I still don't understand. He must have a plan to get enough power that it won't matter who's against him. That is what scares me. We need to figure out what it is."

That's a fair point. If he thinks he can get enough power to wipe us out, he must have a reliable source. "Could it have to do with Tessa? He specifically ordered me to kill her." I think aloud.

Colt walks in the room. "Nah, he was just being an asshole doing that. Think about it, he was the one who got Tessa involved in our lives in the first place. I bet he always planned to kill her. His purpose for her was simply to get you to visit him. We barely knew her; he has no personal reason for her to die. The rest of us do, which means he'll save us all for the grand finale." He takes a bottle of blood out the fridge. "Or he knew Alex would use her and he stopped it."

"I hate to say it, but you are right." Alex agrees. "Lucifer put her into our lives then wrenched her right out." She turns to me. "Do you have any books on supernatural artefacts more powerful than the amulet of sacrifices?"

"No, there is nothing else. That's why it was so special." I answer.

"Lucifer thinks he has a way to kill all of us that we don't know of. If we can figure it out, preferably before he uses it, we are golden. You said you visited a hut or something in Hell to get a chest for Lucifer." Alex thinks.

"If it was in there we are screwed, he already has it." Colt chuckles nervously.

"I did, I don't know what was in it. Colt is probably right, whatever he was using, he has it." We have to outsmart him at this point. Lucifer's best tool is his mind, it's complex and messy.

"Do you think you could portal us to the shack without a demon detecting us?"

"Yeah, demons didn't go near the building."

"They didn't go near it? That means it's probably near the other side... Why would Lucifer hide something all the way over there? That's near Asmodeus territory. If he is in on this, I swear I'll kill him." Alex promises.

Asmodeus is the last one alive of the six Hell royals. Lucifer reigned supreme, then the next demons known to exist; the five princes and the princess. Mammon, Asmodeus, Leviathan, Beelzebub, Belphegor and Kath'tek, who is Flint's mother. Asmodeus was the smartest, and instead of trying to overthrow Lucifer, he made a deal. He lives on the icy side of Hell, full of nightmares and, most importantly, out of Lucifer's way. The second Alex came to rule, Asmodeus tried to take over. He failed miserably and skulked back to his hole, with a worse agreement than he had before. Perhaps he has colluded with Lucifer to get the same agreement he had the last time. "Where are we going first? Asmodeus or the hut?"

"The hut, I want to look at the body. I have never heard of a demon called Annie." Alex waves her hand, the shirt is replaced with a sweater and jeans while her hair does itself. "I'm ready."

Colt groans. "Give me a minute, I don't have magic." Alex lets sparks fly his way, he changes into clothes. "That works." Colt pulls a pouch of hell worms from a cabinet. He kept living hell worms in the kitchen? That is a terrible idea. He dips the worm in the left-over blood from his glass. Swallowing it whole, he chokes it down. "I'm ready."

I create the portal, we land inside the hut, in case Lucifer has demons on patrol. "This is tiny." Colt looks around the one room building. "And smells appalling." The heat has reacted with the body parts; she has started to decompose. The stench is sickening, but manageable for now.

Alex looks at the bloody chains. "I think she was a witch." Alex puts down the chains. "It would explain why she looked human. I imagine Lucifer found a way to keep her down here without the use of hell worms."

I open a small closet, a clear glass box full of hell worms sits inside; it looks like a farm. They reproduce and cause an endless chain of hell worms for her to eat. "Or she was scared of dying."

She would have lived off the hell worms to survive because she was terrified of what would happen if she didn't. I open another drawer, there is an endless supply of water. Chances are that the cuffs are magic reducing. It's ridiculous what people will do to live; centuries of living in torment to avoid death. I put her out of her misery.

"Okay, so she lived here for a decade to stop us from getting our hands on a box? If we had found it, we could simply have taken it." Colt concludes.

Alex shakes her head, lifting up the chains, Latin for 'hail Lucifer' carved into the cuffs. "She could only use magic to serve him. My bet is that she was here for longer than a decade. Centuries, more likely. His own personal witch. The box probably wasn't stored here forever." She puts down the cuffs, glancing out the window. "We are directly on the edge of the other side. I bet Asmodeus knew it was here and never told me. I'm going to kill him."

"What is this?" Colt pulls out a different box with engravings from a loose floorboard. Prising open the lid, chemicals in glass tubes line up in the box. Colt pulls out a pile of old scratchy parchment, dates from the seventeen hundreds scribbled down on the pages. The witch lived here for over three-hundred-years. That must have been rough, but she chose to continue living that way, instead of dying. Possibly in hope she would be free one day, which I highly doubt, considering the circumstances. Colt waves the pages. "It looks like an experiment."

"Yes, Lucifer loves science. Well, if you can call it science." Alex chuffs. "It's probably one of his experiments." She leans over Colt's shoulder. "Morphing? Did he actually do it?" Alex snatches up the sheets curiously. I wouldn't say Lucifer was the only one interested in experiments.

"Colt, anything else in there?" I ask. He opens a small container and a beetle scrambles out of the box. A test subject. How did it live there for so long? The beetle crawls across the floor.

"If you feed it the silver liquid, it will turn back to its original state." Alex picks up the bottle and pours a little on the ground. The beetle drinks it. A demon erupts from the floor, snarling. Instantly, I send out a bolt of magic, killing it.

"Enzo! If you weren't going to let me transform it back to a beetle, you could have at least let me kill it." Alex complains.

"Sorry." I smile. "Is there anything else here?"

"Books." Colt looks at the shelves. "Nothing interesting."

Alex nods. "We should take this back, along with any books with a clasp. If they're locked, they're important."

After scouring through all the books, we find the ones that could be useful and send them through a portal back home, along with the experiment. Alex creates a portal, and we walk through it to the edge of Hell. Hell was divided into two; the hot, fiery side for mayhem and the cold, icy side for everything else. Heaven is meant to be perfect, which means Hell has to have both the worst conditions in one dimension. The icy side shows people's worst fears, the fiery half makes those fears a reality. They don't have separate names; they are both Hell. The icy side is just less relevant because it's not favoured by Lucifer. "The second we walk in, you'll see an image of your worst fear before actually making it through." Alex explains to Colt.

"I think we are already living in my worst nightmare." Colt quips back. "I'll be fine." He may change his answer after going through, but it's nice to see him so confident.

"Remember it's not real." Alex winks, disappearing in the fog. "See you there."

Stepping through, the world tips sideways, like walking through a portal before landing in a frozen scene. We are on Earth, in my house, or what remains. Bodies lie all over the floor, more importantly, whose bodies. A few dozen demons of different kinds. Then there are the ones with faces; Alex, Colt, Flint, Abby, Holly, Tina and myself. Lucifer is the last one alive. He's won. "If you hadn't killed me, we would have won." I spin, the voice belongs to Tessa, looking on at the scene. "You didn't have to kill me, Lucifer gave you a choice. You or me."

I frown. "What do you mean? He forced me to kill you, it was an order."

She shakes her head. "Is that what you tell yourself? He worded his statement very clearly. You could have let me live."

I sigh, he forced me. I should have been able to fight it, and for that I will always feel guilty, but I did not choose myself over her. "That's not true, but I am sorry."

Tessa's shoulders drop. "You don't care, do you? This all could have been avoided if you had killed yourself." She is probably right there, but I failed, nothing can be done about it now. "You killed Colt, like you killed everyone else in your life, to save yourself. You are just too blind to see it."

I take a deep breath, ignoring the voice. I don't want to think she is right. Turning to the scene, all of us are lying dead. This is possible. If I'm realistic, there is more than a fifty percent chance that this is how it will end, which is the terrifying part. Different scenery but Lucifer is smart. Hell, we barely managed to defeat him last time and part of that was luck. We barely survived Silven's attempt, she was nowhere near as powerful as he is.

The image fades, Alex stands before my eyes. Rocks, chunks of ice and a freezing breeze hit me instantly. Mountains covered in a thick layer of ice tower higher than the eye can see. "You took your time." Alex smiles. "What did you see?"

"Lucifer winning and Tessa blaming me for it." I shrug.

"How was it?"

"Not bad. Tessa wasn't very realistic; she would have talked more if she were real. What about you?" I laugh it off. I can't afford to think about whether she is right.

Alex laughs. "Similar. Flint wasn't mad at me in mine, which meant it was fake." Dreams aren't real, it's important to focus on that part to avoid being sucked in. Colt appears between us, wiping tears from his eyes with his t-shirt. He obviously didn't remind himself it wasn't real; it was a nightmare and, hopefully, it will stay that way. "You okay?" I magic him a tissue.

"Yeah." He wipes his eyes and pockets the tissue. "Are we ready?" He doesn't want to talk about what he saw. Fair enough.

We reach the doors of a smaller, broken and less significant castle on a mountain top. Alex welcomes herself inside, slamming open the doors on purpose. Asmodeus sits on a chair, reading. He is tall and lanky, like Lucifer, but with long, straight black hair, bronze skin, smaller horns and green eyes. "Alex, what are you doing here?" He smiles. "And you brought your friends with you."

"You know why I'm here." Alex snaps. "If you thought I wouldn't find out, then you are a bigger imbecile than you look."

"I don't appreciate the insult, Alexagon. I kept to our deal, Lucifer breaking out is not my fault." He closes the book. "You must have known he would come back at some point." He has a big ego for a man overthrown by both Lucifer and Alex, and who had to make deals to stay alive.

"You knew about Lucifer's shack near the border, and never told me because you wanted him to come back. You wanted your old deal, or maybe a better one, and you would get it if you told him you 'assisted' his escape."

"If you didn't know about the shack, then that's not my fault. You are looking for someone to blame, and the only way you can do that is to look in a mirror. Now, if you can go on your merry little way, I have to go meet with Lucifer." He stands. He has a meeting with Lucifer, that is suspicious to say the least. "He requested my presence, I don't know what for. It is not what you are thinking."

Alex flies across the room at full speed, grabbing his head and smashing it into a wall. Asmodeus howls, water appears in his hands, ready to fire back. Alex laughs, hitting him harder and the water splashes to the ground. "Tell me what you did."

"I didn't do anything, I already told you that." He grunts.

A couple of demons crawl into the room, I glance at Colt. He gets the message. Sparks race out of my fingertips, hitting a demon square in the chest. They don't disintegrate, but they do die instantly. I seem to be getting the hang of it, slowly. Colt launches onto the second one, stabbing relentlessly until it stops wiggling under him. That is certainly one way to do it. Alex pummels Asmodeus to the ground. "What did Lucifer keep in the hut?"

"I don't know, I only knew that the hut existed, nothing more. I never told you because I didn't think it was my place." He answers. "Happy?"

"One more thing. You are visiting Lucifer? What about?" Alex orders.

"He requested my presence, I am going to find out. Perhaps he wants my help to defeat his foolish daughter."

Alex kicks him in the head. He howls, feebly. "You are going to find out what he wants and come back and report it to me. Think of it as payment for neglecting to tell me about the secret hut."

"I can't do that. I fight to survive, if there is going to be a war, I will be on the winning side. I will visit Lucifer, if I choose to side with him, I will tell him about your unwanted visit. If I think he will lose, I'll come back and report what Lucifer speaks to me about."

Alex laughs. "You think I would agree to that?"

"You don't have a choice, Lucifer is expecting my company in a few moments. If I don't arrive, he'll know you were here, but if you let me go, you have a fifty percent chance that he won't."

Smartass. I tug Alex's shoulder, pulling her away. I know it'll be tempting for her to kill him, but he's right; if he doesn't show up, Lucifer will know we got to him. On the other hand, we could let him go and he may tell Lucifer himself. At least this way she would get the pleasure of killing him. "What are you going to do?"

"Send him." Alex informs me. "You don't happen to have a video chip with dimensional range, would you?"

"I could summon one." I grin, that plan is not half bad. Watching him could mean we could get one step ahead of Lucifer.

I open my palm and pass the video chip to Alex. Asmodeus grins, brushing off ice from his old-fashioned coat. "I suppose you will be letting me leave now."

"Not yet." Alex pins him to the wall threateningly, hands sliding near his breast pocket. "You said you might join my side, but what if I don't want you? You have already betrayed me."

"Yes, I would like to repay you for that incident and have a clean slate, if you will let me." He nods.

"How do you plan to do that?" Alex quizzes him.

"I'll share a memory of your mother." He proposes.

Alex hesitates. "Why would I want to see that?"

"You get to see where you got your charming good looks from, it certainly wasn't from your father." Asmodeus smiles, reaching for her head. Alex doesn't pull back; she has nothing to lose taking the offer. The camera is planted. He holds her head; her eyes roll back for a minute, then they jolt back to life. "What a bitch." Alex curses.

"Are you pleased?" Asmodeus asks.

"You can go." Alex moves out of his path. "But if you choose him, you'll regret it."

"We'll see about that." Asmodeus marches out of the doors, grinning.

"Would you seriously let that asshole help us?" Colt checks.

"No, I'd get information out of him, then snap his neck." Alex laughs. "We should go back. We need access to a laptop." Creating a portal, she walks through. We follow.

We have about ten or twenty minutes until Asmodeus will reach Lucifer. Alex sets up her laptop, installing the program to watch the footage live. "Alright, what now?"

"We have to sync them up." Colt explains. "I can do it." Alex slides the laptop over to him. Colt taps away on the keys, doing things I don't understand. I understand phones and technology, but Colt has often shown me how to do certain tasks. He grew up with it, I was born before light bulbs were invented. Alex is the same, she was born before electricity was invented.

"Drink, anyone?" Alex offers a bottle appearing in her hand with glasses.

"Hell yeah." Colt smiles.

Alex pours out the drinks, handing them out. She collapses onto the couch. I sip my drink, it's only midday; we missed a few hours from going to Hell. "What did Asmodeus show you?"

"My mother. He's right, I do look like her." Alex shrugs. "I really saw the resemblance when the blood splattered over her face."

"You saw her kill someone?" That sounds unlikely considering she was an angel. Angels are meant to be a breed of everything good in the world. Sadly, they know that and are the biggest snobs for it.

"She tried to but it's obviously Lucifer's point of view, which means Lucifer showed him the memory. I mean it could be coincidental, or it's part of his plan."

"They wouldn't have had time to meet before we got there. I think it is a coincidence. Thousands of years ago, Asmodeus probably was working for Lucifer before the exile." I conclude. "Are you sure it's not his own?"

Alex lifts her hands and grabs my head.

I jolt back into the prison under the castle. A woman howls, the man sprints down the corridor. He runs past one cage, holding a pregnant demon... Flint's mother. She looks identical to the drawings of her. I have no idea where Flint got his genes from, he looks nothing like either of his parents. In the next cell, a woman bathed in blood, her wings hitting both sides of the enlarged cell walls. Blood pools out of her stomach, a knife sticking out of it. Blood stains the woman's hands and face, like

Alex described. She stabbed herself, she is trying to kill Alex before she is born. "It can't live!" The angel screams.

"Who gave her a knife!" Lucifer yells angrily. A hand reaches out to open the gate. The hand is not Lucifer's. It's not boney and transparent. It's Asmodeus's memory, but Lucifer was there. You just can't see him.

Returning, Alex lets go of my head. "What do you think?"

"It's Asmodeus, Lucifer was there. Did you see the hand?"

Alex pauses for a second, remembering. "You are right."

I open my mouth to check how she is doing knowing both her parents were complete assholes, as a portal opens up.

Hayden and Esmeralda fall through, one over each of Flint's shoulders. We jump off the couch, Flint puts them down. Demon goo drips off their skin. "Holy shit Flint, what happened?" Alex panics, cutting open her arm.

"There were at least twenty demons. They were both unconscious when I got there but the demons kept at it, I just hope you can save them." Flint panics.

I open up their mouths, there is no time for magic. Alex pours her blood down their throats. Lucifer sent demons after them, we should have seen that coming; they were both involved in overthrowing Lucifer the first time around, it would make sense that they are targets. Esmeralda's stomach is no longer there. Grey squishy intestines dangle out a gaping hole. Chances are that they were both dead before Flint got there. The demons must have continued attacking them after they died, to try and prevent Alex bringing them back using her blood. They have to be in a certain condition for that to work. Hayden's neck is torn apart, almost detaching his head from his body. "Hayden called me but didn't get any words out." Flint pulls out a broken phone.

Alex pulls her arm away, now we wait to see if they wake. "Can I be a little offended that they called you instead of me?" Alex tries to lighten the mood.

Flint attempts a smile. "Yeah, it means they like me more."

Hayden gasps, jolting up right, clutching his now attached neck. "Esmeralda!" He spins, grabbing her shoulders. "Esmeralda? Is she going to be okay?"

"I don't know." Alex answers honestly. "I've given her my blood."

Shaking her, Hayden's eyes fill with tears. "Wake up! Please." He begs. He peels off the blood-soaked material around her stomach. "It's healing. That's a good sign, right?"

Alex nods, leaning over and checking for breathing. I listen carefully for a heartbeat.

After a minute, I don't hear anything. She's not coming back. Hayden puts an ear to her chest. "Why didn't it work?"

Alex shakes her head. "It's Lucifer, we can't imagine anything will work against his doing. Did they have weapons?"

Hayden nods. "Try again. Please, she can't die." I don't know if he has a choice whether she dies or not. Alex listens, giving her more blood. Hayden tilts her head to make sure it goes down smoothly. "Esmeralda?" Hayden asks hopefully.

My ears pick up a very faint heartbeat. Hayden's eyes widen, as her chest moves a few millimetres. "She's alive." Hayden hugs her limp body.

"Careful." Alex warns him. "She's still weak. Flint, could you go back and see if they left any weapons for us to analyse?"

Flint nods. "I can do that." I create the portal for him, Jade must have got him here. Flint disappears. I lean closer to Esmeralda. Alex tries giving her more blood. Esmeralda groans, blood drooling around her mouth, but doesn't wake up. Flicking my hands, I start assessing the damage with magic. The blood has repaired her organs, but her brain activity is dangerously low and isn't functioning properly. "She's in a coma, but I can try to wake her." I offer.

Hayden nods. "Do it." Magic surges out of my hands, I touch her head carefully. Concentrating, I send magic flooding to her brain; it works on the broken nerve cells. Esmeralda gasps, I open my eyes and the magic cuts off. She's awake, that's a good sign.

"Esmeralda?" Hayden smiles.

She frowns. "Who?" She murmurs, her eyes already fluttering shut.

"What did she say?" Hayden shakes her gently. "Esmeralda?" She doesn't respond, but her heartbeat is strong. She'll need sleep to recover, but she's out of the coma. "Do you think she has forgotten everything? Or was it the drowsiness?"

"She suffered head-trauma. It's likely amnesia. We can't fix it." I answer honestly.

"Fuck." Hayden curses, hands going through his hair. "Couldn't you give her our memories of her? Would that help restore some of her own, trigger them in some way?"

"I doubt it, but it would give her a sense of who she is. We can try it when she wakes up." Alex offers.

"It's working." Colt looks up from the screen. "You should get over here, he's almost there."

"I have a spare room, the second door on the left. Put her in there for now."

Hayden scoops her up in his arms. "Thanks. I'll stay with her; if she wakes up, she'll be confused."

Alex nods. "Alright." We need to fix this before anyone else gets hurt. Turning back to Colt, we lean over and look at the screen.

Two demons open the door for Asmodeus. I squint at the screen; it's blurry, but I can make out the outline of Lucifer on the throne. Lucifer stands as Asmodeus approaches, they walk up to each other and shake hands. "Nice to see you back in charge, Lucifer." Asmodeus smiles. "It's how it's meant to be."

The sound of rubbing fabric interrupts the conversation. "Where is the demon I sent to..." Lucifer's voice is muffled.

"Can you fix it, Colt?" Alex asks, turning up the volume.

"I was trying to, but the connection is bad. I'll try to improve the sound, I don't know about the image." Colt pulls up a tab in the corner of the screen and starts fiddling with the buttons.

"Alex visited?" Lucifer smiles. "It's all on track." I decipher the words.

"The bed, how is it doing?" Asmodeus asks.

Lucifer's answer is broken by Asmodeus moving. The bed? The only bed they would have is the one in the cell with Abby. If the bed was from Asmodeus, it's cursed. Nightmares, most likely. Hopefully, Abby will work it out and sleep on the floor. There is no way for us to tell her. But this means Asmodeus has already chosen Lucifer. It's a good thing we bugged him. The camera view moves, turning to the back doors. A blurry figure walks in, guarded by a demon. Abby is covered in many more bandages than last time. Did she try to escape again? She walks closer, why is she in the room with them? Most of the bandages are around her neck...The video cuts out. "Colt can you get it back?"

He shakes his head. "The camera must have fallen inside his pocket. We can still hear it."

At least we still have the fuzzy audio, if that can help us.

Abby

Groaning, I rub my neck. Wincing in pain, I sit up on the floor. I'm directly next to my bed, they didn't even bother putting me in it. My head throbs, I must have hit it on the way down. The pain was unbearable, the collar was made of metal and it burned. I touch the raw, bloody skin gently. I need a mirror to see how bad it is. What about my fingers! I check, counting carefully. Nine fingers; he didn't take one for passing out. My lungs ache with each breath. "Good, you are awake."

I jump, a woman sits in the corner of the room, pulling equipment out of a bag. "Tessa?"

"Who's Tessa?" The woman turns, she is not Tessa or anyone I know. "Is she part of… whatever this is?"

I inspect the woman; she wears a doctor's uniform, has a small cautious smile on her face, jet black hair and a name tag reading 'Wendy'. She's human. "Tessa died; she was… my friend. What are you doing here?"

"I am here to fix you up. Some animal kidnapped me. Where are we?" Fear glazes her eyes. "Is this some sort of satanic cult?" She has no idea she's in Hell or that the 'animal' was actually a demon. This will be hard to explain; I could tell her the truth or lie. Her hands shake violently as she applies ointment to a cloth. "Stay still."

I gasp, the liquid drips down my neck, the stinging changes to gentle relief. She smiles weakly. "That feels good, huh? What happened to you?"

She is going to keep pushing for answers. I can't blame her, she has been taken to Hell by a demon. I try to think of a different answer than the truth. She has given me the satanic cult idea, but I don't know how much she has seen. I may not know how to answer her other questions with believable answers. Enzo always says it's bad for people to find out. I'll have to try and lie.

"It is a cult. This is a warehouse. I was kidnapped, they think I have some special abilities."

She continues tending to my neck. "Okay… How long have you been here?" She cleans my neck with a clean cloth.

"I don't know, a day?" I guess. I have no idea; Hell doesn't seem to have days or nights. If so, I have not yet seen them.

"You are pretty banged up, whoever treated you before did an awful job." She shakes her head. "I need to sew your finger back together, bandaging it up was a mistake."

"It's all I had to work with." I argue. I had a roll of bandages and water.

"Sorry." She apologies, pulling out a needle and thread. "This might hurt, I don't have any local anaesthetic."

Thirty minutes later, I convince her we are in a warehouse, made to look like Hell from the bible and 'my kidnappers' think I can lead them if they help me unlock my 'hidden ability'. She believes what I say and calms down enough to stop shaking and finish up on my finger. "It is nice talking to you, Abby."

"You too." It has been nice to talk to another human being; I'm honestly surprised Lucifer would send a doctor to tend to my wounds. He must need me badly. Speaking of the devil, Lucifer walks in the doorway of the cell. "Are you done?"

"Yes." The woman packs away some of her equipment without looking up. "She'll need daily check-ups but..."

Lucifer grabs her around the neck, snapping it. Wendy drops dead, falling on top of her bag. "I hope you were watching what she did. You'll be treating yourself from now on." He shrugs. "I'll get a demon to remove her soon." Lucifer walks out, slamming the door, leaving Wendy in my cell. "Have a rest, you'll be needed again shortly."

My neck throbs, Wendy said I was lucky to be alive with the damage to my throat. I don't think I can put that collar on again, unless he wants me to die. Wendy's soulless eyes stare in my direction, her mouth gawping. She didn't deserve to die, and Tessa didn't deserve to die either. I rub my face, taking a deep breath. I wouldn't change knowing about the supernatural world and going back to a normal life, but it is messed up sometimes. It can't be like this for everyone, we just have the pleasure of knowing Lucifer. I close Wendy's eyes and move her neck back into a normal position, for my own peace of mind. I lie back on the bed, the temptation to drink the entire bottle of vodka is getting tougher and tougher to resist.

I open Wendy's bag, finding painkillers instead. I swallow down a number of pills without reading the labels; as long as they help the pain, I don't care what they are. I check the rest of the bag. There are several medical items; a lot of pills, bandages, sanitary products, thread, gloves, rubbing alcohol and hand sanitiser. Falling back on the bed, I close my eyes. The energy transfer is exhausting and painful.

My eyes open to the view of a park. I am lying on a blanket, smiling up to the sun, Colt's hands resting on mine. The cool breeze flutters by, sending a gentle shiver up my arm. It's so good to finally be free from Hell. We won. It was tough, but worth it. I missed real food and people. I wasn't sure if I would ever see Colt or Holly again. Colt sits up abruptly, his hand leaving mine. I frown. "What's up?"

"We need to talk." His face falls.

"About what? We won, it's all fine now." I reassure him.

Colt shakes his head. "Not about that. I mean we need to talk about us."

"Okay… what about us?" I ask, fearful of what direction this is going. If it's a joke, it's a bad one.

"We need to break up." Colt states bluntly. "I'm sorry but it's not going to work."

"What?" My heart sinks in my chest. Where did this come from? I thought we were doing good, we just defeated Lucifer together. "Why?"

"This, it can't go anywhere. Think about it, I'm a vampire, you are human. I'm going to be stuck at seventeen forever, I'm going to need to use fake I.D for the rest of my life. You on the other hand, get to live, and age, and continue life like a normal person. It's not fair on either of us if we stay together." Colt explains.

My shoulders droop, I wasn't expecting that. I open my mouth to say something back, something to change his mind, but I can't; I know he's right. We could try to make it work, but it wouldn't be fair. I can't say I hadn't thought about it either since attending Hayden and Esmeralda's engagement party. Hayden will still look sixteen when she is eighty, they may be alright with that, but I don't know if I will be. I had never thought about the future until that point. I'd say the future doesn't matter. We are still young, only teenagers, thinking like that could wait, and maybe by that point we'd be ready, but I can't. Colt will have his twenty-first birthday in a month, but it's hard to think about that when he doesn't look that old. I nod. "I'm going to go." I pick up my bag. "Bye." I smile, trying not to cry. It's for the best, he's right. I just wish it wasn't happening so soon.

I gasp, I'm back in the cell. None of that happened, it was just another nightmare. I sigh in relief, reaching over Wendy's still body and grabbing a water bottle. Chugging it, I fight the pain as I swallow. My throat is dry and raspy from the collar. The bars shake, a new demon stands at the doors. "Come with me." It can't be time again already? I groan, dragging myself to my feet, I follow it out, rubbing my neck. I don't know if I can suffer through it again. It may be worth risking another finger to get out of this agonising task. I'm likely to have a scar around my neck for the rest of my life.

Going into the throne room, demons wait joyfully for me to kill them. They are twisted creatures, willing to die to let Lucifer become more powerful. A demon with a human-like face stands beside Lucifer. He grins my way. "Hello, human."

I frown, he looks familiar... "Asmodeus, this is Abby." Lucifer beckons me away from the doors. Asmodeus, he's from the history book. He is meant to be very powerful, not Lucifer powerful, but as powerful as Mammon. There were others of their rank, but they are all dead. "Ah, lovely to see you. I can't wait to see how this works."

"Please, don't." I beg. I don't think I can take it again.

"You don't have a choice." Lucifer ushers me over.

I hesitate, I want to run for my life, but I can't. He is faster than me; I wouldn't even get out of the room before I lost my hand. Lucifer moves closer and puts the collar around my neck. I wince in anticipation, the pain stings but not half as badly as last time. "Stop being a wimp, I lined it with rubber." Lucifer growls. He does need me to live if he is willing to make such a gesture.

A demon approaches. I take a deep breath, fighting the pain pulsing through my neck, I put my hands on its dry, crusty skin. I wince in disgust and close my eyes, taking its power. My muscles spasm with the energy, before it is transferred into the collar. The dry figure disappears, my hands slipping through the space where it stood.

"I'm impressed." Asmodeus smiles. "How did you transfer the power into the collar?"

"Abby's body is fragile so, as a reaction to the power being put into it, it naturally wants to leave to save her from dying. Therefore, the collar is conductive, and she unintentionally passes the power into it." Lucifer explains. "Abby, let him examine your collar."

I frown and move over as ordered. I feel like a dog being called upon, and the collar doesn't help. "It's remarkable." Asmodeus touches my neck, I resist the urge to flinch away.

"Kill him." Lucifer mouths behind his back.

He wants me to kill Asmodeus. Asmodeus' hands feel my collar, admiring the work. Does he honestly want me to kill him? Is that why he is here? Killing smaller demons for their power makes sense, but this is a Duke of Hell, I don't know if that will work. Lucifer glares in my direction. "Kill him." He orders.

In fear, I don't wait for him to ask again. I reach out for Asmodeus's head, but he steps out of my reach, without noticing my hands. "How long did it take you to make this? It's incredibly impressive."

Lucifer turns in my direction, a shiver shoots up and down my spine. I messed up; I shouldn't have hesitated. Asmodeus faces me, what do I do now. I can't do it with him watching, he'll fight back.

"It wasn't that hard, all I did was…" Lucifer slices Asmodeus's neck with a dagger before I can blink. "Abby." He instructs.

I jump up and grab for his head full of hair. Asmodeus grabs my hand before I can do it. My back smacks into the floor with force. I groan, unable to move.

"After all this time, this is how you treat me? I expected better, Lucifer." Asmodeus complains. "Maybe I should have sided with your daughter."

He would win if he joined Alex, his loss. He seems like an asshole anyway. Lucifer kicks Asmodeus square in the stomach. He flies in my direction, I struggle to my feet and grab him. Shaking, I close my eyes and put my hands on his heads. Ice cold hands touch my skin, pushing against me, but I ignore it. I'm used to the cold, thanks to Colt. I feel Asmodeus buckle, my hands tremble. The wave of power floods my body, the sheer rush charging it against Asmodeus's struggle. I hear a crack of metal. The hair disappears from my hands and is left in ash after a matter of moments. I gasp, opening my eyes. Lucifer arches an eyebrow. "Took your time."

"Sorry." I say, anxiously; the surge of power and control transferring from my body into the collar leaves me feeling vulnerable. "I didn't…" The knife swoops down, by instinct I flinch away. My hand remains intact. My relief is short lived, Lucifer grabs my right hand and hacks off my pinky. I howl, tears springing to my eyes. My finger drops onto my boot. "I did what you asked." It may have taken a minute or two, but I did it. I clutch my finger, blood seeping through my hand. I can't win, I do what he asks but he doesn't care. I would run or fight back, but I'm completely defenceless. He didn't take my weapons, but they are no use against him. I'm at his mercy and I hate it.

"You shouldn't have hesitated. If you do that with your friends, you'll find out what real punishment is." Lucifer argues, unclipping the collar. My neck burns, but not as bad as before. "I'm done with you for now, you can go back to your cell." He swats me away.

"You plan to do what?" A demon tugs my shoulder, forcing me out of the room. A trail of blood from my hand follows me out the door. He wants to use me against them…

I grab the rubbing alcohol and clean the wound, hissing in pain. I messily stitch the flesh together, each prick attached to a string of curses. Wrapping it in bandages, I wince in pain with each bind. Blood seeps through the bandage and padding. I ignore it and pick up the book. I open the page on Lucifer and get the Latin dictionary. There must be something that I can do, other than wallow in a cell while Lucifer uses me and cuts my fingers off one by one. I know Colt, Holly and the rest of them will come and rescue me at some point. I don't expect them to help unless they know they can win, we can't lose anyone else. I know I'm not going to die; Lucifer isn't going to let me, which I can use to my advantage, I think. He'll be taking my fingers whether I misbehave or not. I might as well try and do something with the time.

CHAPTER SEVENTEEN

Lucifer

I pluck the bloody finger from the ground; I should have taken a bigger one. Thumbs are best, humans don't realise how necessary they are until they lose them. The cut is clean, straight through the bone, I didn't lose any of my talent locked away. I toss it aside, turning back to the collar. There is a small crack in the metal, Asmodeus is the most powerful being I could find to use as a subject. The charge of power bursts through my veins as my finger meets its surface. I sigh in pleasure; that is more like it. Asmodeus' power on top of mine, that is what I need to defeat Alex. Demonic power is much richer than magic.

I can't wait to take Alex's power and have her completely helpless and at my mercy. I want to take all of it, then release her and let her live like a human, with no supernatural abilities. She will be miserable. I've seen it happen to others, it's not pretty. It will be worse for Alex, all the power in the world, then nothing. Sadly, I can't release her to a life of torment, or she would simply return, trying desperately to take her power back. I want it to be quick and efficient; she'll know that I have won when she dies. That is the best reward I could ask for. Along with that, I get to kill the rest of her bastard friends.

I have imagined how to kill them all in a way that will cause Alex the most pain, I have even created an order in which to kill them, from the least to the most important. I have changed it a few times. It's surprising how, over such a short period of time, humans can lose and make connections in the blink of an eye. I'll know the order when it happens, I'll watch who tries to save who the most.

I expect Hayden and Esmeralda will be with Alex by now, if they lived. They have a fifty percent chance. I want them dead, whether it's me who kills them or not. If they live, they'll join Alex's little team of heroes, and I will get to kill them myself. If they are already dead, then good for them. I will have more to kill after that, Jade for starters. Flint will be with Alex and one of them has to stay with the kids. She will be my first order of business after I kill Alex. I want to take my grandchildren and teach them how to be real demons. They will be my next project; they'll be what I tried to do with Alex and Flint, but this time I won't fail. They will be the second and third most powerful beings in the universe after I kill their father and aunt. I will need them when I take over Earth and Heaven. Running three plains on my own will be too much work, I'll need the two of them to do the grunt work.

The ashes of Asmodeus flutter out the window, I'm glad that he is gone. I allowed him to live just for a moment like this; I thought it would be useful to have at least one powerful demon around and, as usual, I was right. Admittedly, I shouldn't have killed Kath'tek, she would have been useful for having more offspring. It all worked out in the end; I have grandchildren to use now. A small, black square sits where Asmodeus stood, the ashes dispersing around it. Kneeling down, I pick it up. I analyse the device, what is it? The small, shiny cuboid is from Earth. It's no bigger than the nail on my thumb. A lens shimmers; it's a mini camera. I thought they might try something like this. I know exactly what to do with it. I get to toy with Abby again too.

I walk down to the cells where Abby is stuffing her face with a type of human food. I should get her more of that, food will help her body heal and keep it strong so she can absorb more demonic power without collapsing. She looks up, eyes wide. "Again?" She asks, face falling in pain. It's already getting to her.

"No. What's this?" I pass the device to her through the bars. I need to see if she'll tell the truth.

She takes it, frowning. She fiddles with it for a moment, thinking hard. "I think it's a miniature bomb."

A bomb? Does she really think I'd fall for that? "How does it work?" I test her.

"I'm not sure, I'm not a bomb expert."

"Then how do you know it's a bomb?"

"Because I've seen them before." Abby lies, her heartbeat rising dramatically. She is a terrible liar. I grab her wrist through the bars, her head thwacks against them. She whimpers, hand clutching onto the chip. "What is it really?" I glare at her.

"A-a...camera." Abby panics. She is scared, which means her heart rate is through the roof, but she is telling the truth. A camera. It probably was recording for Alex. He would have left and given her the footage, but he can't now. The camera is fried. Unless it was live…

I snatch it back. I drop it and squish it under my shoe. If it wasn't broken before, it is now. I assumed that they would use electronics, knowing that I don't know much about them. That's why I installed electronic jammers around the castle after our phone call. If they saw any of that, they wouldn't have gotten much information. Now I have seen their move, I can make mine back. "Is that it?"

"It's what I think. I don't know anything about spy cameras." That is the truth. I stroke a knife against her wrist. "Lie to me again and I will cut the entire hand off."

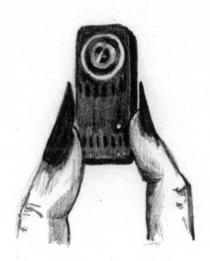

She gulps nodding. "I'm really, really sorry." I can see the hatred in her eyes, not only for me but for herself. She hates herself for being terrified of me and having no power. I let her go and leave her in the cell. The broken camera left just outside the door.

I should have known their move would come with Asmodeus; he probably knew about the camera. He's known for playing both sides. My reputation has been tarnished by Alex, that is why I need to take more than Hell back to prove that I'm stronger. That is my own mistake, it doesn't matter; I have taken precautions. I march off to find a pack of demons. I have my move against them already in place but, before it can happen, I need to make sure they didn't plant something else during their rescue mission for Enzo.

Enzo

Frowning, I hold my notepad, a few dozen words written across the page. The audio is terrible, and the image is black, the camera has fallen inside his pocket. Colt can't make it any better. A flash of fuzzy dirt and Lucifer and the camera lands in the dirt. The image is gone, it is broken.

"Did Lucifer find it?" Alex panics.

"Possibly." I frown. "How? It was inside the pocket, perhaps it fell out?" I shrug. I didn't think Lucifer would find it; last time he saw a camera it was probably the size of a microwave.

"I should have put it in a better place." Alex shakes her head. "Did anyone get anything?"

I look down on my page, I have a few phrases, but not much.

Colt looks down at the notebook I gave him. "I have 'Abby, Asmodeus', 'impressive' and 'daughter'. If that means anything to you."

"It doesn't." Alex responds. Mine is not any better, I think some of my words are wrong as well. I think I got one phrase. 'I should have sided with…' The next word I assume would have been Alex, but that doesn't seem like something Asmodeus would say aloud.

Alex sighs. "Fine, we'll have to work with what we have, we know Abby was there. She was taken out of her cell for a reason. And the words 'impressive' and 'admire' were used. What can we do with that?"

"Well, no offence to Abby but I don't think she would be what they were admiring." I conclude. "She could have been there to prove to Asmodeus that their plan was working."

Alex nods. "Did you hear at the beginning, before Abby came in, Asmodeus told Lucifer we visited, and Lucifer wasn't surprised? He was expecting us to go."

"Which means we are doing exactly what he thinks we will do. We are following his plan." Colt closes the laptop. "We haven't achieved anything today."

"The sun is still up. We have a little information. Abby was in that room for a reason. I think we need booze, food, Flint, wherever he is, and Tina."

I know what my job is, food.

I finish cooking, and everyone begins to eat. Flint is on his way but had to visit his safe house because his kids are getting restless without him. His son, Ricky, is trying to make portals to see him. Tina said she is celebrating what could be her last few days on Earth and will be back later. Holly has been texting Colt; she is trying to find a way into Hell without one of us making her a portal. I don't know what her aim is once she gets one. There are entrances to Hell on Earth for demons who can't make their own portals, but Holly won't be able to locate one. She'll come back when she realises we were right. Colt is texting her hourly to make sure she isn't doing anything stupid. Luckily, she has stopped her parents worrying by using the mind-control Alex put on them to make them forget whenever Abby or Holly said something was for school.

"Abby could have been proof to Asmodeus that Lucifer's plan is on track." Colt suggests.

"Lucifer doesn't think he needs to prove himself to anyone." Alex shakes her head.

"He proved to us Abby was alive."

"It was part of his plan; if we saw the state she was in, it could convince us to make a rash decision to save her immediately instead of thinking it through. He tried to use the fact we care for her well-being against us." Alex explains.

Why else would she be there? He might as well keep her locked away in a cell. Abby isn't really a trophy to be proud of, she has no power. It would be like a child capturing a beetle. Lucifer can't be seen toying with one human, that looks weak. A young human is a newly turned supernatural's territory, not Lucifer's. He should be going after the biggest fish in the ocean... Asmodeus. He isn't just a fish, but a shark. Asmodeus said Lucifer requested him, but they were already in contact.

"Asmodeus knew about Abby, he provided the Bed of Nightmares. But Asmodeus is known for playing both sides, that way he thinks he can't lose. Lucifer may have been using that encounter to enslave Asmodeus. Abby could have been the ploy to get him there, he'd use her if there was an ulterior motive, like he did with us."

Alex nods, considering the possibility. "True."

"It would explain why the camera fell, if they fought it could have easily slipped out." Colt agrees.

"So, Asmodeus is now his loyal slave to help defeat me. I don't know. Lucifer wouldn't rely on anyone else. I bet he would kill him before enslaving him. He is not desperate enough to listen to that man." Alex snorts.

"If Abby was in the room, couldn't we ask her?" Colt suggests.

"How?" I swig my drink. "We can't just waltz in. If we could, we would have rescued her by now."

"We have that morphing experiment Lucifer made. If one of us morphed into a demon, they could slip in right under their noses."

We'd have to learn how to use it first, but he has a point. Abby may have more answers for us than we can imagine, but Lucifer knew we went to Asmodeus, he probably already knows we'll try this too. Lucifer showed the experiment to me, he wouldn't direct us to a clue unless he wanted us to use it.

"It could be a trap. We will have to decide if it is worth the risk." I answer.

"I could try to understand the formula. It's more powerful than a glamour, it physically turns you into the other being, but it shouldn't be too hard to figure out."

"You think it's worth the risk? What if Lucifer is expecting us to do it?" I know we are desperate for answers but putting our lives on the line for something that might not work is not the answer."

"We have nothing better to do." Alex grabs the box from the table. "I'll be in the kitchen." She takes her glass of whiskey with her.

Colt sighs, pouring himself another drink. He looks more dead than he already is, with massive panda rings around his eyes, drooping as he fights the urge to sleep. He looks paler too, if that's possible. "Do you think we are going to succeed?" He interrupts the silence. That is the burning question; will we die horrifically or live 'happily ever after'. The second option has already happened once with Silven, a second chance is practically impossible.

"I don't know." I drink. I won't lie to him, if I swore that we would win, he'd know I was lying, and it would make him more certain that we will fail horrifically. "What did you see in Hell?" He came out of that dream crying, he doesn't do that often, except for break-ups. He cries every time, even if he's the one breaking up with them. I don't know why.

Colt pulls a face. "Nothing."

I glare in his direction. "I'm not daft, what did you see?"

"Sometimes I forget how incredibly old you are. Who uses the word daft anymore?" He quirks a smile. "I'm fine, I was just tired and in need of a drink."

I sigh, I think I'm a bad influence on him; he used to be more open and talkative about his life, now he's more secretive and reserved. I don't think I can be solely to blame, his parents messed him up too, even if he won't admit it. I won't push the subject; he'll tell me if he changes his mind. "Alright, have a nap. You look awful."

"So do you, I have to stay awake. Holly has finally decided she can't save Abby on her own. I told her we were making exceptional progress and she is in a taxi with Selena right now."

"Exceptional? That's a big word for you Colt, and also a lie." I knew Holly would come around; she doesn't really have the resources to save Abby herself. The fact she is taking a taxi means she is still mad, asking for a portal would be much quicker.

He glares. "It's not a lie. We are getting there. We may be saving Abby in a matter of hours if Alex's experimentation goes right."

A massive white light flares out the doorway, the noise of an explosion burning my ears. The fire alarm starts ringing, ash and smoke flaring out of the kitchen. "You had to jinx it, didn't you?" I jog into my flaming kitchen. Alex sweeps away the fires leaping up to the ceiling with her hands.

Alex's hair is slightly frazzled, and her clothes are a wreck, but she is in one piece. "What happened?" A huge chunk of my kitchen counter is missing, the walls are smothered with ash marks.

"Except the obvious?" She gestures to the room. "Lucifer rigged it. The second I went to try it out, it blew up in my face."

"Is there a chance you did it wrong?" Colt raises his eyebrow.

"No, because I understand chemistry." Alex corrects him. "It was Lucifer. I was really looking forward to testing it out." She sighs. "What do we do now?"

We have the knife that was used to attack Hayden and Esmeralda that Flint is meant to be fetching for us but who knows when we will get it, and it won't turn any tides. It's a weapon that didn't do its job. Hayden and Esmeralda are alive. I have the dagger which can kill Alex or Flint, but that won't help; it can't kill Lucifer. The door knocker echoes through the house. It's Holly, we have nothing new to show her. Colt will have fun explaining that. Colt runs off to get the door.

"I'm going for a walk." Alex sighs. "I need to clear my head."

"Do you want me to come with you?"

"I think I can look after myself, thanks." She smiles. "Unless you want to come so I can keep you safe."

I chuckle, shaking my head. "I'm good." Alex nods and saunters out of the room. I bet she ends up in a bar or club.

I lift my hands, cleaning up the mess of a kitchen. I do not know how my home is still standing. I clean the spilled liquor off my shoes and the cuffs of my jeans. Lucifer didn't want us to use his experiment, but he did expect us to find it. He thought we would speak to Asmodeus, we are all doing exactly what he has planned. If we don't break out of the loop soon, we'll be handing ourselves to him on a silver platter. Hayden comes wandering into the room.

"I'm not going to ask." He waves to the mess.

I finish the last few touches, like the hole in my sink. "I was going to train, want to join me? Or does Esmeralda need you?" I have nothing better to do and it gives me a chance to think.

Hayden runs his hands through his hair. "I can train. Es is alive, she woke up for a few minutes but fell back asleep. She still has no idea who she is, or who I am."

"Yeah, I'm sorry about that."

"It's okay, it's not your fault… we'll get through it. I'm just glad she didn't die. I don't know what I'd do if that happened."

We walk to the training room. "She will one day. How will you handle it then?" Hayden knows she isn't going to live forever. You can already see the age difference; she is twenty-six like him, but he looks sixteen. It's only going to get worse over time.

"I don't plan to. For the past year, I've been trying to find a way to become mortal. If we survive this, I'm going to keep trying. I want to die with her."

I pick up a staff and chuck one in his direction. That is a big decision, even if he could do it, they would always have a visible ten-year age gap. Choosing to die and age with one person when you have the chance to be immortal is hard. If he did it, he wouldn't be able to go back and change his mind. "Are you sure?" I aim a blow at Hayden's head.

"Yeah, she means everything to me. People already think we are mother and son, and it will only get worse. It sucks being stuck at one age. I was going to surprise her on our wedding day but that might be a while now." Hayden means it, his heart rate didn't stutter. He wants to die with her.

"I will discuss it with her first, when she's better." I block Hayden's half-assed attempt. "Being immortal is part of your identity, she may not have the reaction you want when you tell her." If he surprised her with that idea, there is an equal chance she would be mad rather than excited. "Becoming mortal would not just impact your life, but hers too." I warn him. She might not want him giving up so much for her and think it's a bad idea. Especially now; she doesn't even know who he is.

"Good point, I just don't want to wait too long... But she doesn't even know who I am, it won't be an issue if we don't live through the next few days. I was just wondering if you thought it was possible."

Chances are, he could become mortal and stay supernatural, he's half werewolf. He wouldn't be the first to try it. I think there have been a few successful attempts, they just don't document them. It would be much easier to use a glamour to look like he is ageing, only he wouldn't be. I sweep Hayden's feet out from under him, he's distracted and out of practice. I doubt he's used his power properly in years. "There are probably ways, if you truly want to be mortal. If not, I could help with an ageing glamour. It wouldn't kill you but then at least you could grow old with her."

His eyes light up. "Seriously?"

I nod. "If we live through the next few days, I'll help you but as long as you promise not to do it until Esmeralda is better and able to give her own opinion."

"Of course. Thanks." Hayden swings the staff at my head. "You don't think I'm making a bad decision, do you?"

"No, as long as you are certain." I poke him in the chest, he stumbles. He should have been able to dodge that and make his own move. Hayden is not using any of his talents. I fake a swing at his side and instead kick him square in the stomach. Hayden doubles over, aiming the staff for my stomach. I propel myself with the staff and soar over his head. He could have intercepted me if he had used super-speed. He is basically living like a human, without realising it. I don't think he would regret becoming mortal.

"Have you ever done it to someone before?"

"No, I haven't. Not many people are willing to be mortal."

"Would you have ever considered it? If you knew how."

I pause, there are a lot of people in my past but giving up my immortality and my power for them has never crossed my mind. It's a large part of my identity, I don't think I could give it up so easily. There was one who I would have considered giving it up for. Ashley, I loved her so much. The only person I'd ever considered marrying. "Yes, one, but she died before I'd had the chance to consider it."

"Do you think you would have regretted it?"

If I had died two hundred years ago, I wouldn't have gotten to enjoy my time since then. So, at that moment, I would have been content with my ending. If I had been able to see my life later on, knowing that I would have never met Colt and that I'd never have helped Alex, I wouldn't have been able to go through with it.

All those memories, I could never give that up now. Dying of old age is not how I was made to go. I expect it'll be in a fiery blaze where I am finally outmatched, which could easily be very soon. I couldn't give up this life, it's a part of me and I'm glad I didn't end it. "Not at the moment."

"Good." Hayden smiles.

"When did you last transform into a wolf?" I ask, in curiosity.

Hayden pauses, thinking. "Six months ago? A little longer, maybe?" He can only last that long without getting cranky because he's a vampire as well. "Try it. You might get a shot in." I smile.

He laughs. "Fine, but we might want to go outside."

CHAPTER EIGHTEEN

Abby

Waking up in a panic, I grab the blanket. Sweat drips down my head, I wipe it from my brow. It was a nightmare, I'm still in Hell. Unless this is a dream too. I rub my face, trying to remember. Holly came to my cell, and we went upstairs to the throne room and everyone was dead except Alex. She was being strangled by Lucifer, dying slowly. She opened up a portal for us, but Holly was dragged away by demons. She pushed me through to safety before they could take me too. I shiver, I don't want them to save me if it costs them their lives. I remember thinking that they should be alive, that none of them should have died because I told them Lucifer's plan using... I scramble out of bed. The camera! I hadn't thought about it before, but maybe it can broadcast live footage. I can talk to them if there is a microphone, or they can read my lips if the camera works. My eyes fall on the chip in the corridor, lying in the dirt.

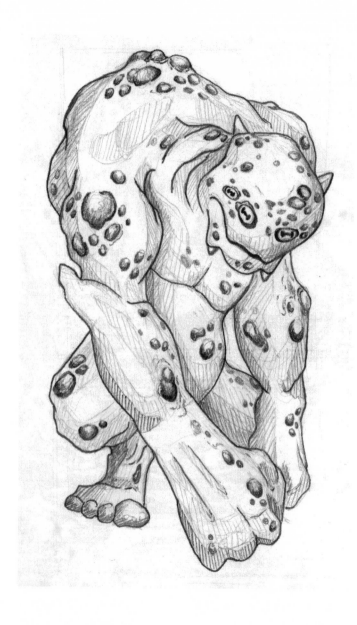

I press my body against the bars and reach through to try to grab it. My fingers fumble on the edge of the chip, why does it have to be so small? Weaving my hand between the bars, I press my body against them. Struggling to get it, I plead with the device to get a millimetre closer. It would be much easier to grab it if I had all my fingers. My middle finger strokes the chip urging it in my direction. Footsteps boom down the corridor, I wrench my hand away, leaving it behind. I curse, turning to my book. I pick it up, but it's too late. A demon leans down to pick up the chip. "What is this you're after?"

"Um… Food. Human food. I dropped it, please can I have it." I put my hand through the bar hoping it would fall for my lie. I have no idea how much knowledge demons have on human life.

"This is human food? It's different to when I last saw it." The demon goes to put the chip in their mouth.

"No!" I panic. "You can't eat it." I shouldn't have said it was food, that was foolish.

"Why not?" It snorts in my direction.

"Because you can't eat it by itself." I rummage in my bag and find a protein bar. I slip a retractable blade underneath the packaging out of view. "You have to eat it with this. Here." I reach through the bars. It goes to take the chip. I flick out the button, the blade stabs their wrist.

It howls in anger. I shove the entire wrapped protein bar in their mouth. Choking, the demon struggles to grab me through the bars. Waving the knife, I plunge it between the demon's eyes. If it had a brain that would have hurt more. Smiling, I stab again and again in the spots Enzo taught us. Demons have thick skin, but they have weak spots. I aim for the last spot…. The demon grabs my wrist. Whacking my head on the bar, I groan. I grab a blade on my belt with my free hand, I jab it in the side of its head. I breathe, released from its grasp. The demon rolls onto the floor, dead. Grinning, I grab the chip through the bars. I have it! The camera lens is broken, cracks all through the screen.

I curse, the cracks move onward to the plastic covering. There is no recording light, but there is a tiny button. I click it, the light doesn't go on. I curse, so much for that plan. If only I had magic, I could just fix it or simply get another one.

I look down at the dead demon. Oh shit! I got caught up in the moment. It was coming to collect me, if I don't show up in about a minute with a demon in tow, he'll know what I've done. I might as well say goodbye to my hand. I clutch my right hand; he'll take my more dominant one. I definitely couldn't use a knife with just my left hand. It was all for nothing. The camera doesn't even work. Hell, I can figure it out, I need to be of some use, and the book has been useless so far. I can try to fix the camera later. I tuck it in the backpack. The cell door doesn't have a key, Enzo told me it was by touch. I reach through the bars and drag the demon across to the handle. I press its hand on the lock, a faint click, and the door swings open, I sigh in relief. I drag the dead demon to the cell which is opposite and down one from mine; it's the last cell in the corridor. Heaving the dead demon upright, I use its hand and carry it in. Panting, I tuck it in the corner as best I can. Grabbing all the limbs and tangling them to squeeze it into the smallest space possible. I shut the door, locking it.

I go back to my cell. Do I go in, shut the door and pretend it never came? Or do I walk myself up there or make a run for it? The first option would be an obvious lie; the demons follow Lucifer's command without question. They would never disobey him. Lucifer will know something is wrong, and I haven't hidden the demon very well. If I walk myself up there, Lucifer will want to know what happened to the demon. I could find a different one and attempt to trick it into taking me? I doubt Lucifer would pay enough attention to realise it was a different one. The last option is to run, but I don't think I will be able to make it. I haven't accomplished it so far, but this time I have the upper hand.

I close my cell door and walk up the corridor out of the prison. As I reach the first floor, a demon immediately spots me.

Charging, it shrieks in my direction. In panic, I draw out my dagger and roll out the way. Razor sharp teeth chomp down on my arm. I curse and stab it in the side of the neck. Yelping, it retreats. I swing my leg out, kicking it in the chest. I punch the beast in the jaw and jab my knife into its neck, yanking it downward. The tough, thick skin rips, splitting the demon open from its neck to its stomach. Ramming my hand inside, I clutch a bundle of sludge and rip the organs out. The demon snarls, falling to the ground. I drop the grey sludge from my hand. I wince, looking at my bloody arm.

"Nice to see you didn't lose your talent along with your fingers." Lucifer chuckles.

My heart stops, shit! "It attacked me. I..." I didn't think this through. I should have shut myself inside and pretended I had never been collected. Of course, the demons would attack me when I'm alone. I looked ready to bolt, they wouldn't let me do that.

"I know. Where is Durgalon?" Lucifer tests me.

I pause, I don't know what to say. Lucifer can hear my heart rate; it must be pounding. "Gone."

"You killed him too?" Lucifer asks.

"No." I lie. Eyes flaring, Lucifer's forked tongue flickers out his mouth as he whistles a breath. I'm screwed. I might as well come clean. He reaches for his pocket, I stumble back, grabbing my wrist.

Lucifer smirks. "I'm impressed. Two demons and only one wound, especially with the missing fingers. You must really be desperate. Tell me, or you can kiss that hand of yours goodbye."

"Um..." I try to think up a believable excuse. "I did it because..." I try to focus on Lucifer, my head spinning in panic.

"If you won't tell me, I can work it out." Lucifer offers. "But in that scenario, you lose your hand."

"The demon stole from me, so I tried to get it back. I accidentally killed it and then I came up to fix the situation by getting another demon to take me but then I got attacked." I try to keep my answer close to the truth to preserve my hand yet not give too much information and pray he doesn't ask too many questions.

"What did the demon steal?" Lucifer asks.

"A protein bar." Which is true, to an extent. "I was very hungry."

"And the camera chip?" Lucifer guesses. "How do I know?" Lucifer takes the words from my mouth. "I figured out that the camera could have live footage instead of being recorded on the device. At first, I was impressed that you could lie to my face and get away with it by telling me that it wasn't. Then I realised you didn't know either, but I knew you would come to the same conclusion eventually. That is why you tried to get it through the bars and got caught. Your ticket to salvation was the only thing worth fighting for, so that is what you did, therefore killing the demon in vain. I assumed you'd just hope for the best when you came up here." I open my mouth to answer, he knew everything already. "Am I wrong?" He asks, knowing that he has the answer.

I don't have a lie to respond with. I can tell the answer is already on my face, thanks to the massive evil smile on his. "No." I admit.

"Good. I have a proposition for you." Lucifer beckons me to follow him to the throne room. I look at my hand, it is in one piece. For now. Scurrying behind, I follow him to the throne. He sits, looking down at me. "I get the camera fixed for you and you can use it at your leisure, but you can only feed your friends the lies I tell you. I need to throw them off the trail of anything they may have witnessed."

I can talk to my friends, but I can't help them. No, worse; I will be leading them to their deaths. I can't do that. "What happens if I say no?"

"I cut off your hand and you do it anyway. I have sent for a warlock to help me this very minute."

I have no choice; I'm doing all of Lucifer's dirty work for him. How did he work it out? There was nothing, no signs or anything, yet he knew exactly what I was going to do. He was waiting for me, there is no way to beat him.

"How would you make sure I would lie?" I ask.

"At first, I thought of a shock collar, painful enough to kill you after three truths to scare you into it, but I remembered that I need you alive so, sadly, I'm resorting to a pain-free option; mind-control."

Mind-control, I will be saying anything he wants me to say. I have no choice in the matter. "Only if you promise not to cut any of my fingers off in the next seventy-two hours." I try to get some sort of deal out of it. He's getting what he wants, whether I try to stop him or not.

"I don't make deals." Lucifer flicks a knife out of his pocket. "But I like the fact you still have spirit, even after all this time. It'll make it much more fun when I crush it beyond return." That's a no then. It was worth a shot. "Go fetch the camera, then come back." Lucifer orders.

My hand remains untouched, but he holds the knife, ready to be used. I take a deep breath and nod, carefully walking a few steps backward, eyes glued to the knife in his hand. Turning my back, I tense, waiting for a knife to fly out of nowhere. Sighing in relief when it doesn't, I scurry off to get the camera, a demon following behind me.

Reaching my cell, the demon opens the door. I pick up the camera. If I get rid of it, he can't use it, but what will be the cost? The demon instructs me to take myself up the stairs, before walking off to the cell where I left the body. I never told him where I put it, yet he knows which cell it is in.

I start walking up the spiral stairs, staring down at the camera. I desperately want to speak to them, but I can't risk their lives. I wanted the camera to help them, but I won't be doing that. If I keep it and let Lucifer use it, I'll be doing the opposite. I have to get rid of it. It's the only camera connected to their computer. They can't make another that'll link to their computer to hear me... Hell, I really hope Alex's blood can bring back limbs. The small broken chip sits in my hand… I could smash it into more pieces, but the warlock could repair it with a flick of their hand. I need to do more than throw it away, I need to get rid of it completely. I can't burn it to ashes, I don't have a lighter. I don't think I could trick a demon into doing it.

I stop outside the throne room. I could swallow it? Lucifer would cut it out of me, but they can't perform surgery, would he risk it? A guard glares at me to enter. I draw out my knife, aiming it for the demon. Its mouth opens, to call for backup. I shove the camera in its mouth. Well, it's in something's stomach. "Abby!" Lucifer hollers.

I wince, walking into the throne room. I'm screwed now. "The demon ate it."

Lucifer nods. "Thought so." Another demon appears, wielding a small camera. "I thought I'd be cautious as you still have a little spirit. The demon you killed swapped out the camera with a fake. The real camera was in Durgalon's possession." My heart sinks in my chest. I should have listened to Alex; he not only knows my next hundred moves, he knows a thousand more after that before I even know them myself. Each step is choreographed by him. I don't know why I even try. Lucifer is unbeatable, we are all going to die. Unless they see sense and run for it and leave me here, I don't know where they would go. Lucifer will be trampling all over Earth soon. We are all screwed. "It's also the reason I didn't promise not to remove any of your fingers." Lucifer waves his knife.

I groan, putting out my hands, there is no point fighting it. I can't escape and I'm going to die in a few days. It won't make a difference if I'm missing another finger. Chances are when I die there won't be a body to look at. Lucifer's eyes sparkle. "Huh, given up, have we?" He smiles. I have tried everything. I can't do any more. I'm utterly useless. Lucifer has it all figured out to the very words I'm going to say, quite literally. My hope has officially been crushed. A miracle couldn't save us at this point. Lucifer grabs my left hand. "One, two, three, four." He puts his blade to each finger in turn. I tense up, waiting for him to pick one. He holds my hand in the air, draws back the blade and swipes. Muffling my scream, I clutch my hand, he narrowly avoided my thumb and took my index finger. Lucifer smiles as I fight the burning hot tears dripping down my face. "You'll also notice, I've taken one finger per day, no matter how annoying you've been to deserve more."

"It's been three days?" I whimper, fighting the pain.

"Humans are stupid, aren't you? Yes, three Earth days. You'll be telling them I'm taking a finger per day of captivity." He passes over the finger along with the pinky I lost yesterday. "Put them in your sock, so you can show them." He places them in my palm.

"How…" I start.

"Socks are a secure, small space for you to hold them." Lucifer explains. "It's simple. Now, let's get started on your lines." His eyes light up, sending a shiver down my spine.

I sit back in the cell, holding the camera. The briefing was short; I can only say things that will help Lucifer. Therefore, lies and other misleading things. For example, my hands; that was specific. A finger a day, then if they don't arrive after ten days, it'll be my toes. I wish he had started with them; toes aren't as important as fingers. I didn't get to see the warlock; a demon went to Earth and got it done while Lucifer prepped me. There is a crack on the lens to make it convincing that I 'scavenged it'. The little light bleeps red, I could just not talk to them? I could leave it, but I don't think Lucifer will let me do that. Lucifer got another light added, if it's green they are online too and can hear me.

I take a deep breath and leave the camera next to me on the bed while I repair my finger. I disinfect, sew and wrap it up like Wendy had done to the other one. I have a new bag of items from the warlock. I smile at the bottle of vodka; I hate the warlock for fixing the camera, but I can't complain about the alcohol. I take the half full one and an apple. I sit and wait, hopefully they won't check the footage, but I know Lucifer wouldn't be going to all this trouble if he thought it wouldn't work. He knows they will check it. I sigh, chugging the bottle.

I giggle, the empty vodka bottle sitting next to me. I smile lazily at the cracked camera, the light is still red. I can't start at the beginning when it turns green; Lucifer said they'll work out that I knew when they were on and offline. I decided to talk pointlessly till the green light appears. "You know... alcohol helps." I slur, to the little screen. "A lot better than painkillers." I chuckle, the fresh stub of my finger numb with pain. I should have taken this approach before. I jump, a green light blaring in my eyes. I drop the camera on the floor. I laugh, they picked up. They are on the other end of the camera. They can see me. I pick up the fingernail sized camera. "I'm so clumsy." I shake my head. "It's the missing fingers." I wave my free hand at the screen revealing the ugly, fresh finger stubs. "Have I said that already? I don't even know if you can hear me." I lie fluently, even while drunk. Mind-control doesn't lessen with alcohol, damn it. "I lose a finger every day!" I complain. "He just slices it off, one second it's here, the next it's gone. Goodbye finger." I pluck the sock. "See, Fingers." I chuck it aside. "Next it'll be my toes, then my ears." I add the detail about the ears myself; the mind-control or the booze made me do it.

"If you care." I slump down on the bed. "Lucifer is going to kill us all. We can't win." I think aloud. "Unless you are watching, I can tell you everything!" I emphasise my point unintentionally. "He's smart. He's going to use me to burst open the gates to Hell. To think we almost died closing them..." I hiccup. "Now it was all for nothing!" I shouldn't be doing this drunk; I'll try not to be next time. "It's hard to believe how times have changed. Last week I was at school, now I'm in a prison cell in Hell. Lucifer told me how we are all going to die, I met Asmodeus, I killed a couple of demons, I thought I saw Tessa." I shrug. Looks like I can tell some of the truth, if it doesn't hurt Lucifer's plan. "You probably don't care about what happened to me. Lucifer is going to…" Vomit churns in my stomach, I grab the disgusting bucket and throw up.

I turn back to the camera, wiping my mouth. I'm going to have a terrible hangover, at least my sleep will be dreamless for once. "Where was I?" I struggle to focus. "Asmodeus was an asshole, I only met him for three minutes." I shake my head, holding up two of the three fingers on my left hand. "Oh, I forgot I was missing one more." I correct the amount. "Lucifer killed him. Apparently, he could join you guys, so Lucifer ended his life. I was there so Lucifer could demonstrate what would happen to me if I tried to disobey him. He didn't do a good job." I chuckle. "I stole the camera. It was a good idea." My eyes droop, I struggle to stay awake. "Lucifer tells me more and more of his plan every day." Lucifer said I had to keep them guessing, miss out a few things, only tell them so much fake useful information. He wants to prevent their visit for a couple of days, which means a couple more fingers. Apparently, knowledge of my torture and fake information in small doses means he can track the exact hour when the big showdown will happen. The bastard is crazy, he has some sort of psychic power. My eyes droop, I open my mouth try to speak. "Good luck." I can't tell them any more fake facts; my mouth won't let me. I yawn, drifting off into a deep sleep.

I wake up gasping, clutching my neck, the skin remains untorn. I sigh in relief, slumping against the wall. It was a dream; stress has made sleep my own personal Hell and when I wake, I'm still here in actual Hell. I splash water onto my face, briefly relieving my head from immense throbbing pain and kicking my brain into action. I look at the empty bottles, I should have saved some. Last night is foggy, I probably fed them the worst bullshit ever. I grab a banana and attempt to swallow a chunk. I hate them but I can't be picky, and the fruit will go bad first. I would hate to have the smell of rotten fruit in my cell. The stench of vomit and piss is bad enough. My throat burns as it goes down. I look down at the camera lying on my floor. I pick it up, the green light isn't on. I could break it, but Lucifer would only get it fixed. Also, I cannot do anything that won't help him. Squishing it under my boot counts, unfortunately. If I repeatedly stomp on it maybe it counts as more than one act. I drop the chip on the ground... A small demon appears at my gate. I frown.

"Again?" The door opens, a non-speaking demon. I am fine with that. "Can I have a minute? I'll go up by myself." I wave it away. "I don't have anywhere to go, do I?"

To my surprise the demon listens, it unlocks the door and wanders off. I look down at the chip, my shoe hovers. I curse, picking it up. What can I do with it? I can't ignore it, Lucifer made sure of that. There must be a way I can help them. I don't expect them to be able to save me, I know that isn't realistic, but even giving them a little true information would be amazing, so they don't all die too. I could sneak the chip into the throne room; I can't say anything, but Lucifer can. He loves to boast about how smart he is and if something were to slip out... I tuck it into my pocket and step out of the cell. I slam the door shut and turn to the staircase. I pause... I can only do actions that please him, and I did all of that without an issue. If I can take this with me, he wants me to do it. I'll be helping him. Then again, if I change my mind and don't do it, that could help him too. He knows which decision I'm going to make, he has probably thought out this very moment. I hover... which is the right choice? I curse, I go back to the cell and chuck the camera back inside. It lands on the bed. I march upstairs before I can change my mind again.

Lucifer grins at my presence tauntingly. "Did it go well yesterday?"

I grumble. "For you." I wince at the light; Hell is dark and dreary, yet there are a dozen more torches lighting up the room today.

"Hangover, huh? Apparently, light makes it worse." Lucifer answers my thoughts. He knows I have a hangover. I'm not going to ask how he knows, that is giving him the opportunity to gloat.

I snatch the collar. I could run off with it, run out those doors and attempt to smash it. I dismiss the idea, it's terrible. Nor would the mind-control allow me to do it.

Cradling my hand, blood pools from my finger. The silver bone glimmering from it. Tears burn in my eyes; it is not getting easier each time he takes one. "Go." Lucifer says, now that he is finished using me.

A demon grabs my arm and yanks me away before I can walk myself. I pull away, storming off in front of the demon with my head down, hoping to hide my tears. I offered him my hand, to pick one, but that wasn't enough for him, he had to wait until my back was turned. He enjoys the game, more than he likes to actually hurt me.

The demon slams the door behind me and leaves. I grab the bandages, trying to fix up the wound as best I can with the materials I have. My entire hand throbs. Despite half my fingers being missing, it feels like they are still there. I stop wrapping up the thick wad of bandages, I can barely move my wrist with the amount. I fight the jolting pain and pick up the book. I've read a quarter of it using the dictionary. It gets easier as I learn more Latin. At least there is one benefit to this.

The bars rattle, I look up from my book but there is no one there. I peer through the bars; a demon pounces on the other side. I jump back, landing on my ass. Silven slithers up the bars. "I told you Lucifer would win." I'm dreaming. I rub my eyes hard, trying to force myself to wake up. I widen my eyes, trying to force the real ones to pop open. Silven's hand passes over the lock. She opens the door. "Lucifer always wins, he's the king." Her tongue flickers. "You shouldn't be the one who gets to be by his side." A scaly hand reaches out from my neck. I step back, drawing my knife. My fingers fumble and it skids along the floor.

I draw another, gripping it tightly in my palm. Dream or not, I'm not letting her kill me. I've dealt with enough bullshit the last few days. Silven chuckles at the switchblade in my hand. "Adorable." She plucks the blade, tip first, out my grasp. I ball up my fist and go to punch her in the face. She catches it, smiling. I can't even win in my dreams. Silven's hand wraps around my throat, they always go for the throat, at least my dreams got that right. I'm choking; if I die, I'll wake up. Silven's spare hand touches my face. "I should be by his side enjoying the victory and there is still one way I can do it." She smiles, eyes lighting up. She releases her grasp, she's not going to kill me; she's going to possess me. Scaly fingers reach for my scalp, I grab her wrist and flip her over my arm. I smile, Colt taught me that move. Scooping up a knife I stab her in the arm. She howls. "You little bastard." Snarling, she kicks me into the wall. I groan, my back throbbing. Silven lifts the switchblade over my head. Holding onto her hands, I stop it moving downward into my chest. She howls, I lose my grip on the blade. Closing my eyes and shielding my face I wait for impact. Nothing. I count to twenty in my head before peeping out from my hands. The knife lies on the ground and the blade isn't out. The door remains closed and Silven is nowhere to be seen. I touch my neck, I can't feel any bruises. It's a dream, I should be waking up. Silven is dead. My heart pounds, Silven couldn't have gone inside me. It's impossible. I try to prise my eyes open into the real world… it doesn't work. I gently prick my skin with the knife, barely enough to draw blood. I wince in real pain. I'm awake… Looking closely at the handle I search for marks. Normally demons leave some sort of grubby fingerprints, but there aren't any. Silven was never here and I'm wide awake…

A scream, I look up. Wendy stands before my eyes, her face dripping away like candle wax. I join her scream with my own, jumping to my feet. I'm hallucinating. I cover my eyes, it's not real! The hairs on my arms rise, feeling a warm hand touch it. It's not real…

Lucifer

I watch the demons light up the room with extra torches. I secure one onto the side of the throne, near where she'll be standing. She'll arrive with an awful hangover. A warlock prepared her bag, warlocks love alcohol, and she is at an all-time low, which equals getting drunk, in human terms. Abby walks in, eyes droopy; she looks much worse than yesterday. "Did it go well yesterday?" I ask, although I already know the answer.

"For you." She murmurs under her breath miserably.

"Hangover? Apparently, lights make it worse." I watch her squint, trying to hide the fact that she is in incredible pain. The girl snatches the collar from my hand wordlessly. She doesn't even bother to ask how I know. Abby's hope is squashed like rotten fruit, it's beautiful to see. I smile, her hand moves to her pocket, hesitates and stops. She left the camera in the room. She wouldn't risk it; she has figured out that I know everything. It doesn't matter either way, the cell signal blockers are up. They won't understand what she is saying. I just wanted to squash her hopes a little more and make her realise that she can't stop me.

Silently, she accepts the demons' energy, one after the other. No arguments or complaints, rather boring to be honest. The twenty demons I personally selected zap into the collar. She detaches it herself after the last one is done and passes it over. She puts out her hands, waiting for me to cleave one off. I miss the arguments, I always do, after they give in, but it makes my life easier. I sigh, the fingers look less appealing when she is waiting for me to do it.

"Not today." I wave for her to leave.

She frowns. "Yeah, right." She waves her hands in my face. "Just get it over with. One a day, you said it yourself."

"Nope, you have listened today. They won't be bothered to count your fingers." Again, I motion for her to leave.

She nods. She turns around to leave. I draw a knife. Silly girl, I chuck the blade. The blade gracefully arcs through the air. It swings around sideways, swiping the second pinky. I have decided to leave her thumbs for now. She howls in surprise. She clutches her hand; the blood loss can't be good for her. I should have started with toes, then she would struggle to walk. I'll start on her toes tomorrow, she'll be useless with no fingers and need assistance from a demon to eat, drink and generally live. I don't have that time to waste. The girl scoops up the finger and leaves. I might need to get another doctor in, I thought Enzo would have taught her first aid properly. I guess he always thought he would be there to help. I chuckle, clutching the collar. A few more days, then it won't matter how they plan to take me down, I'll be too powerful for them to comprehend. Mine and Asmodeus' power combined already matches Alex's. The fiery sparks flicker in my hands.

Tomorrow I'm going to use Abby to open up the portal. I don't plan to go to Earth and start the battle myself. I work better in my own territory. Also, they will think that they are a step ahead of me by bringing the battle to Hell. Not only that, I can't be bothered to keep Abby alive until I kill them all. I'll use her while I have her. Nothing is going to stop me.

I motion for a demon to come to my side. I present the list. "I will need these demons for tomorrow."

I would take them all at once, get Abby's job over and done with, but it could break her like the first time. Small, constant doses are what I have allowed time for. There are a few dukes and duchesses that need killing tomorrow before the portal opening process. I allowed them to live on the stipulation that they always work for me. They should have been smart enough not to bow down to Alex, but they did. They will suffer the price of their weakness. Silven is the only one who deserved the title.

I hear a scream from down in the cells, echoing through the castle. Abby, I guess all that lack of sleep, food and water, as well blood loss, stress and pain has finally caused her to hallucinate. Hell makes humans go crazy, and that process for Abby has just begun with one scream. I stride across to my throne, taking a deep breath. This throne is what I want the most. Ruling Hell is a privilege I took for granted, and I'll do it again once Alex is gone.

CHAPTER NINETEEN

Enzo

I serve dinner to the new gaggle invading my home. Hayden takes plates for himself and Esmeralda upstairs. Holly, Selena and Colt eat together in the kitchen. Holly is pissed at me, but I can live with that. Selena is getting into our business and asking more questions than we can possibly answer. She can stay, but there is no way I'm taking her into Hell. She'll see one demon and die of fright, and Holly will blame me for the mistake. She's struggling with the information she has now; she is trying to support Holly, which is sweet, but she's been flinching at every noise or movement. She's scared of us and hiding it terribly.

Flint is talking to Jade in the dining room. He came back with an evaluation of the knife used on Hayden and Esmeralda. It's nothing too special, a common knife from Hell used to temporarily paralyse victims.

I check my phone; Alex hasn't responded to my message. The front door slams, I walk in the front room to Alex. "Hey." She smiles.

"Was coming through the door for effect or did you actually go for a walk?"

"Effect." Alex smiles. "I'd never walk around aimlessly unless I had time and a bottle of whiskey, of which I had neither. I went to a cafe."

I laugh. "When did the club translate to cafe?"

"It doesn't. I actually went to a cafe for the wifi and the coffee. I thought I'd try it out before I die, never again." She pulls out a laptop from her bag. "Where are the others?"

"They are eating, Flint is on a call. Why?"

"Come with me." She ushers me upstairs. Pulling me into my room, she sits at the desk. She opens the laptop.

"When did you take Colt's laptop?"

"Before I left. I looked at the camera's program because I was stuck, and the connection suddenly started working. Abby found the camera." Alex clicks on the app. "I saved the video."

Abby has the camera in her possession? She has some guts stealing that without Lucifer noticing. Alex plays the video. Abby is mid-sentence and drops the camera. The image is fuzzy and as she talks, we can barely make out any words.

"How does this help?" I ask. "No offence, but I have no idea what she is doing."

"I know it's crap, but look." Alex pauses the video, increasing the resolution, the image becoming slightly clearer. I can make out her body shape, just. Her hand is in view, most of it is bandaged, I think. I see one finger unwrapped, some of it is missing.

"Shit." I curse.

"From the state of her hands and which fingers are covered. I'd say she is missing four fingers, the same number of days she's been down there and listen, she's drunk."

The muffled voice also has a dragging tone to it, definitely like someone who is drunk. I can't blame her for being drunk in her situation. I probably would be too. It's oddly nice of Lucifer to have given her alcohol. I imagine he got someone else to collect supplies for her, and they deemed that a necessity. If I could, I'd thank them; it's probably the only thing keeping her from going insane. The small clip ends with a blur of either a wall or the ceiling.

"She's being tortured." Alex shakes her head.

"I know." We were stupid to think Lucifer would leave her in the cell until he needed her. If Holly or Colt see this, they will insist on going to get her right now, no matter the sacrifice.

Alex rolls back the clip and freezes it. There are purple pixelated wounds on her arms and around the neck. "It looks like he's testing the limits of the human ability to live off adrenaline. She looks half dead." Alex looks at the image on the screen. "My blood only does so much, Enzo. Even if it can regrow fingers, I don't think they'll all come back. After a certain time, the damage becomes permanent."

"Which means we can wait, let her lose a few more fingers, some permanently, and go in with a good plan or rush in without a plan and try to save her while we can."

"Exactly, we have to choose whether Abby gets her fingers back or not. I mean, we still don't know where he plans to get his power from."

"We can't help, can we?" I drag my hands through my hair.

"Well, that's questionable." Alex pulls out a wad of paper from the back pocket of her jeans. "I have the morphing spell, sort of. I wrote as much as I could remember, which is the ingredients, but I don't have the instructions. I've been trying to figure it out, but I still don't know what I need to do with it."

"But if we work it out, one of us could go down and get her?"

"Technically, but it could take days to get close enough without Lucifer noticing and if he knows we have it, he'll expect us to use it."

"I think making the entire thing explode was his back-up to make sure we didn't get it. Even if he expects us to use it, we should try to fix it. It's worth the risk."

"Alright… but we better work fast. Not just for Abby's sake." Alex opens up a new tab on the computer and clicks on the news. A hospital, everyone inside is dead. A gas leak apparently. One doctor is unaccounted for, but the rest are certainly dead. Doctors, nurses and patients. Demons, they are already at it. I didn't think things could get much worse.

"Let me guess, we get food and alcohol, and stay up all night trying to get the potion to work?"

"Exactly that." Alex smiles, she takes out her phone. "Ah, sorry. I just got your message. Nice to know you missed me."

"Do you want me to get Flint?"

"No. His worry will cloud his judgement. Tell him to go home and be with his kids while he still can." Alex sighs.

I walk downstairs. Holly looks up from her seat. "What did Alex want? Did she find something?" Her eyes light up hopefully.

"It was a dead end." I lie. "We are trying to come up with new ideas. If you want, you can train or read books about Lucifer; the more you know, the more helpful you'll be." I offer. That will keep them busy for a little while. I turn to Colt. "Can you make brownies?"

Colt laughs then his face falls. "Wait, you are serious? Last time I almost burned down the kitchen! You said I was banned for life unless I was supervised."

"What did you do?" Selena asks.

"I was trying to make a microwave lava cake and I accidentally left a spoon in the cup." Colt explains. I shake my head, the mess was extraordinary. Colt used blood as the sauce, and it went all over the kitchen. It looked like Colt had tried to cook someone in the microwave. I remember it was more than one spoon, he told me he kept losing them in the cup and just left them there. "How many was it really?"

"Three." Colt admits. "Can I really cook?"

I smirk, I didn't realise he missed it so much. I wave my hand and a recipe appears in Colt's hand. The edges of the page are burnt, I'm still getting the hang of the amount of magic I'm using. "Knock yourself out." I have more problems to deal with than a potentially destroyed kitchen.

Flint enters the room, tucking away his phone. "What can I do?"

"You can go home; if you think of anything text Alex, but we have zero new leads on Lucifer's plan." Flint's ears twitch. He is listening to my heart rate to see if I'm lying. I don't blame him, I'm not completely trustworthy after being under Lucifer's influence. He won't find it spikes enough to think that I'm lying. I have learned how to tame it after years of practice around supernaturals.

"Are you sure?" Flint checks. "I can stay. Jade said the kids have finally settled down."

"And this may be the last few days you have with them. Go have fun." I create a portal. "See you later."

"Alright." He grumbles, feeling unwanted. Alex has a point; Flint's heart is endless, which means he can make unwise decisions. He disappears.

I get back upstairs, creating a chair to sit beside Alex. I put down the bottle of whiskey. Before I can pour, a glass materialises in her hand with a slice of lime and ice. She stares at Abby on the screen. "Watching it over?" I ask. The video we just watched playing on the screen.

"Yeah, thought I might as well while I wait."

"Find anything?"

Alex nods. "Do you see her neck? I'm guessing a shock collar, or something similar. The fresher marks aren't as prominent. I think he over-used it the first time."

"Yeah, he got a little trigger happy." The bandages are gone from her neck, unlike the last time we saw her. There are cuts, but they are not caused by a blade, as well as thick dark bruises and a rash that looks almost gone. "Why isn't she wearing it permanently?"

"I guess to stop himself from going too far again?" Alex guesses. "Or the rash; maybe she is allergic to the metal? That could be torture in itself. Maybe he kept it on too long the first time, and she almost died?"

"Good point. It would have to be some sort of metal from Hell." I can't imagine that many people are allergic to steel or copper. If Abby were allergic, it would have come up in conversation at some point. Lucifer would want to cause the most pain possible, which means the highest charge for electricity. "Zinc, Aluminium, Nickel, Osmium?"

"Osmium is Lucifer's favourite metal; it was in a lot of his books. It's very conductive." Alex agrees. "It irritates human skin." Alex squints at the screen. "That poor girl. I've seen people be decapitated with a collar made of that stuff."

"Thank the devil he needs her." I mutter under my breath, pouring out my own drink.

"Yeah, or we'd be getting a body on our doorstep." She sighs sadly. "Why even torture her? He's risking her life and his freedom, for what? He can't enjoy it that much, he'd have to stop before getting to do anything really fun."

"He hasn't killed anyone in ten years. I think he would torture a squirrel if he had one, even if it could save his life."

She snorts. "Yeah." She shakes the thought out of her mind. "He killed an entire hospital in two days." Sending demons to a hospital to kill the sick is low. Demons don't care if their victims are sick, old or young. If they have a pulse, they are free game.

"There was one doctor unaccounted for. Wendy Rodgers. They attacked a hospital the same day that Abby needed medical attention?"

"The doctor is probably dead then. She did a good job on Abby's hands." Alex praises the surgeon.

A knock on the door. "I'm coming in." Colt calls. Alex switches the screen to the news article. Colt walks in, smiling. "Oh, you are at the desk. Good. Brownies are done." He presents the plate. The edges are burnt yet, somehow, the middle dips and looks very uncooked. He puts the plate down. "That is where my laptop went. I thought we could look to see if the camera is still active."

"It's not, but we will keep an eye on it." Alex lies outright to his face quickly before I can say anything.

"Oh. I sort of need it for something."

"Use mine." I offer. "We already have a bunch of tabs open."

Colt nods slowly. "What? Are there demon e-books on the internet? What are you looking at?"

"Lucifer at work." Alex motions the news article. "He sent demons to take out an entire hospital."

Colt's eyes widen, staring at the pictures on the screen. "Geez. I'll leave you two to it." He leaves the room and the brownies.

I glare at Alex. "You thought I was going to tell him."

"You weren't? I could tell you wanted to. The only reason we didn't die ten years ago was because the minimal amount of people knew about the real plan."

She has a point, I want to tell Colt, of course. He will kill me if he finds out I left him in the dark, but I care about him and want him to live. I will not tell him unless it is to his benefit. "I swear, I won't say a word."

Alex smiles. "Good." She plucks a brownie; she sparks magic and it instantly cooks. She bites into it. "This is amazing." I reach for one, she slaps my hand. "They're mine."

I chuckle, magic moving the plate, leaning in for a kiss. "Nice try." She grabs the plate. In her brief moment of distraction, I pluck the brownie out of her hand and bite into it.

She smirks. "Fair play." She pulls out the list of experiment ingredients.

We stand at my workbench in the adjoining room, Alex swigs her whiskey. I pick out the ingredients from the shelves. We had to translate it to English. With all the ingredients lined up, we add them to a broth, boiling them over water. The thick grey sludge doesn't look right. I add the werewolf claw that the recipe insisted upon.

"The old test tubes had an orange liquid in them." Alex frowns. "What did we do wrong?"

"You think I know? We followed it exactly." I wave the ingredients list. The werewolf claw was the last thing on it.

Alex sighs, looking over at the foul-smelling liquid. "We need this to work." She takes the pages, reading them carefully. "I swear I didn't forget any of the ingredients. Did we put them in the wrong order, does that matter?"

I look at the bubbling liquid on top of the small burner. I take the pot and chuck it in the bin with three other failed attempts. "It does sometimes, but I have cross-referenced all these other potions using similar ingredients and put them in the same order."

"What do we do now?"

I stare at the pages of potions I have collected over the years that cover the entire workbench and floor. "We've been looking at it wrong. This wasn't done by a warlock or a witch, it was made by Lucifer in Hell, but we are using human fire in the burner, and warlock magic to mix the ingredients."

"Hell doesn't have magic." Alex frowns.

"But you can do that thing where you use all four elements at once, that's the closest thing to it."

Alex nods. "Alright." Alex flicks her hand, the fire changes, turning into hot red hellfire. "Walk me through it."

I talk her through the steps as she brews the potion by herself and mixes the ingredients together. She adds all the ingredients slowly until the last step. Alex uses her power on it. The liquid changes colour to orange. I pick it up and pour some in a test tube. "Looks like it worked."

"One way to find out." Alex glances in my direction.

"You have got to be kidding me. You want me to test it?" I should have seen that coming.

"If we have done it right, it should be perfectly harmless." Alex smiles.

That's true, and if we have done it wrong? There are many possibilities of what could happen, none of them are good. "Fine. We need DNA from another creature." I pluck a hair from my head and put it in. That's for turning me back. Alex adds something else to a different test tube. Shaking it, the colour gets brighter. I swap tubes with Alex.

"What did you put in there?" I ask in concern; it didn't look like hair.

"One way to find out." Her eyes sparkle. "Wait, we need more space." She snaps her fingers, creating a portal.

"Why? How big is the creature you're turning me into?"

I walk through the portal with her. We appear in a clearing in a large forest.

"It'll be fine now. Drink it."

"I'm going to regret trusting you one day." I roll my eyes, looking down at the liquid. I down the contents like a shot. Shuddering, I close my eyes. My throat burns like I've just downed a litre of vodka. My hand spasms, skin changing colour. Pain throbs over my body. I double over, the muscles under my skin moving. Panting, I fall to the ground. My body is transforming. The pain is worse than changing into a Hellhound. Groaning, I judder on the ground. My bones snap over the sound of my howl. "Are you okay?" Alex asks.

I jolt, the pain subsiding. I groan, voice hoarse. Alex laughs. "Holy shit, it worked."

Sparks fly out my mouth as I try to speak. My body fills up most of the clearing. Alex holds a giant mirror and moves it so I can see my face. My eyes widen; she picked dragon DNA. My black wings fan out, covering the ground. One wrong move and I'll take down a dozen trees. There are a few dragons in Hell, but they don't come out of their caves often. Most people, and demons for that matter, believe they are mythical. I howl, fire flaring out my mouth. She laughs. "I'm honestly very impressed. I wasn't sure how well it would work."

I glare at her, it's a good thing it did work. I'd rather not be a half human, half dragon mix.

My huge claws dig into the mud, big enough to lift boulders. My magic won't work, dragons don't have that sort of ability. I look in the mirror again, the scaly dragon looking back at me, bright orange eyes burning. One of the dragon's horns is cut, like my own and it has the scar across its left eye. It's unlikely the dragon has those same features, but the formula is close enough with the time we have.

"I think it was quite successful. I mean it would be good to know if you can fly." Alex grins.

I sigh, I should have seen that coming. I lower a wing for her to climb on, she grabs the edge and flips herself up onto my back.

Batting my wings, I fly up into the sky. Sweeping over the top of the trees; flying is a lot easier than I thought. There are mountains ahead, I soar upward. The wind hits my face, fighting against me. Alex laughs on my back, my wings steady as I reach a stable height. My wings cut through the clouds. I can feel Alex walk across my wings, balancing gracefully. I turn to the side, throwing her off balance. She flies to the right, falling off the edge. Clinging to my wing, she howls, swinging back on. "You bastard." I feel her climb up my neck, she holds the potion bottle. If she feeds me that, we'll go crashing down. No, I will. She doesn't need me to fly. I could use magic, but by the time I transformed back it would be too late. I jolt my head away, Alex pours the liquid in. The hot burning sensation takes over my body. Falling, I soar downward. Wheezing, I clutch my ribs. The scales slowly disappear, tears stream down my face in a mixture of air resistance and pain. The air moves too fast to catch a breath. Alex flies down too, not even trying to save herself. Graciously, she flips in the air, hair flying around her. Chances are she's done this a million times before. The trees grow bigger, the pain throbbing through my body. A portal appears in the air, I drop right through it.

Halting to a stop, I land on human feet in my bedroom. My head is spinning, I grab onto the wall for support. Magic sparks from my fingertips and clothes appear on my body. "Damn it." Alex complains.

I roll my eyes. "It works. Painful as hell, but it works."

"That's good. We finally have something useful."

"What do you want to do with it?" I rub the back of my neck, clicking it back into place. "I don't think turning us into dragons is the answer to all our problems."

"That would be amazing to see, and we'd definitely have a better chance, but you're right, it's not." Alex pulls out her phone. "But if one of us were to become a demon, they should be able to walk around in Hell no problem." She puts her phone on the desk. "We could find out what Lucifer is doing."

"That's risky. You're right, Lucifer doesn't make mistakes. If he knows we'd try this, chances are whoever did it will be walking into a trap."

"I know, that's why we have to convince Tina to do it."

At that, a portal opens up. Tina walks through, scowling at the two of us, holding her phone up. "Alex, you can't be serious?" She looks back at the message. "This plan is awful." Shaking her head. "If I got caught, Lucifer would hack my head off and I'd like to keep it."

"I thought you said, you believed I would win? If that's true, you'll do it."

"Don't try that trick on me. Believing I'll live on your side is completely different than believing in this plan."

"Tina, you think everything I do is a bad idea.

So, if you can think of a better one, I'll do it. If not, well..." Alex holds up the potion bottle as her eyes dance.

She groans. "I'm going to regret this, aren't I? You owe me big time for this. I'm talking about my own private island, and shit."

"Obviously." Alex smiles, pouring the liquid into the small vials.

"How will I contact you?" Tina asks.

"Your phone." I wave for her to pass it over.

"Do you honestly think that is a good idea? Alex told me the camera footage was fuzzy."

"So? This is a phone." I send sparks flying over the screen. "I'm equipping it to work in Hell."

"It won't matter. He's probably blocking the signal; he knows our advantage is technology. It's the only thing we know more about than him. He would cover himself with that. Lucifer has Enzo's phone, right? I bet if you text him, it won't deliver."

Alex grabs her phone and types out a message. "You're right."

"Likewise, I bet if you rewind the camera footage, you'll find out while Asmodeus is walking to the castle, the picture will be clear as the day and only messed up once he entered the palace."

"I just assumed I messed up the signal from Hell to Earth. I'm still getting used to the new amount of power." I pass back the phone.

"Well, I'm right which means I'm going to have to leave the castle regularly to give you information or take the cell jammers down without anyone noticing, which we know is near impossible. So, don't expect live updates." She pockets the phone. "Wait, where do I store it? Do demons wear clothes, or bags to hold items?"

"No, hide it somewhere in the building. I need a hair strand or something." She waves for Tina to pass it over.

Tina rolls her eyes, giving her the hair strand. "Nice to know you've thought of everything. What type of demon are you turning me into? Better be a good one, nothing slimy."

"I don't know." Alex pulls out a blade, covered in blood. She puts a few flakes of dry blood in another vial. "Hopefully one with fingers."

Tina shakes her head, cracking a smile. "If I weren't drunk, I'd be running for the hills by now." She takes the vials, magicking a satchel. She puts in her phone and the vial to turn her back. She picks up the one to turn her into a demon. "I can't believe I'm turning myself into a demon for you. This is beyond friendship. Also, know if anything happens to me down there, I will take my revenge out on you."

"Understood." Alex smiles.

"Is there anything I should know before I take this? Maybe how to fit in with the demons?"

"Praise Lucifer and eat hell worms competitively; it's like drinking for them. Do whatever Lucifer asks, play a few harmless pranks on other demons. Nothing big, they find anything funny."

"And make fun of you and Enzo?" Tina grins.

"Low blow, but yeah. Oh, and boast about all the people you've killed." Alex nods.

"Alright…" She groans, looking down at the vial wearily. "Fuck it." She downs the contents, holding her nose. Coughing, she splutters, doubling over. "You bitch, you didn't say it would be this painful."

"Yeah, I may have left that out on purpose, take it as punishment for all the shit you'll say about us in Hell." Alex smirks.

I roll my eyes, Tina collapses to the ground, skin boiling over, turning into a demon.

Tina stands, shaking her head. "This is awful." Her voice croaks. She looks like a typical mid-range demon; she has scales, a semi-human body and small horns. "Open the portal before I change my mind."

Alex whisks her hand, the portal opening. "You'll arrive by the back entrance. Good luck."

"I'll need it." Tina disappears through the portal.

"Do you think it'll work?" I ask.

"Not sure, but if anyone can do it, it's Tina. It's one of the only things going for us, speaking of which, we should check the camera footage."

Ten re-plays later, we stare at the screen. Abby is still on the bed, meaning she hasn't figured out the bed is giving her nightmares. I can't blame her, she probably believes the situation is causing them. Besides, it doesn't look like she has spent much of her time sleeping. There isn't much more to get from the video, it's too blurry to see anything else.

A distorted scream cuts off my thoughts. "What the hell was that?" Alex opens up a new tab, it's the camera's view. The live footage is running in the background of the computer. The camera is facing a blank wall or the ceiling. Abby screams, the camera view shakes. "Is he torturing her?" Lucifer isn't the type of man who would torture a person in their cell. He would do it somewhere the demons could watch, to make it that much more sickening.

A glimpse of Abby appears, she is shielding her face shaking. "Stay away!" She begs.

Leaning closer, I don't see anyone else in the footage. Abby's distorted figure disappears from the screen. She howls out in anger. "Go away! You aren't real! You can't be." There is no one else in the footage. Abby's figure dives, avoiding nothing. The screen goes black except for one corner. I can make out the shape of arms reaching out, possibly a knife in Abby's hands.

"What the hell is she doing?" I panic, holding my breath.

She murmurs something I don't understand. The knife drops from her hand, she waves her arms in the air. I assume she's punching something, but I can't see what she is aiming at. It looks like nothing is there. "She's hallucinating."

"No, she is playing imaginary games with knives like a small child." Alex rolls her eyes. "Yeah, Hell has finally gotten to her. Lucifer should have taken those knives off her."

"But that only adds to his excitement, doesn't it?" Lucifer knows her knives can't harm him so doesn't see the point of taking them off her. It's dangerous for her to be hallucinating while wielding knives, she could kill herself.

"If he doesn't want her to die, he'll take them by tomorrow. He needs her alive, so if she does die, he'd have to contact me for help which won't be all bad." She has a point, but Lucifer isn't stupid. We won't let Abby die, we can't really bargain with him.

"Abby should pass out at some point… I'll leave it on, but I don't think this will give us any information."

It sounds like she is crying through the microphone. She is speaking to the camera, I can barely make out the words she is saying but it sounds like a plea for help. Alex pulls out a notepad and starts scribbling down words. I watch Alex write down words 'light, please, help, Silven, Wendy, I can't and collar.'

The audio ends, and all we can see is a pixelated blur. My heart drops in my chest. We can't get there any quicker. Saving her isn't a flick of a hand, a portal journey and back. I feel awful for her, but there is no-one to blame. I'm sure Abby was desperate to visit Hell without knowing the consequences she could face. Or more likely, she didn't realise how painful it would be. Abby is strong for a human, most would have left when they found out Holly was a werewolf or at least taken time to process the situation.

"Well, can we get anything out from that?" I ask.

"Nothing useful." Alex passes over a book. "Read this."

I pick up the book. It's a scientific article about what would happen if a human could make it to Hell. First day, feeling of terror. Second day, giving up. Third and fourth day, hallucinations and suicidal thoughts. Fifth day, false sense of reality. By the seventh day, if they make it that long, dying of insanity.

I wave at the book. "Why are you only showing this to me now?"

"Not to put any pressure on us to save her. Luckily, Abby is a day behind this schedule." Alex turns back to the video. "Chances are everything she has told us is a lie. An illusion she's made up."

"True. I still think we should use it. She may unintentionally say something useful but let's focus on the first clip where she is talking to us." Alex changes the video back. Putting it slightly before where we started watching it.

We watch it over again. Alex shakes her head. "All I'm getting is her asking for us to hurry up."

"She wouldn't go through all that trouble to steal it only to tell us to rush." Abby wouldn't half-ass her chance at freedom, not after risking it to get the camera.

"There might be a little more to it, but I don't understand, do you?"

"No, can you see the video you haven't saved?" I ask. Most live cameras have a back-up where it can store old footage. It would be odd if this one didn't.

Alex frowns, looking through the old videos. "It won't let me see past yesterday. Any footage of Asmodeus is gone. There's nothing there."

"What?" I frown. "That can't be right."

"Look." Alex speeds it forward to Abby. "The screen doesn't even have a crack in it after it fell. That isn't very realistic and then with the missing footage..."

"You think it's a different camera?" I ask. "But how is it connected to this computer?"

"It could be the same one but it's been fixed."

Abby wouldn't have the skill or equipment to fix it let alone improve it. Lucifer had something to do with it. "Lucifer fixed the camera."

"Exactly, but why? He puts up cell jammers, why let her talk to us?"

"To torment us. We can hear enough to listen to her pleas for help, but we can't make out his plan." Alex explains. "He's messing with us and Abby. She lied, she told us she found it. He's using mind-control to make her lie so if we do hear anything it's fake. It also makes her feel like shit."

"Crap!" I rub my face, trying to keep my eyes open. "What do we do now?"

"She can't constantly be lying, she's only lying to us which means there has to be a trigger. Do you think maybe when she's looking at the camera?"

I shake my head; pointing to the words she has written down. Two of them are 'light off'. "What about this? She talks about a light, what if it's some sort of trigger? Maybe it turns on when we are online?"

"But she said, it was off… unless she hallucinated the trigger incorrectly. She could be telling us the truth. Think about it, she only has to tell lies while we are watching."

"Even if we believe that, it's a mighty big assumption. Especially if she is hallucinating what she's telling us. She may believe it's true, but it might not be."

"Well, that's why we have Tina." Alex checks her phone. "Nothing yet, but it's only been an hour or so."

I stare at the words in the notebook. She mentions a woman called 'Wendy', we originally thought we heard wrong, but it's the name of the woman who is unaccounted for at the hospital. She was probably brought to Hell to treat Abby's numerous wounds. It would explain why she isn't dead yet. I taught Abby to do simple first aid, I doubt what I taught her is helping with the injuries Lucifer has caused. I bet Wendy is dead, probably straight after treating Abby's wounds. I sigh, downing the coffee, it tastes strongly of liquor but I'm not complaining. "Please tell me you have a plan."

"I wish." Alex racks her hands through her hair. "At this point going in plan-less might be our best option. We'd die with some dignity. I mean our one lead is garbage and Tina hasn't messaged back. I think we should take on Abby's plan of getting dead drunk."

"I don't think I have enough bottles left for that." I chuckle, slumping back in my seat.

Alex sighs. "I'm done with this video. Give me a book. We still need to find out what Lucifer is doing to get his power. Probably some ancient artefact or something."

An hour later, we sit with all my books over the floor, a dozen empty bottles and no ideas. The amulet of sacrifices was the only artefact known to suck out power from beings, but it doesn't exist anymore. Supernaturals can acquire powerful weapons to gain status, but you are born or turned with the power you have and get stronger with age unless you are Lucifer who just came into being.

"Do you think he's ageing himself faster? You get more powerful as time goes on. If he somehow managed to speed up time for himself, wouldn't he get stronger? There'd be no downside, he doesn't physically age."

"I think time traveling is less ridiculous than that idea." Alex snorts tipsily. "How would that even work?"

"An ageing potion?" I suggest.

"I've never heard of such a potion. People who stopped ageing at a really young or old age just glamour themselves to the age they want to appear."

"I know but what if that was his experiment? He made morphing possible."

"He'd have to work with a witch; Lucifer uses science. Besides, he'd have to age like seventy thousand years to reach anywhere near to my power. I don't think any sort of experiment or potion could do that without dangerous side-effects."

"Fine." I lie on the floor surrounded by books. "We just have to wait now."

Alex eyes droop out of her control before she can reply. Her hand doesn't reach the book before she falls asleep. I groan, standing up. I scoop her up off the floor and put her in the bed. I should sleep too.

Alex's phone buzzes. Tina's name pops up on the screen. "Alex!" I nudge her gently. She stirs but doesn't wake up. I sigh, picking up the phone and opening the message. 'I hate both of you so much. Lucifer just took a bunch of demons into the throne room with Abby. Abby came out but none of the demons did. I mean the demons literally disappeared into thin air. Abby had something to do with it.'

I curse, that doesn't sound good or make sense. The only way to disappear would be to go through a portal, but there isn't one in the castle. He's using Abby for something in his plan. The torture must have something to do with it. I check the camera footage again, it's still pixelated. I assume Tina can't get to the cell jammers. I rewind the video by half an hour from now, I see the throne room. I can make out the distorted shape of the throne. Abby took the camera in with her. I stare at the screen, looking for whatever made the demons disappear.

CHAPTER TWENTY

Abby

A cold breath tingles my cheek, I drop the camera jumping in my place. Silven fades from her position in the corner of my cell and Wendy's boney face is no longer looming over me. The camera helped distract me, even if they weren't watching. I put it down, my eyes catch a glimpse of green. They are online, it's been one second. Unless they were on before, I could have hallucinated the red light. The light turns off. They wouldn't check for just one second. My heart pounds, I could have successfully told them the truth. They might know. Crap, why didn't I tell them more? I bury my face in my hands, fuck. I could have said so much more but, instead, I just moaned about my conditions. I can turn it around; I'm taking the camera with me today.

"Don't do it."

I jump, spinning, but no one is there. Crap. I take a deep breath, I might not get to talk to them honestly again. They probably don't believe me. I told them Silven was alive, which is impossible. I think. They probably thought it was part of the hallucination… could it be? I shake my head, I won't think like that. It's all been real up to this point. I'll bring the camera to prove my point. I clip the small camera to my jeans. I wish they could speak back to me. Taking the camera will be useless if they aren't watching. I pull my shirt, it covers the camera, but if I move it'll show some of what's going on. I take my water and chug it as I wait to be collected.

Finally, I escape the cell. I walk upstairs with a demon escort. A shadow races past out of the corner of my eye. I spin, the demon prods my back. "Keep going." I nod. I clench my shaking hand and ignore the figure looming just out of my sight. It's not real. We walk up the hallway, passing a demon. It knocks me hard in the shoulder. I stumble, we lock eyes, and it winks before continuing on its way. The demon taking me doesn't bat an eye, another hallucination?

We walk up into the throne room. Lucifer smiles, my eyes dart around the room. There are a few demons in the room, but not many. I search their faces for Silven. She's not here, I sigh in relief. "You alright there?" Lucifer chuckles. He must know I'm hallucinating. I feel my jeans unintentionally checking the camera hasn't fallen.

"Yes." I lie, glimpsing over my shoulder quickly.

"Alright, go ahead." He gestures to a demon, passing over the collar. "I'll be back."

I frown, looking around at the demons. Did I hallucinate it, or did Lucifer leave me with them? I guess he isn't needed until he wants to suck the power out of the collar. I could try and leave, but it has never worked before. Lucifer wouldn't leave me unattended if he thought I could escape. There are half a dozen demons in the room. I clip on the collar, at least I have the camera playing. I wince in pain and grab the first demon.

Lucifer returns at the exact moment I'm done. He unclips the collar and chucks it carelessly to another demon. He winks at the demon and it nods. What was that? The demon pulls out the box that the collar was first kept in and starts working on it. I frown, I don't know what is real and what is not anymore.

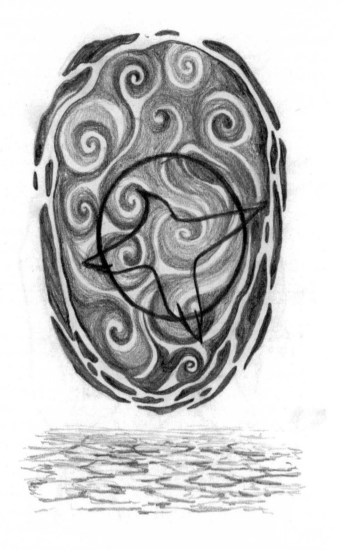

"Come with me." Lucifer waves for me to follow him out the gates. I jog after him, his long legs getting him much further than mine can take me.

We walk right up to the portal. Freedom is right beyond that gateway. He'd stop me before I could make the opening. We must be doing the ritual for his escape. "Wait, you are going for my friends now?" I glance at my pocket, moving the shirt a little. The green light is on, they are getting this. I smile.

"Don't ask questions." Lucifer pulls out a sheet of paper. "Draw this on the portal."

"On the portal?" I take the page. It has a symbol of a bird scrawled across it, much like a crow. It's a vague outline which is good, considering I'm a terrible artist.

"Yes, do it." He insists, passing over a blade.

I nod, reaching out and putting the blade to the swirling dark red liquid. It would be easier if I had all my fingers. The dagger cuts through the portal and leaves a thick black marking where I carve it. I draw the bird symbol, bigger than I intended but it looks good.

"What now?" I glance again at my jeans, though I'm trying not to. It's red. Why would they not be watching now? Preparing possibly. I hope... What if they aren't watching? What if I just hallucinated it. Damn this is bad. Lucifer's hand pushes me into the portal.

Screaming, my body pulses. I feel hot waves of energy connect to me and pulse outward. Howling, pain judders through my body uncontrollably. Agony wrenches through all my muscles. My head spins, my insides feel like they are ripping apart. Vomit churns up in my stomach, my throat burns as I puke. Dizzy lights shine through my eyes. I fall through an endless time tunnel, moving swiftly through nothing. My body spasms out of my control, my limbs feel detached from my body, yet it's so painful. I try to move and leave the portal, but there is nowhere to go. Portals are a wave of coloured nothingness till you get to the other side, but it shouldn't be this painful. The blood leaves my head, leaving me dizzy. Spinning, I scream out in agony. My eyes droop, trying to find the bliss of sleep. I drop onto hard ground, I look around.

I'm still in Hell. I groan, I didn't even go anywhere. The pain slowly fades from my body. Lucifer picks me up by the scruff of my neck. "Get on your feet."

I wince, my legs struggling under my weight. "Are you going to kill them now?" I ask, I would expect an army to be gathering while I broke Lucifer's ritual. The area around us is empty, the demons are all in the castle. Lucifer is powerful, but I expect he would bring some backup.

"No, not yet." He walks away from the portal. He's not even checking to see if it works. I glance at it, the temptation to run in and hope Lucifer isn't fast enough to catch me is overwhelming. "Human!" He yells. I run after him, hating myself as I do so.

I follow him back inside the castle, he doesn't sit on his throne but stands in front of it. "Are you not going to kill them now?" I ask.

"That doesn't concern you. Take off your shoe." He orders.

I look down at my boot, he's going to cut off my toe. I can't say I'm not relieved, I'm running out of fingers.

I didn't realise how few ten fingers really was until I started losing them. I fiddle with the lace, my fingers struggling to undo the bow. "Hurry up!" He hisses angrily, impatiently holding the knife. I untangle the last string and pull off my boot then my sock. Lucifer plays with the knife in his hand. I hold my breath, waiting. The silver flashes, I cry out while grabbing my foot. The toe dangles by a thread, the bone still intact. I muffle my whimper. "Do you want to get the rest of it?"

"Leave."

I frown, am I hallucinating this or is Lucifer different? My foot is a very easy target, and he missed the toe. It is the smallest, but I still can't imagine Lucifer being able to miss it, not with his aim. He took out one of my fingers from across the room. Unless he did it on purpose, I'll probably have to hack the rest off myself. I pick up the boot and sock, and hobble out of the room, leaving a trail of bloody footprints behind me. If I put them on it will hurt and I don't even know if I can. A demon follows, forcing me to move faster. I turn back, Lucifer hovers near his throne instead of sitting down. I shake my head and limp down the stairs with my flapping toe.

Sitting on the bed, I whimper. The toe dangles, blood pooling out of it. I pull out a knife, the skin barely holding on; it's already clean off the bone. I stop and look at the medical bag. I pull out the needle and thread. I curse, I would try, but if I can barely undo bootlaces; I won't be able to sew my toe back on. I take back the knife and swipe off the rest. I whimper as it drops onto the bed. I clean up the wound and let the toe join the fingers. I re-apply my sock; the floor is dirty. I really don't want to deal with an infection. My hands are wrapped up like a mummy, the bandages weaving between my fingers to cover the many stubs.

I struggle to open the water bottle; it'll be easier once the thick wad of bandages is gone. I don't know how I will explain this to my parents. Alex will probably just use mind-control, the truth would be a lot harder to explain, but I don't think we'll have to. I feel my waistband for the little camera... there is nothing there. I lost it. Damn it! I don't know if they saw any of it. Lucifer is planning to attack very soon and if they aren't prepared, we are all doomed. I thought he would go the second that I opened up the portal for him but, of course, he never does what I expect. I chug the water, trying to hydrate. Hell is hot, but I've been here so long that I've gotten used to it. I only notice because of my constant thirst and sweating. I desperately need a shower. My hair is one big, tangled knot and I need real food, preferably hot. A voice echoes up the corridor. Not again, why can't I hallucinate a warm shower instead? Or something equally as calming. I peer out of the bars, looking around. Holly stands there. Damn, I wish she was real. "Hi." I smile. She looks so real; I could almost believe it.

Holly grabs the bars. "Are you alright?"

"What do you think?" I smirk, simply happy to see her face.

"Pass me those bandages." Holly puts her hand through the bars. I pick them up and give them to her. "Thanks." She begins to unravel them.

"Why do you want bandages? Are you hurt?" She doesn't look hurt to me. I mentally curse myself; this isn't real. It would be better if I ignore her, but it's good to see her. Even if it is all fake.

Holly tears off part of the long roll. "No, I'm not. You will be."

Holly reaches through the bars wrapping the bandages around my neck and tightening them. I choke, scratching away at the bandages. Holly holds each end thwacking my head on the bars. I cough, the circulation cutting off. It's not real. Holly smirks, her face morphing into Silven's. I'm doing this to myself, I'm not really choking. I close my eyes, repeating to myself that it's not real. I practise breathing, attempting to stop myself choking, but it doesn't work. I continue losing oxygen. I pull at the bandages on my neck, but they are too tight. Silven whacks my hand away from my knife. I wrench away from the door with everything I have. Collapsing on the floor, my head throbs and the world spins. Silven laughs, pain jolts through my back and I stop squirming. My eyes droop shut as I struggle to breath.

Lucifer

I walk back into the room as Abby leaves, my look-a-like standing beside my throne. I sigh, shaking my head in disappointment. Onnach is a third-class demon that I have chosen to replace me. I do believe I know exactly what Alex is going to do, but I thought I did last time we went head-to-head. This is why I have a decoy. If it all goes to plan, then I can join the fight. I want to see their moves so even if they are smarter than I believe, they can't win. They won't have a second plan; Alex will be too stubborn to believe she can do wrong. That's a trait she got from me, which is why I'm switching it up. I left her a little hint in the hut. It was an easy find; hiding possessions under the floorboards is a classic move. I don't think she will understand the hint, which will make the explanation even sweeter when I reveal it to her.

Abby was my test subject. She didn't seem to notice the switch. Onnach needs a little more training. He could never be exactly like me, but he at least needs to sit on the throne for a start, instead of hovering next to it like the servant he is. "I think they'll work it out." Onnach hisses, with his forked tongue.

"Not unless you are convincing." I pull out the collar. "Take its power." I have more than enough to overpower all of them but preferably not all at once. Especially as they'll realise that they will be outmatched and have to use their shared intelligence to win. Which is why the power is equally as important as the plan; the reason for my decoy. Onnach grips the collar. "Really?"

"Yes."

Today, I chose to drain seven demons of an equal ranking to Onnach and collect their power in the collar. Two made of all the elements he's not and one made up the same as him, amplifying his power two-fold and making him a stronger demon with all elements. Onnach grips the collar and takes its power. He smiles in joy, the sparks in his fire-demon hands growing brighter. I take a syringe and fill it with my blood, I pass it over to him. That'll add to what he already has. Onnach howls in pain, doubling over in agony. I could never make him ready to fight Alex, that would be beyond my capabilities, but he'll be able to give her a decent contest if necessary. Unfortunately, the morphing power, despite making him become me, will only allow him to receive my power up to what his regular body can contain.

It shouldn't matter though; I only expect him to sit on the throne until the demons complete their job. They have power, but I have numbers. There will be at least two thousand demons for each one of them. There is a balcony wrapped around the throne room looking downwards. I'll be working there, using my power. They won't have the time to look up and notice.

There are three ways they might play their cards, depending on how much they work out. The first two options are whether or not they can figure out my plan.

The last way is being unexpected, which is why I have Onnach. I slap his hands, which are playing around with his power in awe. If Alex doesn't kill him, I will, once this is over. "I wouldn't do that, would I?" I shake my head.

"You do." Onnach argues. "It's your power move."

"Don't answer back to me. Now get out of here and re-enter. Pretend you're me, if you succeed, I won't kill you and find a replacement." I snap.

He scurries to the doors. I'm glad I don't act like that weakling. I have just given him enough power to kill any other demon here, yet he cowers like a child. I clap my hands. "Get going." I fling myself onto the throne waiting for the show to start.

Onnach marches in, flinging the doors open. They shut automatically behind him; I don't see it but he's using one of the elements. Satisfying start. Striding forward, he beelines for the throne. Standing before me, he pauses. I watch, without moving from my seat. If it were me, I would have screamed and killed the demon sitting on my throne already. It would only take me this long if I ordered the rest of the demons to watch to show an example. He can't do that, the less demons know what is going on the better. "Get out of my seat!" Onnach orders, frowning.

Did he just call my throne a seat? This isn't an ordinary chair like humans use when they sit at their desks. The throne symbolises the ruler of Hell, I'm the only one who can sit upon it. It's the code. I glare up at him. "No."

Onnach's lips tremble. The demons would never disobey me but if he can't even confront one of them, he won't be able to do the same to Alex let alone look her in the eye when he speaks to her., "Do it!" He demands.

"No." I repeat. Onnach grabs me by the front of my shirt, his hands shaking. I would have done that already.

He chucks me out the way and collapses on the throne. "Leave, before I punish you."

"You've gotten soft." I snort. The blast of fire hits my chest, burning through my clothes. "I didn't... I mean get out of my sight!"

"I'm not going to kill you, but practise. That was borderline abysmal." I snarl. "Now, get off my throne, and never call it a seat again. If you do, your skull will be added to my 'seat'."

"Yes, sir." He nods frantically.

"By the devil." I sigh, rubbing my face. I think a clone might have been a better idea. I pass the potion bottle over for him to de-glamour.

He grasps it. "Are we done?"

"Not yet. Again." I demand. I will force him to do it until he does it right.

A few threats later, Onnach passes the test. He is realistic enough that no one will doubt him for the few moments of interaction that I will need. "Lastly, sneak this into Abby's room some way." I pass over the miniature camera. Abby is hallucinating, which has given her misguided confidence in her friends. When I left to switch with Onnach, I stole the camera from her and put up the cell jammers so her friends wouldn't see me with it. I'll take them down once she receives the camera. She'll believe she hallucinated taking it in with her in the first place. No damage will be done. Admittedly, I wasn't expecting the hallucination to give her hope, but they also have her off guard. She wouldn't stop glancing at her jeans and gently touching it to check it was there.

Enzo

I watch through the gap as Abby's shirt moves, I see what I believe is the throne room. Abby is mad to have the guts to do this. She must have the camera clipped to her jeans and the shirt must be covering it. It doesn't matter, I wouldn't be able to see properly, even if the shirt wasn't covering it. I just have to try to focus and listen. Lucifer talks to Abby forcefully, as though he is giving her instructions. He goes quiet, I don't hear him say anything else. Was he talking to the demons instead? Is he making the demons torture her instead of doing it himself? That's low, he's not even doing it to enjoy it, he's just doing it because he can. I hear Abby whimper in pain. She howls, but I can't see what is happening to her. It's probably something to do with the collar, we saw those marks, or it could be another finger being cut off. The video ends, it goes quiet. I stare at the screen. Tina is right, they do disappear. But how does torturing Abby play into it? I slam the laptop shut in frustration. I slump back in my seat, spinning it around. The door rattles. "Come in." I hope it's someone with a plan.

"Hi." Holly slips inside, lowering her voice to a whisper after seeing Alex asleep. "Can we talk?"

I nod and follow her out of my room.

We reach the living room, it's empty. "Where is everyone?" I ask.

"Selena went home, I don't think she can handle it, I probably shouldn't have asked her to come. Colt is asleep, so are Esmeralda and Hayden." Holly explains. "I wanted to apologise for storming out and blaming you for Abby being kidnapped, and for saying that you weren't helping."

I shrug. "It's fine." I assumed she was sorry when she came back. It's understandable, I would be pissed but it took her longer to come to her senses than I thought it would. "Is that it?"

"No. You act like you've got this far and still don't have a plan. That's bullshit. You and Alex have one, and I want to know what it is."

"I wish we had something useful." I answer. "Truth is we don't have a plan."

"Alright. You must have information. If you don't, you have done a terrible job."

"Nothing worth saying yet." I can't blatantly lie; I can tell by the focus on her face that she is listening to my heart rate.

"I want to know what you have. You can't keep it from me, I'm her sister."

"You don't want to know." I don't think she wants to know that Abby's fingers are being hacked off every day until one of us makes a move. She'll only be more concerned about getting there. "Well, I have something you might want to know. If you tell me." Holly attempts to bargain.

"Really? You want to trade information to help your sister. No, tell me yours first." I roll my eyes. She'll tell me no matter what. She isn't going to prevent us from helping Abby.

"Fine. I have an idea, but I don't know if it's possible." She caves. "I know Lucifer needs Abby to let him out, but I thought there could be more. He lost Silven and will need a replacement, right? Abby didn't need to eat those dreaded worms to save your ass." I try to ignore the bitterness in the last sentence, I didn't think the worms could be that bad. "I did some research in your books and she is able to do some of what Silven could do in Hell. I then studied Silven's powers to see what made her worth Lucifer's time. There was nothing interesting, but I looked into her parents." Holly pulls the book from the couch cushion next to her. "Mammon had the power to take other demons' powers. In the last few pages, it says he was taking so much power to be strong enough to take on Lucifer that it killed him. Could the trait have been passed on to Silven, then Abby?"

I grab the book out of her hands and read it. Lucifer was first, then seven more demons were created for his army. They reproduced. Except for Kath'tek who stayed loyal to Lucifer. Flint doesn't have any siblings except for Alex. Then it was a continuous chain. Thousands and thousands of years of evolution, they mutated to produce eggs and lost the intelligence they had and became more animal-like. Chances are, the first would have extra abilities, how did I not know this? If this is true...

"I was thinking Lucifer could be using Abby as some sort of weapon." Holly explains. "Do you think I'm right?"

Abby could be his weapon, but she doesn't have a demon body, she couldn't withstand the power he needs. Osmium is conductive. Not only for electricity... "Holy shit you are a genius." Osmium is conductive. The collar makes sense. Abby would take the power from other beings and the osmium collar could conduct the power from her. Her body would transfer it automatically to save her from dying of a power overload. Lucifer is a genius. Why the hell does he have to be a genius? He probably has enough power to kill us all by now.

"You think I'm right?" Her eyes light up.

"Yes, I do, but it means we are screwed."

"What do you mean?" Holly's shoulders fall.

"He's had Abby for days, he could be one flaming ball of energy by now." I close the book. "We might as well hand ourselves over."

"No! Mammon died because of his greed. If Lucifer takes too much he'll die." Holly grins. "This is how we can beat him." She points to the book enthusiastically.

Lucifer can't die by taking in too much power. He practically is power inside of a vessel. If it were possible, he would need more than he could get his hands on. "Possibly, I'll talk to Alex. She'll know for sure. Well done." I won't tell her that it's not physically possible, that would crush her. I'll wait till I discuss it with Alex to figure out how to soften the blow, hopefully with a better plan.

"What do you know then?"

I bite my lip; I should tell her something. "We know Abby is alive, she won't sleep for months but Lucifer won't kill her." I promise. "Now, go get some sleep." I order.

"Alright." Holly smiles. "You too."

I start a pot of coffee, forcing my droopy eyes to stay open. Lucifer is using Abby to get power. Possibly, that is what happened to Asmodeus. Who knows what else Lucifer has done to be as strong as possible. I pour the coffee into a mug and Alex saunters in. "I just overheard your conversation. If Holly is right, it would explain why Lucifer hasn't been seen doing anything else. He had his power source already." She snatches my cup. "Her idea to destroy Lucifer won't work. I don't think he has a limit."

I sigh and pour out another. "I know. I didn't have the heart to tell her."

"You are going soft." Alex teases. "The only way her plan could work is if all of us pool our power together and give it to him like a sacrifice. Besides, if it didn't work, we wouldn't be able to put up much of a fight. I mean, imagine being human?"

"Good point." I agree. "He plans to kill us all, taking our power is probably part of it too. I honestly don't think it'll help."

Alex nods. "I know." She wracks her hands through her messy hair. "At least we know what he's doing. We can work off that. He'll be taking in as much power as possible before he attacks. I say we have a day and a half at most."

"You're right. You don't happen to have any genius ideas, do you?" I ask hopefully.

"Nope. It's getting more likely that we'll be using my emergency plan."

"Don't say that, we'll figure out something." I know what I agreed to, but it will be a lot harder to actually do it. I'm still not certain I can.

"Hopefully, we just have to sit and wait for an update from Tina."

"She messaged you while you were asleep. I answered it. Something about demons disappearing."

"I'll see if I can get another update from her, you should sleep. You look like death. I'll wake you up if something happens." Alex pulls out her phone.

"No, I can stay awake." I reach for the pot of coffee.

Alex shakes her head. "You are going to sleep. I was being nice when I said you looked like death. You'll function better if you sleep, and I need your brain to work."

"Fine, wake me up in an hour." I put down the coffee pot.

I wake up in an empty bed. Sunlight streams through the curtains, I jolt upright. I check the time; I've been asleep for the last six hours. Damn it, I knew I shouldn't have trusted Alex to wake me up. I did need those extra five hours. I sigh, I can't go back to sleep now. I jump out of the bed and change clothes. I check the laptop, nothing is showing up on the live footage. It's blurry. I sigh, I guess we don't need it. We know what Lucifer is doing.

I go downstairs, the entire group sits on the sofa while Alex instructs them. I was left out of a meeting. Alex smiles. "I was just telling them Holly's amazing plan." Which is code for the 'fake plan' that she is telling them to prepare for; a plan that won't work.

"Okay. I guess I'm not needed then." I carry Colt's laptop to the kitchen to work on a plan that might actually work, without Alex dying in the process. I can tell by Flint's face that he knows better than to believe this plan will work. I open the laptop. If we can't stop Lucifer getting more powerful in the next few hours, we'll have to assume he could kill us all with ease. Working out what he'll do next, and planning how to work around it is my best option...

I stare at the pages; I have come up with a dozen different endings in which Lucifer is successful in killing us. Each idea is lying on the table, from the most likely, to the least likely. Chances are, it's none of them and I'm simply hopeful.

"You look busy, considering the plan is already finalised." Flint walks in. "Alex is training the others to survive against the demons. So, what's the real plan?"

I curse under my breath. "What do you mean?"

"Alex just said Abby could absorb others' powers. That I believe, but the plan is awful. We are just going to put up a half-ass fight, wait for Lucifer to pin us, take our powers, explode and then our powers will come back, and we will be victorious. It's bullshit." Flint swears. "But I assume you both know I'm not dumb enough to buy that. Whatever fake plan she told you to tell me, save it."

A fake plan to tell Flint would have been a good idea, Alex probably assumed I'd have one ready. My brain whirls for something to tell him... I smile. "I don't have a fake plan to tell you, just the real one."

"Very funny." Flint shakes his head, picking up one of the pages. "These are all plans? You don't have one? Alex said we were leaving at seven in the morning." Flint curses. "Please don't say the real plan is to wing it. I swear..." He chucks down the pages, looking at my face. "This is a ruse." He points to me and the table. "She plans to die, doesn't she?" My face falls, words refusing to come out of my mouth. The answer is written on my face, there is no point lying. "I'm not going to let her die! She's going out of her mind! I'm going to..." He marches away.

I grab his arm to prevent him from yelling at her and get me caught. "She'll do it, whether you yell at her or not. Trust me, I tried. I'm trying to find a way so she doesn't die. The best way you can help is to sit down and brainstorm with me."

Flint hesitates, looking out the doorway. "Fine." Flint slumps onto the chair beside me. "What do you have?"

A dozen coffees later and we finally have some sort of strategy. "I think it'll work." I agree with Flint. There are a few assumptions, a few parts that require luck, but we don't have to tell the others the new plan except for Colt and Alex. We figured it out from the order that he'll take our powers then kill us in. We won't let it get that far, but the plan works. Colt will be happy; he gets to play hero and save Abby which is also why he needs to know.

"There are a few flaws, if it doesn't work, Alex will force you to kill her. I can't let my sister die; I know I can't tell you not to do it but…" He stops mid-sentence. "I'll go find her."

"Wait, I have one more favour to ask you." I beckon him back.

Flint agrees. "I won't tell her." He passes over what I asked for. "I'll be back in a minute." I tuck the scribbled paper into my pocket and pull out the dagger instead. The dagger to kill Alex and Flint.

The pair enter, I slide the dagger over to Alex. She picks it up. "Thanks. Flint said you two came up with a plan?"

"Yeah, we had to. You only had the lie you told everyone else." Flint chuckles.

So, that's what we are going with. Flint promised not to tell Alex that he knew of her emergency last resort, she won't need it. We'll tell her after everything is over. I feel bad for keeping it a secret, but it's for the best.

Alex looks over our plan. "Not as good as I could come up with in three hours, but decent."

"Which means?"

"We don't have anything else; we'll do it. Enzo, you can inform Colt of his part. Flint go home, be back at two am to prepare."

Flint nods. "Will do, if one of you will make me a portal."

Alex chuckles. "Oh yeah, I forgot you aren't as powerful as me." She teases him, creating the portal. Flint flips her the finger before disappearing.

Alex glares in my direction. "Did you tell him?"

"No." I'm not lying, he worked it out.

She nods. "Thank you for finding a different way. I'll stick to my promise, but you need to as well." She passes a small vial of her blood over. "If you need it." I reach out for it, a knife slashes out cutting the tip of my finger.

"What was that for?" I pull back my hand.

Alex presents a document from behind her back with flourish. "Before I give it to you, I want you to sign this. It's a blood oath saying you won't do anything heroic and stupid if your plan doesn't work."

"Can I get you to sign one of these?" I ask dipping the quill on my finger. I sign it, at her request. It'll help her peace of mind.

"No. This was my mess, I'm cleaning it up." She gives me the blood. "Thank you."

"Well, I'm not going to need it, but I'll keep hold of it." I promise. "You'll need to do another; Colt will need it for a different purpose."

"I know." Alex pulls out her phone. "Tina messaged me again. She said Lucifer has already used Abby to open the gates… he's waiting for us to go down there."

"He'll know we'll be trying to get Abby back, which means he's expecting us."

"Exactly, and I would say we should wait, but Abby will not be of use much longer. No doubt if he has used her to open it, he no longer needs her to get power. All he needs is for her to take our power, and he's only so patient."

"Well, we're leaving in the morning."

"Indeed. I would suggest leaving now but we should wait to see if Tina can give us any more of an edge."

"Good idea, now we just have to kill the time." I sigh, rubbing my face.

"Well, I would suggest sleeping, but I don't think we could if we tried. So, do you want to slip away for an hour or two? I don't think they'd notice."

"Sure, what do you have in mind?"

Walking through the portal, humans scurry around before my eyes. Instantly, I glamour my horns before they notice.

Looking around, we are at an ice rink. I look down to my feet, I'm wearing skates. "You have to be kidding me." I curse. This is not what I had in mind. We have about ten hours until we could die horrific deaths. Learning to ice skate isn't on my bucket list.

"Nope." Alex grins. "I need something good to picture if it all goes wrong."

"Haven't you embarrassed me enough over the last few months?" I sigh.

"Nope." Alex tugs my hand. Gliding from the ground to the ice with ease. She's been doing it for thousands of years, even when ice skates weren't a thing. "Come on."

I frown. "I think I would prefer to get drunk or take a nap." I cautiously step on the ice. Alex grabs my hand. "How do you do it?" I stand on the ice, without moving.

"Point your feet outward and push. Make sure to recenter your feet. Talent comes with practice."

I attempt it, gliding forward while using Alex to balance.

"You've had plenty of time to practise. How many thousand years?"

"Ten thousand, give or take. Yet I still look hot as Hell." Alex winks. "Make another comment and I'll let go."

"Please, don't." She is the only thing keeping me up. I shuffle forward at the speed of a tortoise. If I keep this up, our hour will be over before I make it halfway around the rink. I shuffle a little further. Alex lets go of my hand. "Hey! What are you doing?" I stop stationary on the ice as people glide past.

"I taught you the basics, now you have to try to catch me." Alex glides backwards, out of my reach. "Good luck."

I curse under my breath, she has to be kidding me. I look around, I'm not even near the edge to help guide me across. Alex is halfway across the rink, showing off. I look around, the humans are either concentrating on staying on their feet or moving too fast to see their surroundings. My hands flicker, sending sparks trailing to the shoes. I attempt to go forward and move gracefully on the ice. The skates keep me up as I soar forward around the rink to Alex. Alex pulls a face at me, knowing I am cheating. This shouldn't be too hard. Alex is sticking to the outside of the rink, if I try to stick to the centre I should be able to catch up. I follow her around two laps without getting any closer. Dodging a gaggle of women, I think out my route to catch up. Out the corner of my eye, I see one of the women push her friend my way. I stop, catching the girl before she sends us both to the floor and I can't catch Alex. I push her gently towards her friends.

"I'm so sorry." She blushes. "It was…"

"I know, I have to go." I sigh. Looking up, Alex is taunting me from the other end of the rink.

"Can she have your number?" Her friend asks.

"No, sorry. I'm with someone." I look over her shoulder, Alex is gone. "I really have to go." I spin around, but she's nowhere to be seen. I skate, hoping to see her somewhere in the crowd. A shadow appears behind me, I grab the intruder's arm. Alex laughs. "I was hoping to scare you." She pulls her arm free. "Do you want to get a drink? I think I've tortured you enough."

"Definitely."

CHAPTER
TWENTY-ONE

Abby

I sit down in my cell, knees tucked up to my chin. Lucifer has opened the gate, he is free to roam around Earth as he pleases. My heart pounds in my chest, no doubt he wants to attack soon. He could be right now. He wants me to take their power, what if he wants to keep me out the way till the right moment? He could be at Enzo's house, trying to kill them all and there is nothing I can do to help. I'm useless. No, I'm worse than that. I'm helping Lucifer. I could have refused, let him cut off my limbs, but I was too scared to stop him. He still could have used mind-control like he did with the camera, but then at least I wouldn't have been doing it willingly. The odds are stacked against us, meaning Lucifer is going to win, and when he does, he'll kill Holly, Colt, Enzo... All of them, along with me. I was just prolonging my own life by a couple of days. If he wins Hell back and kills us there is nothing stopping him from going to Earth and taking that too. My parents will probably die, along with my friends. I haven't seen Kyle or Lily in ages. I won't ever get to see them

I jump. Turning around, I see a demon at the barred door. "Again?" I don't think I can go through the torture again, it's so draining. I can barely move at all. I've eaten all my food, and I'm running low on water. I've been taking a sip every few hours, or what I believe to be every few hours. I'm re-using bandages as I've run out of fresh ones. My entire body throbs, my neck, feet and hands especially. I've given up wearing shoes and socks in here, I struggle to put them on. Turns out, using that knife with missing fingers was pure adrenaline, I can't do anything properly.

"What do you mean again?" The demon hisses.

"The torture." I frown. Is that not what it's here for? I recognise the demon, I've seen it before. It's the one I thought winked at me in the corridor. Is it a hallucination? An imaginary demon I've made for myself?

"Ah, yes. When you go into that room with the others, what happens in there?"

"What do you mean?" I feel for my knife in my pocket. It slips out my fingertips, clattering to the ground.

"You want to stab me." It snorts. "With this skin, you'd be lucky to even reach a blood vessel, let alone kill me. Look. I got you this." The demon produces a satchel.

I walk forward and take it through the bars. Inside, there is more food and water. I'm hallucinating again. "Why are you here?"

"Lucifer sent me to give you this, obviously. Did staying down here kill your brain cells?" The demon shakes its head. "Sorry, that's how demons speak."

I edge away from the cell door, I don't know what demon this is, but I don't want to be close unless they try something.

"The cell jammers are down." The demon slurs. "You can contact them now."

"What?" Cell jammers stop communications, but Hell doesn't have technology. Why would it have those?

"You wouldn't know. Alright, those spy camera messages to your friends have been blocked, if you try now, they won't be. I took them down."

Talking to the camera, telling countless lies to them all, that wasn't real? They didn't get any of it... Lucifer was messing with me? Making me believe I did it. No, this is another mind game, it's not real at all. It's my guilty consciousness; I'm trying to tell myself I haven't been guiding my friends to their deaths. Lucifer wouldn't make such a big thing over it, forcing me to tell lies if it didn't serve a purpose. It's to distract them from what he's really doing. They had no reason not to believe me, blocking the footage with cell jammers makes no sense. I sit back down on the bed, looking in the bag. I open the water bottle with effort and take a sip. It feels real. I chug the entire thing down.

"Alright, contact them. Okay? Tell them what you are doing in the room with Lucifer, they need to know if they are going to rescue you, got it?"

"You're lying." I shake my head. I need to ignore it. If I feed it on, I'll get lost in the lie.

"For Hell's sake, it's Tina. I've been eating bloody hell worms the last few days, looking like this, talking to some bullshit demons who have the most boring lives in all of history. I've been sneaking information to Alex; the world might end, and I wasted the last ten bloody years being a lawyer when I should have been sitting on a beach drinking. I really miss my magic right now and I almost lost an arm and a leg taking down those cell jammers unnoticed so if you don't tell them what you are doing or tell me, I swear I will open that door and kill you." The demon hisses.

I only met Tina once when we came down for Enzo. I didn't really speak to her, Colt and Holly did most of that, but I am absolutely certain she was not a demon, she was a witch. This is not her. No matter how much I want to believe it. "Goodbye." I turn away, looking towards the wall away from it.

I hear the door swing, the bars clattering against the wall.

"Hey! What are you doing?" A demon yells up the hall. The other demon curses. "The prisoner isn't meant to be disturbed."

I turn around to look again, I can't help it. "Just bringing food and water." The demon closes the door again, leaving me inside. "No harm done." The demon at the gate scowls at me.

"Tina!" Lucifer's voice rockets above it all. The demon's eyes grow. "Shit, I have to get out of here. Contact them or I will come back and kill you." The demon runs away.

I look down at the satchel, the hallway is empty. All the demons are gone, like they were never there. My eyes fall on the camera. I can only tell them lies, they might know… I could try to tell them. Tell an obvious lie, so they would assume the rest was too. Then they could decipher it. I put it back down, the demon can't be right about the cell jammers, it's my hallucinations. Besides, I can't say something useful to them. Lucifer made sure of it. He's thought of everything, there's no point in using it. Everything I just saw and heard was a figment of my imagination.

Lucifer

"Tina!" I scream at the top of my lungs. A demon in the east wing just informed me that the cell jammers are down. There is no way that is an accident or a technical fault, even if they told me no visible damage was done. It means one of them is already here, in the castle. Before I was ready for them. A surprise, but nothing I can't handle. I know it's Tina by process of elimination. They wouldn't send one of the teens down here by themselves, they care about their wellbeing too much because of their youth. Enzo and Alex are needed for brainstorming, Alex cares about Flint too much to let him do the mission, Esmeralda and Hayden would protect each other first, which leaves Tina. The only question is, how long has she been here, how much does she know and how did she do it? I simply need to find her, wherever she is. "You." I point to the demon who informed me. "Gather the demons. You are looking for a witch, five foot seven, auburn hair and brown eyes, or anything else suspicious." It jumps at my demands.

I storm out the room, I need to find her, quickly. The best way is to do it myself. If she took down the cell jammers, it would be for Abby to use the camera or for herself if Enzo made her phone work in Hell. Chances are, she has been gathering information by herself for a day or two, but if she put the cell jammers down, she has informed Abby. She'll be in the cells. I march down the stairs. There is only one way in and out. The demon let me know straight away, which means she is still down there. I march down, bumping into a demon. It dips its head respectfully, another one behind it. I look up the corridor, there is no one in sight. Tina couldn't have made it into a cell, a demon is the only one who could open the door... Tina is one of the demons. They must have figured out morphing. "You, and you." I beckon them. "I need you two to watch the prisoner. I believe we have an intruder; she might be going after our prisoner."

"Yes sir." The second one nods.

They walk with me to the doorway. I analyse their walking patterns and faces. The one on the right has a very humanlike walk, but that could simply be how it is built. I look to the left, our eyes meet. Demon eyes, but I can see the emotions underneath. Eyes are the window to the soul; demons don't have a soul, but witches do.

"I want to talk to you." I pull it aside. I don't recognise the demon that she is portraying. It doesn't matter now.

"Yes, Lucifer." Tina bows, I can hear the dripping sarcasm in her voice despite trying to hide it.

"Follow me." I lead Tina up to the throne room.

We enter and I close the doors behind us. I will let the demons know the threat is over once I've dealt with her. Tina's eyes widen, reaching for something by her side. "Don't try to attack me, you know it won't do anything." I warn her.

"I know, it wasn't a weapon." She pulls out a potion vial. "I thought if you were going to kill me, I'd rather die with my own face instead of this ugly being's." She swigs it back. She shudders, face reconstructing to her own. "How did you know?"

"Your eyes." I look over to her. "How long have you been here? Don't lie, I can make your death very painful."

"I know, that's why I wasn't going to. I've been here for about two days, I think. Time is a little different here." Tina talks, I listen to her heart rate, it's as steady as a rock. She isn't lying. Tina is a slimy being, much like the demons actually. She'll follow whoever she believes will keep her alive, or whoever gives the biggest paycheque. Tina's life the last few thousand years has been funded by Alex, who gave her a large sum of money for some work she did. I'm sure if I gave her enough reason, she'd join me and feel no remorse, but I can't be certain, not after last time. "What else?" She asks.

"What is Alex's plan?" This is the question that will reveal if she is willing to do the switch. I may recruit her if I believe it'll hurt Alex enough.

"I don't know. I was sent down here to gather information for a plan."

"Have you reported back to them yet?"

"A few times. Nothing you would need to worry about. It's why I went to Abby." There were no jumps in her heart rate while she spoke. It's not a surprise that she doesn't know, Alex knows she may slip up. Yet, they are friends, I would at least expect a little more persuasion to get her to talk. It shouldn't be this easy.

"Why are you willing to tell me all this?"

"I'd rather not die, but I don't think I have much of a choice now and it's Alex's fault. Getting back at her is my little goodbye gift, if you get what I mean." She produces a phone out of nowhere. "I can read you our conversation if you'd like, or you could read my mind, or neither. Up to you."

I pause, it's too easy. Tina smiles my way, phone outstretched in her hand willingly. She wants to do it, there is nothing in her eyes saying otherwise.

I reach for the phone and stop. She wants this, not to get back at Alex. She has already told me there is nothing on here to help me. It wasn't a lie either, I have been listening to her heartbeat. I don't need to see proof. She's stalling me. Talking to me about useless information and facts while the cell jammers are down. She might not have information for Alex, but Abby does, and she knows it. She's been running around for days; she'll have noticed Abby coming and going from the throne room. She wants to waste my time on her while Abby communicates back to Earth. She is loyal to Alex, no matter what situations she drags her into. Now she is going to die, and it will be Alex's fault. Tina knows that already; she's stalling in hope she could come up with a miracle, but she has admitted defeat. This is to make her small life have a purpose, right to the end.

"Is that a no?" Tina waves the phone.

I grab her around the neck, she chokes, dropping the phone. Tears drip down her face, the tears of someone who isn't ready to die. The dark depths of the long road to nothingness as the world continues without you is too much to handle for some. They still want to enjoy the small things in life; love, happiness, pain, all of it, because it means they are living. It's especially hard for immortals because they believe they will never die. They have never-ending time; they never have to face that idea of nothingness and the idea of it all ending. I chuck Tina aside, her hands glow with magic. She howls, blasting me with it. I block it easily, shaking my head. Fire flickers in my palms and she gulps, knowing there is no way she can kill me by herself.

"Get it over with then." She stares me dead in the eye.

I grin, fire burning through her skull, melting away the flesh. She screams, collapsing dead, the stink of rotten flesh filling the room. There is no way she can be saved from that, even by Alex. Angel blood is only so powerful. I chuckle, kicking her body. I pull out a blade and cut through her neck. I'll use it as a trophy for Alex to see when she comes in… I just need to put the cell blockers back up.

Enzo

Returning, after only one bottle of scotch we find the rest are sleeping like we should be. We have a couple of hours left. We'll spend an hour checking up on everyone and gearing up. Then go, and pray we win. Alex yawns. "We should probably go to sleep."

"Yeah, I just need to talk to Colt." I kiss her cheek gently.

"Good idea." Alex enters my bedroom.

I knock on Colt's bedroom door, we have a couple hours until we leave. Still no messages from Tina for a last-minute update… Hopefully, it's simply that she can't get away as they are preparing, instead of something more sinister.

"Come in." I walk inside, Colt looks up from his empty desk. "I wasn't able to sleep, guess you couldn't either?"

"I'd be shocked if you were sleeping." I smile. "You alright?"

"Other than the pressure of taking down Lucifer, saving Abby, lack of sleep, possibility that we might die and general fear? I'm good." He tries to quirk a smile. He opens a bottle of blood and chugs. The liquid staining his teeth. "What about you?"

"I'd say about the same at the moment." I pull up a chair next to him.

"Selena's gone home by the way. She didn't want to stay."

"Can't say I blame her." I don't like Selena, but I respect her for at least trying to be there for Holly the last few days, even though it was obvious she would much rather not.

"What's up?" Colt asks. "Did you come here for a reason?"

I did, a very important reason, but I also want to see how he's doing. We've barely spent any time together recently, we've both been trying to work on saving everyone, but I've been doing that with Alex, and he's been with Holly. Now I can let Colt in on what we've been doing.

"Everything Alex told you was a lie. That plan is for Holly to think she solved everything. Also, the less she knows the better."

"Yeah, I know."

"You do?"

"Of course, but I wasn't going to beg you for the real one. I know you've got it sorted. Or I sure hope you do."

I laugh. "We do but it's a little messy."

"Well, you're here to tell me then I have a role to play, right?" His eyes light up. "Something good, where I actually contribute? I'm sick of feeling hopeless."

"Yes." I pull out a vial of blood from my pocket. "It's Alex's. Your job is to collect Abby from her cell unnoticed and bring her. Don't let Lucifer or any other demon get close to her."

Colt takes the small bottle. "You got it. Will I have anyone with me?"

"No, but you'll be fine. You're highly skilled and a quick learner."

"Thanks." He tucks away the tube. "Why am I doing it? No offence, you're right, I'm highly trained, but Flint and Tina are a lot more qualified than I am. Also, wouldn't Lucifer predict that I'll be the one rescuing Abby? Either me or Holly?"

"You're right but... Abby is in bad shape." I should tell him what to expect. Or it may stall him when he collects her from the cells. "Hell is causing Abby to have hallucinations. You'll be the best to convince her it isn't one."

"Is that what the blood is for?"

"No... She's been tortured too. She has burns on her neck and she's missing a few fingers. They might not all come back." I warn him.

"Are you serious?" Colt's face drops in devastation. This is why it was better not to tell him before. He would have rushed down there unprepared and got himself killed to try to stop her suffering. Working with your head instead of your heart is hard, but it needs to be done sometimes to get the results you actually want. "Alright, I'll be prepared." Colt nods. "We've only got a few hours, she'll be fine till then, right?"

"Yeah. We'll be preparing soon." I lean back in my seat.

"Enzo... If we don't make it back. I just want to thank you for everything. You're not who I thought you were and if you weren't there for me when I first turned, I don't know what would have happened."

"You're welcome. I'm glad I met you too. Wait, what did you think I was like?"

"Honestly, I thought you were some asshole who worked for my teacher, but you felt guilty and saved me, that's why I didn't ask why you were there at first. Then I figured out that you weren't, and I then never got around to asking. So, why were you?"

I can't blame him for that assumption. Someone appearing just as you need them is suspicious. I had wondered why he never asked. "I made a promise to someone a long time ago. And I wanted to honour it."

Colt nods. "Sounds about right." He lounges back in his chair. "Want to play cards?" Colt asks, drawing out a pack from his desk. "Neither of us will be able to do anything while we wait."

"I thought you hated cards after I smashed you at them."

"You cheated, we both know it." Colt growls.

"I swear I didn't."

"You did. Your heartbeat may be solid, but I bet you learned to control it. No cheating this time either. I've been practising." Colt hands out the cards.

I holster a dozen knives to my body, along with other weapons. The collection is larger than I expected, Alex brought some weapons from her armoury as well. There is Flint, Jade, Hayden, Alex, Colt, and Holly. Esmeralda is with Flint's kids. She's human for starters, which doesn't help her, and still weak from her wounds. Holly's hands visibly shake inside her gloves, I can't say the rest of us look any calmer. Colt grabs my arm, pulling me away from the others. "What do I do if I can't convince Abby that this is real? I've been trying to think, but I have no idea what to do." He panics.

"Try to remind her of her life out of Hell; school, Holly, all of that. If that doesn't work... knock her out and carry her."

"What? Fine. How long do I have to convince her?"

"Thirty minutes."

Colt nods. Hopefully, it's enough time. I would rather she was conscious, but we don't know the full extent of her wounds or how badly Hell has affected her mentally, it's best if we are cautious. "Alright, don't die."

"You too." I smirk.

Alex pours out eight glasses of scotch. "To drown out the taste of hell worms for those who need to eat them and for the rest of us... Well, we just want a drink." She picks up her glass. They clink together and we drink. It's not a miracle worker, but it helps. "All I can say is don't die and trust me." Alex finishes her motivational speech. "Any questions?"

We remain silent, Flint glances in my direction but doesn't say a word. He knows what will happen if it goes wrong, but our plan is pretty solid... I think. Alex opens up the portal, the group go through one at a time till Alex, Colt and I remain.

I open a new portal for Colt. I can't send him to the cell directly, but I can get him close. I've never been good at goodbyes. We have a plan, but there are a billion other ways we could die. I want to send someone with Colt, to ensure his safety, but if more of us are missing, it will make our plan more obvious. Colt smiles and disappears. "He'll be fine." Alex promises.

"I know." I wouldn't let anything happen to him. Fetching Abby is probably the safest job there is. "We should go."

"You're right. The party doesn't start without us." She smiles. "One last thing." She leans up and kisses me. I grin, kissing her back harder. Alex pulls back. "We really need to go now."

"Damn it." I let her go and we enter the portal.

Jolting through, we stand at the gates. "Holy shit." A head sits at the castle doors, on a pike. Tina's eyes gawp in our direction, blood dripping out her mouth.

"That bastard." Alex snarls, kicking down the doors.

Demons wait for us, filling the room as far as the throne, they stand along the balcony up top, with no space to move. Crap, hopefully Colt will take longer than the thirty minutes, or there is no way to clear them out before he and Abby arrive. My hands light up a bright red, the demons charge our way in fury. A few hundred each... sounds possible.

I flip a demon over my arm, stabbing another. They blur together in a wave of blood, flesh and knives, both theirs and my own. A demon jumps in my direction, wielding claws and razor-sharp teeth. I fall back into a portal. I appear behind him, and stab it through the heart, dragging the blade down and tearing up its insides. Kicking the demon, it sails forward, knocking down two more. Pain rips through my back. I spin, shooting a bolt of magic. I need eyes in the back of my head. Snarling, a Hellhound dares to come out to match their claws and teeth. My back cracks, falling to the ground, flames rising from my skin.

CHAPTER TWENTY-TWO

Abby

I down the last of my water. There is no point saving it. I have one breakfast bar left, I undo the wrapper and bite into it. My foot throbs, the badly done stitches ready to unravel at any moment. It's a miracle that none of my wounds are infected.

"Abby!" A voice hollers down the corridor. I curse, not another one. I don't think I can handle it. I pull the thin blanket over my face and scoff the bar. "Abby!" A male voice calls again, its Colt's voice. It's definitely a hallucination. I close my eyes, praying for it to go away. I know what will happen next, we'll get out of the cell, I will believe I finally am getting to freedom and then next thing I know, I'll be back here. That or he will attempt to kill me.

I hear the bars rattle. He's made it to the cell. Crap, I should have hidden under the bed, maybe he wouldn't have seen me. It's my imagination... he would have found me no matter what. "Abby? It's me, Colt. Can you remove the blanket?" He asks softly. Tears prick my eyes, I've missed him so much. I've missed my sister, all of them. I want to see his face, but then I will just fall for the trick again. "Abby, please." He begs. "At least tell me how to let you out."

I hesitate, peeping out the blanket. Colt stands there; hair a mess, blood splattered over his face, wounds healing under his ripped shirt, holsters for weapons covering his body and a gentle, genuine smile. "Abby, please tell me how to let you out."

I want to ignore him, pull the blanket up and hide until he leaves, but a little glimmer of hope makes me think; what if it is real and I'm missing my shot at freedom? I want to hug him so bad. Fake or not. "A demon's handprint on the lock will open it." I murmur.

"Okay, I'll be right back." He promises, footsteps echoing down the corridor. I remove the blanket from my face.

In a minute, Colt returns clutching a demon's severed hand, he pushes it on the lock, unlatching it, and swings the door open. I freeze, I want to run and collapse in his arms, but I can't. Colt runs to me instead and wraps his arms around me. I flinch away, he lets go. I want to know if he's real, or if I'll be hugging air. Colt stands, letting me have my space.

"Look, Abby. I know you probably think I'm not real, but I promised Enzo it would take me thirty minutes and I already spent fifteen getting here. What can I say to make you believe me?"

I don't know how to answer; he could say anything, and I would believe I imagined it. "I…"

His eyes widen in shock. "Abby, your hands, fucking hell."

"Yeah, one per day, if you include the toe." I waggle my bloody bandaged foot.

"Drink this." Colt passes over a small bottle of Alex's blood. I down it, the aching pain through my body easing. The agonising throb from my foot disappears. I look down at my hands, a few grow back to their original state, uncut and complete. The three older cuts remain stubs.

"Hell, I am hallucinating." This is proof.

"No, if you were, they all would have come back because that would be unrealistic." Colt reassures me. "This is real."

I think for a second. "Or it's my mind tricking me again."

"Alright… would you rather take the risk that this is fake and have a short moment of bliss, or be held up in your cell wondering if you messed up and it's real."

I take a deep breath. I know it has to be real at some point, but that doesn't mean that is now. "But if it's not… I can't do it again. I can't."

Colt wraps his cold arms around me, the familiar scent of his cologne surrounding me. "Trust me, I promise." Tears brim in my eyes. He feels so real, I lean against him carefully. I hit his chest, before collapsing against him. I feel his cool lips touch my forehead, this must be it, right? I desperately want it to be so. "I'm so sorry, I would have come sooner if I could." Colt croaks, holding back tears of his own.

"I know." I lean up to kiss him. I can taste the familiar mixture of blood and alcohol on his lips. This is Colt, it has to be. Colt takes a deep breath, pulling away but keeping me in his arms. He wipes away my tears.

"We should probably get going…" I say sadly. Colt said he was on a time limit, I know he wouldn't tell me if I caused him to overstep it, but I'm not important right now. I can spend as much time as I want with Colt once this is over. I pull back, out of his embrace.

"Yeah, the others are upstairs fighting Lucifer. Can you fight with your hands?"

"Yeah, I killed two demons trying to escape a few days ago." I grab my boots and yank them on. I start on the laces, my fingers fumbling, despite some of them being healed. I curse, maybe I won't be much use.

"Want help?" Colt offers.

I nod. "Please."

"I'll tell you the plan while we gear you up." Colt bends down, tying up the shoes and removing gear from himself and helping me put it on.

I listen, tying a belt around my waist, slipping in duelling knives. I pause at the last part. "Wait, we are doing what?"

"I know, I wasn't keen on the idea either, but we don't have much choice."

"Wait, why does that come last? Surely, Enzo would glamour us to be each other now and won't Lucifer notice?"

"Yeah, probably. It's to stall him for a moment."

"Stall him for what?"

"Plan B I suppose… If our original plan doesn't work out."

"Do you know Plan B?"

"No, I was afraid to ask. Let's hope we don't have to use it."

I suppose if we get glamoured into each other that is the signal for Plan B. It makes sense, Lucifer is using me to gain their power, it takes me out the equation without killing me, which I appreciate.

"Also, Enzo told me whatever you do, don't touch Lucifer while wearing the collar, with all the power he's taken it'll kill you. He advised that you don't touch Alex either, if you can help it, her power would probably kill you too."

"Don't worry, I don't plan to wear it any longer than I have to."

"Is it going to hurt, wearing the collar while we're in there?"

"I'll be fine."

Colt glares in my direction; we both know it'll hurt like hell, but there's not much of a choice. Anything is worth it as long as we make it out alive. I strap on the last of the equipment. I see the initials 'T.B' on the handle of the dagger I choose. It was Tessa's. I smile sadly, she is who I hallucinated the most. Hopefully, no one else will die.

"Ready?" Colt asks.

"One minute." I hug him again, checking he's still there.

He smiles gently. "Once this is over, I swear no demons ever again."

"I'm holding you to that." I don't think I could take any more.

We run up the stairs, charging forward into the throne room. My eyes widen, I have never seen so many demons in one place. Bodies lie all over the floor in a bloody mess. Flames roar overhead, burning demons to a crisp. Alex is smiling, covered in blood splatter. The rest are lost in the crowd. I scan the full throne room for a wolf, but it is pointless, half the demons have fur.

We rush forward into the fray. Pouncing on the nearest demon, I slash the dagger in rage. Tearing through the rubbery flesh, I snarl, the week of captivity and pain fuelling my body. I kick the demon down, blood spilling from its skull. A large beefy hand grabs me by the waist. Before I can react, I fly across the room. I close my eyes waiting for impact. I feel myself stopping in mid-air. I float down unharmed, a witch smiles while guiding the bubble that surrounds me.

"Thanks." I land perfectly on my feet. "Who are you?"

"Jade, nice to meet you." She grins politely. Flint's wife, she's pretty. "Duck!"

I drop, a bolt of magic flies over my head, striking the demon. "Thanks, I'm…"

"Abby." She finishes my sentence. "I'll talk to you later." She smiles, running into the crowd to a figure who I believe to be Flint. She seems nice, if we get a "later" I will talk to her and properly thank her for saving my spine from some serious damage.

I block a demon's attempt to claw at my face. Colt told me to stay alive, but if it looks like a kidnap situation, let them take me but struggle a little to be realistic. I elbow the small demon to my left and, in the brief moment of its haziness, I grab it by the neck and fling it at another. Talons scratch through my shirt and I spin, weapon ready. The demon grabs my arm, carelessly batting the knife out of my hand. I kick it in the shin, but it avoids impact.

"Lucifer is fake." It hisses. "Tell Alex." I frown, the demon releases me from its clutches and disappears out into the crowd. The dagger returns to my hand. What? Are there demons on Alex's side? I thought they all hate her, I suppose there has to be a few exceptions, but Colt has never told me about any of them. None of them helped me while I was stuck in the cell. I scan over the hundreds of heads, dead and alive. My eyes catch Lucifer, sitting on his throne, watching below. His hands dance, but he doesn't bother to stand. Alex is fighting her way towards him, through the endless sea of demons blocking the way. Does the demon mean it's all fake? A message from my subconscious. My thoughts are cut off by a wave of fire. I sprint out of the way, the ground shaking under my feet.

Arms grab me, yanking me away. I desperately try to keep hold of my knife. Claws scratch on my skin as I try to escape their grasp. Lucifer smirks as I'm brought before him. My hands fight to reach a knife, fumbling and dropping it. I scream, but not from fear; Colt told me to do it as a signal to the others. My eyes catch Holly, the demons slowing down enough for me to notice her. Blood dripping from her mouth, tears in her glowing yellow eyes, yet she smiles in my direction. I struggle in their grasp, howling out, kicking and thrashing like a toddler having a tantrum. It's hard to struggle when you are told to pretend to do it, I'm not an actress. Howling, I am led up the steps near the throne where I can overlook the scene.

The demons jump in, like they were also biding their time. I just hope the others are better actors than I am, not that Lucifer knows what we are doing. If he does, we are all going to die. A few sparks fly from Enzo's hands, his clothing badly torn. Colt bites another demon with his fangs, the black goo dripping out of his mouth, before being bombarded by a dozen demons piling onto his body. Holly shrinks back to the size of a human.

The demons look prepared, throwing a blanket of some kind over her. The rest fall down like dominoes, leaving Alex standing. The demons settle down, with no one left to capture. They are all dragged out into a line.

The demons drop me next to the throne. Lucifer chuckles looking down at the group, the collar is strapped around my neck. "Well, it's nice to see all of you." He smirks. "Let me guess, you thought you'd come all the way down here and surprise me, but I knew you'd do that."

"We gathered that from the army waiting for us." Alex stands, the demons don't attempt to manhandle her to her knees. I think she would rather die than kneel to Lucifer. Alex's hands fire up, ready to fight him, but she doesn't move. "Now, get off of my throne before I remove you myself."

"Oh no, Alex. Your friends are all lined up here. If you don't do as I ask I'll make Abby here take their power one by one. The only way to stop me is to kill Abby."

I'm Lucifer's bargaining chip. It makes sense. They want to save everyone, including me. Lucifer knows we won't turn on each other... that's why they have the security blanket... before Plan B.

"You are going to do it anyway, why should I waste my time boosting your self-esteem?"

He motions for a demon to step forward. "I'll show you."

The demon stands before me, I hesitate. Lucifer grabs the collar, pressing the metal into my neck. I whimper and obey his command. They said to follow along for now. I shake and the demon slowly disintegrates to ashes, the remains falling between my fingers. The reactions don't change on my friends' faces, there is no sign of fear, but Lucifer still looks confident.

"You'll have to try harder than that. Only demons will explode like that." Alex snorts.

"Yes, demons explode... like Flint." Their faces fall in realisation, if I successfully take Flint's power, he'll turn to ash like the rest of them. Alex spits an inaudible curse. "Each time

you don't do as I ask, I'll work my way up the ladder to Flint."
Lucifer explains. "Unless you think you can beat me while the
demons pin down Flint and force Abby to kill him." Flint is
strong, it would take a while. That's if I don't die trying. No
matter which one would die, I don't think Alex would be able to
kill him in time. Alex growls. "What do you want?"

"Kneel." Lucifer's eyes gleam.

"You bastard." Alex grits her teeth, eyes darting around to
find a way out of the situation. I don't think there is one, if we
want to continue the plan, then she'll have to kneel for him.

Taking a deep breath, small pits of fire burn in her hand but
she doesn't act on it. Instead, she takes her place before the
throne and drops to one knee. She would rather die, but she isn't
going to risk Flint's life. Lucifer's eyes light up in pure joy.
"Good, it took a few thousand years, but you are finally doing
what you were born to do."

"You were born to be an asshole, I guess we are both fulfilling
our destinies." Alex snaps back.

Lucifer shakes his head. "Abby, approach Hayden." I start
walking forward… something should have happened by now.

Lucifer howls, I spin around. Lucifer wrenches a rope off his
neck. I look up, Tina stands on a ledge. This wasn't part of the
plan; it was meant to be a demon on Alex's side. "How the fuck
are you alive?" Alex splutters.

"We can discuss that later." Tina jumps down.

Lucifer looks at her in equal surprise. Was she meant to be
dead? No one told me. The demon who was meant to distract
him jolts into action. I duck out the way in the direction of Colt,
like instructed. Lucifer yells, hands grab my shirt, yanking me off
my feet. Spasming, my body judders. His hands burn like white
hot fire against my skin. I scream, the searing flesh sending me
into agony. I feel the heat pulse through my body, pain shocking
my nerves. Blood pools out my nose, mixing with my tears. My
eyes droop, I can't take much more. I drop to the ground with a
thud. A buzz rings through my ears, I try to lift my head, but I

can't see anything. Barely able to move, I struggle to breath, vomit churning in my stomach. My eyes flutter, my hand changes with the veins peering out of pale skin. Colt... I have been glamoured into Colt. They've started plan B... My head smacks the concrete.

Lucifer

I watch the scene below, they subdued quickly enough. Onnach isn't doing a terrible job, he's following the script I gave him. I wish I had a camera while watching Alex kneel. It doesn't matter, I'll never forget it. Threatening Flint was the perfect option, Alex will do anything for him. Flint is an early being, which means he might be similar enough to humans to survive, but Alex wouldn't risk it. She begrudgingly drops to one knee before the throne, with one sarcastic bitter comment after another. I did want to force her to kneel like the others, but I knew the demons couldn't force her to do such a thing without my help, so I had to find another way to make her obey.

Onnach continues talking, Alex back chatting to each sentence that comes out of his mouth. He should have blasted her by now, just enough to hurt and show her who's in charge. It's ridiculous. From what I can gather, they are doing the second plan of the three I established they could do. They stop showing off with massive walls of fire, killing a dozen demons in one swipe, flying through portals all over the place, Holly acting like a rabid pit-bull. It all stops, each one barely taking out two at a time. They want me to think that I am winning. Dropping to their knees, ready for me to suck out the last of their power.

Colt flew through the doors with Abby. They all continue fighting, but not as hard. Their grand gestures of power, slowly become less and less extravagant. They allow the demons to beat them down. It's a simple enough plan, allowing themselves to be captured to make me relax enough to be overthrown. I shake my head, to truly think I thought they were smart, I guess I was wrong. I'm sure they'll wait for Abby to start taking their powers, to make their capture look realistic. Then, while Onnach is taking the power out the collar to be used, Alex will take the opportunity to surprise attack him. If it were me down there like they think, it could work, but it's not.

She won't get the chance. Abby will be in for a shock when she grabs Onnach, I have dosed him up with poison. Harmless to demons, potent to humans. Abby stands there uncomfortably; she was fine doing it when her friends weren't there because she couldn't see the effect of what she was doing. Each time she took a demon's strength, she was aiding my win and she knew it, but it changes when she can see who it is hurting.

She starts walking over to Hayden. I have them in a strict order based on connection to Alex, power and my hatred. Hayden is the lowest; my experiment, but nothing special. He was there when Alex took my throne but didn't help her, so my hatred is minimal. Esmeralda was meant to be there too... I first thought she was dead but Jade is here, which means Esmeralda is babysitting. It's going to be even easier to take my grandchildren.

Luckily, the demons still have them in the right order. Next, Holly. Abby will hate hurting her own sister. Jade for her aid in overthrowing me. Colt, to hurt Enzo, the bastard. Then Flint, Enzo and Alex. Killing Flint will crush Alex, but I hate Enzo more and he deserves to suffer Colt's death a little longer. Rope appears out of thin air, wrapping around Onnach's neck. My head snaps up to the attacker; Tina stands there, grinning from ear to ear. How the hell is she alive? I killed her; her head is on display outside. There is no chance Alex would be able to revive her from that, I made sure of that.

Glaring down at Alex, I see she is as shocked as I am. It's not a trick on her part, it really is Tina. A demon jumps onto Onnach, as he struggles to be released from the rope... that's how. Alex has the support of some of the demons. My hands itch to annihilate that abomination of a demon. Tina tricked me. I never killed her. It was a demon; she used another demon to take her place. The head at the door is a demon. She used my own experiment to fool me. And I let her. It doesn't matter, a small bump in the road, that's all. Onnach burns the demon to a crisp, the remaining demon thumping to the floor. Abby runs, darting away while the others break free. As commanded, Onnach grabs her. The fire and flames return, bursting out in colour and new ambition. She screams out in agony. If she's weak enough, she can't argue with helping me. Smoke rises from Abby's back, the cloth turning to ash, revealing boiled red flesh. Abby collapses to the ground, not quite dead. She'll need Alex's blood in the next few hours to survive. At least she's out the way until she's needed again.

They fight, sending demons sprawling worthlessly. Alex, a smug grin across her face, sends demons up into flames while making her way up to Onnach. "Such a disappointment." Onnach growls.

"You should say that to a mirror." Alex grabs him by the throat, throwing him across the room. Wings sprout from her back, the entire human-like glamour falling. Horns appear on her head, eyes blazing a vicious red.

Onnach raises his hands, eyes darting around in panic as sweat drips down his forehead. I would never do that, he looks scared... admittedly he is doomed, which is why I used him and not myself. An unexpected twist; my own kind betraying me for an abomination of a demon was beyond my belief of possibility. Alex howls, an elemental ball charged with magic grows in her hands, the power coursing through her veins, radiating off her body, I can feel it from up here. There is a little bunch of warriors helping her by fending off demons loyal to me. Onnach panics, sending off a surge of his own power. It disperses uselessly at Alex's touch and flies back at him full force. Onnach screams in unimaginable pain. Light streams out of his chest, destroying him from the inside. The energy pulses around the room, Onnach explodes into a million tiny pieces of grub. I was wrong, he couldn't put up any sort of a fight against Alex. Pathetic. I roll my eyes; the demons stop at the sight of 'my' demise.

The little group of superheroes faces light up in joy at the fact I'm gone. They wish. I wait, watching Colt feed Abby another tube of blood, the others staring where Onnach had stood in disbelief. Flint and Jade kiss. Enzo walks over to Alex, to do the same no doubt. I listen to their conversation. "That was too easy." Alex murmurs to him.

He nods. "You're right." I should put them out of their misery before Alex decides to sit on my throne.

Dropping down from the ledge, I land, the ground shaking beneath me. My hands surge, sending the happy group sailing across the room, pinning them down to their original positions; on one knee facing the throne. I sit on the throne, looking down at them all. Alex can't pull any more surprises on me; her little army and her plan has already been used. Once I kill her, I'll execute those rouge demons. Alex curses under her breath, the only one standing.

"Who the hell was that?" Alex spits angrily. The rest are in utter shock, kneeling by the throne powerless.

"Onnach, I even hinted it to you but I was right, you are too stupid to figure it out." I chuckle. Alex's face falls as she works out how I did the morphing and waved it right under her nose. I purposely left the experiment in the hut for her to find.

"You bastard." Her hands light up, flaring in my direction. I lift one hand and the measly ball of energy disperses. Her face falls, I suspect that is the same amount she used to kill Onnach. Abby is dragged along the floor towards Hayden, who is being held down.

"Try again, and he dies." Her hands are tied, caring for people is what makes her vulnerable. Alex's hands spark, firing in my direction. I dodge out the way. Abby grabs hold of Hayden's body automatically, she has no choice. Nothing happens, Abby clutches Hayden tight but nothing is happening. It's not Abby, my eyes dart to the boy, Colt, lying limp on the ground. They glamoured them, that's the simple answer, the demons wouldn't be able to see the difference. I chuck the boy aside, he's useless to me. Racing over, I grab Hayden by the neck, it snaps. He falls, limp in my hands. I drop him and reach out for Abby. Soaring backwards, my back hits the wall. The little gaggle of heroes break free as magic filters across the room. I don't need their power anyway; it was just a sweet addition to my plan. My hands surge with power, blasting Alex. The demons jump back into action.

Alex pounces, wings cutting my face. I stumble, her legs swing up knocking my chin. I spit out blood and she buckles from the legs down. Forcing her to kneel. I send a blast; she screams, her face burning at the touch. She jumps back, the heat scarring her skin. Magic wraps around my body squeezing. I laugh, ripping myself free. Alex's eyes dart up to the corner of the room, Enzo stands there. They're doing something. Wrenching Alex's wing, she skids along the ground, groaning in pain. Flying upward, I grab Enzo. He chokes, dropping his weapons. He's foolish to think I wouldn't notice whatever trick he was trying to prepare. I'm not going to die, but he is.

Enzo

We are kneeling before the throne, Lucifer sits on it. He got a demon to play him. We played out our plan to replicate his. I would never believe he would allow someone to take his place or sit on his throne. That is why he did it. We won against a fake. He wanted us to reveal everything we had, so there would be no surprises when he finally showed up and we fell for it. Alex glances in my direction, I nod. She wants me to do her plan, the small vials clinking in my pocket, ready for the spell. My hands are trapped behind my back and the demons won't budge. She needs to break me out of their hold and give me a distraction so I can perform the spell unbothered.

Alex blasts Lucifer with incredible power. Lucifer blocks with ease, smiling. It's definitely him this time. Luckily, I had time to glamour Colt and Abby as each other before the demons grabbed me. Colt squirms, his hands reaching for Hayden's throat. He clings on to him, nothing happens. Lucifer's face falls before replacing it with a frown. Flashing forward, he grabs Hayden and snaps his neck before Alex can react. Struggling in my hold, the demons press my hands further into my back. Lucifer flies back, Alex hitting him hard before he can touch Colt. He's no use to him, he would very happily kill him for the inconvenience he has caused. Alex's hands flare up again, this time it re-routes, taking out the two guards holding me down. I swing back, magic flaring for Abby. Shocking her, she shakes and goes down. With her out of it, Lucifer doesn't haven't anything to dangle over Alex's head. She smiles my way and charges forward. I fling the demon over my back hitting two more, releasing Flint. A hurricane blows, knocking out the rest, releasing the group. A demon charges my way, I release a portal. It flies through, appearing again and dropping from the ceiling like rain. I race through, appearing on the small ledge Lucifer had been standing on. How didn't I see him? He was in the room, I should have noticed.

Pulling out the vial of blood, I check the labels. I definitely don't want to mix them up. I hold three different tubes. The near empty one is Lucifer's from the syringe. The remnants are enough to perform the spell to connect Alex and Lucifer. I add another small tube of blood and swirl it in the orb. I have prepared the rest of the spell. I add the last few ingredients and start the spell. Screams and howls of pain echo from below, I ignore it, not looking away from the spell. If I help the battle, I'll just be preventing the resolution. If they die, that can be reversed when Lucifer is gone. I murmur the words under my breath, blood pooling from my nose. The spell is just as powerful as the ritual keeping Lucifer in Hell. My fingers judder, the thick red magic surging from my hands. I choke, dropping the bottle. My back flies against the wall; Lucifer's hands burn my throat. Flinging my head forward my horn digs into his eye. Lucifer howls, letting go. Gasping, I kick him, buckling his knees. Lucifer's hands flare, I block his approach, our power connecting. I whimper, I don't have much energy left. My power dwindles, Lucifer's energy bolt penetrates my own.

Smashing into the wall, I lie in a heap. My eyes look towards the orb, daring it not to fall off the ledge. If that breaks, I can't finish the spell and we're all screwed. I whisper a spell, building up the red sparks. Waves circle me, energy pulsing from my body. My head throbs as I focus all my energy, my body struggles to contain it. I let out a cry, charging it in Lucifer's direction. Jolting, Lucifer drops to his knees shaking. Holy shit. I reach for the orb, scooping it up to safety. Lucifer gathers to his feet and I spin, pulling out a dagger. Lucifer grabs my wrist, flipping me over his arm. I groan, hitting the ground. Where the hell is Alex? He waves the blade near my eyes, blood soaking it. That's not anyone's blood. It's Flint's, I asked him for it. There was no way I would use Alex to kill Lucifer, I was going to do it myself.

Pulling out a knife, I raise it up, Lucifer catches my wrist. Shaking his head, he plucks the bloody blade from my hand. "Nice try." He grabs the front of my shirt, lifting me off the ground. Sparks refuse to work at my will, sweat drips down my face. Lucifer slices the blade through my neck. I choke on my own blood while he plunges it and draws it through my insides. Fuck. This isn't how it was meant to go. Lucifer chucks me off the edge, I crash down below unable to move. The rich hot taste of blood fills my mouth, I fumble for my pocket.

"Enzo!" Arms grab me. "Enzo?" My vision blurs, eyes flickering, trying to see the person in front of me, but I know that it is Alex. "Stay still." Blood touches my lips, I cough. It drools out of my mouth, it won't work. The dagger he used was coated with Flint's blood. I had the blade to link Lucifer and I. Then if I used it, he'd suffer with me. He wouldn't die... he's more powerful, and it would affect us in equal measure. He'd go into a coma, a never-ending abyss for him to suffer in. I croak, trying to garble out words. "For fuck sake Enzo, at least try and help me. I'm saving your life." The agony runs through my veins as I struggle to hold on. Alex cuts open her arm, the knife soaked in blood from tip to handle. Driving it through my stomach, I double over, I wheeze out a breath. I grab my neck, touching the skin. It's closed up.

"Do you really think I'd be stupid enough to not figure out your little plan with Flint. I mean, what is it with men and having a fucking hero complex? I'm going to kill you both when we get back." Alex snarls.

"Flint's blood... I swear I used it." The scent was his.

"I faked it obviously, that wasn't even blood. And I switched the labels on our blood vials. Now get your ass up off the floor and help me." Lucifer charges in our direction, I pull Alex down on top of me, rolling out the way. Magic charges in my hands, throbbing in my body. The sparks turn a deep red before I expel them out towards him. Lucifer flies back into a wall. Alex jumps to her feet, her wing slicing through his chest.

CHAPTER
TWENTY-THREE

Abby

Waking up, my head spins. I cough, blood spewing out my mouth. My entire body aches, my back is burning where Lucifer grabbed me. What is going on? I'm alive so we can't have lost yet, and I'm no longer disguised as Colt. I grab my collar and fumble with the clasp. I sigh in relief as the stinging subsides. Chucking it to the ground, I swear I am never wearing that thing again. I pull myself up from the floor to survey my surroundings.

A demon soars in my direction, I duck down. My body is fighting me because it wants to simply give in. I pull out a knife and swing it. The demon howls, its flesh ripping away. That felt good. The demon's talons reach out to scratch me, I lift my arm to shield my face. I curse as blood seeps from my newest injury. I sweep my leg underneath it and it trips. Taking my knife in both hands, I drive it through the demon's skull. I kick it in the stomach before making the final blow to the side of its neck. It drops dead at my feet. I wave my knot of hair out of my face. The wind is coming from every direction, pushing me around so much I can barely keep my footing.

Another demon comes flying through the air. Collapsing, it lands on top of me, my knife falling from my hand. Stupid fingers. Silver teeth flash in my face, I can't reach another weapon. It holds me down against my will, teeth sinking into my collarbone. I howl, blasting it away. It flies, flinging itself off my body and landing beside me... Fuck, I did it. I can use Silven's wind powers too. I swear I couldn't before. The demon charges again, I raise my hands. The demon flies backwards. Teeth catch it by the mid-section and the demon is ripped in two.

Holly stands there, demon goo matting her fur and grinning from ear to ear. She pounces into my arms, licking my face off. I laugh, struggling to hold her up, but I don't want to let go. "I missed you too." I bury my face in her fur, though it smells terrible. Tears spring to my eyes. She jumps down and dances a circle around me.

A demon jolts towards us. Holly snaps her teeth at it protectively. I take out a blade from the collection strapped to my body. Holly leaps up, catching it mid-air. My dagger catches it in the eye, I stab it twice more; once in the heart, the second in the neck. Holly barks, as the light fades from its eyes.

The ground begins to shake, sending me sprawling onto the floor. Holly whines, falling on top of me. Rocks fall from the ceiling, aiming for our heads. I scramble out of the way. The dagger falls out of my grasp. I tug Holly down with me. I shield my head from sharp chunks. A bang echoes throughout the room as timber comes flying down from the roof. Holly and I dart out the way of more incoming wood. I curse as a rock lands on my foot. What is going on? My hands fumble, trying to yank the bricks off my foot. Holly tugs them with her teeth. They fall away, but cracks appear beneath my feet. Holly bites down on my sleeve, tugging me towards the exit. I limp after her. Hopefully, this is part of our plan and not Lucifer's. My eyes catch Colt and everyone else running out. Crap. That is not a good sign.

The doors fly open, the hinges squeal before the doors fly off completely. "Get over here." A voice I don't recognise screams. Dust blinds me, we're dead. That's it, we've lost. A slab of stone drops, taking Colt down.

"No!" Pain explodes in my back, and I fall down too. I lift my head a few inches, coughing up dirt. In a daze, I look around trying to see where Holly went. "Holly! Colt!" I scream. I tug on my leg and gasp in pain. I can't move it, the pile of bricks are trapping it in place. Timber begins to fall, I duck down, my bloody arms going over my head. I can't move. A loud creak above my head, I close my eyes waiting for impact.

A whimper and my eyes burst open. Holly drops beside me; she took the blow for me. "Crap!" I reach out trying to remove the timber from her back. I fail to grip it, pulling against my screaming leg. I put all my weight against the wood, channeling any part of Silven's power I can. It rolls off Holly. She licks my cheek in thanks. She takes the chunk of bricks in her mouth and tries to rip it off my leg. I try to turn to help but I can't. The dust brings tears to my eyes, with a mixture of pain. The bricks roll off my leg. I still can't move it; I think it is broken. I wouldn't be surprised. The rubble moves, and a figure bursts through it. Colt, covered in dust and blood.

"Thank god it's you two." Colt struggles to breath, collapsing next to us, a piece of timber through his stomach.

I look down at the large chunk of wood, it's going to hurt worse when I pull it out, but it will heal faster that way. I put my hands over it. "Ready?" I ask. He nods. I yank it out, he lets out a string of curses. Blood gushes from his stomach like a river.

"Why aren't you healing?"

"I don't know, possibly something to do with..." Colt hisses mid-sentence. "Hell. It hurts like a son of a bitch."

I remove my hoodie and wrap it around his stomach tightly to slow the bleeding. Colt hisses under his breath. "Thanks."

"You're welcome." Brick dust rains down from the ceiling, I can't see any further than a few feet ahead of me. The entire building is collapsing. There is no way out, we are going to be buried alive. "We are all going to die, aren't we?"

"Most likely." Colt curses, clutching his wound. "Sorry, pain talking. I don't know." He answers honestly.

That depends on who is causing this, but I don't believe it's Alex. She wouldn't risk our lives like this, my bet is Lucifer, which means that we are all doomed. Holly whimpers, nudging my leg. I wince in pain and pat her head. A deafening crack and the entire ceiling tumbles down, the walls collapsing in on themselves. Shit. I grab Colt and Holly pulling them down to the floor. Raising my arms to protect them from the incoming rainfall of rubble. I close my eyes in anticipation.

My eyes open, after the last rock hits. My body is covered in bloody bruises, but I am not stuck. I cough, waving the dust from my face. I can barely breath, the air is so thick that I can't see. We are stuck in a small dome of debris. I reach out to find the other two in the darkness, but I can't feel them. "Colt? Holly?" I croak, my throat burning. I crawl forward, dragging my leg along behind me. "Holly?" I feel along the walls of the rubble. "Colt?" They aren't here, but they were. There is nowhere they could have gone… unless they are stuck underneath it all. Tears drop from my eyes, I rub them away with my filthy hand. Even a supernatural couldn't survive underneath all that. They would be squashed to death. "Holly! Colt!" I scream, praying they might answer back but knowing they won't.

I need to find a way out of here, in the small hope that they are alive and might need my help. They can both move quickly, maybe they sped to a safe spot before the rock fell. But they wouldn't have forgotten to take me with them, even at their own risk… maybe that is why I'm here and they aren't. I can't think like that. I have to get out, somehow.

Lucifer

Stumbling out of the rubble, Alex rushes over to Enzo's side. She's strong whenever he's involved; love does that. I brush off my ruined coat. Enzo stirs as she grabs him, it doesn't matter. He'll die. Stupid boy had Flint's blood; it'll burn him from the inside out. It'll be hellishly painful, but it is rightly deserved for the mess he has caused me. Watching from above, I observe Alex desperately trying to feed him her blood. It won't work. A flicker of pain races up my arm, I look down to see a long deep cut healing as quickly as it came. What the hell is this? I've not been hurt... The bloody ritual Enzo was doing. Alex just cut herself and it appeared on me. I draw out a dagger and stab it through my hand. Below, Alex curses, glancing at her palm. There is a small graze, not as bad as the hole through my hand. Enzo didn't get to complete the spell, so the ritual isn't in full effect and the damage to the other person is not as severe. So, I can kill her without killing myself in the process.

Enzo coughs, he's milking his death too much for my liking. The sooner he dies, the better it is for me. I want to watch Alex suffer. Jumping down, I march towards Alex. My hands spark, ready to attack. I pause, as Enzo struggles to his feet with the help of Alex. He's alive, the bastard is alive. Why can't they ever actually die? I need Enzo dead. Howling, I send out power in their direction. Enzo grabs Alex and they roll out the way.

"You fucking bastard!" Alex jumps to her feet and her hands light up with burning red flames. The sparks soar in my direction and hit me in the chest before I can move. I groan stumbling back. Alex gasps, looking at her own shirt, blood seeping through the untouched fabric. Her wound heals instantly, she looks back up in time to see my own wound heal.

"Crap." She's screwed, she can't kill herself to save us both from the long, agonising fight and be the hero. But any attack she does on me, will bounce back to her, making us both more vulnerable with each move we make. Our moves have to be perfect to prevent our own pain as much as possible. Enzo stumbles to his feet beside her, I dart my hand out. He flies backward into the walls like a rag doll. He may not be dead, but he's weak. Those wounds will affect him like they would a human.

The ground begins to shake under my feet. My wings shoot out, she has to do better than that. I charge forward. Alex blocks my approach, rolling across the floor and firing back. I fly back into the wall. My wounds are slowing me down. I need to distract her to gain the advantage. The walls crack and break under the pressure, she wants to bring the castle down on top of me, but she won't. Not with all of her pals inside; they'll die under the rubble. Which is why I'll do it for her.   Raising my hands, all four walls collapse inwards. A force field appears overhead spreading throughout the entire room, refusing to let the bricks fall down. Enzo howls, hands shaking the deep red magic which is soaring from his palms. Even he won't be able to hold that forever, blood is already pouring from his nose and eyes. Once the castle falls, they won't be able to escape, they will all be buried alive, their deaths will be agonising and, with Alex gone, they won't come back.

Boulders soar in my direction and I lift my arms, the wind acting as a barrier around me. The stonework under my feet disappears, crumbling to lava below. My wings flap, Alex will have to try harder than that. I swoop in, my fist connecting with her face. Alex stumbles, barely able to keep upright. Her wing slashes through my cheek, cutting all the way to the other side. I spit out the blood that is rushing into my mouth. I grab her around the neck, slamming her into the rocks. Squirming, she flings herself forward. Our heads connect, I curse. Alex's flaming hand smacks into my face, her eyes meet mine. There is a similar mark on her own face. This is getting better and better every second. Catching her hair, I flip her onto her back into a pile of jagged rocks.

Howling, she tries to get back to her feet. I hold her down, pressing her spine further into the pile. Alex's hands rise, my wing sweeps down cutting through her wrist. Alex screams in agony as her hand drops to the ground. "You asshole!" My other hand bleeds, before sealing itself.

"You must have known you'd lose, didn't you?" I tease her. "Or did you at least hope you could save your precious family? Never mind." My hand sinks into her chest, her ribs crack under the pressure. Alex gasps, blood pooling out of her mouth. A throbbing pain goes through my own chest, but not like anything she'll be experiencing. "I was hoping I could kill Flint in front of you, but I guess letting you die knowing you have failed and that he'll die anyway will have to be enough."

"Son of a bitch." Tears stream down her cheeks, a mixture of pain and sadness. Her wings shrink behind her, eyes turning back to a piercing green. She's turning more human-like, giving in. I don't blame her; I'm surprised she has lasted this long. "Don't worry about Flint's kids, I'll take good care of them." My nails dig into her pumping heart, ripping it out of her chest. Alex's eyes go wide, slumping against the rocks in defeat. Her eyes flutter. I chuck her failing organ onto the ground beside me.

I stand back to admire my work. I knew I'd succeed, there were a few hiccups, but it's done. My hand burns and I lower it down, hovering over her body, ready to set it on fire to kill her once and for all or her heart will simply grow back. With that, I hear Enzo finally collapse. The walls begin to cave, chunks soaring down overhead. A pillar of the castle topples, I lift my hands for cover but it's too late.

Sinking into the ground, I cry out in agony as the rubble piles on top of me. I'll survive, but her friends won't. Blasting away the debris, I crawl out, covered in scratches and bruises. They won't all be my own, some will belong to Alex. I need to kill her now before she heals. I bat away the bricks from Alex, barely anything hit her... that can't be an accident. Enzo aimed the pillar at me on purpose. I set her on fire, starting at her foot.

Hellfire is much worse than any other fire; it'll burn her away until there is nothing but ashes left in a matter of minutes.

Alex's eyes snap open. She grabs my wrist and sends me sailing onto my back. I spew a curse. "You're stupid if you think I'd give up that easy." Alex's eyes change to black. A mixture of elemental powers surge through her hands, exploding against my chest. Groaning, I struggle to my feet. How in Hell's name is she still standing? Enzo. He timed that bloody fall perfectly. It gave Alex time to heal herself enough to move but it cost him the rest of his friends. Enzo knew they'd die anyway.

Alex aims her magic at my head. I howl. Clutching my face, the hot dripping skin smears my hand. My left eye is completely gone. "You little vermin!" I snarl. I scoop up the dagger dripping with Flint's blood. I've given up on inflicting the slow painful death she deserves, she just needs to die. I drive the blade down, Alex twists my wrist, snapping it. I scream in agony, it cracks back into place.

"You'll have wished you used that earlier." Alex spins the knife gracefully between her fingers. Elements spark at my fingertips and silver metal flashes. One of my fingers drops to the ground. She kicks me in the neck and I choke. Hands flaring, she sends a bolt at my chest. I wheeze. Hell is mine, I'm not letting her grubby hands get a hold of it. Not after all the work I put in to keep this place perfect. I'm the most powerful being in the universe, I'm not letting her take anything else from me. Alex lifts the knife over her head, ready to drive it through my heart.

I take her out by her legs, pushing my burning hand into her neck. She's still weak, even if she grew her heart back. Pain throbs through my head, a dagger sticking out of it. Alex rolls out the way. She lifts her dagger. She stops, eyes going wide, juddering back and forth as if she has just had a huge electric shock. What in Hell's name... Hands grab me. I freeze, my blood turning cold. Jolting, my body spasms out of my control and I drop to my knees. Foam froths from my mouth, my head is spinning. I hear a crash ring throughout the room. Alex appears, reaching out behind me. Pain sinks through my chest, I slump to the ground unable to move. What in my name is happening to me? I reach out for Alex, trying to grab the little bastard. She doesn't pay me any attention. My eyes catch a glimpse of brown hair before all I see is a bright light. I'm... I'm dying. How the fuck is that happening? It's impossible. My plan was perfect. I hear sobbing echo around me as I listen to my heart slow down. Alex can't win. Hell belongs to me; it was made for me. I'm the entire reason it exists. My disgrace of a daughter was brought into this world to serve me. She has me to thank for her birth, for her power and this is how she repays me. She doesn't deserve Hell.

I curse, pain enveloping my head as someone's boot connects. Alex. I attempt to fight back with what strength I have left in my body. I lift my hand, I can't see. I let out any power I have left and send it flying, praying I hit Alex. The least she can do is die with me. Agony pulses through my body as she hits me again, not allowing me to die peacefully.

Jolting awake, I can't see anything. My eyes refuse to open. I try to move my limbs. They refuse to work. I'm paralysed, I can't do anything but I'm alive. How? I struggle to move as hot, burning agony throbs throughout my body. I'm frozen. I howl but my mouth doesn't open, I'm stuck. There's nothing left of me to move. It's true… I am unkillable. She can't get rid of me that easily. Where am I? I listen, trying to fathom my surroundings but I can't hear anything except a distant buzzing sound. My ears don't work. I'm useless… I will have to try and learn it all again. I will move again, if I can think. I have to find a way; Alex is not through with me yet.

Abby

My eyes glimpse light, I claw away at the bricks and climb out of the rubble. My head darts around, looking for anyone else… The entire castle is in ruins. All of it, there's nothing left. I can't see Colt, or Holly, or anyone for that matter. If they didn't get out, they're trapped somewhere underneath it. Probably dead. The light hits my eyes, blinding me momentarily. Stepping forward, something squelches under my foot. I squint, peeling it off. A human heart sits in my hand. Fuck. Looking back up, Lucifer looms over Alex. I feel for my weapons, I'm completely out. Scanning the ground frantically, I can't spot anything… except the collar. It sits there, cracked and dirty, but in one piece. I scoop up the dreaded device, strapping it back on. The burn tingles my skin. Limping on my bad leg, I march forward as quickly as possible, fighting the pain. In the distance, I can see a part of a person crushed under the rubble. I think it's Enzo and he's not moving.

As I grow closer, everything Lucifer did to me comes back. The kidnapping, endless torture, cutting off my fingers and toe, trapping me in that cell, making me lie to everyone for his own entertainment, forcing me to wear the collar, helping him gain power at my own expense, using me to kill all the people I care about, making me feel guilty for it all. The endless threats, starvation, dehydration, making me feel hopeless, the hallucinations, the never-ending nightmare, turning Holly into a werewolf. The list doesn't end. Now, he has a chance to win and get exactly what he wants. A reward for forcing us to suffer, for everything he has done. He's trying to kill Holly and Colt, if they aren't already dead, there is no way I can save them and it's all his fault. Everything bad that has happened, starting with Silven, was all because of him. I killed countless people under Silven's control because of him. I know not all of them came back; Enzo and Alex may have told me otherwise, but that was because they knew how bad I felt. I checked the news afterwards, a child died. He did all that in a matter of months, there is no way he can live any longer. He doesn't deserve to.

Alex sends Lucifer soaring and he lands near my feet. Alex draws out her knife at him. "Might want to stand back." She warns me. Before I can comprehend what I'm doing, I grab him by the neck and begin to drain his power into the collar. I watch him fall to the floor in pain, I can feel the anger leave my body. I did that to him. Overwhelming power jolts through me, the energy is stronger than anything the other demons ever gave me. He's a full demon, he should turn to dust. I dig my hands in deeper as he squirms in my grasp. He tries to scratch me, muttering about Alex, but he's too weak to actually fight back. Colt told me that I couldn't hold him for more than a few seconds, or the power would kill me. I don't care at this point, he needs to die. I need him to suffer as much as I have.

Alex screams, dropping to the ground next to him, jolting. Why? Plan B. They must be connected in some way, that must have been their plan to stop him. I attempt to let go; no matter how much I hate Lucifer, I can't willingly kill Alex too. My hands refuse to budge, they are glued to him, sucking out the last ounce of his power. Even by killing him, I'm letting him win. Alex is going to die too. The anger fuels my body, the bastard has to win in some way, doesn't he? The world works in his favour. Hot tears of rage burn on my cheeks. The collar begins to crack struggling to contain the power. I howl, spasming out of control. My body is charging with power it can't contain now the collar is full. The metal scorches my neck, worse than the first time I wore it. Sparks jolt out my body. Lucifer slips in my grasp, but I keep hold. Shaking violently, the veins in my hand throb out of my skin in a horrific glowing red colour. My skin turns a ghostly pale in comparison. Suddenly, Alex springs up grabbing me in her arms. I collapse in them; she's not going to die.

"Abby! Abby! Let go! You're going to die! Let go! Please, please Abby let go." She pulls on my hands, trying to remove them from his body.

Lucifer is going to die. That is what matters. He's not going to win and he's not taking Alex with him either. That is what he wants, more than Hell, and he isn't going to get it. Instead, I get my revenge for all the shit he's done. Power pulses through my body, this has never happened before. I gasp, the pain subsides, leaving me feeling hollow. My eyes catch sight of Lucifer, lying uselessly at the foot of the throne. I smile, feeling the life drain out of me. I murmur, struggling to breath. It was worth it. Alex is alive, even if Holly is stuck under it all, she can be saved. My eyes catch Enzo's amber ones as he shakes me. I can't respond, my body refuses to move as my energy drains away. Distantly, I hear Lucifer howl out in pain as Alex stomps on him, finishing him off.

CHAPTER TWENTY-FOUR

Enzo

Waking, I hold my head in a daze. The forcefield took everything I had, along with the portal. I should have sent them all to safety before I allowed it to collapse, but it was hard to pinpoint where they all were. I couldn't portal the entire floor or the demons would have gone with them. Stumbling to my feet, I see ahead. Abby is wearing the collar and holding onto Lucifer. How is she here? She's going to die. I told Colt to warn her that if she touched Lucifer she would die, there is no way she can hold that amount of power.

I try to rush forward but I'm too exhausted to run at full speed. I'm not going to make it in time. Alex is on the ground. Fuck, they're connected. I grab the orb from my pocket, smashing it to pieces. The splinters fall away, reversing the spell. Alex bounces to her feet, grabbing onto Abby, but it's already too late. Abby is stuck to him; the collar is drawn to him. It won't stop until there is nothing left to take. Sprinting as fast as I can, I see Abby sinking to the ground. It wasn't meant to be her. Clicking my fingers, nothing sparks. Fuck. My heart drops in my chest. Waves of magic flood into the air, hitting Abby and

Lucifer. A scream, Lucifer falls forward but Alex keeps hold of Abby, ripping them apart.

Tina stands there, a few meters away, covered in brick dust. I missed her with the debris, luckily, or she couldn't have saved Abby.

"You sick bastard." Alex stomps on his head. He howls, crawling for a weapon. Alex hands surge, hitting him in the chest. Gagging, he shakes weakly on the ground.

Skidding to a halt, I drop next to Abby, picking her up in my arms. She's still alive, barely. "Abby, please stay alive." She looks like a corpse, deathly pale with neon blue veins showing underneath. She needs Alex. I glance up, she towers over Lucifer. His hand flickers, the energy soaring into the air towards...

"Tina!" I call out. She flies backward hitting the rocks behind her. Fire burns around her. That doesn't look good.

"No!" Alex screams. Furiously, she kicks into Lucifer's face. Bones snapping, blood pools out his mouth and nose. Crashing, Lucifer's head hits the ground, eyes drifting shut, and he stops moving. Alex rushes over. "She's alive?"

"Just, what about Tina?"

"Listen, Enzo… she's dead." Alex's eyes fill with tears. I stop, listening to the silent room, I can hear three heartbeats. Mine, Alex and Abby's. Tina is dead. "But Abby's alive, for now." Alex rips open her arm, pouring the blood into her mouth. Nothing happens. "Worth a shot." Alex sighs rubbing her face.

"There has to be something else we can do." I flick my hands, magic finally forming. Abby's heart rate drops further, barely beating at all and her breathing has stopped. Magic sparks in my hand, surrounding her body but it won't work quickly enough, if at all. We can't lose her, but I don't think we have a choice. "Abby? Abby, can you hear me?" I beg. There must be something we can do. My brain whirls, thinking desperately of anything. Alex's blood is our only option.

She has her whole life ahead of her, we've all lived her lifetime twenty-fold. We had our time to live, we experienced everything we could. Our extra time is a blessing, not a necessity. She deserves to live more than any of us. This is why humans should never get involved with the supernatural world, ever.

Alex studies the room, as if what we need will randomly appear before us. Alex grabs something from the floor. A dirty, bloody heart. I can tell from the scent that it's her own. "Let's try things the human way. She's human, they replace failing organs, right?"

The power source is in her blood, which is spreading it through her entire body via her heart. If we were to completely replace it and remove the energy, it would possibly be enough to save her. The chances are slim, but I'm willing to try anything at this point.

"That asshole isn't winning anything." Alex chucks the organ in her hand aside and sticks her hand in her chest.

"What the hell are you doing?"

Alex rips out her new heart, slumping to her knees. "You know how to transplant organs, right?"

"You want me to put your heart inside of Abby?"

"That's the damn point." Alex lays down in the dirt, hissing in pain. "Now hurry up, we've got a few minutes at most."

I glance at Abby's chest. If this doesn't work, we can never get her back. All those years Abby deserves to live will be gone, and it'll be all my fault for missing her while creating that portal. We can't lose anyone else. I grab a dagger, cutting through the loose flesh. I rip her chest open, going past the ribcage to her heart. I cut it out; it is barely functioning and a sickly, bright blue colour. There are confusing tubes linking to different parts. Damn it, I know this. Magic can only do so much, I know how to replace a heart. I'm panicking, because I know this could be the only solution, if it works. Taking a deep breath, I continue inserting the heart correctly, trying to stop my shaking hands. I'm better than this. Magic streams out my fingertips and starts connecting the tubes with the right parts as quickly as I can.

I finish the job. Nothing happens. "Abby?" I shake her.

"Not yet, here." Alex magics up a needle, injecting it into Abby, the other side connects to Alex. Blood starts flowing through the tube, into Abby.

"You seriously think this will work?" Alex can't bring people back if they are too far gone, like Tessa, but if the heart was the organ messing things up then we have a chance. I still don't know if it'll be enough.

"No, not at all, but we have to try. The energy in her blood is poisoning her, so we have to flush it out. Now, start CPR."

I press on her damaged chest; I hear a rib crack as I try desperately to revive her. I continue, listening for a pulse. This has to work.

Two minutes pass and nothing happens. I pump her chest. "Enzo… I don't think it's working. I'm so sorry." Alex unplugs the tube from her own arm. Her blood did nothing, Abby's is still blue. I nod slowly, it was a long shot. Racking my hands through my hair, I howl. Angrily, I punch the floor, pain throbbing up my arm. I slump down to my knees, hanging my head, barely able to look at Abby. Her skin is pale, her muscles losing their structure, veins throbbing out of her skin, missing fingers. She has experienced more trauma than anyone deserves. She was meant to live a normal human life and was robbed of it. I go to close her eyes, they flicker. I swear to the heavens they flicker.

"She's alive."

"Enzo, her heart isn't beating." Alex says gently. "I know you thought of her as one of your children but… she's gone. You did everything you could."

But save her.

I reach out and close her eyes. They open again. I didn't imagine that. Her hand twitches. Desperately, I listen while watching her chest. The heart begins to beat, slowly, but it's there. "Alex…"

"I heard it. My plan worked, use your magic now."

My hands begin to work, the surges wrapping around her fragile body, working on the wounds carefully. She gasps, the dead gawp disappearing from her face. A blinding white light hurtles from her chest. Rubble scatters, dropping back down like a hailstorm, pelting us. The blue lines disappear, her veins return to their normal colour. There are no signs of where the energy escaped through her chest. She jolts up, grabbing my shoulder for support. "Where am I?"

Relief floods through my body, I slump down. We did it, we actually did it. "If you do anything like that ever again, I swear to Hell. I'll be the one to kill you."

"I… I didn't die?" She looks down at her chest. She watches as the flesh pieces itself together.

"No."

"What did you do?" Abby stares in amazement.

Abby

I stare in awe at my hands, I died. I swear I did, I didn't think I could be brought back but they did it somehow. "How?"

"I'm a genius, that's what." Alex boasts. She continues to explain how they replaced my heart with her own, which she can simply grow back no problem, apparently. Then they pumped her blood through my body, to act like a transfusion while Enzo revived me which released the energy build up. I check my arms, the veins underneath are barely noticeable. They are back to normal.

"Be careful, we don't know what the side effects are of taking Lucifer's power, and so much of it at that."

I nod, I don't regret doing it, even if I did die. I try to recall exactly what happened after I grabbed Lucifer. "Wait, how did you detach me."

"Tina did it."

"Where is she?"

The answer is written across Alex's face. She is dead because she saved me. That's not what I wanted. I didn't even know her that well, yet she saved me. But it wasn't for me, it was for Alex; Tina always made her intentions clear. She was there for Alex. "You're okay. Can you walk or are you still weak?" Alex asks.

"Yes, but what about the others." I look out into the rubble; they could be crushed by now.

"I didn't screw up everything." Enzo raises his hand and a portal opens up. He sent them away before the castle fell. That's smart.

"You're alive!" Colt's voice comes first.

"Abby!" Holly yells, skidding up to me, wrapping her arms around me.

Over Holly's shoulder, I see Alex disappear over to a corner. She scoops a body up into her arms. A body without a head. Carefully, she picks up the head. Guilt fills my body, that's my fault. I'm the reason that happened. I release Holly, she clings onto me, desperately.

"Hey, my turn." Colt nudges her.

"Wait your bloody turn." Holly begrudgingly lets me go.

Colt wraps his arms around me. "I knew you wouldn't die."

"No, you didn't! You were just as scared as me." Holly retorts. "Please say we can get out of here now." Holly begs. "I feel like Lucifer is going to spring back to life any second."

"Yeah." Without the structure of the castle, the entire plain feels eerie. The red orange sky looms over our heads, with the sound of thunder. Lucifer's limp lifeless body adds to the effect.

"You can go." Enzo opens up a fresh portal for us." Alex and I will be there in a minute."

We all sit in a circle around two gravestones. Tessa's name on one and Tina's on the other. Rain pours down from the sky, thunder bellowing. We all sit in silence; it doesn't feel like a victory. Quite the opposite to be honest. I still feel stuck in the nightmare, that I'll wake up or this is a hallucination and Lucifer will appear any second to take me back. I have Tina to thank for being here, and Tessa protected me when we went to rescue Enzo. I didn't know either of them very well, I'm lucky Holly and Colt made it. I don't know what I would have done if they hadn't.

Holly tugs my shoulder. "We should leave them." I look around; Enzo, Alex, Hayden, Flint and Jade look grief stricken; they knew Tina well. She helped them the first time they overthrew Lucifer. I nod, following her. They deserve time to mourn in peace.

Holly pulls out her phone. "Do you want to stay here, or go home to our parents?"

Our parents. I tried not to think about them too much in Hell, I'm used to not seeing them for a week or two at a time. I need to see them after what we have just gone through. Besides, everyone here could use some space, we all need it. "We should go."

"I'll call us a car, it's easier that way. How are you? After... well, you know."

"I'm fine." I lie, none of us are fine, I don't think we'll ever be 'fine' again, but right now all I want to do is see my parents, sleep and pretend it never happened.

Holly nods, putting the phone to her ear, she used to be scared to make calls herself; for pizza, a taxi, any of that stuff. She always made me do it. I guess without me being there, she had to do it herself. Besides, fighting Lucifer makes anything else seem really easy.

"Abby?" Colt appears around the corner, wrapping his arms around me. I collapse into his embrace, like in the cell. It helps me remember that this is reality. "I wanted to check on you, are you bleeding at all."

"No, I'm in one piece, mostly." I glance down at my hands. I'll get used to it eventually. "What about you?"

"Oh, I'm good. A little shaken up, but no more than anyone else. Are you going home?"

"Yeah, I need to see my parents."

"Of course. Can I have a kiss goodbye?"

"Always." I lean up to kiss him. He grins, our lips pressing together. At least this is still the same, I feel Colt's teeth sinking into my bottom lip. The warm blood fills my mouth.

"Sorry about that." He pulls away a little. "I haven't drank anything in a while."

"Don't worry." It happens, I don't mind, except when he stops kissing me to apologise.

A cough behind us. "The car is here, Abby."

I sigh. "See you later." I kiss his cheek, a lip blood stain on his skin.

Walking in the front door, the hallway is empty. It's the middle of the night, they are probably asleep. I flick the switch in the living room. Our parents jump up from the coach, the blanket sprawling over the floor. "What happened to you two! You've been missing for over a day; we always tell you to call us before you stay out all night. We were about to call the police. I hope you two are ashamed of yourselves!" My mother yells.

"Shit, I forgot to use Alex's mojo on them before I left." Holly murmurs under her breath.

I honestly couldn't be happier to see her, even if she is mad.

Holly and I don't answer, the story is going to take a few hours, we can't hide the truth from them any longer, we both know it. We run into their arms, thankful that we still have them. My eyes close, taking in the moment. You never know when it could be over. "Abby, your hands!" My dad panics. "Where are your fingers? What happened? Tell us now!"

I'm too tired to deal with this yet... maybe we should have stayed around Enzo's.

I leave, heading for my bedroom, we've promised to tell our parents everything tomorrow. I text Colt, telling him we got home safely. Not that there is a threat anymore.

I switch the light on in my bedroom, a parcel is sitting on my bed. I pick it up, the cursive calligraphy writing on the paper belongs to Enzo. I always complain that I can never understand his handwriting. I carefully open the parchment paper, a dozen small glass bottles full of cloudy liquid sit in the box. A note on top reads, 'Abby, these should last you for a few days, let me know if you need more. Eye-bags really don't suit you. From, Enzo.' I laugh, I completely forgot he said he'd brew these for me. I don't think they can help very much, not with everything new that has happened. I'm going to have eye-bags forever. I down one of the small vials, gagging. It tastes like rotten fish. I shudder, putting it down. I lie down on my pillow, going out like a light from exhaustion.

Falling, I wake up on my floor. I groan, rubbing my forehead. I gather myself off the carpet. My hand slips on a knife that is still attached to my belt. I curse, a long gash across my palm. I grab a dozen tissues and run to the bathroom. I lock the door and pull out the bandages and medical equipment. I take off the bloody tissues. The gash is gone, I wipe away the blood. It's completely closed up. It's healed. I take the knife again, pricking my finger. It bleeds and I watch it heal in less than thirty seconds.

That is not right. I grab my phone from my room and message Colt. He replies immediately, saying he'd have a portal ready for me in twenty minutes. I suppose I should shower and get dressed while I wait. I must smell terrible.

Enzo

Alex slumps against my shoulder, the rest of them have left already. I would have liked to have seen Abby before she left so I could examine her. She may be alive, but we don't know if there'll be any side effects to what happened. She'll need therapy no doubt, they all will. It's better than being dead, I suppose. The fact Lucifer is actually dead is overwhelming, that asshole has been hanging over our heads for years. It's a relief he's gone, finally.

Alex pours out two glasses of scotch. "Only glasses?" I raise my eyebrow.

"Yeah, as long as we don't count how many times we refill them we don't have to see how much we drink." She downs the first glass.

"I'm sorry about Tina and Tessa." Tina was Alex's best friend. She was the only one who wasn't afraid of her. Hell knows why, she had every reason to be. I know how they met. They almost killed each other.

Alex sighs. "I know, so am I." The first tear slides down her cheek. "At least Lucifer is off our backs." She changes the subject. "Life might get a bit boring soon." She laughs.

I don't think life could ever get boring. Lucifer may have been our biggest threat, but he won't be our last. I can guarantee that.

"Cheers to that." I clink my glass on hers. "Thanks for saving Abby."

"No problem. I know she's like a child to you." Alex finishes off her sixth refill. "I'm glad it worked."

"What are you going to do with Hell?"

"Gather the rest of the demons, rebuild the castle in my own way. Make Lucifer turn in his grave." Alex laughs. "It'll be different without him, but I'm not going to miss him for sure."

"What are you going to do with Lucifer's body?"

"Might hang his head on my new throne, I don't know. He's in one of the cells at the moment, it's the only part of the building that isn't in ruins."

"And what will you do with the demons?"

"I don't know. They need to be punished, but I can't kill them." She shrugs. "I told them to clean the mess for now. I'll get back to it tomorrow." Alex stands up. "But for now, we need to go."

"Where?"

"The spirit realm, Tina will want a visit."

I've heard about the spirit realm; it's where souls go before passing on completely. It's from there that Alex can bring them back if their bodies are in decent enough condition. Tina was burnt to a husk, there wasn't much left of her. We found her head a few meters from the wreckage where it had been blown off by the impact. There was no way she could have been saved. We fixed her head back on for the funeral, it only seemed right but, even then, it wouldn't work. Alex attempted it before we closed the coffin. Tessa will have moved on by now, we never got to see her. We were too busy trying to save everyone else. A perk of being a demon is that Alex can visit the spirit realm whenever she wishes. It's where demons go before they find a body to conduct. "You ready?" Alex asks.

"Go for it." She grabs my skull.

I hear something drop, turning round I see my body lying in the dirt while I remain sitting down. Alex's body falls, but her spirit doesn't move.

"Don't forget you're here, or you'll get stuck here forever."

"Got it." We're not real, we can slip through reality if we aren't careful. The world looks the same, we are still on Earth. Except as ghosts, the only people who can see us are necromancers.

"About damn time." Tina's voice rings out, echoing in the open air. We spin, she leans on her grave. A silver shimmer outlines her body. "I've been watching you taunt me with whiskey for the last half an hour. Anyway, you could have brought that with you?"

"No." Alex laughs.

"I suppose our plan didn't work out quite as we wanted." Tina waves to her grave. "Saying I'm a little disappointed would be an understatement." She shakes her head.

"What do you mean?" Our plan went completely off topic, we changed it about three times after our attempt failed, but she didn't even know the original plan. She was stuck in Hell being our informant. There is no way she could know.

"You never told him." Tina chuckles. "It went exactly how we planned, all but Abby grabbing him. We didn't think she'd do that. That's why I died." She smiles. "Can't blame the kid… well I can, but I won't. She just better feel guilty, you know, just a tad."

"How did you even have time to plan it?" I was with Alex ninety percent of the time the last few days, the only time I saw her with Tina was when I was there too.

"Texting." Tina pulls a face at me. "The reason you couldn't work that out is the same reason you weren't in the know."

"Excuse me?" I can't really complain to her, she saved Abby but I sure as hell want to.

"She has a point." Alex grins.

"You're dead and you're still getting Alex to gang up on me."

"And I expect her to continue when I'm gone." Tina sighs. "Perhaps I'll see the annoying assassin again. As long as Lucifer isn't there, I didn't die for him to follow me here too."

"No, he won't be there, he can't die." Alex answers. "You know that."

"You've got to be bloody kidding me." Tina complains. "He's alive?"

"No, not really. If the facts are correct, he'll be stuck in some hazy fake reality for eternity, like being conscious while you sleep." Alex explains. "But he's not coming back, even if he thinks he is."

"Thank hell for that." Tina's shoulders relax. "You'd never be able to defeat him again without me." We fall back to silence.

"I.. I'll miss you." Alex says slowly. Emotions have never been one of her strong qualities.

"You better." Tina laughs. "I mean, I died and you haven't even hugged me yet."

Their hands fall through each other, as they try to hold on, despite there being nothing to hold onto.

I stand there awkwardly for a minute, until Tina slowly pulls back, wiping away a tear.

"I am sorry, if I'd known you would die, I wouldn't have made you do it." Alex admits. "I really thought it was fool proof."

"Don't be sorry, I thought the same." There is a moment of silence before Tina opens her mouth again. "Honestly, do you think I will see other people when I cross over?"

"You want to see him, don't you?" Alex says gently.

"It would make dying worth it."

"Who?" I ask.

"My son." Tina's lips tremble.

"Your son?"

"Yes, long story short, I had a child with a human, my son was born like his father. I could save him from everything but mortality. That was many thousand years ago now, I doubt he'd even remember me."

"I hope you do see him." Alex answers. "But I won't lie and say you will."

Tina smiles sadly. "That's all I wanted to hear." Her face turns cold sober. "Enzo, if you tell anyone about anything I just said, I'll kill you. I've got to keep my badass reputation, even after I die." Tina threatens, even though there is nothing she could actually do.

"Understood."

"Now, go celebrate the win for me. You both look miserable. We did it. He's dead, or as close to dead as he can be. Fucking celebrate, Lucifer knows I would be."

"You want us to leave?"

"I have some things I want to wrap up. If you're lucky, I'll visit before I go."

There can't be much for her to do, she doesn't have any family that I'm aware of. Alex nods. "We'll leave you to it, thank you."

"Thanks for not putting my head on a pike like Lucifer did." She waves us off, trying to hide a loose tear, forgetting the fact she can't wipe it away.

Alex forces a smile, turning to me. I jolt back into reality, limbs flailing.

I fight the urge to vomit, I much prefer portal travel. Alex stands. "Come on, she's right, if we wallow around, we are letting Lucifer get to us. I killed him; we should be celebrating."

"I thought you were letting Abby believe that she did it." Abby could have killed him if she had held on any longer, but it would have killed her too. It did make Alex's job killing him much easier though.

"Of course, imagine the wreckage that will happen to Lucifer's name when it's told throughout history that he was killed by a teenager. A human teenager. That's the type of story you'd hear about in human novels."

I chuckle. She's right; Lucifer was known as the most feared being in the universe for so long, people won't believe the story that he actually died, especially in such a way. It is quite possibly the best revenge we could ask for. "What do you want to do to celebrate then?"

"Well, this is still a funeral. We should celebrate their lives, we can do something they would have done."

"Like what? We've already drunk, a lot I might add."

"Follow me." Alex grabs my hand pulling me through a portal.

***

Footsteps storm through the house, loud constant banging at my bedroom door wakes me up. I groan, holding my head. Tina lived a crazy life, experiencing even one night of it is enough to last me for eternity. The knocking continues. Alex growls, half asleep, throwing my alarm clock in the direction of the door. The knocking stops and the door is flung open, sunlight streaming in from the doorway. I groan, I'm too hungover and exhausted for this.

Colt stands at the door. "Abby texted me saying there is something wrong with her."

"What?" I jolt awake, rubbing the sleepiness from my eyes. "What's wrong?"

"She said she stabbed herself and it healed like we would."

She did what? I groan, pulling myself from the bed. It doesn't sound like she is in any immediate danger, but it's definitely worth looking at. "Tell her to give me ten minutes."

"Make that twenty." Alex murmurs. "I might be awake by then."

Colt nods, closing the door after him.

"I don't understand why people decide to have children." Alex sighs, climbing out of bed.

"I only picked one. The other two were an accident."

Alex pulls her hair up into a bun. "Alright, let's find out what's wrong with her."

I sit in the living room, scanning Abby's body. She didn't bring Holly with her, she's probably still asleep. I'm only half awake, I didn't have time to shower or eat. "You cut yourself and it healed right."

"Yeah, I checked, and it happened again." Her voice sounds worried. "Do you think it could be Tessa's brother?"

I pause for a minute in confusion. Why would Tessa's brother be healing her? To kill her; she thinks he wants to assassinate her for what happened. Paranoia is a symptom she'll probably experience a lot now, and sometimes her paranoia will be right, but not this time. "No, don't worry. It's not him." He won't want revenge and kill Abby, or any of us, for Tessa. He knows better than to try and Tessa already told Abby how he'd kill someone. He wouldn't use that method to kill her, because if it were true, she'd have already figured it out.

I scan her body. Most of what I can pick up are signs of trauma; the demonic cells from the possession, tissue scars from endless torture and fighting the different DNA in her heart from the transplant. Angel blood works as a universal donor. It will work with any blood type. There is a small difference, she has a power reading, it's weak but unmistakably there. From what I can tell, the heart donation from Alex did more than just save her life. The heart works like Alex's, giving it the power to heal itself. She couldn't grow back a limb like Alex, or her fingers would have returned, but she'll be able to heal wounds no problem. The rest of the power reading is demonic. Not like when she was possessed. It's Lucifer's power, it didn't all escape when we tried to get it out of her. Her body simply rejected enough to keep her alive. It means she may be able to try simple supernatural tricks. Perhaps start a small fire or fill a glass of water with her hands, maybe more if she is taught. But the important thing is that she's okay. Alive and more than well. So is Colt, Holly and Alex. And I can't really ask for more. No doubt people will try to kill us again, there is an eternity for it. We just

need to enjoy the time we have because we don't know when it
will all be over.

About the Author

Trinity-Rose is a teenage writer from Hampshire in the UK who lives off coffee and bubble tea to function as she spends most of her nights thinking up her next book idea. She is the third child and currently lives with her parents, younger sibling and border collie called Izzy. From the age of ten she started writing her own short stories for her family.

The passion of writing came from her love of reading books. She found her love of the supernatural after reading Kelley Armstrong's young adult books in her early teens. This made her want to create her own supernatural world with exciting relatable characters who are fond of sarcasm. She also enjoys incorporating her love of sports cars into her books. The love for sports cars is thanks to her dad who for her fifteenth birthday, took her for an experience day to drive sports cars around a race track.

Trinity-Rose spent most of her early teen years either at school, writing or hanging out with her best-friend who she met on the first day of nursery. At school she was either talking to friends, learning or jotting up notes for her books. Ironically she got better grades in Maths than English.

When it came time at school to consider career paths she looked at becoming a scientist or lawyer but quickly changed her mind when she realised she wouldn't love it as much as writing and decided to devote all her time to dreaming up stories she could share her work with more than just her family and friends. This inspired her to write her first novel *Hell's Daughter,* and now the release of the sequel *Hell's Key.*

Other Books by this Author

For The Latest Information On

New Releases

&

Coming Soon

From this Author

Please Visit

JasamiPublishingLtd.com

Hell's Key